Praise for *Someone Comes to Town,*
Someone Leaves Town

"Doctorow is one of sci-fi's most exciting young writers, and one of the few with a genuine sense of humor. This is, even by his own bizarre standards, his oddest work yet—an absurd, cartoonish fantasy about a man whose father is a mountain, whose mother is a washing machine, and whose brother is a set of Russian nesting dolls. It all takes place in Toronto, where our hero finds love—and discovers a passion for installing wireless Internet connections."

—*Cargo Magazine*

"Dazzles . . . What probably carries the whole project is Doctorow's deft, deep depiction of his characters. I have to say that he's never done a better job of limning real people. However weird they are, they are certainly not cardboard or one-dimensional. They all contain the essential pressure points, drives, caprices, and emotions that power the folks we encounter every day. Damaged yet striving to survive and do good, Alan and his cohorts demand that we empathize with their human foibles. This essential believability pulls us in, easing our acceptance of any grotesqueries."

—Paul Di Filippo, *SciFi.com*

"Cory Doctorow's third novel blends ordinary technology, nerdista tech, myth, horror, sheer astonishing silliness, and the Aspergerish quest of the outsider into a demented non-stop juggling act that struck me as the 1950-ish Absurdism of Eugene Ionesco and Boris Vian melted into the heart-touching whimsy of Jonathan Carroll and Jonathan Lethem, then steeped in the crazed fractured realities of the Goon Show."

—Damien Broderick, *Locus*

"After getting off to what was already an impressive start, Cory Doctorow has finally delivered the book, the one that puts him over the top as one of the rare, demonically original, challenging and gifted writers SF sees about as often as two-headed calves are born. These ranks include the likes of Philip K. Dick, Ballard, and Delany, artists who manage to write mold-breaking, unconventional stories that uproot nearly every preconception about what storytelling ought to do, and yet avoid being alienating or vapid and self-indulgent."

—Thomas M. Wagner, *SFReviews*

"After finishing *Someone Comes to Town, Someone Leaves Town*, I was surprised to find that botherment and uncertainty had vanished into satisfaction. Somehow this loose-jointed, wandering, ramshackle compendium of casual weirdness (perfectly expressed in the title) produces the kind of intimacy—even authenticity—more often associated with a personal journal, a blog, even autobiography. Yes, the mountain's son will have to confront sheer Evil, but he also struggles with the complexities of friendship, outsiderhood, progressive ideals, and the awkward hinterland between sex and love."

—Faren Miller, *Locus*

"Now of course rules, where they apply, are meant to be broken, and you may do so with impunity, if you know them well enough. Cory Doctorow clearly knows the rules. Cory Doctorow must in fact be a freaking dictionary of the rules, because in *Someone Comes to Town, Someone Leaves Town* he breaks them with such breathtaking skill that the enchanted readers of this fine novel will never be the wiser. Doctorow strings together wonderfully witty words into pithy sentences that have no right making as much sense as they do. He brings a powerful but light-hearted magic to a world we very much hope resembles the real world. *Someone Comes to Town, Someone Leaves Town* evades every expectation you might reasonably attempt to apply to it with one exception: expect to enjoy this novel immensely."

—Rick Kleffel, *The Agony Column*

Someone Comes to Town, Someone Leaves Town

CORY DOCTOROW

A TOM DOHERTY ASSOCIATES BOOK
NEW YORK

SOMEONE COMES TO TOWN, SOMEONE LEAVES TOWN

Copyright © 2005 by Cory Doctorow

Edited by Patrick Nielsen Hayden

Book design by Mary A. Worth

A Tor Book
Published by Tom Doherty Associates, LLC
175 Fifth Avenue
New York, NY 10010

www.tor.com

Tor® is a registered trademark of Tom Doherty Associates, LLC.

Library of Congress Cataloging-in-Publication Data

Doctorow, Cory.
　　Someone comes to town, someone leaves town / Cory Doctorow.
　　　　p. cm.
　　"A Tom Doherty Associates book."
　　ISBN-13: 978-0-765-31280-8
　　ISBN-10: 0-765-31280-8
　　1. Toronto (Ont.)—Fiction. 2. Internet—Fiction. I. Title.

　PS3604.O27S67 2005
　813'.6—dc22

　　　　　　　　　　　　　　　　　　　　　　　　　　　　　　2004058025

First Hardcover Edition: July 2005
First Trade Paperback Edition: June 2006

Printed in the United States of America

0 9 8 7 6 5 4 3 2 1

For the family I was born into
and the family I chose—
I got lucky both times

Someone Comes to Town,
Someone Leaves Town

Alan sanded the house on Wales Avenue. It took six months, and the whole time it was the smell of the sawdust, ancient and sweet, and the reek of chemical stripper and the damp smell of rusting steel wool.

Alan took possession of the house on January 1, and paid for it in full by means of an e-gold transfer. He had to do a fair bit of hand-holding with the realtor to get her set up and running on e-gold, but he loved to do that sort of thing, loved to sit at the elbow of a novitiate and guide her through the clicks and taps and forms. He loved to break off for impromptu lectures on the underlying principles of the transaction, and so he treated the poor realtor lady to a dozen addresses on the nature of international currency markets, the value of precious metal as a kind of financial lingua franca to which any currency could be converted, the poetry of vault shelves in a hundred banks around the world piled with the heaviest of metals, glinting dully in the fluorescent tube lighting, tended by gnomish bankers who spoke a hundred languages but communicated with one another by means of this universal tongue of weights and measures and purity.

The clerks who'd tended Alan's many stores—the used clothing store in the Beaches, the used book store in the Annex, the collectible tin-toy store in Yorkville, the antique shop on Queen Street—had both benefited from and had their patience tried by Alan's discursive nature. Alan had pretended never to notice the surreptitious rolling of eyes and twirling fingers aimed temple-wise among his employees when he got himself warmed up to a good oration, but in truth very little ever escaped his attention.

His customers loved his little talks, loved the way he could wax rhapsodic about the tortured prose in a Victorian potboiler, the nearly erotic curve of a beat-up old table leg, the voluminous cuffs of an embroidered silk smoking jacket. The clerks who listened to Alan's lectures went on to open their own stores all about town, and by and large, they did very well.

He'd put the word out when he bought the house on Wales Avenue to all his protégés: Wooden bookcases! His cell phone rang every day, bringing news of another wooden bookcase found at this flea market, that thrift store, this rummage sale or estate auction.

He had a man he used part-time, Tony, who ran a small man-with-van service, and when the phone rang, he'd send Tony over to his protégé's shop with his big panel van to pick up the case and deliver it to the cellar of the house on Wales Avenue, which was ramified by cold storages, root cellars, disused coal chutes and storm cellars. By the time Alan had finished with his sanding, every nook and cranny of the cellar was packed with wooden bookcases of every size and description and repair.

Alan worked through the long Toronto winter at his sanding. The house had been gutted by the previous owners, who'd had big plans for the building but had been tempted away by a job in Boston. They'd had to sell fast, and no amount of realtor magic—flowers on the dining-room table, soup simmering on the stove—could charm away the essential dagginess of the gutted house, the exposed timbers with sagging wires and conduit, the runnels gouged in the floor by careless draggers of furniture. Alan got it for a song, and was delighted by his fortune.

He was drunk on the wood, of course, and would have paid much more had the realtor noticed this, but Alan had spent his whole life drunk on trivial things from others' lives that no one else noticed and he'd developed the alcoholic's knack of disguising his intoxication. Alan went to work as soon as the realtor staggered off, reeling with a New Year's Day hangover. He pulled his pickup truck onto the frozen lawn, unlocked the Kryptonite bike lock he used to secure the camper bed, and dragged out his big belt sander and his many boxes of sandpaper of all grains and sizes, his heat strippers and his jugs of caustic chemical peeler. He still had his jumbled, messy place across town in a nondescript two-bedroom on the Danforth, would keep on paying the rent there until his big sanding project was done and the house on Wales Avenue was fit for habitation.

Alan's sanding project: First, finish gutting the house. Get rid of the substandard wiring, the ancient, lead-leaching plumbing, the cracked tile and water-warped crumbling plaster. He filled a half-dozen dumpsters, working with Tony and Tony's homie Nat, who was happy to help out in exchange for cash on the barrel-head, provided that he wasn't required to report for work on two consecutive days, since he'd need one day to recover from the heroic drinking he'd do immediately after Alan laid the cash across his palm.

Once the house was gutted to brick and timber and delirious wood, the plumbers and the electricians came in and laid down their straight shining ducts and pipes and conduit.

Alan tarped the floors and brought in the heavy sandblaster and stripped the age and soot and gunge off of the brickwork throughout, until it glowed red as a golem's ass.

Alan's father, the mountain, had many golems that called him home. They lived round the other side of his father and left Alan and his brothers alone, because even a golem has the sense not to piss off a mountain, especially one it lives in.

Then Alan tackled the timbers, reaching over his head with palm sanders and sandpaper of ever finer grains until the timbers were as smooth as Adirondack chairs, his chest and arms and shoulders athrob with the agony of two weeks' work. Then it was the floorwork, but *not the floors themselves,* which he was saving for last on the grounds that they were low-hanging fruit.

This materialized a new lecture in his mind, one about the proper role of low-hanging fruit, a favorite topic of MBAs who'd patronize his stores and his person, giving him unsolicited advice on the care and feeding of his shops based on the kind of useless book-learning and jargon-slinging that Fortune 100 companies apparently paid big bucks for. When an

MBA said "low-hanging fruit," he meant "easy pickings," something that could and should be snatched with minimal effort. But *real* low-hanging fruit ripens last, and should be therefore picked as late as possible. Further, picking the low-hanging fruit first meant that you'd have to carry your bushel basket higher and higher as the day wore on, which was plainly stupid. Low-hanging fruit was meant to be picked last. It was one of the ways that he understood people, and one of the kinds of people that he'd come to understand. That was the game, after all—understanding people.

So the floors would come last, after the molding, after the stairs, after the railings and the paneling. The railings, in particular, were horrible bastards to get clean, covered in ten or thirty coats of enamel of varying colors and toxicity. Alan spent days working with a wire brush and pointed twists of steel wool and oozing, stinging paint stripper, until the grain was as spotless and unmarked as the day it came off the lathe.

Then he did the floors, using the big rotary sander first. It had been years since he'd last swung a sander around—it had been when he opened the tin-toy shop in Yorkville and he'd rented one while he was prepping the place. The technique came back to him quickly enough, and he fell into a steady rhythm that soon had all the floors cool and dry and soft with naked, exposed woody heartmeat. He swept the place out and locked up and returned home.

The next day, he stopped at the Portuguese contractor-supply on Ossington that he liked. They opened at five A.M., and the men behind the counter were always happy to sketch out alternative solutions to his amateur construction problems, they never mocked him for his incompetence, and always threw in a ten percent "contractor's discount" for him that made him swell up with irrational pride that confused him. Why should the son of a mountain need affirmation from runty Portugees with pencil stubs behind their ears and scarred fingers? He picked up a pair of foam-rubber knee pads and a ten-kilo box of lint-free shop rags and another carton of disposable paper masks.

He drove to the house on Wales Avenue, parked on the lawn, which was now starting to thaw and show deep muddy ruts from his tires. He spent the next twelve hours crawling around on his knees, lugging a tool bucket filled with sandpaper and steel wool and putty and wood-crayons and shop rags. He ran his fingertips over every inch of floor and molding and paneling, feeling the talc softness of the sifted sawdust, feeling for rough spots and gouges, smoothing them out with his tools. He tried puttying over the gouges in the flooring that he'd seen the day he took possession, but the putty seemed like a lie to him, less honest than the gouged-out boards were, and so he scooped the putty out and sanded the grooves until they were as smooth as the wood around them.

Next came the beeswax, sweet and spicy and shiny. It almost broke his heart to apply it, because the soft, newly exposed wood was so deliciously tender and sensuous. But he knew that wood left to its own would eventually chip and splinter and yellow. So he rubbed wax until his elbows ached, *massaged* the wax into the wood, buffed it with shop rags so that the house shone.

Twenty coats of urethane took forty days—a day to coat and a day to dry. More buffing and the house took on a high shine, a slippery slickness. He nearly broke his neck on the slippery staircase treads, and the Portuguese helped him out with a bag of clear grit made from ground walnut shells. He used a foam brush to put one more coat of urethane on each tread of the stairs, then sprinkled granulated walnut shells on while it was still sticky. He committed a rare error in judgment and did the stairs from the bottom up and trapped himself on the third floor, with its attic ceilings and dormer windows, and felt like a goddamned idiot as he curled up to sleep on the cold, hard, slippery, smooth floor while he waited for his stairs to dry. The urethane must be getting to his head.

The bookcases came out of the cellar one by one. Alan wrestled them onto the front porch with Tony's help and sanded them clean, then turned them over to Tony for urethane and dooring.

The doors were UV-filtering glass, hinged at the top and surrounded by felt on their inside lips so that they closed softly. Each one had a small brass prop-rod on the left side that could brace it open. Tony had been responsible for measuring each bookcase after he retrieved it from Alan's protégés' shops and for sending the measurements off to a glazier in Mississauga.

The glazier was technically retired, but he'd built every display case that had ever sat inside any of Alan's shops and was happy to make use of the small workshop that his daughter and son-in-law had installed in his garage when they retired him to the burbs.

The bookcases went into the house, along each wall, according to a system of numbers marked on their backs. Alan had used Tony's measurements and some CAD software to come up with a permutation of stacking and shouldering cases that had them completely covering every wall—except for the wall by the mantelpiece in the front parlor, the wall over the countertop in the kitchen, and the wall beside the staircases—to the ceiling.

He and Tony didn't speak much. Tony was thinking about whatever people who drive moving vans think about, and Alan was thinking about the story he was building the house to write in.

May smelled great in Kensington Market. The fossilized dog shit had melted and washed away in the April rains, and the smells were all springy ones, loam and blossoms and spilled tetrapak fruit punch left behind by the pan-ethnic street-hockey league that formed up spontaneously in front of his house. When the winds blew from the east, he smelled the fish stalls on Spadina, salty and redolent of Chinese barbecue spices. When it blew from the north, he smelled baking bread in the kosher bakeries and sometimes a rare whiff of roasting garlic from the pizzas in the steaming ovens at Massimo's all the way up on College. The western winds smelled of hospital incinerator, acrid and smoky.

His father, the mountain, had attuned Art to smells, since they were the leading indicators of his moods, sulfurous belches from deep in the caverns when he was displeased, the cold non-smell of springwater when he was thoughtful, the new-mown hay smell from his slopes when he was happy. Understanding smells was something that you did, when the mountain was your father.

Once the bookcases were seated and screwed into the walls, out came the books, thousands of them, tens of thousands of them.

Little kids' books with loose signatures, ancient first-edition hardcovers, outsized novelty art books, mass-market paperbacks, reference books as thick as cinderblocks. They were mostly used when he'd gotten them, and that was what he loved most about them: They smelled like other people and their pages contained hints of their lives: marginalia and pawn tickets, bus transfers gone yellow with age and smears of long-ago meals. When he read them, he was in three places: his living room, the authors' heads, and the world of their previous owners.

They came off his shelves at home, from the ten-by-ten storage down on the lakeshore, they came from friends and enemies who'd borrowed his books years before and who'd "forgotten" to return them, but Alan *never* forgot, he kept every book in a great and deep relational database that had begun as a humble flatfile but which had been imported into successive generations of industrial-grade database software.

This, in turn, was but a pocket in the Ur-database, The Inventory in which Alan had input the value, the cost, the salient features, the unique identifiers, and the photographic record of every single thing he owned, from the socks in his sock drawer to the pots in his cupboard. Maintaining The Inventory was serious business, no less important now than it had been when he had begun it in the course of securing insurance for the bookshop.

Alan was an insurance man's worst nightmare, a customer from hell who'd messenger over five bankers' boxes of detailed, cross-referenced Inventory at the slightest provocation.

The books filled the shelves, row on row, behind the dust-proof, light-proof glass doors. The books began in the foyer and wrapped around the living room, covered the wall behind the dining room in the kitchen, filled the den and the master bedroom and the master bath, climbed the short walls to the dormer ceilings on the third floor. They were organized by idiosyncratic subject categories, and alphabetical by author within those categories.

Alan's father was a mountain, and his mother was a washing machine—he kept a roof over their heads and she kept their clothes clean. His brothers were: a dead man, a trio of nesting dolls, a fortune-teller, and an island. He only had two or three family portraits, but he treasured them, even if outsiders who saw them often mistook them for landscapes. There was one where his family stood on his father's slopes, Mom out in the open for a rare exception, a long tail of extension cords snaking away from her to the cave and the diesel generator's three-prong outlet. He hung it over the mantel, using two hooks and a level to make sure that it came out perfectly even.

Tony helped Alan install the shallow collectibles cases along the house's two-story stairwell, holding the level while Alan worked the cordless power driver. Alan's glazier had built the cases to Alan's specs, and they stretched from the treads to the ceiling. Alan filled them with Made-in-Occupied-Japan tin toys, felt tourist pennants from central Florida gator farms, a stone from Marie Laveau's tomb in the St. Louis I Cemetery in New Orleans, tarnished brass Zippos, small framed comic-book bodybuilding ads, carved Polynesian coconut monkeys, melamine transistor radios, Bakelite snow globes, all the tchotchkes he'd accumulated over a lifetime of picking and hunting and digging.

They were gloriously scuffed and non-mint: he'd always sold off the sterile mint-in-package goods as quickly as he could, squirreling away the items that were marked with "Property of Freddy Terazzo" in shaky ballpoint, the ones with tooth marks and frayed boxes taped shut with brands of stickytape not offered for sale in fifty years.

The last thing to go in was the cellar. They knocked out any wall that wasn't load-bearing, smeared concrete on every surface, and worked in a loose mosaic of beach glass and beach china, smooth and white with spidery blue illustrations pale as a dream. Three coats of urethane made the surfaces gleam.

Then it was just a matter of stringing out the cables for the clip-on halogens whose beams he took care to scatter off the ceilings to keep the glare to a minimum. He moved in his horse-hair sofa and armchairs, his big old bed, his pots and pans and sideboard with its novelty decanters, and his entertainment totem.

A man from Bell Canada came out and terminated the data line in his basement, in a room that he'd outfitted with an uninterruptible power supply, a false floor, dry fire extinguishers and a pipe-break sensor. He installed and configured the router, set up his modest rack and home servers, fished three four-pair wires through to the living room, the den and the attic, where he attached them to unobtrusive wireless access points and thence to weatherproofed omnidirectional antennae made from copper tubing and PVC that he'd affixed to the building's exterior on short masts, aimed out over Kensington Market, blanketing a whole block with free Internet access.

He had an idea that the story he was going to write would require some perambulatory cogitation, and he wanted to be able to take his laptop anywhere in the market and sit down and write and hop online and check out little factoids with a search engine so he wouldn't get hung up on stupid details.

The house on Wales Avenue was done. He'd repainted the exterior a lovely robin's-egg blue, fixed the front step, and planted a low-maintenance combination of outsized rocks from the Canadian Shield and wild grasses on the front lawn. On July first, Alan celebrated Canada Day by crawling out of the attic window onto the roof and watching the fireworks and listening to the collective sighs of the people densely packed around him in the Market, then he went back into the house and walked from room to room, looking for something out of place, some spot still rough and unsanded, and found none. The books and the collections lined the walls, the fans whirred softly in the ceilings, the filters beneath the open windows hummed as they sucked the pollen and particulate out of the rooms—Alan's retail experience had convinced him long ago of the selling power of fresh air and street sounds, so he refused to keep the windows closed, despite the fantastic volume of city dust that blew in.

The house was perfect. The ergonomic marvel of a chair that UPS had dropped off the previous day was tucked under the wooden sideboard he'd set up as a desk in the second-floor den. His brand-new computer sat centered on the desk, a top-of-the-line laptop with a wireless card and a screen big enough to qualify as a home theater in some circles.

Tomorrow, he'd start the story.

Alan rang the next-door house's doorbell at eight A.M. He had a bag of coffees from the Greek diner. Five coffees, one for each bicycle locked to the wooden railing on the sagging porch plus one for him.

He waited five minutes, then rang the bell again, holding it down, listening for the sound of footsteps over the muffled jangling of the buzzer. It took two minutes more, he estimated, but he didn't mind. It was a beautiful summer day, soft and moist and green, and he could already smell the fish market over the mellow brown vapors of the strong coffee.

A young woman in long johns and a baggy tartan T-shirt opened the door. She was excitingly plump, round, and a little jiggly, the kind of woman Alan had always gone for. Of course, she was all of twenty-two, and so was certainly not an appropriate romantic interest for him, but she was fun to look at as she ungummed her eyes and worked the sleep out of her voice.

"Yes?" she said through the locked screen door. Her voice brooked no nonsense, which Alan also liked. He'd hire her in a second, if he were still running a shop. He liked to hire sharp kids like her, get to know them, try to winkle out their motives and emotions through observation.

"Good morning!" Alan said. "I'm Alan, and I just moved in next door. I've brought coffee!" He hefted his sack in her direction.

"Good morning, Alan," she said. "Thanks and all, but—"

"Oh, no need to thank me! Just being neighborly. I brought five—one for each of you and one for me."

"Well, that's awfully nice of you—"

"Nothing at all. Nice morning, huh? I saw a robin just there, on that tree in the park, not an hour ago. Fantastic."

"Great." She unlatched the screen door and opened it, reaching for the sack.

Alan stepped into the foyer and handed it to her. "There's cream and sugar in there," he said. "Lots—don't know how you folks take it, so I just figured better sure than miserable, better to err on the side of caution. Wow, look at this, your place has a completely different layout from mine. I think they were built at the same time, I mean, they look a lot alike. I don't really know much about architecture, but they really do seem the same, don't they, from the outside? But look at this! In my place, I've got a long corridor before you get to the living room, but your place is all open. I wonder if it was built that way, or if someone did that later. Do you know?"

"No," she said, hefting the sack.

"Well, I'll just have a seat while you get your roommates up, all right? Then we can all have a nice cup of coffee and a chat and get to know each other."

She dithered for a moment, then stepped back toward the kitchen and the stairwell. Alan nodded and took a little tour of the living room. There was a very nice media totem, endless shelves of DVDs and videos, including a good selection of Chinese kung-fu VCDs and black and white comedies. There was a stack of guitar magazines on the battered coffee table, and a cozy sofa with an afghan folded neatly on one arm. Good kids, he could tell that just by looking at their possessions.

Not very security-conscious, though. She should have either kicked him out or dragged him around the house while she got her roomies out of bed. He thought about slipping some VCDs into his pocket and returning them later, just to make the point, but decided it would be getting off on the wrong foot.

She returned a moment later, wearing a fuzzy yellow robe

whose belt and seams were gray with grime and wear. "They're coming down," she said.

"Terrific!" Alan said, and planted himself on the sofa. "How about that coffee, hey?"

She shook her head, smiled a little, and retrieved a coffee for him. "Cream? Sugar?"

"Nope," Alan said. "The Greek makes it just the way I like it. Black and strong and aromatic. Try some before you add anything—it's really fantastic. One of the best things about the neighborhood, if you ask me."

Another young woman, rail-thin with a shaved head, baggy jeans, and a tight T-shirt that he could count her ribs through, shuffled into the living room. Alan got to his feet and extended his hand. "Hi there! I'm Adam, your new neighbor! I brought coffees!"

She shook his hand, her long fingernails sharp on his palm. "Natalie," she said.

The other young woman passed a coffee to her. "He brought coffees," she said. "Try it before you add anything to it." She turned to Alan. "I thought you said your name was Alan?"

"Alan, Adam, Andy. Doesn't matter, I answer to any of them. My mom had a hard time keeping our names straight."

"Funny," Natalie said, sipping at her coffee. "Two sugars, three creams," she said, holding her hand out. The other woman silently passed them to her.

"I haven't gotten your name yet," Alan said.

"Right," the other one said. "You sure haven't."

A young man, all of seventeen, with straggly sideburns and a shock of pink hair sticking straight up in the air, shuffled into the room, wearing cutoffs and an unbuttoned guayabera.

"Adam," Natalie said, "this is Link, my kid brother. Link, this is Arthur—he brought coffees."

"Hey, thanks, Arthur," Link said. He accepted his coffee and stood by his sister, sipping reverently.

"So that leaves one more," Alan said. "And then we can get started."

Link snorted. "Not likely. Krishna doesn't get out of bed before noon."

"Krishna?" Alan said.

"My boyfriend," the nameless woman said. "He was up late."

"More coffee for the rest of us, I suppose," Alan said. "Let's all sit and get to know one another, then, shall we?"

They sat. Alan slurped down the rest of his coffee, then gestured at the sack. The nameless woman passed it to him and he got the last one, and set to drinking.

"I'm Andreas, your new next-door neighbor. I've just finished renovating, and I moved in last night. I'm really looking forward to spending time in the neighborhood—I work from home, so I'll be around a bunch. Feel free to drop by if you need to borrow a cup of sugar or anything."

"That's so nice of you," Natalie said. "I'm sure we'll get along fine!"

"Thanks, Natalie. Are you a student?"

"Yup," she said. She fished in the voluminous pockets of her jeans, tugging them lower on her knobby hips, and came up with a pack of cigarettes. She offered one to her brother, who took it, and one to Alan, who declined, then lit up. "Studying fashion design at OCAD. I'm in my last year, so it's all practicum from now on."

"Fashion! How interesting," Alan said. "I used to run a little vintage clothes shop in the Beaches, called Tropicál."

"Oh, I *loved* that shop," she said. "You had the *best* stuff! I used to sneak out there on the streetcar after school." Yup. He didn't remember *her*, exactly, but her *type*, sure. Solo girls with hardcover sketchbooks and vintage clothes home-tailored to a nice fit.

"Well, I'd be happy to introduce you to some of the people I know—there's a vintage shop that a friend of mine runs in Parkdale. He's always looking for designers to help with rehab and repros."

"That would be so cool!"

"Now, Link, what do you study?"

Link pulled at his smoke, ashed in the fireplace grate. "Not much. I didn't get into Ryerson for electrical engineering, so I'm spending a year as a bike courier, taking night classes, and reapplying for next year."

"Well, that'll keep you out of trouble at least," Alan said. He turned to the nameless woman.

"So, what do you do, *Apu*?" she said to him, before he could say anything.

"Oh, I'm retired, Mimi," he said.

"Mimi?" she said.

"Why not? It's as good a name as any."

"Her name is—" Link started to say, but she cut him off.

"Mimi is as good a name as any. I'm unemployed. Krishna's a bartender."

"Are you looking for work?"

She smirked. "Sure. Whatcha got?"

"What can you do?"

"I've got three-quarters of a degree in environmental studies, one year of kinesiology, and a half-written one-act play. Oh, and student debt until the year 3000."

"A play!" he said, slapping his thighs. "You should finish it. I'm a writer, too, you know."

"I thought you had a clothing shop."

"I did. And a bookshop, and a collectibles shop, and an antique shop. Not all at the same time, you understand. But now I'm writing. Going to write a story, then I imagine I'll open another shop. But I'm more interested in *you*, Mimi, and your play. Why half-finished?"

She shrugged and combed her hair back with her fingers. Her hair was brown and thick and curly, down to her shoulders. Alan adored curly hair. He'd had a clerk at the comics shop with curly hair just like hers, an earnest and bright young thing who drew her own comics in the back room on her breaks, using the receiving table as a drawing board. She'd never made much of a go of it as an artist, but she did end up publishing a popular annual anthology of underground comics that had captured the interest of the *New Yorker* the year before. "I just ran out of inspiration," Mimi said, tugging at her hair.

"Well, there you are. Time to get inspired again. Stop by anytime and we'll talk about it, all right?"

"If I get back to it, you'll be the first to know."

"Tremendous!" he said. "I just know it'll be fantastic. Now, who plays the guitar?"

"Krishna," Link said. "I noodle a bit, but he's really good."

"He sure is," Alan said. "He was in fine form last night, about three A.M.!" He chuckled pointedly.

There was an awkward silence. Alan slurped down his second coffee. "Whoops!" he said. "I believe I need to impose on you for the use of your facilities?"

"What?" Natalie and Link said simultaneously.

"He wants the toilet," Mimi said. "Up the stairs, second door on the right. Jiggle the handle after you flush."

The bathroom was crowded with too many towels and too many toothbrushes. The sink was powdered with blusher and marked with lipstick and mascara residue. It made Alan feel at home. He liked young people. Liked their energy, their resentment, and their enthusiasm. Didn't like their guitar-playing at three A.M., but he'd sort that out soon enough.

He washed his hands and carefully rinsed the long curly hairs from the bar before replacing it in its dish, then returned to the living room.

"Abel," Mimi said, "sorry if the guitar kept you up last night."

"No sweat," Alan said. "It must be hard to find time to practice when you work nights."

"Exactly," Natalie said. "Exactly right! Krishna always practices when he comes back from work. He blows off some steam so he can get to bed. We just all learned to sleep through it."

"Well," Alan said, "to be honest, I'm hoping I won't have to learn to do that. But I think that maybe I have a solution we can both live with."

"What's that?" Mimi said, jutting her chin forward.

"It's easy, really. I can put up a resilient channel and a baffle along that wall there, soundproofing. I'll paint it over white and you won't even notice the difference. Shouldn't take me more than a week. Happy to do it. Thick walls make good neighbors."

"We don't really have any money to pay for renovations," Mimi said.

Alan waved his hand. "Who said anything about money? I just want to solve the problem. I'd do it on my side of the wall, but I've just finished renovating."

Mimi shook her head. "I don't think the landlord would go for it."

"You worry too much," he said. "Give me your landlord's number and I'll sort it out with him, all right?"

"All right!" Link said. "That's terrific, Albert, really!"

"All right, Mimi? Natalie?"

Natalie nodded enthusiastically, her shaved head whipping up and down on her thin neck precariously. Mimi glared at Natalie and Link. "I'll ask Krishna," she said.

"All right, then!" Alan said. "Let me measure up the wall and I'll start shopping for supplies." He produced a matte-black, egg-shaped digital tape measure and started shining pinpoints of laser light on the wall, clicking the egg's buttons when he had the corners tight. The Portuguese clerks at his favorite store had dissolved into hysterics when he'd proudly shown them the $300 gadget, but they were consistently impressed by the exacting CAD drawings of his projects that he generated with its output. Natalie and Link stared in fascination as he did his thing with more showmanship than was technically necessary, though Mimi made a point of rolling her eyes.

"Don't go spending any money yet, cowboy," she said. "I've still got to talk to Krishna, and *you've* still got to talk with the landlord."

He fished in the breast pocket of his jean jacket and found a stub of pencil and a little steno pad, scribbled his cell phone number, and tore off the sheet. He passed the sheet, pad, and pencil to Mimi, who wrote out the landlord's number and passed it back to him.

"Okay!" Alan said. "There you go. It's been a real pleasure meeting you folks. I know we're going to get along great. I'll call your landlord right away and you call me once Krishna's up, and I'll see you tomorrow at ten A.M. to start construction, God willin' and the crick don't rise."

Link stood and extended his hand. "Nice to meet you, Albert," he said. "Really. Thanks for the muds, too." Natalie gave him a bony hug, and Mimi gave him a limp handshake, and then he was out in the sunshine, head full of designs and logistics and plans.

The sun set at nine P.M. in a long summertime blaze. Alan sat down on the twig chair on his front porch, pulled up the matching twig table, and set down a wine glass and the bottle of Niagara Chardonnay he'd brought up from the cellar. He poured out a glass and held it up to the light, admiring the new blister he'd gotten on his pinky finger while hauling two-by-fours and gyprock from his truck to his neighbors' front room. Kids rode by on bikes and punks rode by on skateboards. Couples wandered through the park across the street, their murmurous conversations clear on the whispering breeze that rattled the leaves.

He hadn't gotten any writing done, but that was all right. He had plenty of time, and once the soundwall was in, he'd be able to get a good night's sleep and really focus down on the story.

A Chinese girl and a white boy walked down the sidewalk, talking intensely. They were all of six, and the boy had a Russian accent. The Market's diversity always excited Alan. The boy looked a little like Alan's brother Doug (Dan, David, Dearborne) had looked when he was that age.

Doug was the one he'd help murder. All the brothers had helped with the murder, even Charlie (Clem, Carlos, Cory), the island, who'd opened a great fissure down his main fault line and closed it up over Doug's corpse, ensuring that their parents would be none the wiser. Doug was a stubborn son-of-a-bitch, though, and his corpse had tunneled up over the next six years, built a raft from the bamboo and vines that grew in proliferation on Carlos's west coast. He sailed the raft through treacherous seas for a year and a day, beached it on their father's gentle slope, and presented himself to their mother. By that time, the corpse had decayed and frayed and worn away, so that he was little more than a torso and stumps, his tongue withered and stiff, but he pled his case to their mother, and she was so upset that her load overbalanced and they had to restart her. Their father was so angry that he quaked and caved in Billy (Bob, Brad, Benny)'s room, crushing all his tools and all his trophies.

But a lot of time had gone by and the brothers weren't kids anymore. Alan was nineteen, ready to move to Toronto and start scouting for real estate. Only Doug still looked like a little boy, albeit a stumpy and desiccated one. He hollered and stamped until his fingerbones rattled on the floor and his tongue flew across the room and cracked on the wall. When his anger was spent, he crawled atop their mother and let her rock him into a long, long slumber.

Alan had left his father and his family the next morning, carrying a rucksack heavy with gold from under the mountain, and walked down to the town, taking the same trail he'd walked every school day since he was five. He waved to the people that drove past him on the highway as he waited at the bus stop. He was the first son to leave home under his own power, and he'd been full of butterflies, but he had a half-dozen good books that he'd checked out of the Kapuskasing branch library to keep him occupied on the fourteen-hour journey, and before he knew it, the bus was pulling off the Gardiner Expressway by the SkyDome and into the midnight streets of Toronto, where the buildings stretched to the sky, where the blinking lights of the Yonge Street sleaze-strip receded into the distance like a landing strip for a horny UFO.

His liquid cash was tight, so he spent that night in the Rex Hotel, in the worst room in the house, right over the cymbal tree that the jazz drummer below hammered on until nearly two A.M. The bed was small and hard and smelled of bleach and must, the washbasin gurgled mysteriously and spat out moist sewage odors, and he'd read all his books, so he sat in the window and watched the drunks and the hipsters stagger down Queen Street and inhaled the smoky, spicy air, and before he knew it, he'd nodded off in the chair with his heavy coat around him like a blanket.

The Chinese girl abruptly thumped her fist into the Russian boy's ear. He clutched his head and howled, tears streaming down his face, while the Chinese girl ran off. Alan shook his head, got up off his chair, went inside for a cold washcloth and an ice pack, and came back out.

The Russian boy's face was screwed up and blotchy and streaked with tears, and it made him look even more like Doug, who'd always been a crybaby. Alan couldn't understand him, but he took a guess and knelt at his side and wiped the boy's face, then put the ice pack in his little hand and pressed it to the side of his little head.

"Come on," he said, taking the boy's other hand. "Where do your parents live? I'll take you home."

Alan met Krishna the next morning at ten A.M., as Alan was running a table saw on the neighbors' front lawn, sawing studs up to fit the second wall. Krishna came out of the house in a dirty dressing gown, his short hair matted with gel from the night before. He was tall and fit and muscular, his brown calves flashing through the vent of his housecoat. He was smoking a hand-rolled cigarette and clutching a can of Coke.

Alan shut down the saw and shifted his goggles up to his forehead. "Good morning," he said. "I'd stay on the porch if I were you, or maybe put on some shoes. There're lots of nails and splinters around."

Krishna, about to step off the porch, stepped back. "You must be Alvin," he said.

"Yup," Alan said, going up the stairs, sticking out his hand. "And you must be Krishna. You're pretty good with a guitar, you know that?"

Krishna shook briefly, then snatched his hand back and rubbed at his stubble. "I know. You're pretty fucking loud with a table saw."

Alan looked sheepish. "Sorry about that. I wanted to get the heavy work done before it got too hot. Hope I'm not disturbing you too much—today's the only sawing day. I'll be hammering for the next day or two, then it's all wet work—the loudest tool I'll be using is sandpaper. Won't take more than four days, tops, anyway, and we'll be in good shape."

Krishna gave him a long, considering look. "What are you, anyway?"

"I'm a writer—for now. Used to have a few shops."

Krishna blew a plume of smoke off into the distance. "That's not what I mean. What *are* you, Adam? Alan? Andrew? I've met people like you before. There's something not right about you."

Alan didn't know what to say to that. This was bound to come up someday.

"Where are you from?"

"Up north. Near Kapuskasing," he said. "A little town."

"I don't believe you," Krishna said. "Are you an alien? A fairy? What?"

Alan shook his head. "Just about what I seem, I'm afraid. Just a guy."

"Just about, huh?" he said.

"Just about."

"There's a lot of wiggle room in *just about,* Arthur. It's a free country, but just the same, I don't think I like you very much. Far as I'm concerned, you could get lost and never come back."

"Sorry you feel that way, Krishna. I hope I'll grow on you as time goes by."

"I hope that you won't have the chance to," Krishna said, flicking the dog end of his cigarette toward the sidewalk.

Alan didn't like or understand Krishna, but that was okay. He understood the others just fine, more or less. Natalie had taken to helping him out after her classes, mudding and taping the drywall, then sanding it down, priming, and painting it. Her brother Link came home from work sweaty and grimy with road dust, but he always grabbed a beer for Natalie and Alan after his shower, and they'd sit on the porch and kibbitz.

Mimi was less hospitable. She sulked in her room while Alan worked on the soundwall, coming downstairs only to fetch her breakfast and coldly ignoring him then, despite his cheerful greetings. Alan had to force himself not to stare after her as she walked into the kitchen, carrying yesterday's dishes down from her room; then out again, with a sandwich on a fresh plate. Her curly hair bounced as she stomped back and forth, her soft, round buttocks flexing under her long johns.

On the night that Alan and Natalie put the first coat of paint on the wall, Mimi came down in a little baby-doll dress, thigh-high striped tights, and chunky shoes, her face painted with swaths of glitter.

"You look wonderful, baby," Natalie told her as she emerged onto the porch. "Going out?"

"Going to the club," she said. "DJ None Of Your Fucking Business is spinning and Krishna's going to get me in for free."

"Dance music," Link said disgustedly. Then, to Alan, "You know this stuff? It's not playing music, it's playing *records*. Snore."

"Sounds interesting," Alan said. "Do you have any of it I could listen to? A CD or some MP3s?"

"Oh, *that's* not how you listen to this stuff," Natalie said. "You have to go to a club and *dance*."

"Really?" Alan said. "Do I have to take ecstasy, or is that optional?"

"It's mandatory," Mimi said, the first words she'd spoken to him all week. "Great fistfuls of E, and then you have to consume two pounds of candy necklaces at an after-hours orgy."

"Not really," Natalie said, *sotto voce*. "But you *do* have to dance. You should go with, uh, Mimi, to the club. DJ None Of Your Fucking Business is *amazing*."

"I don't think Mimi wants company," Alan said.

"What makes you say that?" Mimi said, making a dare of it with hipshot body language. "Get changed and we'll go together. You'll have to pay to get in, though."

Link and Natalie exchanged a raised eyebrow, but Alan was already headed for his place, fumbling for his keys. He bounded up the stairs, swiped a washcloth over his face, threw on a pair of old cargo pants and a faded Steel Pole Bathtub T-shirt he'd bought from a head shop one day because he liked the words' incongruity, though he'd never heard the band, added a faded jean jacket and a pair of high-tech sneakers, grabbed his phone, and bounded back down the stairs. He was convinced that Mimi would be long gone by the time he got back out front, but she was still there, the stripes in her stockings glowing in the slanting light.

"Retro chic," she said, and laughed nastily. Natalie gave him a thumbs-up and a smile that Alan uncharitably took for a simper, and felt guilty about it immediately afterward. He returned the thumbs-up and then took off after Mimi, who'd already started down Augusta, headed for Queen Street.

"What's the cover charge?" he said, once he'd caught up.

"Twenty bucks," she said. "It's an all-ages show, so they won't be selling a lot of booze, so there's a high cover."

"How's the play coming?"

"Fuck off about the play, okay?" she said, and spat on the sidewalk.

"All right, then," he said. "I'm going to start writing my story tomorrow," he said.

"Your story, huh?"

"Yup."

"What's that for?"

"What do you mean?" he asked playfully.

"Why are you writing a story?"

"Well, I have to! I've completely redone the house, built that soundwall—it'd be a shame not to write the story now."

"You're writing a story about your house?"

"No, *in* my house. I haven't decided what the story's about yet. That'll be job one tomorrow."

"You did all that work to have a place to write? Man, I thought *I* was into procrastination."

He chuckled self-deprecatingly. "I guess you could look at it that way. I just wanted to have a nice, creative environment to work in. The story's important to me, is all."

"What are you going to do with it once you're done? There aren't a whole lot of places that publish short stories these days, you know."

"Oh, I know it! I'd write a novel if I had the patience. But this isn't for publication—yet. It's going into a drawer to be published after I die."

"*What?*"

"Like Emily Dickinson. Wrote thousands of poems, stuck 'em in a drawer, dropped dead. Someone else published 'em and she made it into the canon. I'm going to do the same."

"That's nuts—are you dying?"

"Nope. But I don't want to put this off until I am. Could get hit by a bus, you know."

"You're a goddamned psycho. Krishna was right."

"What does Krishna have against me?"

"I think we both know what that's about," she said.

"No, really, what did I ever do to him?"

Now they were on Queen Street, walking east in the early evening crowd, surrounded by summertime hipsters and wafting, appetizing smells from the bistros and Jamaican roti shops. She stopped abruptly and grabbed his shoulders and gave him a hard shake.

"You're full of shit, Ad-man. I know it and you know it."

"I really don't know what you're talking about, honestly!"

"Fine, let's do this." She clamped her hand on his forearm and dragged him down a side street and turned down an alley. She stepped into a doorway and started unbuttoning her Alice-blue babydoll dress. Alan looked away, embarrassed, glad of the dark hiding his blush.

Once the dress was unbuttoned to her waist, she reached around behind her and unhooked her white underwire bra, which sagged forward under the weight of her heavy breasts. She turned around, treating him to a glimpse of the full curve of her breast under her arm, and shrugged the dress down around her waist.

She had two stubby, leathery wings growing out of the middle of her back, just above the shoulder blades. They sat flush against her back, and as Alan watched, they unfolded and flexed, flapped a few times, and settled back into their position, nested among the soft roll of flesh that descended from her neck.

Involuntarily, he peered forward, examining the wings, which were covered in fine downy brown hairs, and their bases, roped with muscle and surrounded by a mess of ugly scars.

"You . . . *sewed* . . . these on?" Alan said, aghast.

She turned around, her eyes bright with tears. Her breasts swung free of her unhooked bra. "No, you fucking idiot. I sawed them off. Four times a year. They just grow back. If I don't cut them, they grow down to my ankles."

Mimi was curiously and incomprehensibly affectionate after she had buttoned up her dress and resumed walking toward the strip of clubs along Richmond Street. She put her hand on his forearm and murmured funny commentary about the outlandishly attired club kids in their plastic cowboy hats, Sailor Moon outfits, and plastic tuxedoes. She plucked a cigarette from his lips, dragged on it, and put it back into his mouth, still damp with her saliva, an act that sent a shiver down Alan's neck and made the hair on the backs of his hands stand up.

She seemed to think that the wings were self-explanatory and needed no further discussion, and Alan was content to let them stay in his mind's eye, bat-shaped, powerful, restless, surrounded by their gridwork of angry scars.

Once they got to the club, Shasta Disaster, a renovated brick bank with robotic halogen spots that swept the sidewalk out front with a throbbing penis logomark, she let go of his arm and her body stiffened. She said something in the doorman's ear, and he let her pass. When Alan tried to follow her, the bouncer stopped him with a meaty hand on his chest.

"Can I help you sir," he said flatly. He was basically a block of fat and muscle with a head on top, arms as thick as Alan's thighs barely contained in a silver button-down short-sleeve shirt that bound at his armpits.

"Do I pay the cover to you?" Alan asked, reaching for his wallet.

"No, you don't get to pay a cover. You're not coming in."

"But I'm with her," Alan said, gesturing in the direction Mimi had gone. "I'm Krishna's and her neighbor."

"She didn't mention it," the bouncer said. He was smirking now.

"Look," Alan said. "I haven't been to a club in twenty years. Do you guys still take bribes?"

The bouncer rolled his eyes. "Some might. I don't. Why don't you head home, sir."

"That's it, huh?" Alan said. "Nothing I can say or do?"

"Don't be a smart guy," the bouncer said.

"Good night, then," Alan said, and turned on his heel. He walked back up to Queen Street, which was ablaze with TV lights from the open studio out front of the CHUM-City building. Hordes of teenagers in tiny, outrageous outfits milled back and forth from the coffee shops to the studio window, where some band he'd never heard of was performing, generally ambling southward to the clubs. Alan bought himself a coffee with a sixteen-syllable latinate trade name ("Moch-a-latt-a-meraican-a-spress-a-chino," he liked to call them) at the Second Cup and hailed a taxi.

He felt only the shortest moment of anger at Mimi, but it quickly cooled and then warmed again, replaced by bemusement. Decrypting the mystical deeds of young people had been his hobby and avocation since he hired his first cranky-but-bright sixteen-year-old. Mimi had played him, he knew that, deliberately set him up to be humiliated. But she'd also wanted a moment alone with him, an opportunity to confront him with her wings—wings that were taking on an air of the erotic now in his imagination, much to his chagrin. He imagined that they were soft and pliable as lips but with spongy cartilage beneath that gave way like livid nipple flesh. The hair must be silky, soft, and slippery as a pubic thatch oiled with sweat and juices. Dear oh dear, he was really getting himself worked into a lather, imagining the wings drooping to the ground, unfolding powerfully in his living room, encircling him, enveloping him as his lips enveloped the tendons on her neck, as her vagina enveloped him . . . Whew!

The taxi drove right past his place and that gave Alan a much-needed distraction, directing the cabbie through the maze of Kensington Market's one-way streets back around to his front door. He tipped the cabbie a couple of bucks over his customary ten percent and bummed a cigarette off him, realizing that Mimi had asked him for a butt but never returned the pack.

He puffed and shook his head and stared up the street at the distant lights of College Street, then turned back to his porch.

"Hello, Albert," two voices said in unison, speaking from the shadows on his porch.

"Jesus," he said, and hit the remote on his keyring that switched on the porch light. It was his brother Edward, the eldest of the nesting dolls, the bark of their trinity, coarse and tough and hollow. He was even fatter than he'd been as a little boy, fat enough that his arms and legs appeared vestigial and unjointed. He struggled, panting, to his tiny feet—feet like undersized exclamation points beneath the tapered Oh of his body. His face, though doughy, had not gone to undefined softness. Rather, every feature had acquired its own rolls of fat, rolls that warred with one another to define his appearance—nose and cheekbones and brow and lips all grotesque and inflated and blubbery.

"Eugene," Alan said. "It's been a very long time."

Edward cocked his head. "It has, indeed, big brother. I've got bad news."

"What?"

Edward leaned to the left, the top half of his body tipping over completely, splitting at his narrow leather belt, so that his trunk, neck, and head hung upside down beside his short, cylindrical legs and tiny feet.

Inside of him was Frederick, the perennial middle child. Frederick planted his palms on the dry, smooth edges of his older brother's waist and levered himself up, stepping out of Ed's legs with the unconscious ease of a lifetime's practice. "It's good to see you, Andy," he said. He was pale and wore his habitual owlish expression of surprise at seeing the world without looking through his older brother's eyes.

"It's nice to see you, too, Frederick," Alan said. He'd always gotten along with Frederick, always liked his ability to play peacemaker and to lend a listening ear.

Frederick helped Edward upright, methodically circumnavigating his huge belly, retucking his grimy white shirt. Then he hitched up his sweatshirt over the hairy pale expanse of his own belly and tipped to one side.

Alan had been expecting to see Gregory, the core, but instead there was nothing inside Frederick. The Gregory-shaped void was empty. Frederick righted himself and hitched up his belt.

"We think he's dead," Edward said, his rubbery features distorted into a Greek tragedy mask. "We think that Doug killed him." He pinwheeled his round arms and then clapped his hands to his face, sobbing. Frederick put a hand on his arm. He, too, was crying.

Once upon a time, Alan's mother gave birth to three sons in three months. Birthing sons was hardly extraordinary—before these three came along, she'd already had four others. But the interval, well, that was unusual.

As the eldest, Alan was the first to recognize the early signs of her pregnancy. The laundry loads of diapers and play clothes he fed into her belly unbalanced more often, and her spin cycle became almost lackadaisical, so the garments had to hang on the line for days before they stiffened and dried completely. Alan liked to sit with his back against his mother's hard enamel side while she rocked and gurgled and churned. It comforted him.

The details of her conception were always mysterious to Alan. He'd been walking down into town to attend day school for five years, and he'd learned all about the birds and the bees, and he thought that maybe his father—the mountain—impregnated his mother by means of some strange pollen carried on the gusts of winds from his deep and gloomy caves. There was a gnome, too, who made sure that the long hose that led from Alan's mother's back to the spring pool in his father's belly remained clear and unfouled, and sometimes Alan wondered if the gnome dove for his father's seed and fed it up his mother's intake. Alan's life was full of mysteries, and he'd long since learned to keep his mouth shut about his home life when he was at school.

He attended all three births, along with the smaller kids—Bill and Donald (Charlie, the island, was still small enough to float in the middle of their father's heart-pool)—waiting on tenterhooks for his mother's painful off-balance spin cycle to spend itself before reverently opening the round glass door and removing the infant within.

Edward was fat, even for a baby. He looked like an elongated soccer ball with a smaller ball on top. He cried healthily, though, and gave hearty suck to their mother's exhaust valve once Alan had cleaned the soap suds and fabric softener residue from his little body. His father gusted proud, warm, blustery winds over them and their little domestic scene.

Alan noticed that little Edward, for all his girth, was very light, and wondered if the baby was full of helium or some other airy substance. Certainly he hardly appeared to be full of *baby*, since everything he ate and drank passed through him in a matter of seconds, hardly digested at all. Alan had to go into town twice to buy new twelve-pound boxes of clean white shop rags to clean up the slime trail the baby left behind him. Drew, at three, seemed to take a perverse delight in the scummy water, spreading it around the cave as much as possible. The grove in front of the cave mouth was booby-trapped with clothesline upon clothesline, all hung with diapers and rags drying out in the early spring sunlight.

Thirty days later, Alan came home from school to find the younger kids surrounding his mother as she rocked from side to side, actually popping free of the grooves her small metal feet had worn in the cave floor over the years.

Two babies in thirty days! Such a thing was unheard of in their father's cave. Edward, normally a sweet-tempered baby, howled long screams that resonated through Alan's milk teeth and made his testicles shrivel up into hard stones. Alan knew his mother liked to be left alone when she was in labor, but he couldn't just stand there and watch her shake and shiver.

He went to her and pressed his palms to her top, tried to soothe and restrain her. Bill, the second eldest and still only four years old, followed suit. Edward's screams grew even louder, loud and hoarse and utterly terrified, echoing off their father's walls and back to them. Soon Alan was sobbing, too, biting his lip to keep the sounds inside, and so were the other children. Dillon wrinkled his brow and screamed a high-pitched wail that could have cut glass.

Alan's mother rocked harder, and her exhaust hose dislodged itself. A high-pressure jet of cold, soapy water spurted from her back parts, painting the cave wall with suds. Edward crawled into the puddle it formed and scooped small handsful of the liquid into his mouth between howls.

And then, it stopped. His mother stopped rocking, stopped shaking. The stream trailed off into a trickle. Alan stopped crying, and soon the smaller kids followed suit, even Edward. The echoes continued for a moment, and then they, too, stopped. The silence was as startling—and nearly as unbearable—as the cacophony had been.

With a trembling hand, Alan opened his mother's door and extracted little Frederick. The baby was small and cyanotic blue. Alan tipped the baby over and shook him gently, and the baby vomited up a fantastic quantity of wash water, a prodigious stream that soaked the front of Alan's school trousers and his worn brown loafers. Finally it ended, and the baby let out a healthy

yowl. Alan shifted the infant to one arm and gingerly recon-
nected the exhaust hose and set the baby down alongside of its
end. The baby wouldn't suck, though.

Across the cave, from his soggy seat in the puddle of wastewater, Edward watched the new baby with curious eyes. He
crawled across the floor and nuzzled his brother with his high
forehead. Frederick squirmed and fussed, and Edward shoved
him to one side and sucked. His little diaper dripped as the liquid passed directly through him.

Alan patiently picked dripping Edward up and put him over
one shoulder, and gave Frederick the tube to suck. Frederick
gummed at the hose's end, then fussed some more, whimper-
ing. Edward squirmed in his arms, nearly plummeting to the
hard stone floor.

"Billy," Alan said to the solemn little boy, who nodded. "Can
you take care of Edward for a little while? I need to clean up."
Billy nodded again and held out his pudgy arms. Alan grabbed
some clean shop rags and briskly wiped Frederick down, then
laid another across Billy's shoulder and set Edward down. The
baby promptly set to snoring. Danny started screaming again,
with no provocation, and Alan took two swift steps to bridge the
distance between them and smacked the child hard enough to
stun him silent.

Alan grabbed a mop and bucket and sloshed the puddles
into the drainage groove where his mother's wastewater usually
ran, out the cave mouth and into a stand of choking mountain
grass that fed greedily and thrived riotous in the phosphates
from the detergent.

Frederick did not eat for thirty days, and during that time
he grew so thin that he appeared to shrivel like a raisin, going
hard and folded in upon himself. Alan spent hours patiently
spooning sudsy water into his little pink mouth, but the baby
wouldn't swallow, just spat it out and whimpered and fussed. Edward liked to twine around Alan's feet like a cat as he joggled
and spooned and fretted over Frederick. It was all Alan could
do not to go completely mad, but he held it together, though his
grades slipped.

His mother vibrated nervously, and his father's winds grew so unruly that two of the golems came around to the cave to make their slow, peevish complaints. Alan shoved a baby into each of their arms and seriously lost his shit upon them, screaming himself hoarse at them while hanging more diapers, more rags, more clothes on the line, tossing his unfinished homework in their faces.

But on the thirtieth day, his mother went into labor again—a labor so frenzied that it dislodged a stalactite and sent it crashing and chundering to the cave floor in a fractious shivering of flinders. Alan took a chip in the neck and it opened up a small cut that nevertheless bled copiously and ruined, *ruined* his favorite T-shirt, with Snoopy sitting atop his doghouse in an aviator's helmet, firing an imaginary machine gun at the cursed Red Baron.

That was nearly the final straw for Alan, but he held fast and waited for the labor to pass and finally unlatched the door and extracted little George, a peanut of a child, a lima-bean infant, curled and fetal and eerily quiet. He set the little half-baby down by the exhaust hose, where he'd put shriveled Frederick in a hopeless hope that the baby would suck, would ingest, finally.

And ingest Frederick did. His dry and desiccated jaw swung open like a snake's, unhinged and spread wide, and he *swallowed* little George, ate him up in three convulsive swallows, the new baby making Frederick's belly swell like a balloon. Alan swallowed panic, seized Frederick by the heels, and shook him upside down. "Spit him out," Alan cried. "Spat him free!"

But Frederick kept his lips stubbornly together, and Alan tired of the terrible business and set the boy with the newest brother within down on a pile of hay he'd brought in to soak up some of Edward's continuous excretions. Alan put his hands over his face and sobbed, because he'd failed his responsibilities as eldest of their family and there was no one he could tell his woes to.

The sound of baby giggles stopped his crying. Edward had belly-crawled to Frederick's side and he was eating *him,* jaw unhinged and gorge working. He was up to Frederick's little bottom, dehydrated to a leathery baby-jerky, and then he was past, swallowing the arms and the chin and the *head,* the giggling, smiling head, the laughing head that had done nothing but whine and fuss since Alan had cleared it of its volume of detergenty water, fresh from their mother's belly.

And then Frederick was gone. Horrified, Alan rushed over and picked up Edward—now as heavy as a cannonball—and pried his mouth open, staring down his gullet, staring down into *another mouth,* Frederick's mouth, which gaped open, revealing a *third* mouth, George's. The smallest mouth twisted and opened, then shut. Edward squirmed furiously and Alan nearly fumbled him. He set the baby down in the straw and watched him crawl across to their mother, where he sucked hungrily. Automatically, Alan gathered up an armload of rags and made ready to wipe up the stream that Edward would soon be ejecting.

But no stream came. The baby fed and fed, and let out a deep burp in three-part harmony, spat up a little, and drank some more. Somehow, Frederick and George were in there feeding, too. Alan waited patiently for Edward to finish feeding, then put him over his shoulder and joggled him until he burped up, then bedded him down in his little rough-hewn crib—the crib that the golems had carved for Alan when he was born—cleaned the cave, and cried again, leaned up against their mother.

F rederick huddled in on himself, half behind Edward on the porch, habitually phobic of open spaces. Alan took his hand and then embraced him. He smelled of Edward's clammy guts and of sweat.

"Are you two hungry?" Alan asked.

Edward grimaced. "Of course we're hungry, but without George there's nothing we can do about it, is there?"

Alan shook his head. "How long has he been gone?"

"Three weeks," Edward whispered. "I'm so hungry, Alan."

"How did it happen?"

Frederick wobbled on his feet, then leaned heavily on Edward. "I need to sit down," he said.

Alan fumbled for his keys and let them into the house, where they settled into the corners of his old overstuffed horsehide sofa. He dialed up the wall sconces to a dim, homey lighting, solicitous of Frederick's sensitive eyes. He took an Apollo 8 Jim Beam decanter full of stunning Irish whiskey off the sideboard and poured himself a finger of it, not offering any to his brothers.

"Now, how did it happen?"

"He wanted to speak to Dad," Frederick said. "He climbed out of me and wandered down through the tunnels into the spring pool. The goblin told us that he took off his clothes and waded in and started whispering." Like most of the boys, George had believed that their father was most aware in his very middle, where he could direct the echoes of the water's rippling, shape them into words and phrases in the hollow of the great cavern.

"So the goblin saw it happen?"

"No," Frederick said, and Edward began to cry again. "No. George asked him for some privacy, and so he went a little way up the tunnel. He waited and waited, but George didn't come back. He called out, but George didn't answer. When he went to look for him, he was gone. His clothes were gone. All that he could find was this." He scrabbled to fit his chubby hand into his jacket's pocket, then fished out a little black pebble. Alan took it and saw that it wasn't a pebble, it was a rotted-out and dried-up fingertip, pierced with unbent paperclip wire.

"It's Dave's, isn't it?" Edward said.

"I think so," Alan said. Dave used to spend hours wiring his dropped-off parts back onto his body, gluing his teeth back into his head. "Jesus."

"We're going to die, aren't we?" Frederick said. "We're going to starve to death."

Edward held his pudgy hands one on top of the other in his lap and began to rock back and forth. "We'll be okay," he lied.

"Did anyone see Dave?" Alan asked.

"No," Frederick said. "We asked the golems, we asked Dad, we asked the goblin, but no one saw him. No one's seen him for years."

Alan thought for a moment about how to ask his next question. "Did you look in the pool? On the bottom?"

"He's not there!" Edward said. "We looked there. We looked all around Dad. We looked in town. Alan, they're both gone."

Alan felt a sear of acid jet up esophagus. "I don't know what to do," he said. "I don't know where to look. Frederick, can't you, I don't know, *stuff* yourself with something? So you can eat?"

"We tried," Edward said. "We tried rags and sawdust and clay and bread and they didn't work. I thought that maybe we could get a *child* and put him inside, maybe, but God, Albert, I don't want to do that, it's the kind of thing Dan would do."

Alan stared at the softly glowing wood floors, reflecting highlights from the soft lighting. He rubbed his stocking toes over the waxy finish and felt its shine. "Don't do that, okay?" he said. "I'll think of something. Let me sleep on it. Do you want to sleep here? I can make up the sofa."

"Thanks, big brother," Edward said. "Thanks."

Alan walked past his study, past the tableau of laptop and desk and chair, felt the pull of the story, and kept going, pulling his housecoat tighter around himself. The summer morning was already hotting up, and the air in the house had a sticky, dewy feel.

He found Edward sitting on the sofa, with the sheets and pillowcases folded neatly next to him.

"I set out a couple of towels for you in the second-floor bathroom and found an extra toothbrush," Alan said. "If you want them."

"Thanks," Edward said, echoing in his empty chest. The thick rolls of his face were contorted into a caricature of sorrow.

"Where's Frederick?" Alan asked.

"Gone!" Edward said, and broke into spasms of sobbing.

"He's gone he's gone he's gone, I woke up and he was gone."

Alan shifted the folded linens to the floor and sat next to Edward. "What happened?"

"You *know* what happened, Alan," Edward said. "You know as well as I do! Dave took him in the night. He followed us here and he came in the night and stole him away."

"You don't know that," Alan said, softly stroking Edward's greasy fringe of hair. "He could have wandered out for a walk or something."

"Of course I know it!" Edward yelled, his voice booming in the hollow of his great chest. "Look!" He handed Alan a small, desiccated lump, like a black bean pierced with a paperclip wire.

"You showed me this yesterday—" Alan said.

"It's from a *different finger*!" Edward said, and he buried his face in Alan's shoulder, sobbing uncontrollably.

"Have you looked for him?" Alan asked.

"I've been waiting for you to get up. I don't want to go out alone."

"We'll look together," Alan said. He got a pair of shorts and a T-shirt, shoved his feet into Birkenstocks, and led Edward out the door.

The previous night's humidity had thickened to a gray cloudy soup, swift thunderheads coming in from all sides. The foot traffic was reduced to sparse, fast-moving umbrellas, people rushing for shelter before the deluge. Ozone crackled in the air and thunder roiled seemingly up from the ground, deep and sickening.

They started with a circuit of the house, looking for footprints, body parts. He found a shred of torn gray thrift-store shirt, caught on a rose bramble near the front of his walk. It smelled of the homey warmth of Edward's innards, and had a few of Frederick's short, curly hairs stuck to it. Alan showed it to Edward, then folded it into the change pocket of his wallet.

They walked the length of the sidewalk, crossed Wales, and began to slowly cross the little park. Edward circumnavigated the little cement wading pool, tracing the political runes left behind by the Market's cheerful anarchist taggers, painfully bent almost double at his enormous waist.

"What are we looking for, Alan?"

"Footprints. Finger bones. Clues."

Edward puffed back to the bench and sat down, tears streaming down his face. "I'm so *hungry*," he said.

Alan, crawling around the torn sod left when someone had dragged one of the picnic tables, contained his frustration. "If we can find Daniel, we can get Frederick and George back, okay?"

"All right," Edward snuffled.

The next time Alan looked up, Edward had taken off his scuffed shoes and grimy-gray socks, rolled up the cuffs of his tent-sized pants, and was wading through the little pool, piggy eyes cast downward.

"Good idea," Alan called, and turned to the sandbox.

A moment later, there was a booming yelp, almost lost in the roll of thunder, and when Alan turned about, Edward was gone.

Alan kicked off his Birks and splashed up to the hems of his shorts in the wading pool. In the pool's center, the round fountainhead was a twisted wreck, the concrete crumbled and the dry steel and brass fixtures contorted and ruptured. They had long streaks of abraded skin, torn shirt, and blood on them, leading down into the guts of the fountain.

Cautiously, Alan leaned over, looking well down the dark tunnel that had been scraped out of the concrete centerpiece. The thin gray light showed him the rough walls, chipped out with some kind of sharp tool. "Edward?" he called. His voice did not echo or bounce back to him.

Tentatively, he reached down the tunnel, bending at the waist over the rough lip of the former fountain. Deep he reached and reached and reached, and as his fingertips hit loose dirt, he leaned farther in and groped blindly, digging his hands into the plug of soil that had been shoveled into the tunnel's bend a few feet below the surface. He straightened up and climbed in, sinking to the waist, and tried to kick the dirt out of the way, but it wouldn't give—the tunnel had caved in behind the plug of earth.

He clambered out, feeling the first fat drops of rain on his bare forearms and the crown of his head. *A shovel.* There was one in the little coach house in the back of his place, behind the collapsed boxes and the bicycle pump. As he ran across the street, he saw Krishna, sitting on his porch, watching him with a hint of a smile.

"Lost another one, huh?" he said. He looked as if he'd been awake all night, now hovering on the brink of sleepiness and wiredness. A roll of thunder crashed and a sheet of rain hurtled out of the sky.

Alan never thought of himself as a violent person. Even when he'd had to throw the occasional troublemaker out of his shops, he'd done so with an almost cordial force. Now, though, he trembled and yearned to take Krishna by the throat and ram his head, face first, into the column that held up his front porch, again and again, until his fingers were slick with the blood from Krishna's shattered nose.

Alan hurried past him, his shoulders and fists clenched. Krishna chuckled nastily and Alan thought he knew who got the job of sawing off Mimi's wings when they grew too long, and thought, too, that Krishna must relish the task.

"Where you going?" Krishna called.

Alan fumbled with his keyring, desperate to get in and get the keys to the coach house and to fetch the shovel before the new tunnels under the park collapsed.

"You're too late, you know," Krishna continued. "You might as well give up. Too late, too late!"

Alan whirled and shrieked, a wordless, contorted war cry, a sound from his bestial guts. As his eyes swam back into focus, he saw Mimi standing beside Krishna, barefoot in a faded house-coat. Her eyes were very wide, and as she turned away from him, he saw that her stubby wings were splayed as wide as they'd go, forming a tent in her robe that pulled it up above her knees. Alan bit down and clamped his lips together and found his keys. He tracked mud over the polished floors and the ancient, threadbare Persian rugs as he ran to the kitchen, snatching the coach-house keys from their hook over the sink.

He ran back across the street to the little park, clutching his shovel. He jammed his head into the centerpiece and tried to see which way the tunnel had curved off when it turned, but it was too dark, the dirt too loose. He pulled himself out and took the shovel in his hands like a spear and stabbed it into the concrete bed of the wading pool, listening for a hollowness in the returning sound like a man thudding for a stud under drywall.

The white noise of the rain was too high, the rolling thunder too steady. His chest heaved and his tears mingled with the rain streaking down his face as he stabbed, again and again, at the pool's bottom. His mind was scrambled and saturated, his vision clouded with the humid mist rising off his exertion-heated chest and the raindrops caught in his eyelashes.

He splashed out of the wading pool and took the shovel to the sod of the park's lawn, picking an arbitrary spot and digging inefficiently and hysterically, the bent shovel tip twisting with each stroke.

Suddenly strong hands were on his shoulders, another set prizing the shovel from his hands. He looked up and blinked his eyes clear, looking into the face of two young Asian police officers. They were bulky from the Kevlar vests they wore under their rain slickers, with kind and exasperated expressions on their faces.

"Sir," the one holding the shovel said, "what are you doing?"

Alan breathed himself into a semblance of composure. "I . . ." he started, then trailed off. Krishna was watching from his porch, grinning ferociously, holding a cordless phone.

The creature that had howled at Krishna before scrambled for purchase in Alan's chest. Alan averted his eyes from Krishna's shit-eating, 911-calling grin. He focused on the cap of the officer in front of him, shrouded in a clear plastic shower cap to keep its crown dry. "I'm sorry," he said. "It was a—a dog. A stray, or maybe a runaway. A little Scottie dog, it jumped down the center of the fountain there and disappeared. I looked down and thought it had found a tunnel that caved in on it."

The officer peered at him from under the brim of his hat, dubiousness writ plain on his young, good-looking face. "A tunnel?"

Alan wiped the rain from his eyes, tried to regain his composure, tried to find his charm. It wasn't to be found. Instead, every time he reached for something witty and calming, he saw the streaks of blood and torn clothing, dark on the loose soil of the fountain's center, and no sooner had he dispelled those images than they were replaced with Krishna, sneering, saying, "Lost another one, huh?" He trembled and swallowed a sob.

"I think I need to sit down," he said, as calmly as he could, and he sank slowly to his knees. The hands on his biceps let him descend.

"Sir, do you live nearby?" one of the cops asked, close in to his ear. He nodded into his hands, which he'd brought up to cover his face.

"Across the street," he said. They helped him to his feet and supported him as he tottered, weak and heaving, to his porch. Krishna was gone once they got there.

The cops helped him shuck his drenched shoes and socks and put him down on the overstuffed horsehide sofa. Alan recovered himself with an effort of will and gave them his ID.

"I'm sorry, you must think I'm an absolute lunatic," he said, shivering in his wet clothes.

"Sir," the cop who'd taken the shovel from him said, "we see absolute lunatics every day. I think you're just a little upset. We all go a little nuts from time to time."

"Yeah," Alan said. "Yeah. A little nuts. I had a long night last night. Family problems."

The cops shifted their weight, showering the floor with raindrops that beaded on the finish.

"Are you going to be all right on your own? We can call someone if you'd like."

"No," Alan said, pasting on a weak smile. "No, that's all right.

I'll be fine. I'm going to change into some dry clothes and clean up and, oh, I don't know, get some sleep. I think I could use some sleep."

"That sounds like an excellent idea," the cop who'd taken the shovel said. He looked around at the bookcases. "You've read all of these?" he asked.

"Naw," Alan said, falling into the rote response from his proprietorship of the bookstore. "What's the point of a bunch of books you've already read?" The joke reminded him of better times and he smiled a genuine smile.

Though the stinging hot shower revived him somewhat, he kept quickening into panic at the thought of David creeping into his house in the night, stumping in on desiccated black child-legs, snaggled rictus under mummified lips.

He spooked at imagined noises and thudding rain and the dry creaking of the old house as he toweled off and dressed.

There was no phone in the mountain, no way to speak to his remaining brothers, the golems, his parents. He balled his fists and stood in the center of his bedroom, shaking with impotent worry.

David. None of them had liked David very much. Billy, the fortune-teller, had been born with a quiet wisdom, an eerie solemnity that had made him easy for the young Alan to care for. Carlos, the island, had crawled out of their mother's womb and pulled himself to the cave mouth and up the face of their father, lying there for ten years, accreting until he was ready to push off on his own.

But Daniel, Daniel had been a hateful child from the day he was born. He was colicky, and his screams echoed through their father's caverns. He screamed from the moment he emerged and Alan tipped him over and toweled him gently dry and he didn't stop for an entire year. Alan stopped being able to tell day from night, lost track of the weeks and months. He'd developed a taste for food, real people food, that he'd buy in town at the Loblaws Superstore, but he couldn't leave Davey alone in the cave, and he certainly couldn't carry the howling, shitting, puking, pissing, filthy baby into town with him.

So they ate what the golems brought them: sweet grasses, soft berries, frozen winter fruit dug from the base of the orchards in town, blind winter fish from the streams. They drank snowmelt and ate pine cones and the baby Davey cried and cried until Alan couldn't remember what it was to live in a world of words and conversations and thought and reflection.

No one knew what to do about Davey. Their father blew warm winds scented with coal dust and loam to calm him, but still Davey cried. Their mother rocked him on her gentlest spin cycle, but still Davey cried. Alan walked down the slope to Carl's landmass, growing with the dust and rains and snow, and set him down on the soft grass and earth there, but still Davey cried, and Carlos inched farther and farther toward the St. Lawrence seaway, sluggishly making his way out to the ocean and as far away from the baby as possible.

After his first birthday, David started taking breaks from his screaming, learning to crawl and then totter, becoming a holy terror. If Alan left his schoolbooks within reach of the boy, they'd be reduced to shreds of damp mulch in minutes. By the time he was two, his head was exactly at Alan's crotch height and he'd greet his brother on his return from school by charging at full speed into Alan's nuts, propelled at unlikely speed on his thin legs.

At three, he took to butchering animals—the rabbits that little Bill kept in stacked hutches outside of the cave mouth went first. Billy rushed home from his grade-two class, eyes crazed with precognition, and found David methodically wringing the animals' necks and then slicing them open with a bit of sharpened chert. Billy had showed David how to knap flint and chert the week before, after seeing a filmstrip about it in class. He kicked the makeshift knife out of Davey's hand, breaking his thumb with the toe of the hard leather shoes the golems had made for him, and left Davey to bawl in the cave while Billy dignified his pets' corpses, putting their entrails back inside their bodies and wrapping them in shrouds made from old diapers. Alan helped him bury them, and then found Davey and taped his thumb to his hand and spanked him until his arm was too tired to deal out one more wallop.

Alan made his way down to the living room, the floor streaked with mud and water. He went into the kitchen and filled a bucket with soapy water and gathered up an armload of rags from the rag bag. Methodically, he cleaned away the mud. He turned his sopping shoes on end over the grate and dialed the thermostat higher. He made himself a bowl of granola and a cup of coffee and sat down at his old wooden kitchen table and ate mindlessly, then washed the dishes and put them in the drying rack.

He'd have to go speak to Krishna.

Natalie answered the door in a pretty sundress, combat boots, and a baseball hat. She eyed him warily.

"I'd like to speak to Krishna," Alan said from under the hood of his poncho.

There was an awkward silence. Finally, Natalie said, "He's not home."

"I don't believe you," Alan said. "And it's urgent, and I'm not in the mood to play around. Can you get Krishna for me, Natalie?"

"I told you," she said, not meeting his eyes, "he's not here."

"That's enough," Alan said in his boss voice, his more-in-anger-than-in-sorrow voice. "Get him, Natalie. You don't need to be in the middle of this—it's not right for him to ask you to. Get him."

Natalie closed the door and he heard the deadbolt turn. *Is she going to fetch him, or is she locking me out?*

He was on the verge of hammering the buzzer again, but he got his answer. Krishna opened the door and stepped onto the dripping porch, bulling Alan out with his chest.

He smiled grimly at Alan and made a well-go-on gesture.

"What did you see?" Alan said, his voice tight but under control.

"Saw you and that fat guy," Krishna said. "Saw you rooting around in the park. Saw him disappear down the fountain."

"He's my brother," Alan said.

"So what, he ain't heavy? He's fat, but I expect there's a reason for that. I've seen your kind before, Adam. I don't like you, and I don't owe you any favors." He turned and reached for the screen door.

"No," Alan said, taking him by the wrist, squeezing harder than was necessary. "Not yet. You said, 'Lost another one.' What other one, Krishna? What else did you see?"

Krishna gnawed on his neatly trimmed soul patch. "Let go of me, Andrew," he said, almost too softly to be heard over the rain.

"Tell me what you saw," Alan said. "Tell me, and I'll let you go." His other hand balled into a fist. "Goddammit, *tell me!*" Alan yelled, and twisted Krishna's arm behind his back.

"I called the cops," Krishna said. "I called them again and they're on their way. Let me go, freak show."

"I don't like you, either, Krishna," Alan said, twisting the arm higher. He let go suddenly, then stumbled back as Krishna scraped the heel of his motorcycle boot down his shin and hammered it into the top of his foot.

He dropped to one knee and grabbed his foot while Krishna slipped into the house and shot the lock. Then he hobbled home as quickly as he could. He tried to pace off the ache in his foot, but the throbbing got worse, so he made himself a drippy ice pack and sat on the sofa in the immaculate living room and rocked back and forth, holding the ice to his bare foot.

A t five, Davey graduated from torturing animals to beating up on smaller children. Alan took him down to the school on the day after Labor Day to sign him up for kindergarten. He was wearing his stiff new blue jeans and sneakers, his knapsack stuffed with fresh binders and pencils. Finding out about these things had been Alan's first experience with the wide world, a kindergartner sizing up his surroundings at speed so that he could try to fit in. David was a cute kid and had the benefit of Alan's experience. He had a foxy little face and shaggy blond hair, all clever smiles and awkward winks, and for all that he was still a monster.

They came and got Alan twenty minutes after classes started, when his new home-room teacher was still briefing them on the rules and regulations for junior high students. He was painfully aware of all the eyes on his back as he followed the office lady out of the portable and into the old school building where the kindergarten and the administration was housed.

"We need to reach your parents," the office lady said, once they were alone in the empty hallways of the old building.

"You can't," Alan said. "They don't have a phone."

"Then we can drive out to see them," the office lady said. She smelled of artificial floral scent and Ivory soap, like the female hygiene aisle at the drugstore.

"Mom's still real sick," Alan said, sticking to his traditional story.

"Your father, then," the office lady said. He'd had variations on this conversation with every office lady at the school, and he knew he'd win it in the end. Meantime, what did they want?

"My dad's, you know, gone," he said. "Since I was a little kid." That line always got the office ladies, "since I was a little kid," made them want to write it down for their family Christmas newsletters.

The office lady smiled a powdery smile and put her hand on his shoulder. "All right, Alan, come with me."

Davey was sitting on the dusty sofa in the vice principal's office. He punched the sofa cushion rhythmically. "Alan," he said when the office lady led him in.

"Hi, Dave," Alan said. "What's going on?"

"They're stupid here. I hate them." He gave the sofa a particularly vicious punch.

"I'll get Mr. Davenport," the office lady said, and closed the door behind her.

"What did you do?" Alan asked.

"She wouldn't let me play!" David said, glaring at him.

"Who wouldn't?"

"A girl! She had the blocks and I wanted to play with them and she wouldn't let me!"

"What did you hit her with?" Alan asked, dreading the answer.

"A block," David said, suddenly and murderously cheerful. "I hit her in the eye!"

Alan groaned. The door opened and the vice principal, Mr. Davenport, came in and sat behind his desk. He was the punishment man, the one that no one wanted to be sent in to see.

"Hello, Alan," he said gravely. Alan hadn't ever been personally called before Mr. Davenport, but Billy got into some spot of precognitive trouble from time to time, rushing out of class to stop some disaster at home or somewhere else in the school. Mr. Davenport knew that Alan was a straight arrow, not someone he'd ever need to personally take an interest in.

He crouched down next to Darren, hitching up his slacks. "You must be David," he said, ducking down low to meet Davey's downcast gaze.

Davey punched the sofa.

"I'm Mr. Davenport," he said, and extended a hand with a big class ring on it and a smaller wedding band.

Davey kicked him in the nose, and the vice principal toppled over backward, whacking his head on the sharp corner of his desk. He tumbled over onto his side and clutched his head. "Mother*fucker*!" he gasped, and Davey giggled maniacally.

Alan grabbed Davey's wrist and bent his arm behind his back, shoving him across his knee. He swatted the little boy on the ass as hard as he could, three times. "Don't you ever—" Alan began.

The vice principal sat up, still clutching his head. "That's enough!" he said, catching Alan's arm.

"Sorry," Alan said. "And David's sorry, too, right?" He glared at David.

"You're a stupid mother*fucker*!" David said, and squirmed off of Alan's lap.

The vice principal's lips tightened. "Alan," he said quietly, "take your brother into the hallway. I am going to write a note that your mother will have to sign before David comes back to school, after his two-week suspension."

David glared at them each in turn. "I'm not coming back to this mother*fucker* place!" he said.

He didn't.

The rain let up by afternoon, leaving a crystalline, fresh-mown air hanging over the Market.

Andrew sat in his office by his laptop and watched the sun come out. He needed to find Ed, needed to find Frank, needed to find Grant, but he was out of practice when it came to the ways of the mountain and its sons. Whenever he tried to imagine a thing to do next, his mind spun and the worldless howling thing inside him stirred. The more he tried to remember what it was like to be a son of the mountain, the more he felt something he'd worked very hard for, his delicate normalcy, slipping away.

So he put his soaked clothes in the dryer, clamped his laptop under his arm, and went out. He moped around the park and the fountain, but the stroller moms whose tots were splashing in the wading pool gave him sufficient dirty looks that he walked up to the Greek's, took a table on the patio, and ordered a murderously strong cup of coffee.

He opened up the screen and rotated around the little café table until the screen was in the shade and his wireless card was aligned for best reception from the yagi antenna poking out of his back window. He opened up a browser and hit MapQuest, then brought up a street-detailed map of the Market. He pasted it into his CAD app and started to mark it up, noting all the different approaches to his house that Davey might take the next time he came. The maps soothed him, made him feel like a part of the known world.

Augusta Avenue and Oxford were both out; even after midnight, when the stores were all shuttered, there was far too much foot traffic for Davey to pass by unnoticed. But the alleys that mazed the back ways were ideal. Some were fenced off, some were too narrow to pass, but most of them—he'd tried to navigate them by bicycle once and found himself utterly lost. He'd had to turn around slowly until he spotted the CN Tower and use it to get his bearings.

He poked at the map, sipping the coffee, then ordering another from the Greek's son, who hadn't yet figured out that he was a regular and so sneered at his laptop with undisguised contempt. "Computers, huh?" he said. "Doesn't anyone just read a book anymore?"

"I used to own a bookstore," Alan said, then held up a finger and moused over to his photo album and brought up the thumbnails of his old bookstore. "See?"

The Greek's son, thirty with a paunch and sweat rings under the pits of his white "The Greek's" T-shirt, sat down and looked at the photos. "I remember that place, on Harbord Street, right?"

Alan smiled. "Yup. We lost the store when they blew up the abortion clinic next door," he said. "Insurance paid out, but I wasn't ready to start over with another bookstore."

The Greek's son shook his head. "Another coffee, right?"

"Right," Alan said.

Alan went back to the map, realigning the laptop for optimal reception again.

"You got a wireless card in that?" a young guy at the next table asked. He was dressed in Kensington Market crusty-punk chic, tatts and facial piercings, filth-gray bunchoffuckinggoofs tee, cutoffs, and sweaty high boots draped with chains.

"Yeah," Alan said. He sighed and closed the map window. He wasn't getting anywhere, anyway.

"And you get service here? Where's your access point?" Crusty-punk or no, he sounded as nerdy as any of the Webheads you'd find shopping for bargains on CD blanks on College Street.

"Three blocks that way," Alan said, pointing. "Hanging off my house. The network name is 'walesave.'"

"Shit, that's you?" the kid said. "Goddammit, you're clobbering our access points!"

"What access point?"

"Access *points*. ParasiteNet." He indicated a peeling sticker on the lapel of his cut-down leather jacket showing a skull with crossed radio towers underneath it. "I'm trying to get a mesh-net running though all of the Market, and you're hammering me. Jesus, I was ready to rat you out to the radio cops at the Canadian Radio and Television Commission. Dude, you've got to turn down the freaking *gain* on those things."

"What's a mesh-net?"

The kid moved his beer over to Alan's table and sat down. "Okay, so pretend that your laptop is the access point. It radiates more or less equally in all directions, depending on your antenna characteristics and leaving out the RF shadows that microwaves and stucco and cordless phones generate." He arranged the coffee cup and the beer at equal distances from the laptop, then moved them around to demonstrate the coverage area. "Right, so what happens if I'm out of range, over *here*" —he put his beer back on his own table—"and you want to reach me? Well, you could just turn up the gain on your access point, either by increasing the power so that it radiates farther in all directions, or by focusing the transmissions so they travel farther in a line of sight."

"Right," Alan said, sipping his coffee.

"Right. So both of those approaches suck. If you turn up the power, you radiate over everyone else's signal, so if I've got an access point *here*"—he held his fist between their tables—"no one can hear it because you're drowning it out. It's like you're shouting so loud that no one else can carry on a conversation."

"So why don't you just use my network? I want to be able to get online anywhere in the Market, but that means that anyone can, right?"

The crusty-punk waved his hand dismissively. "Sure, whatever. But what happens if your network gets shut down? Or if you decide to start eavesdropping on other people? Or if someone wants to get to the printer in her living room? It's no good."

"So, what, you want me to switch to focused antennae?"

"That's no good. If you used a focused signal, you're going to have to be perfectly aligned if you're going to talk back to your base, so unless you want to provide a connection to one tiny pin-point somewhere a couple kilometers away, it won't do you any good."

"There's no solution, then? I should just give up?"

The crusty-punk held up his hands. "Hell, no! There's just no *centralized* solution. You can't be Superman, blanketing the whole world with wireless using your almighty antennaprick, but so what? That's what mesh networks are for. Check it out." He arranged the beer and the laptop and the coffee cup so that they were strung out along a straight line. "Okay, you're the laptop and I'm the coffee cup. We both have a radio and we want to talk to each other.

"We *could* turn up the gain on our radios so that they can shout loud enough to be heard at this distance, but that would drown out this guy here." He gestured at the now-empty beer. "We *could* use a focused antenna, but if I move a little bit off the beam"—he nudged the coffee cup to one side—"we're dead. But there's a third solution."

"We ask the beer to pass messages around?"

"Fucking right we do! That's the mesh part. Every station on the network gets *two* radios—one for talking in one direction, the other for relaying in the other direction. The more stations you add, the lower the power on each radio—and the more pathways you get to carry your data."

Alan shook his head.

"It's a fuckin' mind-blower, isn't it?"

"Sure," Alan said. "Sure. But does it work? Don't all those hops between point *a* and point *b* slow down the connection?"

"A little, sure. Not so's you'd notice. They don't have to go that far—the farthest any of these signals has to travel is 151 Front Street."

"What's at 151 Front?"

"TorIX—the main network interchange for the whole city! We stick an antenna out a window there and downlink it into the cage where UUNet and PSINet meet—voilà, instant eleven-megabit city-wide freenet!"

"Where do you get the money for that?"

"Who said anything about money? How much do you think UUNet and PSI charge each other to exchange traffic with one another? Who benefits when UUNet and PSI cross-connect? Is UUNet the beneficiary of PSI's traffic, or vice versa? Internet access only costs money at the *edge*—and with a mesh-net, there is no edge anymore. It's penetration at the center, just like the Devo song."

"I'm Adrian," Alan said.

"I'm Kurt," the crusty-punk said. "Buy me a beer, Adrian?"

"It'd be my pleasure," Alan said.

Kurt lived in the back of a papered-over storefront on Oxford. The front two-thirds were a maze of peeling, stickered-over stamped-metal shelving units piled high with junk tech: ancient shrink-wrapped software, stacked-up low-capacity hard drives, cables and tapes and removable media. Alan tried to imagine making sense of it all, flowing it into The Inventory, and felt something like vertigo.

In a small hollow carved out of the back, Kurt had arranged a cluttered desk, a scuffed twin bed and a rack of milk crates filled with T-shirts and underwear.

Alan picked his way delicately through the store and found himself a seat on an upturned milk crate. Kurt sat on the bed and grinned expectantly.

"So?" he said.

"So what?" Alan said.

"So what is *this*! Isn't it great?"

"Well, you sure have a lot of *stuff*, I'll give you that," Alan said.

"It's all dumpstered," Kurt said casually.

"Oh, you dive?" Alan said. "I used to dive." It was mostly true. Alan had always been a picker, always on the lookout for bargoons, even if they were sticking out of someone's trash bin. Sometimes *especially* if they were sticking out of someone's trash bin—seeing what normal people threw away gave him a rare glimpse into their lives.

Kurt walked over to the nearest shelving unit and grabbed a PC mini-tower with the lid off. "But did you ever do this?" He stuck the machine under Alan's nose and swung the gooseneck desk lamp over it. It was a white-box PC, generic commodity hardware, with a couple of network cards.

"What's that?"

"It's a junk access point! I made it out of trash! The only thing I bought were the network cards—two wireless, one Ethernet. It's running a FreeBSD distribution off a CD, so the OS can never get corrupted. It's got lots of sweet stuff in the distro, and all you need to do is plug it in, point the antennae in opposite directions, and you're up. It does its own power management, it automagically peers with other access points if it can find 'em, and it does its own dynamic channel selection to avoid stepping on other access points."

Alan turned his head this way and that, making admiring noises. "You made this, huh?"

"For about eighty bucks. It's my fifteenth box. Eventually, I wanna have a couple hundred of these."

"Ambitious," Alan said, handing the box back. "How do you pay for the parts you have to buy? Do you have a grant?"

"A grant? Shit, no! I've got a bunch of street kids who come in and take digital pix of the stuff I have no use for, research them online, and post them to eBay. I split the take with them. Brings in a couple grand a week, and I'm keeping about fifty street kids fed besides. I go diving three times a week out in Concord and Oakville and Richmond Hill, anywhere I can find an industrial park. If I had room, I'd recruit fifty more kids— I'm bringing it in faster than they can sell it."

"Why don't you just do less diving?"

"Are you kidding me? It's all I can do not to go out every night! You wouldn't believe the stuff I find—all I can think about is all the stuff I'm missing out on. Some days I wish that my kids were less honest; if they ripped off some stuff, I'd have room for a lot more."

Alan laughed. Worry for Edward and Frederick and George nagged at him, impotent anxiety, but this was just so fascinating. Fascinating and distracting, and, if not normal, at least not nearly so strange as he could be. He imagined the city gridded up with junk equipment, radiating Internet access from the lakeshore to the outer suburbs. The grandiosity took his breath away.

"Look," Kurt said, spreading out a map of Kensington Market on the unmade bed. "I've got access points here, here, here, and here. Another eight or ten and I'll have the whole Market covered. Then I'm going to head north, cover the U of T campus, and push east towards Yonge Street. Bay Street and University Avenue are going to be tough—how can I convince bankers to let me plug this by their windows?"

"Kurt," Alan said, "I suspect that the journey to University Avenue is going to be a lot slower than you expect it to be."

Kurt jutted his jaw out. "What's that supposed to mean?"

"There's a lot of real estate between here and there. A lot of trees and high-rises, office towers and empty lots. You're going to have to knock on doors every couple hundred meters—at best—and convince them to let you install one of these boxes, made from garbage, and plug it in, to participate in what?"

"Democratic communication!" Kurt said.

"Ah, well, my guess is that most of the people who you'll need to convince won't really care much about that. Won't be able to make that abstract notion concrete."

Kurt mumbled into his chest. Alan could see that he was fuming.

"Just because you don't have the vision to appreciate this—"

Alan held up his hand. "Stop right there. I never said anything of the sort. I think that this is big and exciting and looks like a lot of fun. I think that ringing doorbells and talking people into letting me nail an access point to their walls sounds like a *lot* of fun. Really, I'm not kidding.

"But this is a journey, not a destination. The value you'll get out of this will be more in the doing than the having done. The having done's going to take decades, I'd guess. But the doing's going to be something." Alan's smile was so broad it ached. The idea had seized him. He was drunk on it.

The buzzer sounded and Kurt got up to answer it. Alan craned his neck to see a pair of bearded neohippies in rasta hats.

"Are you Kurt?" one asked.

"Yeah, dude, I'm Kurt."

"Marcel told us that we could make some money here? We're trying to raise bus fare to Burning Man? We could really use the work?"

"Not today, but maybe tomorrow," Kurt said. "Come by around lunchtime."

"You sure you can't use us today?"

"Not today," Kurt said. "I'm busy today."

"All right," the other said, and they slouched away.

"Word of mouth," Kurt said, with a jingling shrug. "Kids just turn up, looking for work with the trash."

"You think they'll come back tomorrow?" Alan was pretty good at evaluating kids and they hadn't looked very reliable.

"Those two? Fifty-fifty chance. Tell you what, though: There's always enough kids and enough junk to go around."

"But you need to make arrangements to get your access points mounted and powered. You've got to sort it out with people who own stores and houses."

"You want to knock on doors?" Kurt said.

"I think I would," Alan said. "I suspect it's a possibility. We can start with the shopkeepers, though."

"I haven't had much luck with merchants," Kurt said, shrugging his shoulders. His chains jingled and a whiff of armpit wafted across the claustrophobic hollow. "Capitalist pigs."

· "I can't imagine why," Alan said.

Wales Avenue, huh?" Kurt said.

They were walking down Oxford Street, and Alan was seeing it with fresh eyes, casting his gaze upward, looking at the lines of sight from one building to another, mentally painting in radio-frequency shadows cast by the transformers on the light poles.

"Just moved in on July first," Alan said. "Still getting settled in."

"Which house?"

"The blue one, with the big porch, on the corner."

"Sure, I know it. I scored some great plumbing fixtures out of the dumpster there last winter."

"You're welcome," Alan said.

They turned at Spadina and picked their way around the tourist crowds shopping the Chinese importers' sidewalk displays of bamboo parasols and Hello Kitty slippers, past the fogged-up windows of the dim-sum restaurants and the smell of fresh pork buns. Alan bought a condensed milk and kiwi snow-cone from a sidewalk vendor and offered to treat Kurt, but he declined.

"You never know about those places," Kurt said. "How clean is their ice, anyway? Where do they wash their utensils?"

"You dig around in dumpsters for a living," Alan said. "Aren't you immune to germs?"

Kurt turned at Baldwin, and Alan followed. "I don't eat garbage, I pick it," he said. He sounded angry.

"Hey, sorry," Alan said. "Sorry. I didn't mean to imply—"

"I know you didn't," Kurt said, stopping in front of a dry-goods store and spooning candied ginger into a baggie. He handed it to the age-hunched matron of the shop, who dropped it on her scale and dusted her hands on her black dress. Kurt handed her a two-dollar coin and took the bag back. "I'm just touchy, okay? My last girlfriend split because she couldn't get past it. No matter how much I showered, I was never clean enough for her."

"Sorry," Alan said again.

"I heard something weird about that blue house on the corner," Kurt said. "One of my kids told me this morning, he saw something last night when he was in the park."

Alan pulled up short, nearly colliding with a trio of cute university girls in wife-beaters pushing bundle-buggies full of newspaper-wrapped fish and bags of soft, steaming bagels. They stepped around him, lugging their groceries over the curb and back onto the sidewalk, not breaking from their discussion.

"What was it?"

Kurt gave him a sideways look. "It's weird, okay? The kid who saw it is never all that reliable, and he likes to embellish."

"Okay," Alan said. The crowd was pushing around them now, trying to get past. The dry-goods lady sucked her teeth in annoyance.

"So this kid, he was smoking a joint in the park last night, really late, after the clubs shut down. He was alone, and he saw what he thought was a dog dragging a garbage bag down the steps of your house."

"Yes?"

"So he went over to take a look, and he saw that it was too big to be a garbage bag, and the dog, it looked sick, it moved wrong. He took another step closer and he must have triggered a motion sensor because the porch light switched on. He says . . ."

"What?"

"He's not very reliable. He says it wasn't a dog, he said it was like a dried-out mummy or something, and it had its teeth sunk into the neck of this big, fat, naked guy, and it was dragging the fat guy out into the street. When the light came on, though, it gave the fat guy's neck a hard shake, then let go and turned on this kid, walking toward him on stumpy little feet. He says it made a kind of growling noise and lifted up its hand like it was going to slap the kid, and the kid screamed and ran off. When he got to Dundas, he turned around and saw the fat guy get dragged into an alley between two of the stores on Augusta."

"I see," Alan said.

"It's stupid, I know," Kurt said.

Natalie and Link rounded the corner, carrying slices of pizza from Pizzabilities, mounded high with eggplant and cauliflower and other toppings that were never intended for use in connection with pizza. They startled on seeing Alan and Kurt, then started to walk away.

"Wait," Alan called. "Natalie, Link, wait." He smiled apologetically at Kurt. "My neighbors," he said.

Natalie and Link had stopped and turned around. Alan and Kurt walked to them.

"Natalie, Link, this is Kurt," he said. They shook hands all around.

"I wanted to apologize," Alan said. "I didn't mean to put you between Krishna and me. It was very unfair."

Natalie smiled warily. Link lit a cigarette with a great show of indifference. "It's all right," Natalie said.

"No, it's not," Alan said. "I was distraught, but that's no excuse. We're going to be neighbors for a long time, and there's no sense in our not getting along."

"Really, it's okay," Natalie said.

"Yeah, fine," Link said.

"Three of my brothers have gone missing," Alan said. "That's why I was so upset. One disappeared a couple of weeks ago, another last night, and one this morning. Krishna . . ." He thought for a moment. "He taunted me about it. I really wanted to find out what he saw."

Kurt shook his head. "Your brother went missing last night?"

"From my house."

"So what the kid saw . . ."

Alan turned to Natalie. "A friend of Kurt's was in the park last night. He says he saw my brother being carried off."

Kurt shook his head. "Your brother?"

"What do you mean, 'carried off'?" Natalie said. She folded her slice in half to keep the toppings from spilling.

"Someone is stalking my brothers," Alan said. "Someone very strong and very cunning. Three are gone that I know about. There are others, but I could be next."

"Stalking?" Natalie said.

"My family is a little strange," Alan said. "I grew up in the north country, and things are different there. You've heard of blood feuds?"

Natalie and Link exchanged a significant look.

"I know it sounds ridiculous. You don't need to be involved. I just wanted to let you know why I acted so strangely last night."

"We have to get back," Natalie said. "Nice to meet you, Kurt. I hope you find your brother, Andy."

"Brothers," Alan said.

"Brothers," Natalie said, and walked away briskly.

Alan was the oldest of the brothers, and that meant that he was the one who blazed all the new trails in the family.

He met a girl in the seventh grade. Her name was Marci, and she had just transferred in from Scotland. Her father was a mining engineer, and she'd led a gypsy life that put her in stark contrast to the third-generation homebodies that made up most of the rest of their class.

She had red hair and blue eyes and a way of holding her face in repose that made her look cunning at all times. No one understood her accent, but there was a wiry ferocity in her movement that warned off any kid who thought about teasing her about it.

Alan liked to play in a marshy corner of the woods that bordered the playground after school, crawling around in the weeds, catching toads and letting them go again, spying on the crickets and the secret lives of the larvae that grubbed in the milkweed. He was hunkered down on his haunches one afternoon when Marci came crunching through the tall grass. He ducked down lower, then peered out from his hiding spot as she crouched down and he heard the unmistakable patter of urine as she peed in the rushes.

His jaw dropped. He'd never seen a girl pee before, had no idea what the squatting business was all about. The wet ground sucked at his sneaker and he tipped back on his ass with a yelp. Marci straightened abruptly and crashed over to him, kicking him hard in the ribs when she reached him, leaving a muddy toeprint on his fall windbreaker.

She wound up for another kick and he hollered something wordless and scurried back, smearing marsh mud across his jeans and jacket.

"You pervert!" she said, pronouncing it, *Yuh peervurrt!*

"I am not!" he said, still scooting back.

"Watching from the bushes!" she said.

"I wasn't—I was already here, and you—I mean, what were *you* doing? I was just minding my own business and you came by, I just didn't want to be bothered, this is *my* place!"

"You don't own it," she said, but she sounded slightly chastened. "Don't tell anyone I had a piss here, all right?"

"I won't," he said.

She sat down beside him, unmindful of the mud on her denim skirt. "Promise," she said. "It's so embarrassing."

"I promise," he said.

"Swear," she said, and poked him in the ribs with a bony finger.

He clutched his hands to his ribs. "Look," he said, "I swear. I'm good at secrets."

Her eyes narrowed slightly. "Oh, aye? And I suppose you've lots of secrets, then?"

He said nothing, and worked at keeping the smile off the corners of his mouth.

She poked him in the ribs, then got him in the stomach as he moved to protect his chest. "Secrets, huh?"

He shook his head and clamped his lips shut. She jabbed a flurry of pokes and prods at him while he scooted back on his butt, then dug her clawed hands into his tummy and tickled him viciously. He giggled, then laughed, then started to hiccup uncontrollably. He shoved her away roughly and got up on his knees, gagging.

"Oh, I like you," she said, "just look at that. A wee tickle and you're ready to toss your lunch." She tenderly stroked his hair until the hiccups subsided, then clawed at his belly again, sending him rolling through the mud.

Once he'd struggled to his feet, he looked at her, panting. "Why are you doing this?"

"You're not serious! It's the most fun I've had since we moved to this terrible place."

"You're a sadist!" He'd learned the word from a book he'd bought from the ten-cent pile out front of the used bookstore. It had a clipped-out recipe for liver cutlets between the pages and lots of squishy grown-up sex things that seemed improbable if not laughable. He'd looked "sadist" up in the class dictionary.

"Aye," she said. "I'm that." She made claws of her hands and advanced on him slowly. He giggled uncontrollably as he backed away from her. "C'mere, you, you've more torture comin' to ye before I'm satisfied that you can keep a secret."

He held his arms before him like a movie zombie and walked toward her. "Yes, mathter," he said in a monotone. Just as he was about to reach her, he dodged to one side, then took off.

She chased him, laughing, halfway back to the mountain, then cried off. He stopped a hundred yards up the road from her, she doubled over with her hands planted on her thighs, face red, chest heaving. "You go on, then," she called. "But it's more torture for you at school tomorrow, and don't you forget it!"

"Only if you catch me!" he called back.

"Oh, I'll catch you, have no fear."

She caught him at lunch. He was sitting in a corner of the schoolyard, eating from a paper sack of mushrooms and dried rabbit and keeping an eye on Edward-Frederick-George as he played tag with the other kindergartners. She snuck up behind him and dropped a handful of gravel down the gap of his pants and into his underpants. He sprang to his feet, sending gravel rattling out the cuffs of his jeans.

"Hey!" he said, and she popped something into his mouth. It was wet and warm from her hand and it squirmed. He spat it out and it landed on the schoolyard with a soft splat.

It was an earthworm, thick with loamy soil.

"You!" he said, casting about for a curse of sufficient vehemence. "You!"

She hopped from foot to foot in front of him, clearly delighted with this reaction. He reached out for her and she danced back. He took off after her and they were chasing around the yard, around hopscotches and tag games and sand castles and out to the marshy woods. She skidded through the puddles and he leapt over them. She ducked under a branch and he caught her by the hood of her windbreaker.

Without hesitating, she flung her arms in the air and slithered out of the windbreaker, down to a yellow T-shirt that rode up her back, exposing her pale freckles and the knobs of her spine, the fingers of her ribs. She took off again and he balled the windbreaker up in his fist and took off after her.

She stepped behind a bushy pine, and when he rounded the corner she was waiting for him, her hands clawed, digging at his tummy, leaving him giggling. He pitched back into the pine needles and she followed, straddling his waist and tickling him until he coughed and choked and gasped for air.

"Tell me!" she said. "Tell me your secrets!"

"Stop!" Alan said. "Please! I'm going to piss myself!"

"What's that to me?" she said, tickling more vigorously.

He tried to buck her off, but she was too fast. He caught one wrist, but she pinned his other arm with her knee. He heaved and she collapsed on top of him.

Her face was inches from his, her breath moist on his face. They both panted, and he smelled her hair, which was over his face and neck. She leaned forward and closed her eyes expectantly.

He tentatively brushed his lips across hers, and she moved closer, and they kissed. It was wet and a little gross, but not altogether unpleasant.

She leaned back and opened her eyes, then grinned at him. "That's enough torture for one day," she said. "You're free to go."

She "tortured" him at morning and afternoon recess for the next two weeks, and when he left school on Friday afternoon after the last bell, she was waiting for him in the schoolyard.

"Hello," she said, socking him in the arm.

"Hi," he said.

"Why don't you invite me over for supper this weekend?" she said.

"Supper?"

"Yes. I'm your girlfriend, yeah? So you should have me around to your place to meet your parents. Next weekend you can come around my place and meet my dad."

"I can't," he said.

"You can't."

"No."

"Why not?"

"It's a secret," he said.

"Oooh, a secret," she said. "What kind of secret?"

"A family secret. We don't have people over for dinner. That's the way it is."

"A secret! They're all child molesters?"

He shook his head.

"Horribly deformed?"

He shook his head.

"What, then? Give us a hint?"

"It's a secret."

She grabbed his ear and twisted it. Gently at first, then harder. "A secret?" she said.

"Yes," he gasped. "It's a secret, and I can't tell you. You're hurting me."

"I should hope so," she said. "And it will go very hard for you indeed if you don't tell me what I want to know."

He grabbed her wrist and dug his strong fingers into the thin tendons on their insides, twisting his fingertips for maximal effect. Abruptly, she released his ear and clutched her wrist hard, sticking it between her thighs.

"Owwww! That bloody hurt, you bastard. What did you do that for?"

"My secrets," Alan said, "are secret."

She held her wrist up and examined it. "Heaven help you if you've left a bruise, Alvin," she said. "I'll kill you." She turned her wrist from side to side. "All right," she said. "All right. Kiss it better, and you can come to my place for supper on Saturday at six P.M." She shoved her arm into his face and he kissed the soft skin on the inside of her wrist, putting a little tongue in it.

She giggled and punched him in the arm. "Saturday, then!" she called as she ran off.

Edward-Felix-Gerald were too young to give him shit about his schoolyard romance, and Brian was too sensitive, but Dave had taken to lurking about the schoolyard, spying on the children, and he'd seen Marci break off from a clench with Alan, take his hand, and plant it firmly on her tiny breast, an act that had shocked Danny to the core.

"Hi, pervert," David said, as he stepped into the cool of the cave. "Pervert" was Davey's new nickname for him, and he had a finely honed way of delivering it so that it dripped with contempt. "Did you have sex with your *girlfriend* today, *pervert*?"

Allan turned away from him and helped E-F-G take off his shoes and roll up the cuffs of his pants so that he could go down to the lake in the middle of their father and wade in the shallows, listening to Father's winds soughing through the great cavern.

"Did you touch her boobies? Did she suck your pee-pee? Did you put your finger in her?" The litany would continue until Davey went to bed, and even then he wasn't safe. One night, Allen had woken up to see Darren standing over him, hands planted on his hips, face twisted into an elaborate sneer. "Did you put your penis inside of her?" he'd hissed, then gone back to bed.

Alby went out again, climbing the rockface faster than Doug could keep up with him, so that by the time he'd found his perch high over the woodlands, where he could see the pines dance in the wind and the ant-sized cars zooming along the highways, Doug was far behind, likely sat atop their mother, sucking his thumb and sulking and thinking up new perversions to accuse Alan of.

Saturday night arrived faster than Alan could have imagined. He spent Saturday morning in the woods, picking mushrooms and checking his snares, then headed down to town on Saturday afternoon to get a haircut and to haunt the library.

Converting his father's gold to cash was easier than getting a library card without an address. There was an old assayer whom the golems had described to him before his first trip to town. The man was cheap but he knew enough about the strangeness on the mountain not to cheat him too badly. The stern librarian who glared at him while he walked the shelves, sometimes looking at the titles, sometimes the authors, and sometimes the Dewey Decimal numbers had no such fear.

The Deweys were fascinating. They traced the fashions in human knowledge and wisdom. It was easy enough to understand why the arbiters of the system placed subdivided Motorized Land Vehicles (629.2) into several categories, but here in the 629.22s, where the books on automobiles were, you could see the planners' deficiencies. Automobiles divided into dozens of major subcategories (taxis and limousines, buses, light trucks, cans, lorries, tractor-trailers, campers, motorcycles, racing cars, and so on), then ramified into a combinatorial explosion of sub-sub-subcategories. There were Dewey numbers on some of the automotive book spines that had twenty digits or more after the decimal, an entire Dewey Decimal system hidden between 629.2 and 629.3.

To the librarian, this shelf-reading looked like your garden-variety screwing around, but what really made her nervous were Alan's excursions through the card catalogue, which required constant tending to replace the cards that errant patrons made unauthorized reorderings of.

The subject headings in the third bank of card drawers were the most interesting of all. They, too, branched and forked and rejoined themselves like the meanderings of an ant colony on the march. He'd go in sequence for a while, then start following cross-references when he found an interesting branch, keeping notes on scraps of paper on top of the file drawer. He had spent quite some time in the mythology categories, looking up golems and goblins, looking up changelings and monsters, looking up seers and demigods, but none of the books that he'd taken down off the shelves had contained anything that helped him understand his family better.

His family was uncatalogued and unclassified in human knowledge.

He rang the bell on Marci's smart little brick house at bang-on six, carrying some daisies he'd bought from the grocery store, following the etiquette laid down in several rather yucky romance novels he'd perused that afternoon.

She answered in jeans and a T-shirt, and punched him in the arm before he could give her the flowers. "Don't you look smart?" she said. "Well, you're not fooling anyone, you know." She gave him a peck on the cheek and snatched away the daisies. "Come along, then, we're eating soon."

Marci sat him down in the living room, which was furnished with neutral sofas and a neutral carpet and a neutral coffee table. The bookcases were bare. "It's horrible," she said, making a face. She was twittering a little, dancing from foot to foot. Alan was glad to know he wasn't the only one who was uncomfortable. "Isn't it? The company put us up here. We had a grand flat in Scotland."

"It's nice," Alan said, "but you look like you could use some books."

She crossed her eyes. "Books? Sure—I've got *ten boxes* of them in the basement. You can come by and help me unpack them."

"Ten *boxes*?" Alan said. "You're making that up." *Ten boxes of books!* Things like books didn't last long under the mountain, in the damp and with the ever-inquisitive, ever-destructive Davey exploring every inch of floor and cave and corridor in search of opportunities for pillage.

"I ain't neither," she said. "At least ten. It was a grand flat and they were all in alphabetical order, too."

"Can we go see?" Alan asked, getting up from the sofa.

"See boxes?"

"Yes," Alan said. "And look inside. We could unbox them after dinner, okay?"

"That's more of an afternoon project," said a voice from the top of the stairs.

"That's my Da," she said. "Come down and introduce yourself to Alan, Da," she said. "You're not the voice of God, so you can bloody well turn up and show your face."

"No more sass, gel, or it will go very hard for you," said the voice. The accent was like Marci's squared, thick as oatmeal, liqueur-thick. Nearly incomprehensible, but the voice was kind and smart and patient, too.

"You'll have a hard time giving me any licks from the top of the stairs, Da, and Alan looks like he's going to die if you don't at least come down and say hello."

Alan blushed furiously. "You can come down whenever you like, sir," he said. "That's all right."

"That's mighty generous of you, young sir," said the voice. "Aye. But before I come down, tell me, are your intentions toward my daughter honorable?"

His cheeks grew even hotter, and his ears felt like they were melting with embarrassment. "Yes, sir," he said in a small voice.

"He's a dreadful pervert, Da," Marci said. "You should see the things he tries, you'd kill him, you would." She grinned foxish and punched him in the shoulder. He sank into the cushions, face suddenly drained of blood.

"What?" roared the voice, and there was a clatter of slippers on the neutral carpet of the stairs. Alan didn't want to look but found that he couldn't help himself, his head inexorably turned toward the sound, until a pair of thick legs hove into sight, whereupon Marci leapt into his lap and threw her arms around his neck.

"Ge'orff me, pervert!" she said, as she began to cover his face in darting, pecking kisses.

He went rigid and tried to sink all the way into the sofa.

"All right, all right, that's enough of that," her father said. Marci stood and dusted herself off. Alan stared at his knees.

"She's horrible, isn't she?" said the voice, and a great, thick hand appeared in his field of vision. He shook it tentatively, noting the heavy class ring and the thin, plain wedding band. He looked up slowly.

Marci's father was short but powerfully built, like the wrestlers on the other kids' lunchboxes at school. He had a shock of curly black hair that was flecked with dandruff, and a thick bristling mustache that made him look very fierce, though his eyes were gentle and bookish behind thick glasses. He was wearing wool trousers and a cable-knit sweater that was unraveling at the elbows.

"Pleased to meet you, Albert," he said. They shook hands gravely. "I've been after her to unpack those books since we moved here. You could come by tomorrow afternoon and help, if you'd like—I think it's the only way I'll get herself to stir her lazy bottom to do some chores around here."

"Oh, *Da!*" Marci said. "Who cooks around here? Who does the laundry?"

"The take-away pizza man does the majority of the cooking, daughter. And as for laundry, the last time I checked, there were two weeks' worth of laundry to do."

"Da," she said in a sweet voice, "I love you Da," she said, wrapping her arms around his trim waist.

"You see what I have to put up with?" her father said, snatching her up and dangling her by her ankles.

She flailed her arms about and made outraged choking noises while he swung her back and forth like a pendulum, releasing her at the top of one arc so that she flopped onto the sofa in a tangle of thin limbs.

"It's a madhouse around here," her father continued as Marci righted herself, knocking Alan in the temple with a tennis shoe, "but what can you do? Once she's a little bigger, I can put her to work in the mines, and then I'll have a little peace around here." He sat down on an overstuffed armchair with a fussy antimacassar.

"He's got a huge life-insurance policy," Marci said conspiratorially. "I'm just waiting for him to kick the bucket and then I'm going to retire."

"Oh, aye," her father said. "Retire. Your life is an awful one, it is. Junior high is a terrible hardship, I know."

Alan found himself grinning.

"What's so funny?" Marci said, punching him in the shoulder.

"You two are," he said, grabbing her arm and then digging his fingers into her tummy, doubling her over with tickles.

There were *twelve* boxes of books. The damp in the basement had softened the cartons to cottage-cheese mush, and the back covers of the bottom layer of paperbacks were soft as felt. To Alan, these seemed unremarkable—all paper under the mountain looked like this after a week or two, even if Doug didn't get to it—but Marci was heartbroken.

"My books, my lovely books, they're roont!" she said as they piled them on the living room carpet.

"They're fine," Alan said. "They'll dry out a little wobbly, but they'll be fine. We'll just spread the damp ones out on the rug and shelve the rest."

And that's what they did, book after book—old books, hardcover books, board-back kids' books, new paperbacks, dozens of green- and orange-spined Penguin paperbacks. He fondled them, smelled them. Some smelled of fish and chips, and some smelled of road dust, and some smelled of Marci, and they had dog ears where she'd stopped and cracks in their spines where she'd bent them around. They fell open to pages that had her favorite passages. He felt wobbly and drunk as he touched each one in turn.

"Have you read all of these?" Alan asked as he shifted the John Mortimers down one shelf to make room for the Ed McBains.

"Naw," she said, punching him in the shoulder. "What's the point of a bunch of books you've already read?"

She caught him in the schoolyard on Monday and dragged him by one ear out to the marshy part. She pinned him down and straddled his chest and tickled him with one hand so that he cried out and used the other hand to drum a finger across his lips, so that his cries came out "bibble."

Once he'd bucked her off, they kissed for a little while, then she grabbed hold of one of his nipples and twisted.

"All right," she said. "Enough torture. When do I get to meet your family?"

"You can't," he said, writhing on the pine needles, which worked their way up the back of his shirt and pricked him across his lower back, feeling like the bristles of a hairbrush.

"Oh, I can, and I will," she said. She twisted harder.

He slapped her hand away. "My family is really weird," he said. "My parents don't really ever go out. They're not like other people. They don't talk." All of it true.

"They're mute?"

"No, but they don't talk."

"They don't talk much, or they don't talk at all?" She pronounced it *a-tall*.

"Not at all."

"How did you and your brothers learn to talk, then?"

"Neighbors." Still true. The golems lived in the neighboring caves. "And my father, a little." True.

"So you have neighbors who visit you?" she asked, a triumphant gleam in her eye.

Damn. "No, we visit them." Lying now. Sweat on the shag of hair over his ears, which felt like they had coals pressed to them.

"When you were a baby?"

"No, my grandparents took care of me when I was a baby." Deeper. "But they died." Bottoming out now.

"I don't believe you," she said, and he saw tears glisten in her eyes. "You're too embarrassed to introduce me to your family."

"That's not it." He thought fast. "My brother. David. He's not well. He has a brain tumor. We think he'll probably die. That's why he doesn't come to school. And it makes him act funny. He hits people, says terrible things." Mixing truth with lies was a *lot* easier. "He shouts and hurts people and he's the reason I can't ever have friends over. Not until he dies."

Her eyes narrowed. "If that's a lie," she said, "it's a terrible one. My Ma died of cancer, and it's not something anyone should make fun of. So, it better not be a lie."

"It's not a lie," he said, mustering a tear. "My brother David, we don't know how long he'll live, but it won't be long. He acts like a monster, so it's hard to love him, but we all try."

She rocked back onto her haunches. "It's true, then?" she asked softly.

He nodded miserably.

"Let's say no more about it, then," she said. She took his hand and traced hieroglyphs on his palm with the ragged edges of her chewed-up fingernails.

The recess bell rang and they headed back to school. They were about to leave the marshland when something hard hit Alan in the back of the head. He spun around and saw a small, sharp rock skitter into the grass, saw Davey's face contorted with rage, lips pulled all the way back off his teeth, half-hidden in the boughs of a tree, winding up to throw another rock.

He flinched away and the rock hit the paving hard enough to bounce. Marci whirled around, but David was gone, high up in the leaves, invisible, malicious, biding.

"What was that?"

"I dunno," Alan lied, and groaned.

Kurt and Alan examined every gap between every storefront on Augusta, no matter how narrow. Kurt kept silent as Alan fished his arm up to the shoulder along miniature alleys that were just wide enough to accommodate the rain gutters depending from the roof.

They found the alley that Frederick had been dragged down near the end of the block, between a mattress store and an egg wholesaler. It was narrow enough that they had to traverse it sideways, but there, at the entrance, were two smears of skin and blood, just above the ground, stretching off into the sulfurous, rotty-egg depths of the alleyway.

They slid along the alley's length, headed for the gloom of

the back. Something skittered away from Alan's shoe and he bent down, but couldn't see it. He ran his hands along the ground and the walls and they came back with a rime of dried blood and a single strand of long, oily hair stuck to them. He wiped his palms off on the bricks.

"I can't see," he said.

"Here," Kurt said, handing him a miniature maglight whose handle was corrugated by hundreds of toothmarks. Alan saw that he was intense, watching.

Alan twisted the light on. "Thanks," he said, and Kurt smiled at him, seemed a little taller. Alan looked again. There, on the ground, was a sharpened black tooth, pierced by a piece of pipe-cleaner wire.

He pocketed the tooth before Kurt saw it and delved farther, approaching the alley's end, which was carpeted with a humus of moldering cardboard, leaves, and road turds blown or washed there. He kicked it aside as best he could, then crouched down to examine the sewer grating beneath. The greenish brass screws that anchored it to the ground had sharp cuts in their old grooves where they had been recently removed. He rattled the grating, which was about half a meter square, then slipped his multitool out of his belt holster. He flipped out the Phillips driver and went to work on the screws, unconsciously putting Kurt's flashlight in his mouth, his front teeth finding purchase in the dents that Kurt's own had left there.

He realized with a brief shudder that Kurt probably used this flashlight while nipple-deep in dumpsters, had an image of Kurt transferring it from his gloved hands to his mouth and back again as he dug through bags of kitchen and toilet waste, looking for discarded technology. But the metal was cool and clean against his teeth and so he bit down and worked the four screws loose, worked his fingers into the mossy slots in the grate, lifted it out, and set it to one side.

He shone the light down the hole and found another finger-bone, the tip of a thumb, desiccated to the size of a large raisin, and he pocketed that, too. There was a lot of blood here, a little puddle that was still wet in the crusted middle. Frederick's blood.

He stepped over the grating and shone the light back down the hole, inviting Kurt to have a look.

"That's where they went," he said as Kurt bent down.

"That hole?"

"That hole," he said.

"Is that blood?"

"That's blood. It's not easy to fit someone my brother's size down a hole like that." He set the grate back, screwed it into place, and passed the flashlight back to Kurt. "Let's get out of here," he said.

On the street, Alan looked at his blood- and moss-grimed palms. Kurt pushed back his floppy, frizzed-out, bleach-white mohawk and scratched vigorously at the downy brown fuzz growing in on the sides of his skull.

"You think I'm a nut," Alan said. "It's okay, that's natural."

Kurt smiled sheepishly. "If it's any consolation, I think you're a *harmless* nut, okay? I like you."

"You don't have to believe me, so long as you don't get in my way," Alan said. "But it's easier if you believe me."

"Easier to do what?"

"Oh, to get along," Alan said.

Davey leapt down from a rock outcropping as Alan made his way home that night, landing on his back. Alan stumbled and dropped his school bag. He grabbed at the choking arm around his neck, then dropped to his knees as Davey bounced a fist-sized stone off his head, right over his ear.

He slammed himself back, pinning Davey between himself and the sharp stones on the walkway up to the cave entrance, then mashed backward with his elbows, his head ringing like a gong from the stone's blow. His left elbow connected with Davey's solar plexus and the arm around his throat went slack.

He climbed to his knees and looked Davey in the face. He was blue and gasping, but Alan couldn't work up a lot of sympathy for him as he reached up to the side of his head and felt the goose egg welling there. His fingertips came back with a few strands of hair blood-glued to them.

He'd been in a few schoolyard scraps and this was always the moment when a teacher intervened—one combatant pinned, the other atop him. What could you do after this? Was he going to take the rock from Davey's hand and smash him in the face with it, knocking out his teeth, breaking his nose, blacking his eyes? Could he get off of Davey without getting back into the fight?

He pinned Davey's shoulders under his knees and took him by the chin with one hand. "You can't do this, Danny," he said, looking into his hazel eyes, which had gone green as they did when he was angry.

"Do *what*?"

"Spy on me. Try to hurt me. Try to hurt my friends. Tease me all the time. You can't do it, okay?"

"I'll stab you in your sleep, Andy. I'll break your fingers with a brick. I'll poke your eyes out with a fork." He was fizzling like a baking-soda volcano, saliva slicking his cheeks and nostrils and chin, his eyes rolling.

Alan felt helplessness settle on him, weighing down his limbs. How could he let him go? What else could he do? Was he going to have to sit on Davey's shoulders until they were both old men?

"Please, Davey. I'm sorry about what I said. I just can't bring her home, you understand," he said.

"Pervert. She's a slut and you're a pervert. I'll tear her titties off."

"Don't, Danny, please. Stop, okay?"

Darren bared his teeth and growled, jerking his head forward and snapping at Alan's crotch, heedless of the painful thuds his head made when it hit the ground after each lunge.

Alan waited to see if he would tire himself out, but when it was clear that he would not tire, Alan waited for his head to thud to the ground and then, abruptly, he popped him in the chin, leapt off of him, turned him on his belly, and wrenched him to his knees, twisting one arm behind his back and pulling his head back by the hair. He brought Davey to his feet, under his control, before he'd recovered from the punch.

"I'm telling Dad," he said in Davey's ear, and began to frog-march him through to the cave mouth and down into the lake in the middle of the mountain. He didn't even slow down when they reached the smooth shore of the lake, just pushed on, sloshing in up to his chest, Davey's head barely above the water.

"He won't stop," Alan said, to the winds, to the water, to the vaulted ceiling, to the scurrying retreat of the goblin. "I think he'll kill me if he goes on. He's torturing me. You've seen it. Look at him!"

Davey was thrashing in the water, his face swollen and bloody, his eyes rattling like dried peas in a maraca. Alan's fingers, still buried in Davey's shiny blond hair, kept brushing up against the swollen bruises there, getting bigger by the moment. "I'll *fucking* kill you!" Davey howled, screaming inchoate into the echo that came back from his call.

"Shhh," Alan said into his ear. "Shhh. Listen, Davey, please, shhh."

Davey's roar did not abate. Alan thought he could hear the whispers and groans of their father in the wind, but he couldn't make it out. "Please, shhh," he said, gathering Davey in a hug that pinned his arms to his sides, putting his lips up against Davey's ear, holding him still.

"Shhh," he said, and Davey stopped twitching against him, stopped his terrible roar, and they listened.

At first the sound was barely audible, a soughing through the tunnels, but gradually the echoes chased each other 'round the great cavern and across the still, dark surface of the lake, and then a voice, illusive as a face in the clouds.

"My boys," the voice said, their father said. "My sons. David, Alan. You must not fight like this."

"He—!" Davey began, the echoes of his outburst scattering their father's voice.

"Shhh," Alan said again.

"Daniel, you must love your brother. He loves you. I love you. Trust him. He won't hurt you. I won't let you come to any harm. I love you, son."

Alan felt Danny tremble in his arms, and he was trembling, too, from the icy cold of the lake and from the voice and the words and the love that echoed from every surface.

"Adam, my son. Keep your brother safe. You need each other. Don't be impatient or angry with him. Give him love."

"I will," Alan said, and he relaxed his arms so that he was holding Danny in a hug and not a pinion. Danny relaxed back into him. "I love you, Dad," he said, and they trudged out of the water, out into the last warmth of the day's sun, to dry out on the slope of the mountainside, green grass under their bodies and wispy clouds in the sky that they watched until the sun went out.

M arci followed him home a week before Christmas break. He didn't notice her at first. She was cunning, and followed his boot prints in the snow. A blizzard had blown up halfway through the school day, and by the time class let out, there was fresh knee-deep powder and he had to lift each foot high to hike through it, the shush of his snow pants and the huff of his breath the only sounds in the icy winter evening.

She followed the deep prints of his boots on the fresh snow, stalking him like he stalked rabbits in the woods. When he happened to turn around at the cave mouth, he spotted her in her yellow snowsuit, struggling up the mountainside, barely visible in the twilight.

He'd never seen an intruder on the mountain. The dirt trail that led up to the cave branched off a side road on the edge of town, and it was too rocky even for the dirt-bike kids. He stood at the cave mouth, torn by indecision. He wanted to keep walking, head away farther uphill, away from the family's den, but now she'd seen him, had waved to him. His cold-numb face drained of blood and his bladder hammered insistently at him. He hiked down the mountain and met her.

"Why are you here?" he said, once he was close enough to see her pale, freckled face.

"Why do you think?" she said. "I followed you home. Where do you live, Alan? Why can't I even see where you live?"

He felt tears prick at his eyes. "You just *can't*! I can't bring you home!"

"You hate me, don't you?" she said, hands balling up into mittened fists. "That's it."

"I don't hate you, Marci. I—I love you," he said, surprising himself.

She punched him hard in the arm. "Shut up." She kissed his cheek with her cold, dry lips and the huff of her breath thawed his skin, making it tingle.

"Where do you live, Alan?"

He sucked air so cold it burned his lungs. "Come with me." He took her mittened hand in his and trudged up to the cave mouth.

They entered the summer cave, where the family spent its time in the warm months, now mostly empty, save for some straw and a few scattered bits of clothing and toys. He led her through the cave, his eyes adjusting to the gloom, back to the right-angle bend behind a stalactite baffle, toward the sulfur reek of the hot spring on whose shores the family spent its winters.

"It gets dark," he said. "I'll get you a light once we're inside."

Her hand squeezed his tighter and she said nothing.

It grew darker and darker as he pushed into the cave, helping her up the gentle incline of the cave floor. He saw well in the dark—the whole family did—but he understood that for her this was a blind voyage.

They stepped out into the sulfur-spring cavern, the acoustics of their breathing changed by the long, flat hollow. In the dark, he saw Edward-Frederick-George playing with his Matchbox cars in one corner; Davey leaned up against their mother, sucking his thumb. Billy was nowhere in sight, probably hiding out in his room—he would, of course, have foreseen this visit.

He put her hand against the cave wall, then said, "Wait here." He let go of her and walked quickly to the heap of winter coats and boots in the corner and dug through them for the flashlight he used to do his homework by. It was a hand-crank number, and as he squeezed it to life, he pointed it at Marci, her face wan and scared in its light. He gave the flashlight a few more pumps to get its flywheel spinning, then passed it to her.

"Just keep squeezing it," he said. "It doesn't need batteries." He took her hand again. It was limp.

"You can put your things on the pile," he said, pointing to the coats and boots. He was already shucking his hat and mittens and boots and snow pants and coat. His skin flushed with the warm vapors coming off of the sulfur spring.

"You *live* here?" she said. The light from the flashlight was dimming and he reached over and gave it a couple of squeezes, then handed it back to her.

"I live here. It's complicated."

Davey's eyes were open and he was staring at them with squinted eyes and a frown.

"Where are your parents?" she said.

"It's complicated," he said again, as though that explained everything. "This is my secret. No one else knows it."

Edward-Frederick-George tottered over to them with an armload of toy cars, which he mutely offered to Marci, smiling a drooly smile. Alan patted him on the head and knelt down. "I don't think Marci wants to play cars, okay?" Ed nodded solemnly and went back to the edge of the pool and began running his cars through the nearly scalding water.

Marci reached out a hand ahead of her into the weak light, looked at the crazy shadows it cast on the distant walls. "How can you live here? It's a cave, Alan. How can you live in a cave?"

"You get used to it," Alan said. "I can't explain it all, and the parts that I can explain, you wouldn't believe. But you've been to my home now, Marci. I've shown you where I live."

Davey approached them, a beatific smile on his angelic face.

"This is my brother, Daniel," Alan said. "The one I told you about."

"You're his slut," Davey said. He was still smiling. "Do you touch his peter?"

Alan flinched, suppressing a desire to smack Davey, but Marci just knelt down and looked him in the eye. "Nope," she said. "Are you always this horrible to strangers?"

"Yes!" Davey said cheerfully. "I hate you, and I hate *him*." He cocked his head Alanward. "And you're all *motherfuckers*."

"But we're not wee horrible shits, Danny," she said. "We're not filthy-mouthed brats who can't keep a civil tongue."

Davey snapped his head back and then forward, trying to get her in the bridge of the nose, a favorite tactic of his, but she was too fast for him and ducked it, so that he stumbled and fell to his knees.

"Your mother's going to be very cross when she finds out how you've been acting. You'll be lucky if you get any Christmas pressies," she said as he struggled to his feet.

He swung a punch at her groin, and she caught his wrist and then hoisted him to his tiptoes by his arm, then lifted him off the floor, bringing his face up level with hers. "Stop it," she said. "*Now.*"

He fell silent and narrowed his eyes as he dangled there, thinking about this. Then he spat in her face. Marci shook her head slowly as the gob of spit slid down her eyebrow and over her cheek, then she spat back, nailing him square on the tip of his nose. She set him down and wiped her face with a glove.

Davey started toward her, and she lifted a hand and he flinched back and then ran behind their mother, hiding in her tangle of wires and hoses. Marci gave the flashlight a series of hard cranks that splashed light across the washing machine and then turned to Alan.

"That's your brother?"

Alan nodded.

"Well, I see why you didn't want me to come home with you, then."

K**urt was properly appreciative** of Alan's bookcases and trophies, ran his fingertips over the wood, willingly accepted some iced mint tea sweetened with honey, and used a coaster without having to be asked.

"A washing machine and a mountain," he said.

"Yes," Alan said. "He kept a roof over our heads and she kept our clothes clean."

"You've told that joke before, right?" Kurt's foot was bouncing, which made the chains on his pants and jacket jangle.

"And now Davey's after us," Alan said. "I don't know why it's now. I don't know why Davey does *anything*. But he always hated me most of all."

"So why did he snatch your brothers first?"

"I think he wants me to sweat. He wants me scared, all the time. I'm the eldest. I'm the one who left the mountain. I'm the one who came first, and made all the connections with the outside world. They all looked to me to explain the world, but I never had any explanations that would suit Davey."

"This is pretty weird," he said.

Alan cocked his head at Kurt. He was about thirty, old for a punk, and had a kind of greasy sheen about him, like he didn't remember to wash often enough, despite his protestations about his cleanliness. But at thirty, he should have seen enough to let him know that the world was both weirder than he suspected and not so weird as certain mystically inclined people would like to believe.

Arnold didn't like this moment of disclosure, didn't like dropping his carefully cultivated habit of hiding this, but he also couldn't help but feel relieved. A part of his mind nagged him, though, and told him that too much of this would waken the worry for his brothers from its narcotized slumber.

"I've told other people, just a few. They didn't believe me. You don't have to. Why don't you think about it for a while?"

"What are you going to do?"

"I'm going to try to figure out how to find my brothers. I can't go underground like Davey can. I don't think I can, anyway. I never have. But Davey's so . . . *broken* . . . so small and twisted. He's not smart, but he's cunning and he's determined. I'm smarter than he is. So I'll try to find the smart way. I'll think about it, too."

"Well, I've got to get ready to go diving," Kurt said. He stood up with a jangle. "Thanks for the iced tea, Adam."

"It was nice to meet you, Kurt," Alan said, and shook his hand.

Alan woke with something soft over his face. It was pitch-dark, and he couldn't breathe. He tried to reach up, but his arms wouldn't move. He couldn't sit up. Something heavy was sitting on his chest. The soft thing—a pillow?—ground against his face, cruelly pressing down on the cartilage in his nose, filling his mouth as he gasped for air.

He shuddered hard, and felt something give near his right wrist and then his arm was loose from the elbow down. He kept working the arm, his chest afire, and then he'd freed it to the shoulder, and something bit him, hard little teeth like knives, in the fleshy underside of his bicep. Flailing dug the teeth in harder, and he knew he was bleeding, could feel it seeping down his arm. Finally, he got his hand onto something, a desiccated, mummified piece of flesh. Davey. Davey's ribs, like dry stones, cold and thin. He felt up higher, felt for the place where Davey's arm met his shoulder, and then twisted as hard as he could, until the arm popped free in its socket. He shook his head violently and the pillow slid away.

The room was still dark, and the hot, moist air rushed into his nostrils and mouth as he gasped it in. He heard Davey moving in the dark, and as his eyes adjusted, he saw him unfolding a knife. It was a clasp knife with a broken hasp and it swung open with the sound of a cockroach's shell crunching underfoot. The blade was rusty.

Alan flung his freed arm across his body and tried to tug himself loose. He was being held down by his own sheets, which had been tacked or stapled to the bed frame. Using all his strength, he rolled over, heaving and bucking, and felt/heard the staples popping free down one side of the bed, just as Davey slashed at where his face had been a moment before. The knife whistled past his ear, then scored deeply along his shoulder. His arm flopped uselessly at his side and now they were both fighting one-armed, though Davey had a knife and Adam was wrapped in a sheet.

His bedroom was singularly lacking in anything that could be improvised into a weapon—he considered trying getting a heavy encyclopedia out to use as a shield, but it was too far a distance and too long a shot.

He scooted back on the bed, trying to untangle the sheet, which was still secured at the foot of the bed and all along one side. He freed his good arm just as Davey slashed at him again, aiming for the meat of his thigh, the big arteries there that could bleed you out in a minute or two. He grabbed for Davey's shoulder and caught it for an instant, squeezed and twisted, but then the skin he had hold of sloughed away and Davey was free, dancing back.

Then he heard, from downstairs, the sound of rhythmic pounding at the door. He'd been hearing it for some time, but hadn't registered it until now. A muffled yell from below. Police? Mimi? He screamed out, "Help!" hoping his voice would carry through the door.

Apparently, it did. He heard the sound of the small glass pane over the doorknob shatter, and Davey turned his head to look in the direction of the sound. Alan snatched up the pillow that he'd been smothering under and swung it as hard as he could at Davey's head, knocking him around, and the door was open now, the summer night air sweeping up the stairs to the second-floor bedroom.

"Alan?" It was Kurt.

"Kurt, up here, he's got a knife!"

Boots on the stairs, and Davey standing again, cornered, with the knife, slashing at the air toward him and toward the bedroom door, toward the light coming up the stairs, bobbing, Kurt's maglight, clenched in his teeth, and Davey bolted for the door with the knife held high. The light stopped moving and there was an instant's tableau, Davey caught in the light, cracked black lips peeled back from sharp teeth, chest heaving, knife bobbing, and then Alan was free, diving for his knees, bringing him down.

Kurt was on them before Davey could struggle up to his good elbow, kicking the knife away, scattering fingerbones like dice.

Davey screeched like a rusty hinge as Kurt twisted his arms up behind his back and Alan took hold of his ankles. He thrashed like a raccoon in a trap, and Alan forced the back of his head down so that his face was mashed against the cool floor, muffling his cries.

Kurt shifted so that his knee and one hand were pinning Davey's wrists, fished in his pockets, and came out with a bundle of hairy twine. He set it on the floor next to Alan and then shifted his grip back to Davey's arms.

As soon as Alan released the back of Davey's head, he jerked it up and snapped his teeth into the top of Kurt's calf, just above the top of his high, chain-draped boot. Kurt hollered and Adam reached out and took the knife, moving quickly before he could think, and smashed the butt into Davey's jaw, which cracked audibly. Davey let go of Kurt's calf and Alan worked quickly to lash his feet together, using half the bundle of twine, heedless of how he cut into the thin, cracking skin. He used the knife to snip the string and then handed the roll to Kurt, who went to work on Danny's wrists.

Alan got the lights and rolled his brother over, looked into his mad eyes. Dale was trying to scream, but with his jaw hanging limp and his teeth scattered, it came out in a rasp. Alan stood and found that he was naked, his shoulder and bicep dripping blood down his side into a pool on the polished floor.

"We'll take him to the basement," he told Kurt, and dug through the laundry hamper at the foot of the bed for jeans. He found a couple of pairs of boxer shorts and tied one around his bicep and the other around his shoulder, using his teeth and chin as a second hand. It took two tries before he had them bound tight enough to still the throb.

The bedroom looked like someone had butchered an animal

in it, and the floor was gritty with Darrel's leavings, teeth and nails and fingerbones. Picking his way carefully through the mess, he hauled the sheet off the bed, popping out the remaining staples, which pinged off the bookcases and danced on the polished wood of the floor. He folded it double and laid it on the floor next to Davey.

"Help me roll him onto it," he said, and then saw that Kurt was staring down at his shriveled, squirming, hateful brother in horror, wiping his hands over and over again on the thighs of his jeans.

He looked up and his eyes were glazed and wide. "I was passing by and I saw the shadows in the window. I thought you were being attacked—" He hugged himself.

"I was," Alan said. He dug another T-shirt out of his hamper. "Here, wrap this around your hands."

They rolled Davey into the sheet and then wrapped him in it. He was surprisingly heavy, dense. Hefting his end of the sheet one-handed, hefting that mysterious weight, he remembered picking up Ed-Fred-Geoff in the cave that first day, remembered the weight of the brother-in-the-brother-in-the-brother, and he had a sudden sickening sense that perhaps Davey was so heavy because he'd eaten them.

Once they had him bound snugly in the sheet, Danny stopped thrashing and became very still. They carried him carefully down the dark stairs, the walnut-shell grit echoing the feel of teeth and flakes of skin on the bare soles of Alan's feet.

They dumped him unceremoniously on the cool mosaic of tile on the floor. They stared at the unmoving bundle for a moment. "Wait here, I'm going to get a chair," Alan said.

"Jesus, don't leave me alone here," Kurt said. "That kid, the one who saw him . . . take . . . your brother? No one's seen him since." He looked down at Davey with wide, crazed eyes.

Alan's shoulder throbbed. "All right," he said. "You get a chair from the kitchen, the captain's chair in the corner with the newspaper recycling stacked on it."

While Kurt was upstairs, Alan unwrapped his brother. Danny's eyes were closed, his jaw hanging askew, his wrists bound behind him. Alan leaned carefully over him and took his jaw and rotated it gently until it popped back into place.

"Davey?" he said. The eyes were closed, but now there was an attentiveness, an alertness to him. Alan stepped back quickly, feeling foolish at his fear of this pathetic, disjointed bound thing on his floor. No two ways about it, though: Davey gave him the absolutely willies, making his testicles draw up and the hair on the back of his arms prickle.

"Set the chair down there," Alan said, pointing. He hoisted Davey up by his dry, papery armpits and sat him in the seat. He took some duct tape out of a utility drawer under the basement staircase and used it to gum Danny down in the chair.

"Davey," he said again. "I know you can hear me. Stop pretending."

"That's your brother?" Kurt said. "The one who—"

"That's him," Alan said. "I guess you believe me now, huh?"

Davey grinned suddenly, mirthless. "Still making friends and influencing people, brother?" he said. His voice was wet and hiccuping, like he was drowning in snot.

"We're not going to play any games here, Davey. You're going to tell me where Edward, Felix, and Griffin are, or I'm going to tear your fingers off and smash them into powder. When I run out of fingers, I'll switch to teeth."

Kurt looked at him in alarm. He moaned. "Jesus, Adam—"

Adam whirled on him, something snapping inside. "Don't, Kurt, just don't, okay? He tried to kill me tonight. He may already have killed my brothers. This is life or death, and there's no room for sentiment or humanity. Get a hammer out of the toolbox, on that shelf." Kurt hesitated. "Do it!" Alan said, pointing at the toolbox.

Kurt shrank back, looking as though he'd been slapped. He moved as if in a dream, opening the toolbox and pawing through it until he came up with a scarred hammer, one claw snapped off.

Davey shook his head. "You don't scare me, Albert. Not for an instant. I have a large supply of fingers and teeth—all I need. And you—you're like him. You're a sentimentalist. Scared of yourself. Scared of me. Scared of everything. That's why you ran away. That's why you got rid of me. Scared."

Alan dug in his pocket for the fingerbones and teeth he'd collected. He found the tip of a pinky with a curled-over nail as thick as an oyster's shell, crusted with dirt and blood. "Give me the hammer, Kurt," he said.

Davey's eyes followed him as he set the fingertip down on the tiles and raised the hammer. He brought it down just to one side of the finger, hard enough to break the tile. Kurt jumped a little, and Alan held the hammer up again.

"Tell me or this time I won't miss," he said, looking Davey in the eye.

Davey shrugged in his bonds.

Alan swung the hammer again. It hit the fingertip with a jarring impact that vibrated up his arm and resonated through his hurt shoulder. He raised the hammer again. He'd expected the finger to crush into powder, but instead it fissured into three jagged pieces, like a piece of chert fracturing under a hammerstone.

Davey's eyes were squeezed down to slits now. "You're the scared one. You can't scare me," he said, his voice choked with phlegm.

Alan sat on the irregular tile and propped his chin in his palm. "Okay, Davey, you're right. I'm scared. You've kidnapped our brothers, maybe even killed them. You're terrorizing me. I can't think, I can't sleep. So tell me, Danny, why shouldn't I just kill you again, and get rid of all that fear?"

"I know where the brothers are," he said instantly. "I know where there are more people like us. All the answers, Albert, every answer you've ever looked for. I've got them. And I won't tell you any of them. But so long as I'm walking around and talking, you think that I might."

Alan took Marci back to his bedroom, the winter bedroom that was no more than a niche in the hot-spring cavern, a pile of rags and a sleeping bag for a bed. It had always been enough for him, but now he was ashamed of it. He took the flashlight from Marci and let it wind down, so that they were sitting in darkness.

"Your parents—" she said, then broke off.

"It's complicated."

"Are they dead?"

He reached out in the dark and took her hand.

"I don't know how to explain it," he said. "I can lie, and you'll probably think I'm telling the truth. Or I can tell the truth, and you'll think that I'm lying."

She squeezed his hand. Despite the sweaty heat of the cave, her fingers were cold as ice. He covered her hand with his free hand and rubbed at her cold fingers.

"Tell me the truth," she whispered. "I'll believe you."

So he did, in mutters and whispers. He didn't have the words to explain it all, didn't know exactly how to explain it, but he tried. How he knew his father's moods. How he felt his mother's love.

After keeping this secret all his life, it felt incredible to be letting it out. His heart thudded in his chest, and his shoulders felt progressively lighter, until he thought he might rise up off his bedding and fly around the cave.

If it hadn't been dark, he wouldn't have been able to tell it. It was the dark, and the faint lunar glow of Marci's face that showed no expression, that let him open up and spill out all the secrets. Her fingers squeezed tighter and tighter, and now he felt like singing and dancing, because surely between the two of them they could find a book in the library or maybe an article in the microfilm cabinets that would *really* explain it to him.

He wound down. "No one else knows this," he said. "No one except you." He leaned in and planted a kiss on her cold lips. She sat rigid and unmoving as he kissed her.

"Marci?"

"Alan," she breathed. Her fingers went slack. She pulled her hand free.

Suddenly Alan was cold, too. The scant inches between them felt like an unbridgeable gap.

"You think I'm lying," he said, staring out into the cave.

"I don't know—"

"It's okay," he said. "I can help you get home now, all right?" She folded her hands on her lap and nodded miserably.

On the way out of the cave, Eddie-Freddie-Georgie tottered over, still holding his car. He held it out to her mutely. She knelt down solemnly and took it from him, then patted him on the head. "Merry Christmas, kiddo," she said. He hugged her leg, and she laughed a little and bent to pick him up. She couldn't. He was too heavy. She let go of him and nervously pried his arms from around her thigh.

Alan took her down the path to the side road that led into town. The moonlight shone on the white snow, making the world glow bluish. They stood by the roadside for a long and awkward moment.

"Good night, Alan," she said, and turned and started trudging home.

There was no torture at school the next day. She ignored him through the morning, and he couldn't find her at recess, but at lunch she came and sat next to him. They ate in silence, but he was comforted by her presence beside him, a warmth that he sensed more than felt.

She sat beside him in afternoon classes, too. Not a word passed between them. For Alan, it felt like anything they could say to one another would be less true than the silence, but that realization hurt. He'd never been able to discuss his life and nature with anyone and it seemed as though he never would.

But the next morning, in the schoolyard, she snagged him as he walked past the climber made from a jumble of bolted-together logs and dragged him into the middle. It smelled faintly of pee and was a rich source of mysterious roaches and empty beer bottles on Monday mornings after the teenagers had come and gone.

She was crouched down on her haunches in the snow there, her steaming breath coming in short huffs. She grabbed him by the back of his knit toque and pulled his face to hers, kissing him hard on the mouth, shocking the hell out of him by forcing her tongue past his lips.

They kissed until the bell rang, and as Alan made his way to class, he felt like his face was glowing like a lightbulb. His home-room teacher asked him if he was feeling well, and he stammered out some kind of affirmative while Marci, sitting in the next row, stifled a giggle.

They ate their lunches together again, and she filled the silence with a running commentary of the deficiencies of the sandwich her father had packed her, the strange odors coming from the brown bag that Alan had brought, filled with winter mushrooms and some soggy bread and cheese, and the hairiness of the mole on the lunch lady's chin.

When they reached the schoolyard, she tried to drag him back to the logs, but he resisted, taking her instead to the marsh where he'd first spied her. The ground had frozen over and the rushes and reeds were stubble, poking out of the snow. He took her mittened hands in his and waited for her to stop squirming.

Which she did, eventually. He'd rehearsed what he'd say to her all morning: *Do you believe me? What am I? Am I like you? Do you still love me? Are you still my friend? I don't understand it any better than you do, but now, now there are two of us who know about it, and maybe we can make sense of it together. God, it's such a relief to not be the only one anymore.*

But now, standing there with Marci, in the distant catcalls of the playground and the smell of the new snow and the soughing of the wind in the trees, he couldn't bring himself to say it. She either knew these things or she didn't, and if she didn't, he didn't know what he could do to help it.

"What?" she said at last.

"Do you—" he began, then fell silent. He couldn't say the words.

She looked irritated, and the sounds and the smells swept over him as the moment stretched. But then she softened. "I don't understand it, Alan," she said. "Is it true? Is it really how you say it is? Did I see what I saw?"

"It's true," he said, and it was as though the clouds had parted, the world gone bright with the glare off the snow and the sounds from the playground now joyous instead of cruel. "It's true, and I don't understand it any more than you do, Marci."

"Are you . . . *human*, Alan?"

"I *think* so," he said. "I bleed. I eat. I sleep. I think and talk and dream."

She squeezed his hands and darted a kiss at him. "You kiss," she said.

And it was all right again.

The next day was Saturday, and Marci arranged to meet him at the cave mouth. In the lee of the wind, the bright winter sun reflected enough heat off the snow that some of it melted away, revealing the stunted winter grass beneath. They sat on the dry snow and listened to the wind whistle through the pines and the hiss of loose snow blowing across the crust.

"Will I get to meet your Da, then?" she said, after they'd watched a jackrabbit hop up the mountainside and disappear into the woods.

He sniffed deeply, and smelled the coalface smell of his father's cogitation.

"You want to?" he said.

"I do."

And so he led her inside the mountain, through the winter cave, and back and back to the pool in the mountain's heart. They crept along quietly, her fingers twined in his. "You have to put out the flashlight now," he said. "It'll scare the goblin." His voice shocked him, and her, he felt her startle. It was so quiet otherwise, just the sounds of breathing and of cave winds.

So she let the whirring dynamo in the flashlight wind down, and the darkness descended on them. It was cool, but not cold, and the wind smelled more strongly of coalface than ever. "He's in there," Alan said. He heard the goblin scamper away. His words echoed over the pool around the corner. "Come on." Her fingers were very cool. They walked in a slow, measured step, like a king and queen of elfland going for a walk in the woods.

He stopped them at the pool's edge. There was almost no light here, but Alan could make out the smooth surface of his father's pool.

"Now what?" she whispered, the hissing of her words susurrating over the pool's surface.

"We can only talk to him from the center," he whispered. "We have to wade in."

"I can't go home with wet clothes," she whispered.

"You don't wear clothes," he said. He let go of her hand and began to unzip his snowsuit.

And so they stripped, there on his father's shore. She was luminous in the dark, a pale girl-shape picked out in the ripples of the pool, skinny, with her arms crossed in front of her chest. Even though he knew she couldn't see him, he was self-conscious in his nudity, and he stepped into the pool as soon as he was naked.

"Wait," she said, sounding panicked. "Don't leave me!"

So he held out his hand for her, and then, realizing that she couldn't see it, he stepped out of the pool and took her hand, brushing her small breast as he did so. He barely registered the contact, though she startled and nearly fell over. "Sorry," he said. "Come on."

The water was cold, but once they were in up to their shoulders, it warmed up, or they went numb.

"Is it okay?" she whispered, and now that they were in the center of the cavern, the echoes crossed back and forth and took a long time to die out.

"Listen," Andy said. "Just listen."

And as the echoes of his words died down, the winds picked up, and then the words emerged from the breeze.

"Adam," his father sighed. Marci jumped a foot out of the water, and her splashdown sent watery ripples rebounding off the cavern walls.

Alan reached out for her and draped his arm around her

shoulders. She huddled against his chest, slick cold naked skin goose-pimpled against his ribs. She smelled wonderful, like a fox. It *felt* wonderful, and solemn, to stand there nude, in the heart of his father, and let his secrets spill away.

Her breathing stilled again.

"Alan," his father said.

"We want to understand, Father," Alan whispered. "What am I?" It was the question he'd never asked. Now that he'd asked it, he felt like a fool: Surely his father *knew*, the mountain knew everything, had stood forever. He could have found out anytime he'd thought to ask.

"I don't have the answer," his father said. "There may be no answer. You may never know."

Adam let go of Marci, let his arms fall to his sides.

"No," he said. "No!" he shouted again, and the stillness was broken. The wind blew cold and hard, and he didn't care. *"NO!"* he screamed, and Marci grabbed him and put her hand over his mouth. His ears roared with echoes, and they did not die down, but rather built atop one another, to a wall of noise that scared him.

She was crying now, scared and openmouthed sobs. She splashed him and water went up his nose and stung his eyes. The wind was colder now, cold enough to hurt, and he took her hand and sloshed recklessly for the shore. He spun up the flashlight and handed it to her, then yanked his clothes over his wet skin, glaring at the pool while she did the same.

In the winter cave, they met a golem.

It stood like a statue, brick-red with glowing eyes, beside Alan's mother, hands at its sides. Golems didn't venture to this side of his father very often, and almost never in daylight. Marci caught him in the flashlight's beam as they entered the warm humidity of the cave, shivering in the gusting winds. She fumbled the flashlight and Alan caught it before it hit the ground.

"It's okay," he said. His chest was heaving from his tantrum, but the presence of the golem calmed him. You could say or do anything to a golem, and it couldn't strike back, couldn't answer back. The sons of the mountain that sheltered—and birthed?—the golems owed nothing to them.

He walked over to it and folded his arms.

"What is it?" he said.

The golem bent its head slightly and looked him in the eye. It was man-shaped, but baggier, muscles like frozen mud. An overhang of belly covered its smooth crotch like a kilt. Its chisel-shaped teeth clacked together as it limbered up its jaw.

"Your father is sad," it said. Its voice was slow and grinding, like an avalanche. "Our side grows cold."

"I don't care," Alan said. "*Fuck* my father," he said. Behind him, perched atop their mother, Davey whittered a mean little laugh.

"You shouldn't—"

Alan shoved the golem. It was like shoving a boulder. It didn't give at all.

"You don't tell me what to do," he said. "You can't tell me what to do. I want to know what I am, how we're possible, and if you can't help, then you can leave now."

The winds blew colder, smelling now of the golem's side of the mountain, of clay and the dry bones of their kills, which they arrayed on the walls of their cavern.

The golem stood stock-still.

"Does it . . . *understand*?" Marci asked. Davey snickered again.

"It's not stupid," Alan said, calming a little. "It's . . . *slow.* It thinks slowly and acts slowly. But it's not stupid." He paused for a moment. "It taught me to speak," he said.

That did it. He began to cry, biting his lip to keep from making a sound, but the tears rolled down his cheeks and his shoulders shook. The flashlight's beam pinned him, and he wanted to run to his mother and hide behind her, wanted to escape the light.

"Go," he said softly to the golem, touching its elbow. "It'll be all right."

Slowly, gratingly, the golem turned and lumbered out of the cave, clumsy and ponderous.

Marci put her arm around him and he buried his face in her skinny neck, the hot tears coursing down her collarbones.

Davey came to him that night and pinned him in the light of the flashlight. He woke staring up into the bright bulb, shielding his eyes. He groped out for the light, but Darryl danced back out of reach, keeping the beam in his eyes. The air crackled with the angry grinding of its hand-dynamo.

He climbed out of bed naked and felt around on the floor. He had a geode there, he'd broken it and polished it by hand, and it was the size of a softball, the top smooth as glass, the underside rough as a coconut's hide.

Wordless and swift, he wound up and threw the geode as hard as he could at where he judged Davey's head to be.

There was a thud and a cry, and the light clattered to the ground, growing more dim as its dynamo whirred to a stop. Green blobs chased themselves across his vision, and he could only see Darren rolling on the ground by turning his head to one side and looking out of the corner of his eye.

He groped toward Davey and smelled the blood. Kneeling down, he found Davey's hand and followed it up to his shoulder, his neck. Slick with blood. Higher, to Davey's face, his forehead, the dent there sanded ragged by the rough side of the geode. The blood flowed freely and beneath his other hand Danny's chest heaved as he breathed, shallowly, rapidly, almost panting.

His vision was coming back now. He took off his T-shirt and wadded it up, pressed it to Davey's forehead. They'd done first aid in class. You weren't supposed to move someone with a head injury. He pressed down with the T-shirt, trying to stanch the blood.

Then, quick as a whip, Davey's head twisted around and he bit down, hard, on Alan's thumbtip. Albert reeled back, but it was too late: Davey had bitten off the tip of his right thumb. Alan howled, waking up Ed-Fred-Geoff, who began to cry. Davey rolled away, scampering back into the cave's depths.

Alan danced around the cave, hand clamped between his

thighs, mewling. He fell to the floor and squeezed his legs together, then slowly brought his hand up before his face. The ragged stump of his thumb was softly spurting blood in time with his heartbeat. He struggled to remember his first aid. He wrapped his T-shirt around the wound and then pulled his parka on over his bare chest and jammed his bare feet into his boots, then made his way to the cave mouth and scooped up snow under the moon's glow, awkwardly packing a snowball around his hand. He shivered as he made his way back into the winter cave and propped himself up against his mother, holding his hurt hand over his head.

The winter cave grew cold as the ice packed around his hand. Bobby, woken by his clairvoyant instincts, crept forward with a blanket and draped it over Alan. He'd foreseen this, of course—had foreseen all of it. But Bobby followed his own code, and he kept his own counsel, cleaning up after the disasters he was powerless to prevent.

Deep in the mountains, they heard the echoes of Davey's tittering laughter.

It was wrong to bring her here, Adam," Billy said to him in the morning, as he fed Alan the crusts of bread and dried apples he'd brought him, packing his hand with fresh snow.

"I didn't bring her here, she followed me," Adam said. His arm ached from holding it aloft, and his back and tailbone were numb with the ache of a night spent sitting up against their mother's side. "And besides, why should it be wrong? Whose rules? What rules? What are the *fucking* rules?"

"You can feel the rules, brother," he said. He couldn't look Alan in the eye, he never did. This was a major speech, coming from Bobby.

"I can't feel any rules," Alan said. He wondered if it was true. He'd never told anyone about the family before. Had he known all along that he shouldn't do this?

"I can. She can't know. No one can know. Even we can't know. We'll never understand it."

"Where is Davey?"

"He's doing a . . . ritual. With your thumb."

They sat silent and strained their ears to hear the winds and the distant shuffle of the denizens of the mountain.

Alan shifted, using his good hand to prop himself up, looking for a comfortable position. He brought his injured hand down to his lap and unwrapped his blood-soaked T-shirt from his fist, gently peeling it away from the glue of dried blood that held it there.

His hand had shriveled in the night, from ice and from restricted circulation, and maybe from Davey's ritual. Alan pondered its crusty, clawed form, thinking that it looked like it belonged to someone—some*thing*—else.

Buddy scaled the stalactite that served as the ladder up to the lofty nook where he slept and came back down holding his water bottle. "It's clean, it's from the pool," he said, another major speech for him. He also had an armload of scavenged diapers, much-washed and worn soft as flannel. He wet one and began to wipe away the crust of blood on Alan's arm and hand, working his way up from the elbow, then tackling the uninjured fingers, then, very gently, gently as a feather-touch, slow as a glacier, he worked on Alan's thumb.

When he was done, Alan's hand was clean and dry and cold, and the wound of his thumb was exposed and naked, a thin crust of blood weeping liquid slowly. It seemed to Alan that he could see the stump of bone protruding from the wound. He was amazed to see his bones, to get a look at a cross-section of himself. He wondered if he could count the rings and find out how old he was, as he had never been really certain on that score. He giggled ghoulishly.

He held out his good hand. "Get me up, okay?" Bobby hauled him to his feet. "Get me some warm clothes, too?"

And he did, because he was Bobby, and he was always only too glad to help, only too glad to do what service he could for you, even if he would never do you the one service that would benefit you the most: telling you of his visions, helping you avoid the disasters that loomed on your horizon.

Standing up, walking around, being clean—he began to feel

like himself again. He even managed to get into his snow pants and parka and struggle out to the hillside and the bright sunshine, where he could get a good look at his hand.

What he had taken for a bone wasn't. It was a skinny little thumbtip, growing out of the raggedy, crusty stump. He could see the whorl of a fingerprint there, and narrow, nearly invisible cuticles. He touched the tip of his tongue to it and it seemed to him that he could feel a tongue rasping over the top of his missing thumbtip.

It's disgusting, keep it away," Marci said, shrinking away from his hand in mock horror. He held his proto-thumb under her nose and waggled it.

"No joking, okay? I just want to know what it *means*. I'm *growing a new thumb*."

"Maybe you're part salamander. They regrow their legs and tails. Or a worm—cut a worm in half and you get two worms. It's in one of my Da's books."

He stared at his thumb. It had grown perceptibly, just on the journey into town to Marci's place. They were holed up in her room, surrounded by watercolors of horses in motion that her mother had painted. She'd raided the fridge for cold pork pies and cheese and fizzy lemonade that her father had shipped from the Marks & Spencer in Toronto. It was the strangest food he'd ever eaten but he'd developed a taste for it.

"Wiggle it again," she said.

He did, and the thumbtip bent down like a scale model of a thumbtip, cracking the scab around it.

"We should go to a doctor," she said.

"I don't go to doctors," he said flatly.

"You *haven't* gone to a doctor—doesn't mean you can't."

"I don't go to doctors." X-ray machines and stethoscopes, blood tests and clever little flashlights in your ears—who knew what they'd reveal? He wanted to be the first to discover it, he didn't want to have to try to explain it to a doctor before he understood it himself.

"Not even when you're sick?"

"The golems take care of it," he said.

She shook her head. "You're a weirdo, you know that?"

"I know it," he said.

"I thought my family was strange," she said, stretching out on her tummy on the bed. "But they're not a patch on you."

"I know it."

He finished his fizzy lemonade and lay down beside her, belching.

"We could ask my Da. He knows a lot of strange things."

He put his face down in her duvet and smelled the cotton covers and her nighttime sweat, like a spice, like cinnamon. "I don't want to do that. Please don't tell anyone, all right?"

She took hold of his wrist and looked again at the teensy thumb. "Wiggle it again," she said. He did. She giggled. "Imagine if you were like a worm. Imagine if your thumbtip was out there growing another *you*."

He sat bolt upright. "Do you think that's possible?" he said. His heart was thudding. "Do you think so?"

She rolled on her side and stared at him. "No, don't be daft. How could your thumb grow another *you*?"

"Why wouldn't it?"

She had no answer for him.

"I need to go home," he said. "I need to know."

"I'm coming with," she said. He opened his mouth to tell her no, but she made a fierce face at him, her foxy features wrinkled into a mock snarl.

"Come along, then," he said. "You can help me do up my coat."

The winter cave was deserted. He listened at the mouths of all the tunnels, straining to hear Davey. From his high nook, Brian watched them.

"Where is he, Billy?" Alan called. "Tell me, godfuckit!"

Billy looked down from him perch with his sad, hollow eyes—had he been forgetting to eat again?—and shook his head.

They took to the tunnels. Even with the flashlights Marci couldn't match him for speed. He could feel the tunnels through the soles of his boots, he could smell them, he could pick them apart by the quality of their echoes. He moved fast, dragging Marci along with his good hand while she cranked the flashlight as hard as she could. He heard her panting, triangulated their location from the way that the shallow noises reflected off the walls.

When they found Davey at last, it was in the golem's cave, on the other side of the mountain. He was hunkered down in a corner, while the golems moved around him slowly, avoiding him like he was a boulder or a stalagmite that had sprung up in the night. Their stony heads turned to regard Marci and Adam as they came upon them, their luminous eyes lighting on them for a moment and then moving on. It was an eloquent statement for them: *This is the business of the mountain and his sons. We will not intervene.*

There were more golems than Alan could remember seeing at once, six, maybe seven. The golems made more of their kind from the clay they found at the riverbank whenever they cared to or needed to, and allowed their number to dwindle when the need or want had passed by the simple expedient of deconstructing one of their own back to the clay it had come from.

The golems' cave was lined with small bones and skulls, rank and row climbing the walls, twined with dried grasses in ascending geometries. These were the furry animals that the golems patiently trapped and killed, skinned, dressed, and smoked, laying them in small, fur-wrapped bundles in the family's cave when they were done. It was part of their unspoken bargain with the mountain, and the tiny bones had once borne the flesh of nearly every significant meal Alan had ever eaten.

Davey crouched among the bones at the very back of the cave, his back to them, shoulders hunched.

The golems stood stock-still as Marci and he crept up on Davey. So intent was he on his work that he didn't notice them, even as they loomed over his shoulder, staring down on the thing he held in his hands.

It was Alan's thumb, and growing out of it—Allen. Tiny, the size of a pipe-cleaner man, and just as skinny, but perfectly formed, squirming and insensate, face contorted in a tiny expression of horror.

Not so perfectly formed, Alan saw, once he was over the initial shock. One of the pipe-cleaner-Allen's arms was missing, protruding there from Davey's mouth, and he crunched it with lip-smacking relish. Alan gawped at it, taking it in, watching his miniature doppelgänger, hardly bigger than the thumb it sprouted from, thrash like a worm on a hook.

Davey finished the arm, slurping it back like a noodle. Then he dangled the tiny Allen from the thumb, shaking it, before taking hold of the legs, one between the thumb and forefinger of each hand, and he gently, almost lovingly pulled them apart. The Allen screamed, a sound as tiny and tortured as a cricket song, and then the left leg wrenched free of its socket. Alan felt his own leg twist in sympathy, and then there was a killing rage in him. He looked around the cave for the thing that would let him murder his brother for once and for all, but it wasn't to be found.

Davey's murder was still to come.

Instead, he leapt on Davey's back, arm around his neck, hand gripping his choking fist, pulling the headlock tighter and tighter. Marci was screaming something, but she was lost in the crash of the blood-surf that roared in his ears. Davey pitched over backward, trying to buck him off, but he wouldn't be thrown, and he flipped Davey over by the neck, so that he landed it a thrash of skinny arms and legs. The Allen fell to the floor, weeping and dragging itself one-armed and one-legged away from the melee.

Then Davey was on him, squeezing his injured hand, other thumb in his eye, screeching like a rusted hinge. Alan tried to see through the tears that sprang up, tried to reach Davey with his good hand, but the rage was leaking out of him now. He rolled desperately, but Davey's weight on his chest was like a cannonball, impossibly heavy.

Suddenly Davey was lifted off of him. Alan struggled up into a sitting position, clutching his injured hand. Davey dangled by his armpits in the implacable hands of one of the golems, face contorted into unrecognizability. Alan stood and confronted him, just out of range of his kicking feet and his gnashing teeth, and Darrel spat in his face, a searing gob that landed in his eye.

Marci took his arm and dragged him back toward the cave mouth. He fought her, looking for the little Allen, not seeing him. Was that him, there, in the shadows? No, that was one of the little bone tableaux, a field mouse's dried bones splayed in an anatomically correct mystic hieroglyph.

Marci hauled him away, out into the bright snow and the bright sun. His thumb was bleeding anew, dripping fat drops the color of a red crayon into the sun, blood so hot it seemed to sizzle and sink into the snow.

You need to tell an adult, Alan," she said, wrapping his new little thumb in gauze she'd taken from her pocket.

"My father knows. My mother knows." He sat with his head between his knees, not daring to look at her, in his nook in the winter cave.

She just looked at him, squinting.

"They count," he said. "They understand it."

She shook her head.

"They understand it better than any adult you know would. This will get better on its own, Marci. Look." He wiggled his thumb at her. It was now the size of the tip of his pinky, and had a well-formed nail and cuticle.

"That's not all that has to get better," she said. "You can't just let this fester. Your brother. That *thing* in the cave . . ." She shook her head. "Someone needs to know about this. You're not safe."

"Promise me you won't tell anyone, Marci. This is important. No one except you knows, and that's how it has to be. If you tell—"

"What?" She got up and pulled her coat on. "What, Alan? If I tell and try to help you, what will you do to me?"

"I don't know," he mumbled into his chest.

"Well, you do whatever you have to do," she said, and stomped out of the cave.

Davey escaped at dawn. Kurt had gone outside to repark his old Buick, the trunk bungeed shut over his haul of LCD flat panels, empty laser-toner cartridges, and open gift baskets of pricey Japanese cosmetics. Alan and Davey just glared at each other, but then Davey closed his eyes and began to snore softly, and even though Alan paced and pinched the bridge of his nose and stretched out his injured arm, he couldn't help it when he sat down and closed his eyes and nodded off.

Alan woke with a start, staring at the empty loops of duct tape and twine hanging from his captain's chair, dried strings of skin like desiccated banana peel fibers, hanging from them. He swore to himself quietly, and shouted Shit! at the low basement ceiling. He couldn't have been asleep for more than a few seconds, and the half-window that Davey had escaped through gaped open at him like a sneer.

He tottered to his feet and went out to find Kurt, bare feet jammed into sneakers, bare chest and bandages covered up with a jacket. He found Kurt cutting through the park, dragging his heels in the bloody dawn light.

Kurt looked at his expression, then said, "What happened?" He had his fists at his sides, he looked tensed to run. Alan felt that he was waiting for an order.

"He got away."

"How?"

Alan shook his head. "Can you help me get dressed? I don't think I can get a shirt on by myself."

They went to the Greek's, waiting out front on the curb for the old man to show up and unchain the chairs and drag them out around the table. He served them tall coffees and omelets sleepily, and they ate in silence, too tired to talk.

"Let me take you to the doctor?" Kurt asked, nodding at the bandage that bulged under his shirt.

"No," Alan said. "I'm a fast healer."

Kurt rubbed at his calf and winced. "He broke the skin," he said.

"You got all your shots?"

"Hell, yeah. Too much crap in the dumpsters. I once found a styro cooler of smashed blood vials in a Red Cross trash."

"You'll be okay, then," Alan said. He shifted in his seat and winced. He grunted a little ouch. Kurt narrowed his eyes and shook his head at him.

"This is pretty fucked up right here," Kurt said, looking down into his coffee.

"It's only a little less weird for me, if that's any comfort."

"It's not," Kurt said.

"Well, that's why I don't usually tell others. You're only the second person to believe it."

"Maybe I could meet up with the first and form a support group?"

Alan pushed his omelet away. "You can't. She's dead."

Davey haunted the schoolyard. Alan had always treated the school and its grounds as a safe haven, a place where he could get away from the inexplicable, a place where he could play at being normal.

But now Davey was everywhere, lurking in the climber, hiding in the trees, peering through the tinsel-hung windows during class. Alan only caught the quickest glimpses of him, but he had the sense that if he turned his head around quickly enough, he'd see him. Davey made himself scarce in the mountain, hiding in the golems' cave or one of the deep tunnels.

Marci didn't come to class after Monday. Alan fretted every morning, waiting for her to turn up. He worried that she'd told her father, or that she was at home sulking, too angry to come to school, glaring at her Christmas tree.

Davey's grin was everywhere.

On Wednesday, he got called into the vice principal's office. As he neared it, he heard the rumble of Marci's father's thick voice and his heart began to pound in his chest.

He cracked the door and put his face in the gap, looking at the two men there: Mr. Davenport, the vice principal, with his gray hair growing out his large ears and cavernous nostrils, sitting behind his desk, looking awkwardly at Marci's father, eyes bugged and bagged and bloodshot, face turned to the ground, looking like a different man, the picture of worry and loss.

Mr. Davenport saw him and crooked a finger at him, looking stern and stony. Alan was sure, then, that Marci'd told it all to her father, who'd told it all to Mr. Davenport, who would tell the world, and suddenly he was jealous of his secret, couldn't bear to have it revealed, couldn't bear the thought of men coming to the mountain to catalogue it for the subject index at the library, to study him and take him apart.

And he was . . . afraid. Not of what they'd all do to him. What Davey would do to them. He knew, suddenly, that Davey would not abide their secrets being disclosed.

He forced himself forward, his feet dragging like millstones, and stood between the two men, hands in his pockets, nervously twining at his underwear.

"Alan," Marci's father croaked. Mr. Davenport held up a hand to silence him.

"Alan," Mr. Davenport said. "Have you seen Marci?"

Alan had been prepared to deny everything, call Marci a liar, betray her as she'd betrayed him, make it her word against his. Protect her. Protect her father and the school and the town from what Davey would do.

Now he whipped his head toward Marci's father, suddenly understanding.

"No," he said. "Not all week! Is she all right?"

Marci's father sobbed, a sound Alan had never heard an adult make.

And it came tumbling out. No one had seen Marci since Sunday night. Her presumed whereabouts had moved from a friend's place to Alan's place to runaway to fallen in a lake to hit by a car and motionless in a ditch, and if Alan hadn't seen her—

"I haven't," Alan said. "Not since the weekend. Sunday morning. She said she was going home."

Another new sound, the sound of an adult crying. Marci's father, and his sobs made his chest shake and Mr. Davenport awkwardly came from behind his desk and set a box of kleenexes on the hard bench beside him.

Alan caught Mr. Davenport's eye and the vice principal made a shoo and pointed at the door.

Alan didn't bother going back to class. He went straight to the golems' cave, straight to where he knew Davey would be—must be—hiding, and found him there, playing with the bones that lined the walls.

"Where is she?" Alan said, after he'd taken hold of Davey's hair and, without fanfare, smashed his face into the cold stone floor hard enough to break his nose. Alan twisted his wrists behind his back and when he tried to get up, Alan kicked his legs out from under him, wrenching his arms in their sockets. He heard a popping sound.

"Where is she?" Alan said again, amazing himself with his own calmness. Davey was crying now, genuinely scared, it seemed, and Alan reveled in the feeling. "I'll kill you," he whispered in Davey's ear, almost lovingly. "I'll kill you and put the body where no one will find it, unless you tell me where she is."

Davey spat out a milk tooth, his right top incisor, and cried around the blood that coursed down his face. "I'm—I'm *sorry*, Alan," he said. "But it was the *secret*." His sobs were louder and harsher than Marci's father's had been.

"Where is she?" Alan said, knowing.

"With Caleb," Davey said. "I buried her in Caleb."

He found his brother the island midway down the mountain, sliding under cover of winter for the seaway. He climbed the island's slope, making for the ring of footprints in the snow, the snow peppered brown with soil and green with grass, and he dug with his hands like a dog, tossing snow soil grass through his legs, digging to loose soil, digging to a cold hand.

A cold hand, protruding from the snow now, from the soil, some of the snow red-brown with blood. A skinny, freckled hand, a fingernail missing, torn off leaving behind an impression, an inverse fingernail. A hand, an arm. Not attached to anything. He set it to one side, dug, found another hand. Another arm. A leg. A head.

She was beaten, bruised, eyes swollen and two teeth missing, ear torn, hair caked with blood. Her beautiful head fell from his shaking cold hands. He didn't want to dig anymore, but he had to, because it was the secret, and it had to be kept, and—

—he buried her in Caleb, piled dirt grass snow on her parts, and his eyes were dry and he didn't sob.

It was a long autumn and a long winter and a long spring that year, unwiring the Market. Alan fell into the familiar rhythm of the work of a new venture, rising early, dossing late, always doing two or three things at once: setting up meetings, sweet-talking merchants, debugging his process on the fly.

His first victory came from the Greek, who was no pushover. The man was over seventy, and had been pouring lethal coffee and cheap beer down the throats of Kensington's hipsters for decades and had steadfastly refused every single crackpot scheme hatched by his customers.

"Larry," Andy said, "I have a proposal for you and you're going to hate it."

"I hate it already," the Greek said. His dapper little mustache twitched. It was not even seven A.M. yet, and the Greek was tinkering with the guts of his espresso delivery system, making it emit loud hisses and tossing out evil congealed masses of sin-black coffee grounds.

"What if I told you it wouldn't cost you anything?"

"Maybe I'd hate it a little less."   '

"Here's the pitch," Alan said, taking a sip of the thick, steaming coffee the Greek handed to him in a minuscule cup. He shivered as the stuff coated his tongue. "Wow."

The Greek gave him half a smile, which was his version of roaring hilarity.

"Here's the pitch. Me and that punk kid, Kurt, we're working on a community Internet project for the Market."

"Computers?" the Greek said.

"Yup," Alan said.

"Pah," the Greek said.

Anders nodded. "I knew you were going to say that. But don't think of this as a computer thing, okay? Think of this as a free speech thing. We're putting in a system to allow people all over the Market—and someday, maybe, the whole city—to communicate for free, in private, without permission from anyone. They can send messages, they can get information about the world, they can have conversations. It's like a library and a telephone and a café all at once."

Larry poured himself a coffee. "I hate when they come in here with computers. They sit forever at their tables, and they don't talk to nobody, it's like having a place full of statues or zombies."

"Well, *sure*," Alan said. "If you're all alone with a computer, you're just going to fall down the rabbit hole. You're in your own world and cut off from the rest of the world. But once you put those computers on the network, they become a way to talk to anyone else in the world. For free! You help us with this network—all we want from you is permission to stick up a box over your sign and patch it into your power, you won't even know it's there—and those customers won't be antisocial, they'll be socializing, over the network."

"You think that's what they'll do if I help them with the network?"

He started to say, *Absolutely*, but bit it back, because Larry's bullshit antennae were visibly twitching. "No, but some of them will. You'll see them in here, talking, typing, typing, talking. That's how it goes. The point is that we don't know how people are going to use this network yet, but we know that it's a social benefit."

"You want to use my electricity?"

"Well, yeah."

"So it's not free."

"Not entirely," Alan said. "You got me there."

"Aha!" the Greek said.

"Look, if that's a deal-breaker, I'll personally come by every day and give you a dollar for the juice. Come on, Larry—the box we want to put in, it's just a repeater to extend the range of the network. The network already reaches to here, but your box will help it go farther. You'll be the first merchant in the Market to have one. I came to you first because you've been here the longest. The others look up to you. They'll see it and say, 'Larry has one, it must be all right.' "

The Greek downed his coffee and smoothed his mustache. "You are a bullshit artist, huh? All right, you put your box in. If my electricity bills are too high, though, I take it down."

"That's a deal," Andy said. "How about I do it this morning, before you get busy? Won't take more than a couple minutes."

The Greek's was midway between his place and Kurt's, and Kurt hardly stirred when he let himself in to get an access point from one of the chipped shelving units before going back to his place to get his ladder and Makita drill. It took him most of the morning to get it securely fastened over the sign, screws sunk deep enough into the old, spongy wood to survive the buildup of ice and snow that would come with the winter. Then he had to wire it into the sign, which took longer than he thought it would, too, but then it was done, and the idiot lights started blinking on the box Kurt had assembled.

"And what, exactly, are you doing up there, Al?" Kurt said, when he finally stumbled out of bed and down the road for his afternoon breakfast coffee.

"Larry's letting us put up an access point," he said, wiping the pigeon shit off a wire preparatory to taping it down. He descended the ladder and wiped his hands off on his painter's pants. "That'll be ten bucks, please."

Kurt dug out a handful of coins and picked out enough loonies and toonies to make ten dollars, and handed it over. "You talked the Greek into it?" he hissed. "How?"

"I kissed his ass without insulting his intelligence."

"Neat trick," Kurt said, and they had a little partner-to-partner high-five. "I'd better login to that thing and get it onto the network, huh?"

"Yeah," Anders said. "I'm gonna order some lunch, lemme get you something."

What they had done was, they had hacked the shit out of those boxes that Kurt had built in his junkyard of a storefront of an apartment.

"These work?" Alan said. He had three of them in a big catering tub from his basement that he'd sluiced clean. The base stations no longer looked like they'd been built out of garbage. They'd switched to low-power Mini-ATX motherboards that let them shrink the hardware down to small enough to fit in a fifty-dollar all-weather junction box from Canadian Tire.

Adam vaguely recognized the day's street-kids as regulars who'd been hanging around the shop for some time, and they gave him the hairy eyeball when he had the audacity to question Kurt. These kids of Kurt's weren't much like the kids he'd had working for him over the years. They might be bright, but they were a lot . . . angrier. Some of the girls were cutters, with knife scars on their forearms. Some of the boys looked like they'd been beaten up a few times too many on the streets, like they were spoiling for a fight. Alan tried to unfocus his eyes when he was in the front of Kurt's shop, to not see any of them too closely.

"They work," Kurt said. He smelled terrible, a combination of garbage and sweat, and he had the raccoon-eyed jitters he got when he stayed up all night. "I tested them twice."

"You built me a spare?" Alan said, examining the neat lines of hot glue that gasketed the sturdy rubberized antennae in place, masking the slightly melted edges left behind by the drill press.

"You don't need a spare," Kurt said. Alan knew that when he got touchy like this, he had to be very careful or he'd blow up, but he wasn't going to do another demo Kurt's way. They'd done exactly one of those, at a Toronto District School Board superintendents meeting, when Alan had gotten the idea of using schools' flagpoles and backhaul as test beds for building out the net. It had been a debacle, needless to say. Two of the access points had been permanently installed on either end of Kurt's storefront and the third had been in storage for a month since it was last tested.

"They'll work," Kurt had said when Alan told him that he wanted to test the access points out before they took them to the meeting. "It's practically solid-state. They're running off the standard distribution. There's almost no configuration."

One of the street kids, a boy with a pair of improbably enormous raver shoes, looked up at Alan. "We've tested these all. They work."

Kurt puffed up and gratefully socked the kid in the shoulder. "We did."

"Fine," Adam said patiently. "But can we make sure they work now?"

Which may or may not have been true—it certainly sounded plausible to Alan's lay ear—but it didn't change the fact that once they powered up the third box, the other two seized up and died. The blinking network lights fell still, and as Kurt hauled out an old VT-100 terminal and plugged it into the serial ports on the backs of his big, ugly, bestickered, and cig-burned PC cases, it became apparent that they had ceased to honor all requests for routing, association, deassociation, DHCP leases, and the myriad of other networking services provided for by the software.

"It's practically solid-state," Kurt said, nearly *shouted*, after he'd powered down the third box and found that the other two— previously routing and humming along happily—refused to come back up into their known-good state. He gave Alan a dirty look, as though his insistence on preflighting were the root of their problems.

The street-kid who'd spoken up had jumped when Kurt raised his voice, then cringed away. Now as Kurt began to tear around the shop, looking through boxes of CDs and dropping things on the floor, the kid all but cowered, and the other three all looked down at the table.

"I'll just reinstall," Kurt said. "That's the beauty of these things. It's a standard distro, I just copy it over, and biff-bam, it'll come right back up. No problem. Take me ten minutes. We've got plenty of time."

Then, five minutes later, "Shit, I forgot that this one has a different mo-bo than the others."

"Mo-bo?" Alan said, amused. He'd spotted the signs of something very finicky gone very wrong and he'd given up any hope of actually doing the demo, so he'd settled in to watch the process without rancor and to learn as much as he could.

"Motherboard," Kurt said, reaching for a spool of blank CDs. "Just got to patch the distribution, recompile, burn it to CD, and reboot, and we're on the road."

Ten minutes later, "Shit."

"Yes?" Alan said.

"Back off, okay?"

"I'm going to call them and let them know we're going to be late."

"We're *not* going to be late," Kurt said, his fingers going into claws on the keyboard.

"We're already late," Alan said.

"Shit," Kurt said.

"Let's do this," Alan said. "Let's bring down the two that you've got working and show them those, and explain the rest."

They'd had a fight, and Kurt had insisted, as Alan had suspected he would, that he was only a minute or two away from bringing everything back online. Alan kept his cool, made mental notes of the things that went wrong, and put together a plan for avoiding all these problems the next time around.

"Is there a spare?" Alan said.

Kurt sneered and jerked a thumb at his workbench, where another junction box sat, bunny-ear antennae poking out of it. Alan moved it into his tub. "Great," he said. "Tested, right?"

"All permutations tested and ready to go. You know, you're not the boss around here."

"I know it," he said. "Partners." He clapped Kurt on the shoulder, ignoring the damp gray grimy feeling of the clammy T-shirt under his palm.

The shoulder under his palm sagged. "Right," Kurt said. "Sorry."

"Don't be," Alan said. "You've been hard at it. I'll get loaded while you wash up."

Kurt sniffed at his armpit. "Whew," he said. "Yeah, okay."

When Kurt emerged from the front door of his storefront ten minutes later, he looked like he'd at least made an effort. His mohawk and its fins were slicked back and tucked under a baseball hat, his black jeans were unripped and had only one conservative chain joining the wallet in his back pocket to his belt loop. Throw in a clean T-shirt advertising an old technology conference instead of the customary old hardcore band, and you had an approximation of the kind of geek that everyone knew was in possession of secret knowledge and hence must be treated with attention, if not respect.

"I feel like such a dilbert," he said.

"You look totally disreputable," Alan said, hefting the tub of their access points into the bed of his truck and pulling the bungees tight around it. "Punk as fuck."

Kurt grinned and ducked his head. "Stop it," he said. "Flatterer."

"Get in the truck," Alan said.

Kurt drummed his fingers nervously on his palms the whole way to Bell offices. Alan grabbed his hand and stilled it. "Stop worrying," he said. "This is going to go great."

"I still don't understand why we're doing this," Kurt said. "They're the phone company. They hate us, we hate them. Can't we just leave it that way?"

"Don't worry, we'll still all hate each other when we get done."

"So why bother?" He sounded petulant and groggy, and Alan reached under his seat for the thermos he'd had filled at the Greek's before heading to Kurt's place. "Coffee," he said, and handed it to Kurt, who groaned and swigged and stopped bitching.

"Why bother is this," Alan said. "We're going to get a lot of publicity for doing this." Kurt snorted into the thermos. "It's going to be a big deal. You know how big a deal this can be. We're going to communicate that to the press, who will communicate it to the public, and then there will be a shitstorm. Radio cops, telco people, whatever—they're going to try to discredit us. I want to know what they're liable to say."

"Christ, you're dragging me out for that? I can tell you what they'll say. They'll drag out the Four Horsemen of the Infocalypse: kiddie porn, terrorists, pirates, and the mafia. They'll tell us that any tool for communicating that they can't tap, log, and switch off is irresponsible. They'll tell us we're stealing from ISPs. It's what they say every time some tries this: Philly, New York, London. All around the world same song."

Alan nodded. "That's good background—thanks. I still want to know *how* they say it, what the flaws are in their expression of their argument. And I wanted us to run a demo for some people who we could never hope to sway—that's a good audience for exposing the flaws in the show. This'll be a good prep session."

"So I pulled an all-nighter and busted my nuts to produce a demo for a bunch of people we don't care about? Thanks a lot."

Alan started to say something equally bitchy back, and then he stopped himself. He knew where this would end up—a screaming match that would leave both of them emotionally overwrought at a time when they needed cool heads. But he couldn't think of what to tell Kurt in order to placate him. All his life, he'd been in situations like this: confronted by people who had some beef, some grievance, and he'd had no answer for it. Usually he could puzzle out the skeleton of their cause, but sometimes—times like this—he was stumped.

He picked at the phrase. *I pulled an all-nighter.* Kurt pulled an all-nighter because he'd left this to the last minute, not because Alan had surprised him with it. He knew that, of course. Was waiting, then, for Kurt to bust him on it. To tell him, *This is your fault, not mine.* To tell him, *If this demo fails, it's because you fucked off and left it to the last minute.* So he was angry, but not at Alan, he was angry at himself.

A bunch of people we don't care about, what was that about? Ah. Kurt knew that they didn't take him seriously in the real world. He was too dirty, too punk-as-fuck, too much of his identity was wrapped up in being alienated and alienating. But he couldn't make his dream come true without Alan's help, either, and so Alan was the friendly face on their enterprise, and he resented that—feared that in order to keep up his appearance of punk-as-fuckitude, he'd have to go into the meeting cursing and sneering and that Alan would bust him on that, too.

Alan frowned at the steering wheel. He was getting better at understanding people, but that didn't make him necessarily better at being a person. What should he say here?

"That was a really heroic effort, Kurt," he said, biting his lip. "I can tell you put a lot of work into it." He couldn't believe that praise this naked could possibly placate someone of Kurt's heroic cynicism, but Kurt's features softened and he turned his face away, rolled down the window, lit a cigarette.

"I thought I'd never get it done," Kurt said. "I was so sleepy, I felt like I was half-baked. Couldn't concentrate."

You were up all night because you left it to the last minute, Alan thought. But Kurt knew that, was waiting to be reassured about it. "I don't know how you get as much done as you do. Must be really hard."

"It's not so bad," Kurt said, dragging on his cigarette and not quite disguising his grin. "It gets easier every time."

"Yeah, we're going to get this down to a science someday," Alan said. "Something we can teach anyone to do."

"That would be so cool," Kurt said, and put his boots up on the dash. "God, you could pick all the parts you needed out of the trash, throw a little methodology at them, and out would pop this thing that destroyed the phone company."

"This is going to be a fun meeting," Alan said.

"Shit, yeah. They're going to be terrified of us."

"Someday. Maybe it starts today."

The Bell boardroom looked more like a retail operation than a back office, decked out in brand-consistent livery, from the fabric-dyed rag carpets to the avant-garde lighting fixtures. They were given espressos by a young secretary-barista whose skirt-and-top number was some kind of reinterpreted ravewear outfit toned down for a corporate workplace.

"So this is the new Bell," Kurt said, once she had gone. "Our tax dollars at work."

"This is good work," Alan said, gesturing at the blown-up artwork of pan-ethnic models who were extraordinary- but not beautiful-looking on the walls. The Bell redesign had come at the same time as the telco was struggling back from the brink of bankruptcy, and the marketing firm they'd hired to do the work had made its name on the strength of the campaign. "Makes you feel like using a phone is a really futuristic, cutting-edge activity," he said.

His contact at the semiprivatized corporation was a young kid who shopped at one of his protégés' designer furniture stores. He was a young turk who'd made a name for himself quickly in the company through a couple of ISP acquisitions at fire-sale prices after the dot-bomb, which he'd executed flawlessly, integrating the companies into Bell's network with hardly a hiccup. He'd been very polite and guardedly enthusiastic when Alan called him, and had invited him down to meet some of his colleagues.

Though Alan had never met him, he recognized him the minute he walked in as the person who had to go with the confident voice he'd heard on the phone.

"Lyman," he said, standing up and holding out his hand. The guy was slightly Asian-looking, tall, with a sharp suit that managed to look casual and expensive at the same time.

He shook Alan's hand and said, "Thanks for coming down." Alan introduced him to Kurt, and then Lyman introduced them both to his colleagues, a gender-parity posse of young, smart-looking people, along with one graybeard (literally—he had a Unix beard of great rattiness and gravitas) who had no fewer than seven devices on his belt, including a line tester and a GPS.

Once they were seated, Alan snuck a look at Kurt, who had narrowed his eyes and cast his gaze down onto the business cards he'd been handed. Alan hadn't been expecting this— he'd figured on finding himself facing down a group of career bureaucrats—and Kurt was clearly thrown for a loop, too.

"Well, Alan, Kurt, it's nice to meet you," Lyman said. "I hear you're working on some exciting stuff."

"We are," Alan said. "We're building a city-wide mesh wireless network using unlicensed spectrum that will provide high-speed Internet connectivity absolutely gratis."

"That's ambitious," Lyman said, without the skepticism that Alan had assumed would greet his statement. "How's it coming?"

"Well, we've got a bunch of Kensington Market covered," Alan said. "Kurt's been improving the hardware design and we've come up with something cheap and reproducible." He opened his tub and handed out the access points, housed in gray high-impact plastic junction boxes.

Lyman accepted one solemnly and passed it on to his graybeard, then passed the next to an East Indian woman in horn-rim glasses whose bitten-down fingernails immediately popped the latch and began lightly stroking the hardware inside, tracing the connections. The third landed in front of Lyman himself.

"So, what do they do?"

Alan nodded at Kurt. Kurt put his hands on the table and took a breath. "They've got three network interfaces; we can do any combination of wired and wireless cards. The OS is loaded on a flash card; it auto-detects any wireless cards and auto-configures them to seek out other access points. When it finds a peer, they negotiate a client-server relationship based on current load, and the client then associates with the server. There's a key exchange that we use to make sure that rogue APs don't sneak into the mesh, and a self-healing routine we use to switch routes if the connection drops or we start to see too much packet loss."

The graybeard looked up. "It izz a radio vor talking to Gott!"

he said. Lyman's posse laughed, and after a second, so did Kurt.

Alan must have looked puzzled, for Kurt elbowed him in the ribs and said, "It's from Indiana Jones," he said.

"Ha," Alan said. That movie had come out long before he'd come to the city—he hadn't seen a movie until he was almost twenty. As was often the case, the reference to a film made him feel like a Martian.

The graybeard passed his unit on to the others at the table. "Does it work?" he said.

"Yeah," Kurt said.

"Well, that's pretty cool," he said.

Kurt blushed. "I didn't write the firmware," he said. "Just stuck it together from parts of other peoples' projects."

"So, what's the plan?" Lyman said. "How many of these are you going to need?"

"Hundreds, eventually," Alan said. "But for starters, we'll be happy if we can get enough to shoot down to 151 Front."

"You're going to try to peer with someone there?" The East Indian woman had plugged the AP into a riser under the boardroom table and was examining its blinkenlights.

"Yeah," Alan said. "That's the general idea." He was getting a little uncomfortable—these people weren't nearly hostile enough to their ideas.

"Well, that's very ambitious," Lyman said. His posse all nodded as though he'd paid them a compliment, though Alan wasn't sure. Ambitious could certainly be code for "ridiculous."

"How about a demo?" the East Indian woman said.

"Course," Kurt said. He dug out his laptop, a battered thing held together with band stickers and gaffer tape, and plugged in a wireless card. The others started to pass him back his access points but he shook his head. "Just plug 'em in," he said. "Here or in another room nearby—that'll be cooler."

A couple of the younger people at the table picked up two of the APs and headed for the hallway. "Put one on my desk," Lyman told them, "and the other at reception."

Alan felt a sudden prickle at the back of his neck, though he didn't know why—just a random premonition that they were on the brink of something very bad happening. This wasn't the kind of vision that Brad would experience, that faraway look followed by a snap-to into the now, eyes filled with certitude about the dreadful future. More like a goose walking over his grave, a tickle of badness.

The East Indian woman passed Kurt a VGA cable that snaked into the table's guts and down into the riser on the floor. She hit a button on a remote and an LCD projector mounted in the ceiling began to hum, projecting a rectangle of white light on one wall. Kurt wiggled it into the backside of his computer and spun down the thumbscrews, hit a button, and then his desktop was up on the wall, ten feet high. His wallpaper was a picture of a group of black-clad, kerchiefed protesters charging a police line of batons and gas grenades. A closer look revealed that the protester running in the lead was probably Kurt.

He tapped at his touchpad and a window came up, showing relative strength signals for two of the access points. A moment later, the third came online.

"I've been working with this network visualizer app," Kurt said. "It tries to draw logical maps of the network topology, with false coloring denoting packet loss between hops—that's a pretty good proxy for distance between two APs."

"More like the fade," the graybeard said.

"Fade is a function of distance," Kurt said. Alan heard the dismissal in his voice and knew they were getting into a dick-swinging match.

"Fade is a function of geography and topology," the graybeard said quietly.

Kurt waved his hand. "Whatever—sure. Geography. Topology. Distance. It's a floor wax and a desert topping."

"I'm not being pedantic," the graybeard said.

"You're not just being pedantic," Lyman said gently, watching the screen on which four animated jaggy boxes were jumbling and dancing as they reported on the throughput between the routers and the laptop.

"Not just pedantic," the graybeard said. "If you have a *lot* of these boxes in known locations with known nominal throughput, you can use them as a kind of sensor array. When throughput drops between point foo and point bar, it will tell you something about the physical world between foo and bar."

Kurt looked up from his screen with a thoughtful look. "Huh?"

"Like, whether a tree had lost its leaves in the night. Or whether there were a lot of people standing around in a normally desolate area. Or whether there are lots of devices operating between foo and bar that are interfering with them."

Kurt nodded slowly. "The packets we lose could be just as interesting as the packets we don't lose," he said.

A light went on in Alan's head. "We could be like jazz critics, listening to the silences instead of the notes," he said. They all looked at him.

"That's very good," Lyman said. "Like a jazz critic." He smiled.

Alan smiled back.

"What are we seeing, Craig?" Lyman said.

"Kurt," Alan said.

"Right, Kurt," he said. "Sorry."

"We're seeing the grid here. See how the access points go further up the spectrum the more packets they get? I'm associated with that bad boy right there." He gestured to the box blinking silently in the middle of the boardroom table. "And it's connected to one other, which is connected to a third."

Lyman picked up his phone and dialed a speed-dial number. "Hey, can you unplug the box on my desk?"

A moment later, one of the boxes on the display winked out. "Watch this," Kurt said, as the remaining two boxes were joined by a coruscating line. "See that? Self-healing. Minimal packet loss. Beautiful."

"That's hot," Lyman said. "That makes me all wet."

They chuckled nervously at his crudity. "Seriously."

"Here," Kurt said, and another window popped up, showing twenty or more boxes with marching ant trails between them. "That's a time-lapse of the Kensington network. The boxes are running different versions of the firmware, so you can see that in some edge cases, you get a lot more oscillation between two similar signals. We fixed that in the new version."

The graybeard said, "How?"

"We flip a coin," Kurt said, and grinned. "These guys in Denmark ran some simulations, proved that a random toss-up worked as well as any other algorithm, and it's a lot cheaper, computationally."

"So what's going on just to the northeast of center?"

Alan paid attention to the patch of screen indicated. Three access points were playing musical chairs, dropping signal and reacquiring it, dropping it again.

Kurt shrugged. "Bum hardware, I think. We've got volunteers assembling those boxes, from parts."

"Parts?"

Kurt's grin widened. "Yeah. From the trash, mostly. I dumpster-dive for 'em."

They grinned back. "That's very hot," Lyman said.

"We're looking at normalizing the parts for the next revision," Alan said. "We want to be able to use a single distro that works on all of them."

"Oh, sure," Lyman said, but he looked a little disappointed, and so did Kurt.

"Okay, it works," Lyman said. "It works?" he said, nodding the question at his posse. They nodded back. "So what can we do for you?"

Alan chewed his lip, caught himself at it, stopped. He'd anticipated a slugfest, now he was getting strokes.

"How come you're being so nice to us?" Kurt said. "You guys are The Man." He shrugged at Alan. "Someone had to say it."

Lyman smiled. "Yeah, we're the phone company. Big lumbering dinosaur that is thrashing in the tarpit. The spazz dinosaur that's so embarrassed all the other dinosaurs that none of them want to rescue us."

"Heh, spazz dinosaur," the East Indian woman said, and they all laughed.

"Heh," Kurt said. "But seriously."

"Seriously," Lyman said. "Seriously. Think a second about the scale of a telco. Of this telco. The thousands of kilometers of wire in the ground. Switching stations. Skilled linesmen and cable pullers. Coders. Switches. Backhaul. Peering arrangements. We've got it all. Ever get on a highway and hit a flat patch where you can't see anything to the horizon except the road and the telephone poles and the wires? Those are *our wires*. It's a lot of goodness, especially for a big, evil phone company.

"So we've got a lot of smart hackers. A lot of cool toys. A gigantic budget. The biggest network any of us could ever hope to manage—like a model train set the size of a city.

"That said, we're hardly nimble. Moving a Bell is like shifting a battleship by tapping it on the nose with a toothpick. It can be done, but you can spend ten years doing it and still not be sure if you've made any progress. From the outside, it's easy to mistake 'slow' for 'evil.' It's easy to make that mistake from the inside, too.

"But I don't let it get me down. It's *good* for a Bell to be slow and plodding, most of the time. You don't want to go home and discover that we've dispatched the progress-ninjas to upgrade all your phones with video screens and a hush mode that reads your thoughts. Most of our customers still can't figure out voice mail. Some of them can't figure out touch-tone dialing. So we're slow. Conservative. But we can do lots of killer R&D, we can roll out really hot upgrades on the back end, and we can provide this essential service to the world that underpins its ability to communicate. We're not just cool, we're essential.

"So you come in and you show us your really swell and interesting meshing wireless data boxes, and I say, 'That is damned cool.' I think of ways that it could be part of a Bell's business plan in a couple decades' time."

"A couple decades?" Kurt squawked. "Jesus Christ, I expect to have a chip in my brain and a jetpack in a couple decades' time."

"Which is why you'd be an idiot to get involved with us," Lyman said.

"Who wants to get involved with you?" Kurt said.

"No one," Alan said, putting his hands on the table, grateful that the conflict had finally hove above the surface. "That's not what we're here for.'

"Why are you here, Alvin?" Lyman said.

"We're here because we're going into the moving-data-around trade, in an ambitious way, and because you folks are the most ambitious moving-data-around tradespeople in town. I thought we'd come by and let you know what we're up to, see if you have any advice for us."

"Advice, huh?"

"Yeah. You've got lots of money and linesmen and switches and users and so forth. You probably have some kind of well-developed cosmology of connectivity, with best practices and philosophical ruminations and tasty metaphors. And I hear that you, personally, are really good at making geeks and telcos play together. Since we're going to be a kind of telco"—Kurt startled and Alan kicked him under the table—"I thought you could help us get started right."

"Advice," Lyman said, drumming his fingers. He stood up and paced.

"One: Don't bother. This is at least two orders of magnitude harder than you think it is. There aren't enough junk computers in all of Toronto's landfills to blanket the city in free wireless. The range is nothing but three hundred feet, right? Less if there are trees and buildings, and this city is all trees and buildings.

"Two: Don't bother. The liability here is stunning. The gear you're building is nice and all, but you're putting it into people's hands and you've got no idea what they're going to do with it. They're going to hack in bigger antennae and signal amplifiers. The radio cops will be on your ass day and night.

"What's more, they're going to open it up to the rest of the world and any yahoo who has a need to hide what he's up to is going to use your network to commit unspeakable acts—you're going to be every pirate's best friend and every terrorist's safest haven.

"Three: Don't bother. This isn't going to work. You've got a cute little routing algorithm that runs with three nodes, and you've got a model that may scale up to three hundred, but by the time you get to thirty thousand, you're going to be hitting so much latency and dropping so many packets on the floor and incurring so much signaling overhead that it'll be a gigantic failure.

"You want my advice? Turn this into a piece of enterprise technology: a cheap way of rolling out managed solutions in hotels and office towers and condos—building-wide meshes, not city-wide. Those guys will pay—they pay a hundred bucks per punchdown now for wired networking, so they'll gladly cough up a thousand bucks a floor for these boxes, and you'll only need one on every other story. And those people *use* networks, they're not joe consumer who doesn't have the first clue what to do with a network connection."

Kurt had stiffened up when the rant began, and once he heard the word "consumer," he began to positively vibrate. Alan gave him a warning nudge with his elbow.

"You're shitting me, right?" he said.

"You asked me for advice—" Lyman said mildly.

"You think we're going to bust our balls to design and deploy all this hardware so that business hotels can save money on cable pullers? Why the hell would we want to do that?"

"Because it pays pretty well," Lyman said. He was shaking his head a little, leaning back from the table, and his posse picked up on it, going slightly restless and fidgety, with a room-wide rustle of papers and clicking of pens and laptop latches.

Alan held up his hand. "Lyman, I'm sorry, we've been unclear. We're not doing this as a moneymaking venture—" Kurt snorted. "It's about serving the public interest. We want to give our neighbors access to tools and ideas that they wouldn't have had before. There's something fundamentally undemocratic about charging money for communications: It means that the more money you have, the more you get to communicate. So we're trying to fix that, in some small way. We are heartily appreciative of your advice, though—"

Lyman held up a hand. "Sorry, Alan, I don't mean to interrupt, but there was something I wanted to relate to you two, and I've got to go in about five minutes." Apparently, the meeting was at an end. "And I had made myself a note to tell you two about this when I discovered it last week. Can I have the floor?"

"Of course," Alan said.

"I took a holiday last week," Lyman said. "Me and my girlfriend. We went to Switzerland to see the Alps and to visit her sister, who's doing something for the UN in Geneva. So her sister, she's into, I don't know, saving children from vampires in Afghanistan or something, and she has Internet access at the office, and can't see any reason to drop a connection in at home. So there I was, wandering the streets of Geneva at seven in the morning, trying to find a WiFi connection so I can get my email and find out how many ways I can enlarge my penis this week.

"No problem—outside every hotel and most of the cafés, I can find a signal for a network called Swisscom. I log on to the network and I fire up a browser and I get a screen asking me for my password. Well, I don't have one, but after poking around, I find out that I can buy a card with a temporary password on it. So I wait until some of the little smoke shops open and start asking them if they sell Swisscom Internet Cards, in my terrible, miserable French, and after chuckling at my accent, they look at me and say, 'I have no clue what you're talking about,' shrug, and go back to work.

"Then I get the idea to go and ask at the hotels. The first one, the guy tells me that they only sell cards to guests, since they're in short supply. The cards are in short supply! Three hotels later, they allow as how they'll sell me a thirty-minute card. Oh, that's fine. Thirty whole minutes of connectivity. Whoopee. And how much will that be? Only about a zillion Swiss pesos. Don't they sell cards of larger denominations? Oh, sure, two hours, twenty-four hours, seven days—and each one costs about double the last, so if you want, you can get a seven-day card for about as much as you'd spend on a day's worth of connectivity in thirty-minute increments—about three hundred dollars Canadian for a week, just FYI.

"Well, paying three hundred bucks for a week's Internet is ghastly, but very Swiss, where they charge you if you have more than two bits of cheese at breakfast, and hell, I could afford it. But three hundred bucks for a day's worth of thirty-minute cards? Fuck that. I was going to have to find a seven-day card or bust. So I ask at a couple more hotels and finally find someone who'll explain to me that Swisscom is the Swiss telco, and that they have a retail storefront a couple blocks away where they'd sell me all the cards I wanted, in whatever denominations I require.

"By this time, it's nearly nine A.M. and I'm thinking that my girlfriend and her sister are probably up and eating a big old breakfast and wondering where the fuck I am, but I've got too much invested in this adventure to give up when I'm so close to finding the treasure. And so I hied myself off to the Swisscom storefront, which is closed, even though the sign says they open at nine and by now it's nine-oh-five, and so much for Swiss punctuality. But eventually this sneering kid with last year's faux-hawk comes out and opens the door and then disappears up the stairs at the back of the showroom to the second floor, where I follow him. I get up to his counter and say, *'Pardonnez moi,'* but he holds up a hand and points behind me and says, *'Numero!'* I make an elaborate shrug, but he just points again and says, *'Numero!'* I shrug again and he shakes his head like he's dealing with some kind of unbelievable moron, and then he steps out from behind his counter and stalks over to a little touchscreen. He takes my hand by the wrist and plants my palm on the touchscreen and a little ribbon of paper with zero-zero-one slides out. I take it and he goes back behind his counter and says, *'Numero un!'*

"I can tell this is not going to work out, but I need to go through the motions. I go to the counter and ask for a seven-day card. He opens his cash drawer and paws through a pile of cards, then smiles and shakes his head and says, sorry, all sold out. My girlfriend is probably through her second cup of coffee and reading brochures for nature walks in the Alps at this point, so I say, fine, give me a one-day card. He takes a moment to snicker at my French, then says, so sorry, sold out those, too. Two hours? Nope. Half an hour? Oh, those we got.

"Think about this for a second. I am sitting there with my laptop in hand, at six in the morning, on a Swiss street, connected to Swisscom's network, a credit card in my other hand, wishing to give them some money in exchange for the use of their network, and instead I have to go chasing up and down every hotel in Geneva for a card, which is not to be found. So I go to the origin of these cards, the Swisscom store, and they're sold out, too. This is not a T-shirt or a loaf of bread: There's no inherent scarcity in two-hour or seven-day cards. The cards are just a convenient place to print some numbers, and all you need to do to make more numbers is pull them out of thin air. They're just numbers. We have as many of them as we could possibly need. There's no sane, rational universe in which all the 'two-hour' numbers sell out, leaving nothing behind but 'thirty-minute' numbers.

"So that's pretty bad. It's the kind of story that net-heads tell about Bell-heads all around the world. It's the kind of thing I've made it my business to hunt down and exterminate here wherever I find it. So I just wrote off my email for that week and came home and downloaded a hundred thousand spams about my cock's insufficient dimensions and went in to work and I told everyone I could find about this, and they all smiled nervously and none of them seemed to find it as weird and ridiculous as me, and then, that Friday, I went into a meeting about our new high-speed WiFi service that we're piloting in Montreal and the guy in charge of the program hands out these little packages to everyone in the meeting, a slide deck and some of the marketing collateral and—a little prepaid thirty-minute access card.

"That's what we're delivering. Prepaid cards for Internet access. *Complet avec* number shortages and business travelers prowling the bagel joints of Rue St. Urbain looking for a shopkeeper whose cash drawer has a few seven-day cards kicking around.

"And you come in here, and you ask me, you ask the ruling Bell, what advice do we have for your metro-wide free info-hippie wireless dumpster-diver anarcho-network? Honestly—I don't have a fucking clue. We don't have a fucking clue. We're a telephone company. We don't know how to give away free communications—we don't even know how to charge for it."

"That was refreshingly honest," Kurt said. "I wanna shake your hand."

He stood up and Lyman stood up and Lyman's posse stood up and they converged on the doorway in an orgy of handshaking and grinning. The graybeard handed over the access point, and the East Indian woman ran off to get the other two, and before they knew it, they were out on the street.

"I liked him," Kurt said.

"I could tell," Alan said.

"Remember you said something about an advisory board? How about if we ask him to join?"

"That is a *tremendous* and deeply weird idea, partner. I'll send out the invite when we get home."

K̲urt said that the anarchist bookstore would be a slam dunk, but it turned out to be the hardest sell of all.

"I spoke to them last month, they said they were going to run it down in their weekly general meeting. They love it. It's anarcho-radio. Plus, they all want high-speed connectivity in the store so they can webcast their poetry slams. Just go on by and introduce yourself, tell 'em I sent you."

Ambrose nodded and skewered up a hunk of omelet and swirled it in the live yogurt the Greek served, and chewed. "All right," he said, "I'll do it this afternoon. You look exhausted, by the way. Hard night in the salt mines?"

Kurt looked at his watch. "I got about an hour's worth of diving in. I spent the rest of the night breaking up with Monica."

"Monica?"

"The girlfriend."

"Already? I thought you two just got together last month."

Kurt shrugged. "Longest fucking month of my life. All she

wanted to do was go clubbing all night. She hated staying over at my place because of the kids coming by in the morning to work on the access points."

"I'm sorry, pal," Andy said. He never knew what to do about failed romance. He'd had no experience in that department since the seventh grade, after all. "You'll find someone else soon enough."

"Too soon!" Kurt said. "We screamed at each other for five hours before I finally got gone. It was probably my fault. I lose my temper too easy. I should be more like you."

"You're a good man, Kurt. Don't forget it."

Kurt ground his fists into his eyes and groaned. "I'm such a fuck-up," he said.

Alan tugged Kurt's hand away from his face. "Stop that. You're an extraordinary person. I've never met anyone who has the gifts you possess, and I've met some gifted people. You should be very proud of the work you're doing, and you should be with someone who's equally proud of you."

Kurt visibly inflated. "Thanks, man." They gripped one another's hand for a moment. Kurt swiped at his moist eyes with the sleeve of his colorless gray sweatshirt. "Okay, it's way past my bedtime," he said. "You gonna go to the bookstore today?"

"Absolutely. Thanks for setting them up."

"It was about time I did some of the work, after you got the nut-shop and the cheese place and the Salvadoran pupusa place."

"Kurt, I'm just doing the work that you set in motion. It's all you, this project. I'm just your helper. Sleep well."

Andy watched him slouch off toward home, reeling a little from sleep deprivation and emotional exhaustion. He forked up the rest of his omelet, looked reflexively up at the blinkenlights on the AP over the Greek's sign, just above the apostrophe, where he'd nailed it up two months before. Since then, he'd nailed up five more, each going more smoothly than the last. At this rate, he'd have every main drag in the Market covered by summer. Sooner, if he could offload some of the labor onto one of Kurt's eager kids.

He went back to his porch then and watched the Market

wake up. The traffic was mostly bicycling bankers stopping for a fresh bagel on their way down to the business district. The Market was quite restful. It shuffled like an old man in carpet slippers, setting up streetside produce tables, twiddling the dials of its many radios looking for something with a beat. He watched them roll past, the Salvadoran pupusa ladies, Jamaican Patty Kings, Italian butchers, Vietnamese pho-tenders, and any number of thrift-store hotties, crusty-punks, strung-out artistes, trustafarians, and pretty-boy skaters.

As he watched them go past, he had an idea that he'd better write his story soon, or maybe never. Maybe never nothing: Maybe this was his last season on earth. Felt like that, apocalyptic. Old debts, come to be settled.

He shuffled upstairs and turned on the disused computer, which had sat on his desk for a couple of seasons and was therefore no longer top-of-the-line, no longer nearly so exciting, no longer so fraught with promise. Still, he made himself sit in his seat for two full hours before he allowed himself to get up, shower, dress, and head over to the anarchist bookstore, taking a slow route that gave him the chance to eyeball the lights on all the APs he'd installed.

The anarchist bookstore opened lackadaisically at eleven or eleven-thirty or sometimes noon, so he'd brought along a nice old John D. MacDonald paperback with a gun-toting bikini girl on the cover to read. He liked MacDonald's books: You could always tell who the villainesses were because the narrator made a point of noting that they had fat asses. It was as good a way as any to shorthand the world, he thought.

The guy who came by to open the store was vaguely familiar to Alfred, a Kensington stalwart of about forty, whose thrifted slacks and unraveling sweater weren't hip so much as they were just plain old down and out. He had a frizzed-out, no-cut haircut, and carried an enormous army-surplus backpack that sagged with beat-up left books and bags of organic vegetariania.

"Hi, there!" Arnold said, pocketing the book and dusting off his hands.

"Hey," the guy said into his stringy beard, fumbling with a

keyring. "I'll be opening up in a couple minutes, okay? I know I'm late. It's a bad day. Okay?"

Arnold held his hands up, palms out. "Hey, no problem at all! Take as much time as you need. I'm in no hurry."

The anarchist hustled around inside the shop, turning on lights, firing up the cash register and counting out a float, switching on the coffee machine. Alan waited patiently by the doorway, holding the door open with his toe when the clerk hauled out a rack of discounted paperbacks and earning a dirty look for his trouble.

"Okay, we're open," the anarchist said, looking Alan in the toes. He turned around and banged back into the shop and perched himself behind the counter, opening a close-typed punk newspaper and burying his nose in it.

Adam walked in behind him and stood at the counter, politely, waiting. The anarchist looked up from his paper and shook his head exasperatedly. "Yes?"

Alan extended his hand. "Hi, I'm Archie, I work with Kurt, over on Augusta?"

The anarchist stared at his hand, then shook it limply.

"Okay," he said.

"So, Kurt mentioned that he'd spoken to your collective about putting a wireless repeater up over your sign?"

The anarchist shook his head. "We decided not to do that, okay?" He went back to his paper.

Andrew considered him for a moment. "So, what's your name?"

"I don't like to give out my name," the anarchist said. "Call me Waldo, all right?"

"All right," Andy said, smiling. "That's fine by me. So, can I ask why you decided not to do it?"

"It doesn't fit with our priorities. We're here to make print materials about the movement available to the public. They can get Internet access somewhere else. Internet access is for people who can afford computers, anyway."

"Good point," Art said. "That's a good point. I wonder if I

could ask you to reconsider, though? I'd love a chance to try to explain why this should be important to you."

"I don't think so," Waldo said. "We're not really interested."

"I think you *would* be interested, if it were properly explained to you."

Waldo picked up his paper and pointedly read it, breathing heavily.

"Thanks for your time," Avi said, and left.

T hat's *bullshit*," Kurt said. "Christ, those people—"

"I assumed that there was some kind of politics," Austin said, "and I didn't want to get into the middle of it. I know that if I could get a chance to present to the whole group, I could win them over."

Kurt shook his head angrily. His shop was better organized now, with six access points ready to go and five stuck to the walls as a test bed for new versions of the software. A couple of geeky Korean kids were seated at the communal workbench, eating donuts and wrestling with drivers.

"It's all politics with them. Everything. You should hear them argue about whether it's cool to feed meat to the store cat! Who was working behind the counter?"

"He wouldn't tell me his name. He told me to call him—"

"Waldo."

"Yeah."

"Well, that could be any of about six of them, then. That's what they tell the cops. They probably thought you were a narc or a fed or something."

"I see."

"It's not total paranoia. They've been busted before—it's always bullshit. I raised bail for a couple of them once."

Andrew realized that Kurt thought he was offended at being mistaken for a cop, but he got that. He was weird—visibly weird. Out of place wherever he was.

"So they owe me. Let me talk to them some more."

"Thanks, Kurt. I appreciate it."

"Well, you're doing all the heavy lifting these days. It's the least I can do."

Alan clapped a hand on his shoulder. "None of this would exist without you, you know." He waved his hand to take in the room, the Korean kids, the whole Market. "I saw a bunch of people at the Greek's with laptops, showing them around to each other and drinking beers. In the park, with PDAs. I see people sitting on their porches, typing in the twilight. Crouched in doorways. Eating a bagel in the morning on a bench. People are finding it, and it's thanks to you."

Kurt smiled a shy smile. "You're just trying to cheer me up," he said.

"Course I am," Andy said. "You deserve to be full of cheer."

Don't bother," Andy said. "Seriously, it's not worth it. We'll just find somewhere else to locate the repeater. It's not worth all the bullshit you're getting."

"Screw that. They told me that they'd take one. They're the only ones *I* talked into it. My contribution to the effort. And they're fucking *anarchists*—they've *got* to be into this. It's totally irrational!" He was almost crying.

"I don't want you to screw up your friendships, Kurt. They'll come around on their own. You're turning yourself inside out over this, and it's just not worth it. Come on, it's cool." He turned around his laptop and showed the picture to Kurt. "Check it out, people with tails. An entire gallery of them!" There were lots of pictures like that on the net. None of people without belly buttons, though.

Kurt took a pull off his beer. "Disgusting," he said, and clicked through the gallery.

The Greek looked over their shoulder. "It's real?"

"It's real, Larry," Alan said. "Freaky, huh?"

"That's terrible," the Greek said. "Pah." There were five or six other network users out on the Greek's, and it was early yet. By five-thirty, there'd be fifty of them. Some of them brought their own power strips so that they could share juice with their coreligionists.

"You really want me to give up?" Kurt asked, once the Greek had given him a new beer and a scowling look over the litter of picked-at beer label on the table before him.

"I really think you should," Alan said. "It's a poor use of time."

Kurt looked ready to cry again. Adam had no idea what to say.

"Okay," Kurt said. "Fine." He finished his beer in silence and slunk away.

B̲ut it wasn't fine, and Kurt wouldn't give it up. He kept on beating his head against the blank wall, and every time Alan saw him, he was grimmer than the last.

"Let it *go*," Adam said. "I've done a deal with the vacuum-cleaner repair guy across the street." A weird-but-sweet old Polish Holocaust survivor who'd listened attentively to AJ's pitch before announcing that he'd been watching all the hardware go up around the Market and had simply been waiting to be included in the club. "That'll cover that corner just fine."

"I'm going to throw a party," Kurt said. "Here, in the shop. No, I'll rent out one of the warehouses on Oxford. I'll invite them, the kids, everyone who's let us put up an access point, a big mill-and-swill. Buy a couple kegs. No one can resist free beer."

Alan had started off frustrated and angry with Kurt, but this drew him up and turned him around. "That is a *fine* idea," he said. "We'll invite Lyman."

L̲yman had taken to showing up on Alan's stoop in the morning sometimes, on his way to work, for a cup of coffee. He'd taken to showing up at Kurt's shop in the afternoon, sometimes, on his way home from work, to marvel at the kids' industry. His graybeard had written some code that analyzed packet loss and tried to make guesses about the crowd density in different parts of the Market, and Lyman took a proprietary interest in it, standing out by Bikes on Wheels or the Portuguese furniture store and watching the data on his PDA, comparing it with the actual crowds on the street.

He'd only hesitated for second when Andrew asked him to be the inaugural advisor on ParasiteNet's board, and once he'd said yes, it became clear to everyone that he was endlessly fascinated by their little adhocracy and its experimental telco potential.

"This party sounds like a great idea," he said. He was buying the drinks, because he was the one with five-hundred-dollar glasses and a full-suspension racing bike. "Lookit that," he said.

From the Greek's front window, they could see Oxford Street and a little of Augusta, and Lyman loved using his PDA and his density analysis software while he sat, looking from his colored map to the crowd scene. "Lookit the truck as it goes down Oxford and turns up Augusta. That signature is so distinctive, I could spot it in my sleep. I need to figure out how to sell this to someone—maybe the cops or something." He tipped Andy a wink.

Kurt opened and shut his mouth a few times, and Lyman slapped his palm down on the table. "You look like you're going to bust something," he said. "Don't worry. I kid. Damn, you've got you some big, easy-to-push buttons."

Kurt made a face. "You wanted to sell our stuff to luxury hotels. You tried to get us to present at the *SkyDome*. You're capable of anything."

"The SkyDome would be a great venue for this stuff," Lyman said, settling into one of his favorite variations of bait-the-anarchist.

"The SkyDome was built with tax dollars that should have been spent on affordable housing, then was turned over to rich pals of the premier for a song, who then ran it into the ground, got bailed out by the province, and then it got turned over to different rich pals. You can just shut up about the goddamned Sky-Dome. You'd have to break both of my legs and *carry me* to get me to set foot in there."

"About the party," Adam said. "About the party."

"Yes, certainly," Lyman said. "Kurt, behave."

Kurt belched loudly, provoking a scowl from the Greek.

The Waldos all showed up in a bunch, with plastic brown liter bottles filled with murky homemade beer and a giant bag of skunk-weed. The party had only been on for a couple hours, but it had already balkanized into inward-facing groups: merchants, kids, hackers. Kurt kept turning the music way up ("If they're not going to talk with one another, they might as well dance." "Kurt, those people are old. Old people don't dance to music like this." "Shut up, Lyman." "Make me."), and Andy kept turning it down.

The bookstore people drifted in, then stopped and moved vaguely toward the middle of the floor, there to found their own breakaway conversational republic. Lyman startled. "Sara?" he said, and one of the anarchists looked up sharply.

"Lyman?" She had two short ponytails and a round face that made her look teenage young, but on closer inspection she was more Lyman's age, mid-thirties. She laughed and crossed the gap to their little republic and threw her arms around Lyman's neck. "Crispy Christ, what are *you* doing here?"

"I work with these guys!" He turned to Arnold and Kurt. "This is my cousin Sara," he said. "These are Albert and Kurt. I'm helping them out."

"Hi, Sara," Kurt said.

"Hey, Kurt," she said, looking away. It was clear even to Alan that they knew each other already. The other bookstore people were looking on with suspicion, drinking their beer out of refillable coffee-store thermos cups.

"It's great to meet you!" Alan said, taking her hand in both of his and shaking it hard. "I'm really glad you folks came down."

She looked askance at him, but Lyman interposed himself. "Now, Sara, these guys really, really wanted to talk something over with you all, but they've been having a hard time getting a hearing."

Kurt and Alan traded uneasy glances. They'd carefully planned out a subtle easeway into this conversation, but Lyman was running with it.

"You didn't know that I was involved, huh?"

"Surprised the hell outta me," Lyman said. "Will you hear them out?"

She looked back at her collective. "What the hell? Yeah, I'll talk 'em into it."

It starts with the sinking of the *Titanic*," Kurt said. They'd arranged their mismatched chairs in a circle in the cramped back room of the bookstore and were drinking and eating organic crumbly things with the taste and consistency of mud-brick. Sara told him that they'd have ten minutes, and Alan had told Kurt that he could take it all. Alan'd spent the day reading on the net, remembering the arguments that had swayed the most people, talking it over. He was determined that Kurt would win this fight.

"There's this ship going down, and it's signaling S-O-S, S-O-S, but the message didn't get out, because the shipping lanes were full of other ships with other radios, radios that clobbered the *Titanic*'s signal. That's because there were no rules for radio back then, so anyone could light up any transmitter and send out any signal at any frequency. Imagine a room where everyone shouted at the top of their lungs, nonstop, while setting off air horns.

"After that, they decided that fed regulators would divide up the radio spectrum into bands, and give those bands to exclusive licensees who'd know that their radio waves would reach their destination without being clobbered, because any clobberers would get shut down by the cops.

"But today, we've got a better way: We can make radios that are capable of intelligently cooperating with each other. We can make radios that use databases or just finely tuned listeners to determine what bands aren't in use, at any given moment, in any place. They can talk between the gaps in other signals. They can relay messages for other radios. They can even try to detect the presence of dumb radio devices, like TVs and FM tuners, and grab the signal they're meant to be receiving off of the Internet and pass it on, so that the dumb device doesn't even realize that the world has moved on.

"Now, the original radio rules were supposed to protect free expression because if everyone was allowed to speak at once, no one would be heard. That may have been true, but it was a pretty poor system as it went: Mostly, the people who got radio licenses were cops, spooks, and media barons. There aren't a lot of average people using the airwaves to communicate for free with one another. Not a lot of free speech.

"But now we have all this new technology where computers direct the operation of flexible radios, radios whose characteristics are determined by software, and it's looking like the scarcity of the electromagnetic spectrum has been pretty grossly overstated. It's hard to prove, because now we've got a world where lighting up a bunch of smart, agile radios is a crime against the 'legit' license-holders.

"But Parliament's not going to throw the airwaves open because no elected politician can be responsible for screwing up the voters' televisions, because that's the surest-fire way to not get reelected. Which means that when you say, 'Hey, our freedom of speech is being clobbered by bad laws,' the other side can say, 'Go study some physics, hippie, or produce a working network, or shut up.'

"The radios we're installing now are about one-millionth as smart as they could be, and they use one-millionth as much spectrum as they could without stepping on anyone else's signal, but they're legal, and they're letting more people communicate than ever. There are people all over the world doing this, and whenever the policy wonks go to the radio cops to ask for more radio spectrum to do this stuff with, they parade people like us in front of them. We're like the Pinocchio's nose on the face of the radio cops: They say that only their big business buddies can be trusted with the people's airwaves, and we show them up for giant liars."

He fell silent and looked at them. Adam held his breath.

Sara nodded and broke the silence. "You know, that sounds pretty cool, actually."

Kurt insisted on putting up that access point, while Alan and Lyman steadied the ladder. Sara came out and joked with Lyman, and Alan got distracted watching them, trying to understand this notion of "cousins." They had an easy rapport, despite all their differences, and spoke in a shorthand of family weddings long past and crotchety relatives long dead.

So none of them were watching when Kurt overbalanced and dropped the Makita, making a wild grab for it, foot slipping off the rung, and toppled backward. It was only Kurt's wild bark of panic that got Adam to instinctively move, to hold out his arms and look up, and he caught Kurt under the armpits and gentled him to the ground, taking the weight of Kurt's fall in a bone-jarring crush to his rib cage.

"You okay?" Alan said, once he'd gotten his breath back.

"Oof," Kurt said. "Yeah."

They were cuddled together on the sidewalk, Kurt atop him, and Lyman and Sara bent to help them apart. "Nice catch," Lyman said. Kurt was helped to his feet, and he declared that he'd sprained his ankle and nothing worse, and they helped him back to his shop, where a couple of his kids doted over him, getting him an ice pack and a pillow and his laptop and one of the many dumpster-dived discmen from around the shop and some of the CDs of old punk bands that he favored.

There he perched, growly as a wounded bear, master of his kingdom, for the next two weeks, playing online and going twitchy over the missed dumpsters going to the landfill every night without his expert picking-over. Alan visited him every day and listened raptly while Kurt gave him the stats for the day's network usage, and Kurt beamed proud the whole while.

One morning, Alan threw a clatter of toonies down on the Greek's counter and walked around the Market, smelling the last night's staggering pissers and the morning's blossoms.

Here were his neighbors, multicolored heads at the windows of their sagging house adjoining his, Link and Natalie in the adjacent windows farthest from his front door, Mimi's face suspicious at her window, and was that Krishna behind her, watching over her shoulder, hand between her wings, fingers tracing the scars descending from the muscles there?

He waved at them. The reluctant winter made every day feel like the day before a holiday weekend. The bankers and the retail slaves coming into and out of the Market had a festive air.

He waved at the neighbors, and Link waved back, and then so did Natalie, and he hefted his sack of coffees from the Greek's suggestively, and Mimi shut her curtains with a snap, but Natalie and Link smiled, and a moment later they were sitting in twig chairs on his porch in their jammies, watching the world go past as the sun began to boil the air and the coffee tasted as good as it smelled.

"Beautiful day," Natalie said, rubbing the duckling fuzz on her scalp and closing her eyes.

"Found any work yet?" Alan said, remembering his promise to put her in touch with one of his fashionista protégés.

She made a face. "In a video store. Bo-ring."

Link made a rude noise. "You are *so* spoiled. Not just any video store, she's working at Martian Signal on Queen Street."

Alan knew it, a great shop with a huge selection of cult movies and a brisk trade in zines, transgressive literature, action figures, and T-shirts.

"It must be great there," he said.

She smiled and looked away. "It's okay." She bit her lip. "I don't think I like working retail," she said.

"Ah, retail!" he said. "Retail would be fantastic if it wasn't for the fucking customers."

She giggled.

"Don't let them get to you," he said. "Get to be really smart about the stock, so that there's always something you know more about than they do, and when that isn't true, get them to *teach you* more so you'll be in control the next time."

She nodded.

"And have fun with the computer when it's slow," he said.

"What?"

"A store like that, it's got the home phone number of about seventy percent of the people in Toronto you'd want to ever hang out with. Most of your school friends, even the ones you've lost track of. All the things they've rented. All their old addresses—you can figure out who's living together, who gave their apartment to whom, all of that stuff. That kind of database is way more fun than you realize. You can get lost in it for months."

She was nodding slowly. "I can see that," she said. She up-ended her coffee and set it down. "Listen, Arbus—" she began, then bit her lip again. She looked at Link, who tugged at his fading pink shock of hair.

"It's nothing," he said. "We get emotionally overwrought about friends and family. I have as much to apologize for as . . . Well, I owe you an apology." They stared at the park across the street, at the damaged wading pool where Edward had vanished.

"So, sorries all 'round and kisses and hugs, and now we're all friends again, huh?" Link said. Natalie made a rude noise and ruffled his hair, then wiped her hand off on his shirt.

Alan, though, solemnly shook each of their hands in turn, and thanked them. When he was done, he felt as though a weight had been lifted from him. Next door, Mimi's window slammed shut.

"What is it you're doing around here, Akin?" Link said. "I keep seeing you running around with ladders and tool belts. I thought you were a writer. Are you soundproofing the whole Market?"

"I never told you?" Alan said. He'd been explaining wireless networking to anyone who could sit still and had been begin-ning to believe that he'd run it down for every denizen of Kens-ington, but he'd forgotten to clue in his own neighbors!

"Right," he said. "Are you seated comfortably? Then I shall begin. When we connect computers together, we call it a network.

There's a *big* network of millions of computers, called the Internet."

"Even *I* know this," Natalie said.

"Shush," Alan said. "I'll start at the beginning, where I started a year ago, and work my way forward. It's weird, it's big, and it's cool." And he told them the story, the things he'd learned from Kurt, the arguments he'd honed on the shopkeepers, the things Lyman had told him.

"So that's the holy mission," he said at last. "You give everyone a voice and a chance to speak on a level playing field with the rich and powerful, and you make democracy, which is good."

He looked at Link and Natalie, who were looking to one another rather intensely, communicating in some silent idiom of sibling body language.

"Plate-o-shrimp," Natalie said.

"Funny coincidence," Link said.

"We were just talking about this yesterday."

"Spectrum?" Alan quirked his eyebrows.

"No, not exactly," Natalie said. "About making a difference. About holy missions. Wondering if there were any left."

"I mean," Link said, "riding a bike or renting out videos are honest ways to make a living and all, and they keep us in beer and rent money, but they're not—"

"—*important,*" Natalie said.

"Ah," Alan said.

"Ah?"

"Well, that's the thing we all want, right? Making a difference."

"Yeah."

"Which is why you went into fashion," Link said, giving her skinny shoulder a playful shove.

She shoved him back. "And why *you* went into electrical engineering!"

"Okay," Alan said. "It's not necessarily about what career you pick. It's about how you do what you do. Natalie, you told me you used to shop at Tropicál."

She nodded.

"You liked it, you used to shop there, right?"

"Yeah."

"And it inspired you to go into fashion design. It also provided employment for a couple dozen people over the years. I sometimes got to help out little alternative girls from North Toronto buy vintage prom dresses at the end of the year, and I helped Motown revival bands put together matching outfits of red blazers and wide trousers. Four or five little shops opened up nearby selling the same kind of thing, imitating me—that whole little strip down there started with Tropicál."

Natalie nodded. "Okay, I knew that, I guess. But it's not the same as *really* making a difference, is it?"

Link flicked his butt to the curb. "You're changing people's lives for the better either way, right?"

"Exactly," Alan said.

Then Link grinned. "But there's something pretty, oh, I dunno, *ballsy* about this wireless thing, yeah? It's not the same."

"Not the same," Alan said, grinning. "Better."

"How can we help?"

Kurt had an assembly line cranking out his access points now. Half a dozen street kids worked in the front of his place, in a cleared-out space with a makeshift workbench made from bowed plywood and scratched IKEA table legs. It made Alan feel better to watch them making sense of it all, made him feel a little like he felt when he was working on The Inventory. The kids worked from noon, when Kurt got back from breakfast, until nine or ten, when he went out to dive.

The kids were smart, but screwed up: half by teenaged hormones and half by bad parents or bad drugs or just bad brain chemistry. Alan understood their type, trying to carve some atom of individual identity away from family and background, putting pins through their bodies and affecting unconvincing tough mannerisms. They were often bright—the used bookstore had been full of their type, buying good, beat-up books off the sale rack for fifty cents, trading them back for twenty cents' credit the next day, and buying more.

Natalie and Link were in that morning, along with some newcomers, Montreal street punks trying their hand at something other than squeegee bumming. The punks and his neighbors gave each other uneasy looks, but Alan had deliberately put the sugar for the coffee at the punks' end of the table and the cream in front of Natalie and the stirs by the bathroom door with the baklava and the napkins, so a rudimentary social intercourse was begun.

First, one of the punks (who had a rusty "NO FUTURE" pin that Alan thought would probably go for real coin on the collectors' market) asked Natalie to pass her the cream. Then Link and another punk (foppy silly black hair and a cut-down private school blazer with the short sleeves pinned on with rows of safety pins) met over the baklava, and the punk offered Link a napkin. Another punk spilled her coffee on her lap, screeching horrendous Quebecois blasphemies as curses, and that cracked everyone up, and Arnold, watching from near the blanket that fenced off Kurt's monkish sleeping area, figured that they would get along.

"Kurt," he said, pulling aside the blanket, handing a double-double coffee over to Kurt as he sat up and rubbed his eyes. He was wearing a white T-shirt that was the grimy gray of everything in his domain, and baggy jockeys. He gathered his blankets around him and sipped reverently.

Kurt cocked his head and listened to the soft discussions going on on the other side of the blanket. "Christ, they're at it already?"

"I think your volunteers showed up a couple hours ago—or maybe they were up all night."

Kurt groaned theatrically. "I'm running a halfway house for geeky street kids."

"All for the cause," Alan said. "So, what's on the plate for today?"

"You know the church kittycorner from your place?"

"Yeah?" Alan said cautiously.

"Its spire is just about the highest point in the Market. An omnidirectional up there . . ."

"The church?"

"Yeah."

"What about the new condos at the top of Baldwin? They're tall."

"They are. But they're up on the northern edge. From the bell tower of that church, I bet you could shoot half the houses on the west side of Oxford Street, along with the backs of all the shops on Augusta."

"How are we going to get the church to go along with it? Christ, what are they, Ukranian Orthodox?"

"Greek Orthodox," Kurt said. "Yeah, they're pretty conservative."

"So?"

"So, I need a smooth-talking, upstanding cit to go and put the case to the pastor. Priest. Bishop. Whatever."

"Groan," Alex said.

"Oh, come on, you're good at it."

"If I get time," he said. He looked into his coffee for a moment. "I'm going to go home," he said.

"Home?"

"To the mountain," he said. "Home," he said. "To my father," he said.

"Whoa," Kurt said. "Alone?"

Alan sat on the floor and leaned back against a milk crate full of low-capacity hard drives. "I have to," he said. "I can't stop thinking of . . ." He was horrified to discover that he was on the verge of tears. It had been three weeks since Davey had vanished into the night, and he'd dreamt of Eugene-Fabio-Greg every night since, terrible dreams, in which he'd dug like a dog to uncover their hands, their arms, their legs, but never their heads. He swallowed hard.

He and Kurt hadn't spoken of that night since.

"I sometimes wonder if it really happened," Kurt said.

Alan nodded. "It's hard to believe. Even for me."

"I believe it," Kurt said. "I won't ever not believe it. I think that's probably important to you."

Alan felt a sob well up in his chest and swallowed it down again. "Thanks," he managed to say.

"When are you leaving?"

"Tomorrow morning. I'm going to rent a car and drive up," he said.

"How long?"

"I dunno," he said. He was feeling morose now. "A couple days. A week, maybe. No longer."

"Well, don't sweat the Bishop. He can wait. Come and get a beer with me tonight before I go out?"

"Yeah," he said. "That sounds good. On a patio on Kensington. We can people-watch."

How Alan and his brothers killed Davey: very deliberately.

Alan spent the rest of the winter in the cave, and Davey spent the spring in the golem's cave, and through that spring, neither of them went down to the school, so that the younger brothers had to escort themselves to class. When the thaws came and icy melt-off carved temporary streams in the mountainside, they stopped going to school, too—instead, they played on the mountainside, making dams and canals and locks with rocks and imagination.

Their father was livid. The mountain rumbled as it warmed unevenly, as the sheets of ice slid off its slopes and skittered down toward the highway. The sons of the mountain reveled in their dark ignorance, their separation from the school and from the nonsensical and nonmagical society of the town. They snared small animals and ate them raw, and didn't wash their clothes, and grew fierce and guttural through the slow spring.

Alan kept silent through those months, becoming almost nocturnal, refusing to talk to any brother who dared to talk to him. When Ed-Fred-George brought home a note from the vice principal asking when he thought he'd be coming back to school, Alan shoved it into his mouth and chewed and chewed and chewed, until the paper was reduced to gruel, then he spat it by the matted pile of his bedding.

The mountain grumbled and he didn't care. The golems came to parley, and he turned his back to them. The stalactites crashed to the cave's floor until it was carpeted in ankle-deep chips of stone, and he waded through them.

He waited and bided. He waited for Davey to try to come home.

W hat have we here?" Alan said, as he wandered into Kurt's shop, which had devolved into joyous bedlam. The shelves had been pushed up against the wall, clearing a large open space that was lined with long trestle tables. Crusty-punks, goth kids, hippie kids, geeks with vintage video-game shirts, and even a couple of older, hard-done-by street people crowded around the tables, performing a conglomeration of arcane tasks. The air hummed with conversation and coffee smells, the latter emanating from a catering-sized urn in the corner.

He was roundly ignored—and before he could speak again, one of the PCs on the floor started booming out fuzzy, grungy rockabilly music that made him think of Elvis cassettes that had been submerged in salt water. Half of the assembled mass started bobbing their heads and singing along while the other half rolled their eyes and groaned.

Kurt came out of the back and hunkered down with the PC, turning down the volume a little. "Howdy!" he said, spreading his arms and taking in the whole of his dominion.

"Howdy yourself," Alan said. "What do we have here?"

"We have a glut of volunteers," Kurt said, watching as an old rummy carefully shot a picture of a flat-panel LCD that was minus its housing. "I can't figure out if those laptop screens are worth anything," he said, cocking his head. "But they've been taking up space for far too long. Time we moved them."

Alan looked around and realized that the workers he'd

taken to be at work building access points were, in the main, shooting digital pictures of junk from Kurt's diving runs and researching them for eBay listings. It made him feel good— great, even. It was like watching an Inventory being assembled from out of chaos.

"Where'd they all come from?"

Kurt shrugged. "I dunno. I guess we hit critical mass. You recruit a few people, they recruit a few people. It's a good way to make a couple bucks, you get to play with boss crap, you get paid in cash, and you have colorful co-workers." He shrugged again. "I guess they came from wherever the trash came from. The city provides."

The homeless guy they were standing near squinted up at them. "If either of you says something like, *Ah, these people were discarded by society, but just as with the junk we rescue from landfills, we have seen the worth of these poor folks and rescued them from the scrap heap of society,* I'm gonna puke."

"The thought never crossed my mind," Alan said solemnly.

"Keep it up, Wes," Kurt said, patting the man on the shoulder. "See you at the Greek's tonight?"

"Every night, so long as he keeps selling the cheapest beer in the Market," Wes said, winking at Alan.

"It's cash in the door," Kurt said. "Buying components is a lot more efficient than trying to find just the right parts." He gave Alan a mildly reproachful look. Ever since they'd gone to strictly controlled designs, Kurt had been heartbroken by the amount of really nice crap that never made its way into an access point.

"This is pretty amazing," Alan said. "You're splitting the money with them?"

"The profit—anything leftover after buying packaging and paying postage." He walked down the line, greeting people by name, shaking hands, marveling at the gewgaws and gimcracks that he, after all, had found in some nighttime dumpster and brought back to be recycled. "God, I love this. It's like Napster for dumpsters."

"How's that?" Alan asked, pouring himself a coffee and

adding some UHT cream from a giant, slightly dented box of little creamers.

"Most of the music ever recorded isn't for sale at any price. Like eighty percent of it. And the labels, they've made copyright so strong, no one can figure out who all that music belongs to—not even them! Costs a fortune to clear a song. Pal of mine once did a CD of Christmas music remixes, and he tried to figure out who owned the rights to all the songs he wanted to use. He just gave up after a year—and he had only cleared one song!

"So along comes Napster. It finds the only possible way of getting all that music back into our hands. It gives millions and millions of people an incentive to rip their old CDs—hell, their old vinyl and tapes, too!—and put them online. No label could have afforded to do that, but the people just did it for free. It was like a barn-raising: a library-raising!"

Alan nodded. "So what's your point—that companies' dumpsters are being Napstered by people like you?" A napsterized Inventory. Alan felt the *rightness* of it.

Kurt picked a fragile LCD out of a box of dozens of them and smashed it on the side of the table. "Exactly!" he said. "This is garbage—it's like the deleted music that you can't buy today, except at the bottom of bins at Goodwill or at yard sales. Tons of it has accumulated in landfills. No one could afford to pay enough people to go around and rescue it all and figure out the copyrights for it and turn it into digital files and upload it to the net—but if you give people an incentive to tackle a little piece of the problem and a way for my work to help you . . ." He went to a shelf and picked up a finished AP and popped its latches and swung it open.

"Look at that—I didn't get its guts out of a dumpster, but someone else did, like as not. I sold the parts I found in my dumpster for money that I exchanged for parts that someone else found in *her* dumpster—"

"Her?"

"Trying not to be sexist," Kurt said.

"Are there female dumpster divers?"

"Got me," Kurt said. "In ten years of this, I've only run into other divers twice or three times. Remind me to tell you about the cop later. Anyway. We spread out the effort of rescuing this stuff from the landfill, and then we put our findings online, and we move it to where it needs to be. So it's not cost-effective for some big corporation to figure out how to use or sell these—so what? It's not cost-effective for some big dumb record label to figure out how to keep music by any of my favorite bands in print, either. We'll figure it out. We're spookily good at it."

"Spookily?"

"Trying to be more poetic." He grinned and twisted the fuzzy split ends of his newly blue mohawk around his fingers. "Got a new girlfriend, she says there's not enough poetry in my views on garbage."

They found one of Davey's old nests in March, on a day when you could almost believe that the spring would really come and the winter would go and the days would lengthen out to more than a few hours of sour grayness huddled around noon. The reference design for the access point had gone through four more iterations, and if you knew where to look in the Market's second-story apartments, rooftops, and lamp-posts, you could trace the evolution of the design from the clunky PC-shaped boxen in Alan's attic on Wales Avenue to the environment-hardened milspec surplus boxes that Kurt had rigged from old circuit boxes he'd found in Bell Canada's Willowdale switching station dumpster.

Alan steadied the ladder while Kurt tightened the wing nuts on the antenna mounting atop the synagogue's roof. It had taken three meetings with the old rabbi before Alan hit on the idea of going to the temple's youth caucus and getting *them* to explain it to the old cleric. The synagogue was one of the oldest buildings in the Market, a brick-and-stone beauty from 1930.

They'd worried about the fight they'd have over drilling through the roof to punch down a wire, but they needn't have:

The wood up there was soft as cottage cheese, and showed gaps wide enough to slip the power cable down. Now Kurt slathered Loctite over the nuts and washers and slipped dangerously down the ladder, toe-tips flying over the rungs.

Alan laughed as he touched down, thinking that Kurt's heart was aburst with the feeling of having finished, at last, at last. But then he caught sight of Kurt's face, ashen, wide-eyed.

"I saw something," he said, talking out of the sides of his mouth. His hands were shaking.

"What?"

"Footprints," he said. "There's a lot of leaves that have rotted down to mud up there, and there were a pair of little footprints in the mud. Like a toddler's footprints, maybe. Except there were two toes missing from one foot. They were stamped down all around this spot where I could see there had been a lot of pigeon nests, but there were no pigeons there, only a couple of beaks and legs—so dried up that I couldn't figure out what they were at first.

"But I recognized the footprints. The missing toes, they left prints behind like unbent paperclips."

Alan moved, as in a dream, to the ladder and began to climb it.

"Be careful, it's all rotten up there," Kurt called. Alan nodded.

"Sure, thank you," he said, hearing himself say it as though from very far away.

The rooftop was littered with broken glass and scummy puddles of meltwater and little pebbles and a slurry of decomposing leaves, and there, yes, there were the footprints, just as advertised. He patted the antenna box absently, feeling its solidity, and he sat down cross-legged before the footprints and the beaks and the legs. There were no tooth marks on the birds. They hadn't been eaten, they'd been torn apart, like a label from a beer bottle absently shredded in the sunset. He pictured Davey sitting here on the synagogue's roof, listening to the evening prayers, and the calls and music that floated over the Market, watching the gray winter nights come on and slip away, a pigeon in his hand, writhing.

He wondered if he was catching Bradley's precognition, and if that meant that Bradley was dead now.

Bradley was born with the future in his eyes. He emerged from the belly of their mother with bright brown eyes that did not roll aimlessly in the manner of babies, but rather sought out the corners of the cave where interesting things were happening, where movement was about to occur, where life was being lived. Before he developed the muscle strength and coordination necessary to crawl, he mimed crawling, seeing how it was that he would someday move.

He was the easiest of all the babies to care for, easier even than Carlo, who had no needs other than water and soil and cooing reassurance. Toilet training: As soon as he understood what was expected of him—they used the downstream-most bend of one of the underground rivers—Benny could be relied upon to begin tottering toward the spot in sufficient time to drop trou and do his business in just the right spot.

(Alan learned to pay attention when Bruce was reluctant to leave home for a walk during those days—the same premonition that made him perfectly toilet-trained at home would have him in fretting sweats at the foreknowledge that he has destined to soil himself during the recreation.)

His nightmares ran twice: once just before bed, in clairvoyant preview, and again in the depths of REM sleep. Alan learned to talk him down from these crises, to soothe the worry, and in the end it worked to everyone's advantage, defusing the nightmares themselves when they came.

He never forgot anything—never forgot to have Alan forge a signature on a permission form, never forgot to bring in the fossil he'd found for show-and-tell, never forgot his mittens in the cloakroom and came home with red, chapped hands. Once he started school, he started seeing to it that Alan never forgot anything, either.

He did very well on quizzes and tests, and he never let the pitcher fake him out when he was at bat.

After four years alone with the golems, Alan couldn't have been more glad to have a brother to keep him company.

Billy got big enough to walk, then big enough to pick mushrooms, then big enough to chase squirrels. He was big enough to play hide-and-go-seek with, big enough to play twenty questions with, big enough to horse around in the middle of the lake at the center of the mountain with.

Alan left him alone during the days, in the company of their parents and the golems, went down the mountain to school, and when he got back, he'd take his kid brother out on the mountain face and teach him what he'd learned, even though he was only a little kid. They'd write letters together in the mud with a stick, and in the winter they'd try to spell out their names with steaming pee in the snow, laughing.

"That's a fraction," Brad said, chalking "¾" on a piece of slate by the side of one of the snowmelt streams that coursed down the springtime mountain.

"That's right, three-over-four," Alan said. He'd learned it that day in school, and had been about to show it to Billy, which meant that Brad had remembered him doing it and now knew it. He took the chalk and drew his own ¾—you had to do that, or Billy wouldn't be able to remember it in advance.

Billy got down on his haunches. He was a dark kid, dark hair and eyes the color of chocolate, which he insatiably craved and begged for every morning when Alan left for school, "Bring me, bring me, bring me!"

He'd found something. Alan leaned in and saw that it was a milkweed pod. "It's an egg," Bobby said.

"No, it's a weed," Alan said. Bobby wasn't usually given to flights of fancy, but the shape of the pod was reminiscent of an egg.

Billy clucked his tongue. "I *know* that. It's also an egg for a bug. Living inside there. I can see it hatching. Next week." He closed his eyes. "It's orange! Pretty. We should come back and find it once it hatches."

Alan hunkered down next to him. "There's a bug in here?"

"Yeah. It's like a white worm, but in a week it will turn into an orange bug and chew its way out."

He was about three then, which made Alan seven. "What if I chopped down the plant?" he said. "Would the bug still hatch next week?"

"You won't," Billy said.

"I could, though."

"Nope," Brad said.

Alan reached for the plant. Took it in his hand. The warm skin of the plant and the woody bole of the pod would be so easy to uproot.

He didn't do it.

That night, as he lay himself down to sleep, he couldn't remember why he hadn't. He couldn't sleep. He got up and looked out the front of the cave, at the countryside unrolling in the moonlight and the far lights of the town.

He went back inside and looked in on Benji. He was sleeping, his face smooth and his lips pouted. He rolled over and opened his eyes, regarding Alan without surprise.

"Told you so," he said.

Alan had an awkward relationship with the people in town. Unaccompanied little boys in the grocery store, at the Gap, in the library, and in toy section of the Canadian Tire were suspect. Alan never "horsed around"—whatever that meant—but nevertheless, he got more than his share of the hairy eyeball from the shopkeepers, even though he had money in his pocket and had been known to spend it on occasion.

A lone boy of five or six or seven was suspicious, but let him show up with the tiny hand of his dark little brother clasped in his, quietly explaining each item on the shelf to the solemn child, and everyone got an immediate attitude adjustment. Shopkeepers smiled and nodded, shoppers mouthed, "So cute," to each other. Moms with babies in snuglis bent to chuckle them under their chins. Store owners spontaneously gave them candy, and laughed aloud at Bryan's cries of, "Chocolate!"

When Brian started school, he foresaw and avoided all trouble, and delighted his teachers with his precociousness. Alan ate lunch with him once he reached the first grade and started eating in the cafeteria with the rest of the nonkindergartners.

Brad loved to play with Craig after he was born, patiently mounding soil and pebbles on his shore, watering him and patting him smooth, planting wild grasses on his slopes as he crept toward the mouth of the cave. Those days—before Darcy's arrival—were a long idyll of good food and play in the hot sun or the white snow and brotherhood.

Danny couldn't sneak up on Brad and kick him in the back of the head. He couldn't hide a rat in his pillow or piss on his toothbrush. Billy was never one to stand pat and eat shit just because Davey was handing it out. Sometimes he'd just wind up and take a swing at Davey, seemingly out of the blue, knocking him down, then prying open his mouth to reveal the chocolate bar he'd nicked from under Brad's pillow, or a comic book from under his shirt. He was only two years younger than Brad, but by the time they were both walking, he hulked over Brad and could lay him out with one wild haymaker of a punch.

Billy came down from his high perch when Alan returned from burying Marci, holding out his hands wordlessly. He hugged Alan hard, crushing the breath out of him.

The arms felt good around his neck, so he stopped letting himself feel them. He pulled back stiffly and looked at Brian.

"You could have told me," he said.

Bram's face went expressionless and hard and cold. Telling people wasn't what he did, not for years. It hurt others—and it hurt him. It was the reason for his long, long silences. Alan knew that sometimes he couldn't tell what it was that he knew that others didn't. But he didn't care, then.

"You should have told me," he said.

Bob took a step back and squared up his shoulders and his feet, leaning forward a little as into a wind.

"You *knew* and you didn't *tell me* and you didn't *do anything* and as far as I'm concerned, you killed her and cut her up and buried her along with Darryl, you coward." Adam knew he was crossing a line, and he didn't care. Brian leaned forward and jutted his chin out.

Avram's hands were clawed with cold and caked with mud and still echoing the feeling of frozen skin and frozen dirt, and balled up into fists, they felt like stones.

He didn't hit Barry. Instead, he retreated to his niche and retrieved the triangular piece of flint that he'd been cherting into an arrowhead for school and a hammer stone and set to work on it in the light of a flashlight.

He sharpened a knife for Davey, there in his room in the cave, as the boys ran feral in the woods, as the mountain made its slow and ponderous protests.

He sharpened a knife, a hunting knife with a rusty blade and a cracked handle that he'd found on one of the woodland trails beside a hunter's snare, not lost but pitched away in disgust one winter and not discovered until the following spring.

But the nicked blade took an edge as he whetted it with the round stone, and the handle regained its grippiness as he wound a cord tight around it, making tiny, precise knots with each turn, until the handle no longer pinched his hand, until the blade caught the available light from the cave mouth and glinted dully.

The boys brought him roots and fruits they'd gathered, sweets and bread they'd stolen, small animals they'd caught. Ed-Fred-George were an unbeatable team when it came to catching and killing an animal, though they were only small, barely out of the second grade. They were fast, and they could coordinate their actions without speaking, so that the bunny or the squirrel could never duck or feint in any direction without encountering the thick, neck-wringing outstretched hands of the pudgy boys. Once, they brought him a cat. It went in the night's stew.

Billy sat at his side and talked. The silence he'd folded himself in unwrapped and flapped in the wind of his beating gums.

He talked about the lessons he'd had in school and the lessons he'd had from his big brother, when it was just the two of them on the hillside and Alan would teach him every thing he knew, the names of and salient facts regarding every thing in their father's domain. He talked about the truths he'd gleaned from reading chocolate-bar wrappers. He talked about the things that he'd see Davey doing when no one else could see it.

One day, George came to him, the lima-bean baby grown to toddling about on two sturdy legs, fat and crispy red from his unaccustomed time out-of-doors and in the sun. "You know, he *worships* you," Glenn said, gesturing at the spot in his straw bedding where Brad habitually sat and gazed at him and chattered.

Alan stared at his shoelaces. "It doesn't matter," he said. He'd dreamt that night of Davey stealing into the cave and squatting beside him, watching him the way that he had before, and of Alan knowing, *knowing* that Davey was there, ready to rend and tear, knowing that his knife with its coiled handle was just under his pillow, but not being able to move his arms or legs. Paralyzed, he'd watched Davey grin and reach behind him with agonizing slowness for a rock that he'd lifted high above his head and Andrew had seen that the rock had been cherted to a razor edge that hovered a few feet over his breastbone, Davey's arms trembling with the effort of holding it aloft. A single drop of sweat had fallen off of Davey's chin and landed on Alan's nose, and then another, and finally he'd been able to open his eyes and wake himself, angry and scared. The spring rains had begun, and the condensation was thick on the cave walls, dripping onto his face and arms and legs as he slept, leaving behind chalky lime residue as it evaporated.

"He didn't kill her," Greg said.

Albert hadn't told the younger brothers about the body buried in Craig, which meant that Brad had been talking to them, had told them what he'd seen. Alan felt an irrational streak of anger at Brad—he'd been blabbing Alan's secrets. He'd been exposing the young ones to things they didn't need to know. To the nightmares.

"He didn't stop her from being killed," Alan said. He had

the knife in his hand and hunted through his pile of belongings for the whetstone to hone its edge.

Greg looked at the knife, and Andy followed his gaze to his own white knuckles on the hilt. Greg took a frightened step back, and Alan, who had often worried that the smallest brother was too delicate for the real world, felt ashamed of himself.

He set the knife down and stood, stretching his limbs and leaving the cave for the first time in weeks.

Brad found him standing on the slopes of the gentle, soggy hump of Charlie's slope, a few feet closer to the seaway than it had been that winter when Alan had dug up and re-buried Marci's body there.

"You forgot this," Brad said, handing him the knife.

Alan took it from him. It was sharp and dirty and the handle was grimed with sweat and lime.

"Thanks, kid," he said. He reached down and took Billy's hand, the way he'd done when it was just the two of them. The three eldest sons of the mountain stood there touching and watched the outside world rush and grind away in the distance, its humming engines and puffing chimneys.

Brendan tugged his hand free and kicked at the dirt with a toe, smoothing over the divot he'd made with the sole of his shoe. Andy noticed that the sneaker was worn out and had a hole in the toe, and that it was only laced up halfway.

"Got to get you new shoes," he said, bending down to relace them. He had to stick the knife in the ground to free his hands while he worked. The handle vibrated.

"Davey's coming," Benny said. "Coming now."

Alan reached out as in his dream and felt for the knife, but it wasn't there, as in his dream. He looked around as the skin on his face tightened and his heart began to pound in his ears, and he saw that it had merely fallen over in the dirt. He picked it up and saw that where it had fallen, it had knocked away the soil that had barely covered up a small, freckled hand, now gone black and curled into a fist like a monkey's paw. Marci's hand.

"He's coming." Benny took a step off the hill. "You won't lose," he said. "You've got the knife."

The hand was small and fisted, there in the dirt. It had been just below the surface of where he'd been standing. It had been there, in Clarence's soil, for months, decomposing, the last of Marci going. Somewhere just below that soil was her head, her face sloughing off and wormed. Her red hair fallen from her loosened scalp. He gagged and a gush of bile sprayed the hillside.

Danny hit him at the knees, knocking him into the dirt. He felt the little rotting fist digging into his ribs. His body bucked of its own accord, and he knocked Danny loose of his legs. His arm was hot and slippery, and when he looked at it he saw that it was coursing with blood. The knife in his other hand was bloodied and he saw that he'd drawn a long ragged cut along his bicep. A fountain of blood bubbled there with every beat of his heart, blub, blub, blub, and on the third blub, he felt the cut, like a long pin stuck in the nerve.

He climbed unsteadily to his feet and confronted Danny. Danny was naked and the color of the red golem clay. His ribs showed and his hair was matted and greasy.

"I'm coming home," Danny said, baring his teeth. His breath reeked of corruption and uncooked meat, and his mouth was ringed with a crust of dried vomit. "And you're not going to stop me."

"You don't have a home," Alan said, pressing the hilt of the knife over the wound in his bicep, the feeling like biting down on a cracked tooth. "You're not welcome."

Davey was monkeyed over low, arms swinging like a chimp, teeth bared, knees splayed and ready to uncoil and pounce. "You think you'll stab me with that?" he said, jerking his chin at the knife. "Or are you just going to bleed yourself out with it?"

Alan steadied his knife hand before him, unmindful of the sticky blood. He knew that the pounce was coming, but that didn't help when it came. Davey leapt for him and he slashed once with the knife, Davey ducking beneath the arc, and then

Davey had his forearm in his hands, his teeth fastened onto the meat of his knife thumb.

Andre rolled to one side and gripped down hard on the knife, tugging his arm ineffectually against the grip of the cruel teeth and the grasping bony fingers. Davey had lost his boyish charm, gone simian with filth and rage, and the sore and weak blows Alan was able to muster with his hurt arm didn't seem to register with Danny at all as he bit down harder.

Arnold dragged his arm up higher, dragging the glinting knifetip toward Davey's face. Drew kicked at his shins, planted a knee alongside his groin. Alan whipped his head back, then brought it forward as fast and hard as he could, hammering his forehead into the crown of Davey's head so hard that his head rang like a bell.

He stunned Davey free of his hand and stunned himself onto his back. He felt small hands beneath each armpit, dragging him clear of the hill. Brian. And George. They helped him to his feet and Breton handed him the knife again. Darren got onto his knees, and then to his feet, holding the back of his head.

They both swayed slightly, standing to either side of Chris's rise. Alan's knife hand was red with blood streaming from the bite wounds and his other arm felt unaccountably heavy now.

Davey was staggering back and forth a little, eyes dropping to the earth. Suddenly he dropped to one knee and scrabbled in the dirt, then scrambled back with something in his hand.

Marci's fist.

He waggled it at Andrew mockingly, then charged, crossing the distance between them with long, loping strides, the fist held out before him like a lance. Alan forgot the knife in his hand and shrank back, and then Davey was on him again, dropping the fist to the mud and taking hold of Alan's knife wrist, digging his ragged nails into the bleeding bites there.

Now Alan released the knife, so that it, too, fell to the mud, and the sound it made woke him from his reverie. He pulled his hand free of Davey's grip and punched him in the ear as hard as he could, simultaneously kneeing him in the groin. Davey hissed and punched him in the eye, a feeling like his eyeball was going to break open, a feeling like he'd been stabbed in the back of his eye socket.

He planted a foot in the mud for leverage, then flipped Danny over so that Alan was on top, knees on his skinny chest. The knife was there beside Davey's head, and Alan snatched it up, holding it ready for stabbing.

Danny's eyes narrowed.

Alan could do it. Kill him altogether dead finished yeah. Stab him in the face or the heart or the lung, somewhere fatal. He could kill Davey and make him go away forever.

Davey caught his eye and held it. And Alan knew he couldn't do it, and an instant later, Davey knew it, too. He smiled a crusty smile and went limp.

"Oh, don't hurt me, *please*," he said mockingly. "Please, big brother, don't stab me with your big bad knife!"

Alan hurt all over, but especially on his bicep and his thumb. His head sang with pain and blood loss.

"Don't hurt me, please!" Davey said.

Billy was standing before him, suddenly.

"That's what Marci said when he took her, 'Don't hurt me, please,'" he said. "She said it over and over again. While he dragged her here. While he choked her to death."

Alan held the knife tighter.

"He said it over and over again as he cut her up and buried her. He *laughed*."

Danny suddenly bucked hard, almost throwing him, and before he had time to think, Alan had slashed down with the knife, aiming for the face, the throat, the lung. The tip landed in the middle of his bony chest and skated over each rib, going *tink, tink, tink* through the handle, like a xylophone. It scored along the emaciated and distended belly, then sank in just to one side of the smooth patch where a real person—where Marci—would have a navel.

Davey howled and twisted free of the seeking edge, skipping back three steps while holding in the loop of gut that was trailing free of the incision.

"She said, 'Don't hurt me.' She said, 'Please.' Over and over. He said it, too, and he laughed at her." Benny chanted it at him, standing just behind him, and the sound of his voice filled Alan's ears.

Suddenly Davey reeled back as a stone rebounded off of his shoulder. They both looked in the direction it had come from, and saw George, with the tail of his shirt aproned before him, filled with small, jagged stones from the edge of the hot spring in their father's depths. They took turns throwing those stones, skimming them over the water, and Ed and Fred and George had a vicious arm.

Davey turned and snarled and started upslope toward George, and a stone took him in the back of the neck, thrown by Freddie, who had sought cover behind a thick pine that couldn't disguise the red of his windbreaker, red as the inside of his lip, which pouted out as he considered his next toss.

He was downslope, and so Drew was able to bridge the distance between them very quickly—he was almost upon Felix when a third stone, bigger and faster than the other, took him in the back of the head with terrible speed, making a sound like a hammer missing the nail and hitting solid wood instead.

It was Ernie, of course, standing on Craig's highest point, winding up for another toss.

The threesome's second volley hit him all at once, from three sides, high, low, and medium.

"Killed her, cut her up, buried her," Benny chanted. "Sliced her open and cut her up," he called.

"SHUT UP!" Davey screamed. He was bleeding from the back of his head, the blood trickling down the knobs of his spine, and he was crying, sobbing.

"KILLED HER, CUT HER UP, SLICED HER OPEN," Ed-Fred-George chanted in unison.

Alan tightened his grip on the cords wound around the handle of his knife, and his knife hand bled from the puncture wounds left by Davey's teeth.

Davey saw him coming and dropped to his knees, crying. Sobbing.

"Please," he said, holding his hands out before him, palms together, begging.

"Please," he said, as the loop of intestine he'd been holding in trailed free.

"Please," he said, as Alan seized him by the hair, jerked his head back, and swiftly brought the knife across his throat.

Benny took his knife, and Ed-Fred-George coaxed Clarence into a slow, deep fissuring. They dragged the body into the earthy crack and Clarence swallowed up their brother.

Benny led Alan to the cave, where they'd changed his bedding and laid out a half-eaten candy bar, a shopping bag filled with bramble-berries, and a lock of Marci's hair, tied into a knot.

Alan dragged all of his suitcases up from the basement to the living room, from the tiny tin valise plastered with genuine vintage deco railway stickers to the steamer trunk that he'd always intended to refurbish as a bathroom cabinet. He hadn't been home in fifteen years. Nearly half his life. What should he bring?

Clothes were the easiest. It was coming up on the cusp of July and August, and he remembered boyhood summers on the mountain's slopes abuzz with blackflies and syrupy heat. White T-shirts, lightweight trousers, high-tech hiking boots that breathed, a thin jacket for the mosquitoes at dusk.

He decided to pack four changes of clothes, which made a very small pile on the sofa. Small suitcase. The little rolling carry-on? The wheels would be useless on the rough cave floor.

He paced and looked at the spines of his books, and paced more, into the kitchen. It was a beautiful summer day and the tall grasses in the back yard nodded in the soft breeze. He stepped through the screen door and out into the garden and let the wild grasses scrape over his thighs. Ivy and wild sunflowers climbed the fence that separated his yard from his neighbors, and through the chinks in the green armor, he saw someone moving.

Mimi.

Pacing her garden, neatly tended vegetable beds, some flowering bulbs. Skirt and a cream linen blazer that rucked up over her shoulders, moving restlessly. Powerfully.

Alan's breath caught in his throat. Her pale, round calves flashed in the sun. He felt himself harden, painfully. He must have gasped, or given some sign, or perhaps she heard his skin tighten over his body into a great goosepimply mass. Her head turned.

Their eyes met and he jolted. He was frozen in his footsteps by her gaze. One cheek was livid with a purple bruise, the eye above it slitted and puffed. She took a step toward him, her jacket opening to reveal a shapeless gray sweatshirt stained with food and—blood?

"Mimi?" he breathed.

She squeezed her eyes shut, her face turning into a fright mask.

"Abel," she said. "Nice day."

"Are you all right?" he said. He'd had his girls, his employees, show up for work in this state before. He knew the signs. "Is he in the house now?"

She pulled up a corner of her lip into a sneer and he saw that it was split, and a trickle of blood wet her teeth and stained them pink.

"Sleeping," she said.

He swallowed. "I can call the cops, or a shelter, or both."

She laughed. "I gave as good as I got," she said. "We're more than even."

"I don't care," he said. " 'Even' is irrelevant. Are you *safe*?"

"Safe as houses," she said. "Thanks for your concern." She turned back toward her back door.

"Wait," he said. She shrugged and the wings under her jacket strained against the fabric. She reached for the door. He jammed his fingers into the chain-link near the top and hauled himself, scrambling, over the fence, landing on all fours in a splintering of tomato plants and sticks.

He got to his feet and bridged the distance between them.

"I don't believe you, Mimi," he said. "I don't believe you. Come over to my place and let me get you a cup of coffee and an ice pack and we'll talk about it, please?"

"Fuck off," she said, tugging at the door. He wedged his toe in it, took her wrist gently.

"Please," she said. "We'll wake him."

"Come over," he said. "We won't wake him."

She cracked her arm like a whip, shaking his hand off her wrist. She stared at him out of her swollen eye and he felt the jolt again. Some recognition. Some shock. Some mirror, his face tiny and distorted in her eye.

She shivered.

"Help me over the fence," she said, pulling her skirt between her knees—bruise on her thigh—and tucking it behind her into her waistband. She jammed her bare toes into the link and he gripped one hard, straining calf in one hand and put the other on her padded, soft bottom, helping her up onto a perch atop the fence. He scrambled over and then took one bare foot, one warm calf, and guided her down.

"Come inside," he said.

She'd never been in his house. Natalie and Link went in and out to use his bathroom while they were enjoying the sunset on his porch, or to get a beer. But Mimi had never crossed his threshold. When she did, it felt like something he'd been missing there had been finally found.

She looked around with a hint of a smile on her puffed lips. She ran her fingers over the cast-iron gas range he'd restored, caressing the Bakelite knobs. She peered at the titles of the books in the kitchen bookcases, over the honey wood of the mismatched chairs and the smoothed-over scars of the big, simple table.

"Come into the living room," Alan said. "I'll get you an ice pack."

She let him guide her by the elbow, then crossed decisively to the windows and drew the curtains, bringing on twilight. He moved aside his piles of clothes and stacked up the suitcases in a corner.

"Going somewhere?"

"To see my family," he said. She smiled and her lip cracked anew, dripping a single dark droplet of blood onto the gleaming wood of the floor, where it beaded like water on wax paper.

"Home again, home again, jiggety jig," she said. Her nearly closed eye was bright and it darted around the room, taking in shelves, fireplace, chairs, clothes.

"I'll get you that ice pack," he said. As he went back into the kitchen, he heard her walking around in the living room, and he remembered the first time he'd met her, of walking around her living room and thinking about slipping a VCD into his pocket.

He found her halfway up the staircase with one of the shallow bric-a-brac cabinets open before her. She was holding a Made-in-Occupied-Japan tin robot, the paint crazed with age into craquelure like a Dutch Master painting in a gallery.

"Turn it upside down," he said.

She looked at him, then turned it over, revealing the insides of the tin, revealing the gaudily printed tuna-fish label from the original can that it had been fashioned from.

"Huh," she said, and peered down into it. He hit the light switch at the bottom of the stairs so that she could see better. "Beautiful," she said.

"Have it," he said, surprising himself. He'd have to remove it from The Inventory. He restrained himself from going upstairs and doing it before he forgot.

For the first time he could remember, she looked flustered. Her unbruised cheek went crimson.

"I couldn't," she said.

"It's yours," he said. He went up the stairs and closed the cabinet, then folded her fingers around the robot and led her by the wrist back down to the sofa. "Ice pack," he said, handing it to her, releasing her wrist.

She sat stiff-spined in on the sofa, the hump of her wings behind her keeping her from reclining. She caught him staring.

"It's time to trim them," she said.

"Oh, yes?" he said, mind going back to the gridwork of old scars by her shoulders.

"When they get too big, I can't sit properly or lie on my back. At least not while I'm wearing a shirt."

"Couldn't you, I don't know, cut the back out of a shirt?"

"Yeah," she said. "Or go topless. Or wear a halter. But not in public."

"No, not in public. Secrets must be kept."

"You've got a lot of secrets, huh?" she said.

"Some," he said.

"Deep, dark ones?"

"All secrets become deep. All secrets become dark. That's in the nature of secrets."

She pressed the towel-wrapped bag of ice to her face and rolled her head back and forth on her neck. He heard pops and crackles as her muscles and vertebrae unlimbered.

"Hang on," he said. He ran up to his room and dug through his T-shirt drawer until he found one that he didn't mind parting with. He brought it back downstairs and held it up for her to see. "Steel Pole Bathtub," he said. "Retro chic. I can cut the back out for you, at least while you're here."

She closed her eyes. "I'd like that," she said in a small voice.

So he got his kitchen shears and went to work on the back of the shirt, cutting a sizable hole in the back of the fabric. He folded duct tape around the ragged edges to keep them from fraying. She watched bemusedly.

"Freakshow Martha Stewart," she said.

He smiled and passed her the shirt. "I'll give you some privacy," he said, and went back into the kitchen and put away the shears and the tape. He tried not to listen to the soft rustle of clothing in the other room.

"Alan," she said—*Alan* and not *Asshole* or *Abel*—"I could use some help."

He stepped cautiously into the living room and saw there, in the curtained twilight, Mimi. She was topless, heavy breasts marked red with the outline of her bra straps and wires. They hung weightily, swaying, and stopped him in the doorway. She had her arms lifted over her head, tugging her round belly up, stretching her navel into a cat-eye slit. The T-shirt he'd given her was tangled in her arms and in her wings.

Her magnificent wings.

They were four feet long each, and they stretched, one through the neck hole and the other through the hole he'd cut in the T-shirt's back. They were leathery as he remembered, covered in a downy fur that glowed where it was kissed by the few shafts of light piercing the gap in the drapes. He reached for the questing, almost prehensile tip of the one that was caught in the neck hole. It was muscular, like a strong finger, curling against his palm like a Masonic handshake.

When he touched her wing, she gasped and shivered, indeterminately between erotic and outraged. They were as he imagined them, these wings, strong and primal and dark and spicy-smelling like an armpit after sex.

He gently guided the tip down toward the neck hole and marveled at the intricate way that it folded in on itself, at the play of mysterious muscle and cartilage, the rustle of bristling hair, and the motility of the skin.

It accordioned down and he tugged the shirt around it so that it came free, and then he slid the front of the shirt down over her breasts, painfully aware of his erection as the fabric rustled down over her rounded belly.

As her head emerged through the shirt, she shook her hair out and then unfolded her wings, slowly and exquisitely, like a cat stretching out, bending forward, spreading them like sails. He ducked beneath one, feeling its puff of spiced air on his face, and found himself staring at the hash of scars and the rigid ropes of hyperextended muscle and joints. Tentatively, he traced the scars with his thumbs, then, when she made no move to stop him, he dug his thumbs into the muscles, into their tension.

He kneaded at her flesh, grinding hard at the knots and feeling them give way, briskly rubbing the spots where they'd been to get the blood going. Her wings flapped gently around him as he worked, not caring that his body was pretzeled into a knot of its own to reach her back, since he didn't want to break the spell to ask her to move over to give him a better angle.

He could smell her armpit and her wings and her hair and he closed his eyes and worked by touch, following scar to muscle, muscle to knot, working his way the length and breadth of her back, following the muscle up from the ridge of her iliac crest like a treasure trail to the muscle of her left wing, which was softly twitching with pleasure.

She went perfectly still again when he took the wing in his hands. It had its own geometry, hard to understand and irresistible. He followed the mysterious and powerful muscles and bones, the vast expanses of cartilage, finding knots and squeezing them, kneading her as he'd kneaded her back, and she groaned and went limp, leaning back against him so that his face was in her hair and smelling her scalp oil and stale shampoo and sweat. It was all he could do to keep himself from burying his face in her hair and gnawing at the muscles at the base of her skull.

He moved as slow as a seaweed and ran his hands over to her other wing, giving it the same treatment. He was rock-hard, pressed against her, her wings all around him. He traced the line of her jaw to her chin, and they were breathing in unison, and his fingers found the tense place at the hinge and worked there, too.

Then he brushed against her bruised cheek and she startled, and that shocked him back to reality. He dropped his hands to his sides and then stood, realized his erection was straining at his shorts, sat back down again in one of the club chairs, and crossed his legs.

"Well," he said.

Mimi unfolded her wings over the sofa-back and let them spread out, then leaned back, eyes closed.

"You should try the ice pack again," he said weakly. She groped blindly for it and draped it over her face.

"Thank you," she sighed.

He suppressed the urge to apologize. "You're welcome," he said.

"It started last week," she said. "My wings had gotten longer. Too long. Krishna came home from the club and he was drunk and he wanted sex. Wanted me on the bottom. I couldn't. My wings. He wanted to get the knife right away and cut them off. We do it about four times a year, using a big serrated hunting knife he bought at a sporting-goods store on Yonge Street, one of those places that sells dud grenades and camou pants and tasers."

She opened her eyes and looked at him, then closed them. He shivered and a goose walked over his grave.

"We do it in the tub. I stand in the tub, naked, and he saws off the wings right to my shoulders. I don't bleed much. He gives me a towel to bite on while he cuts. To scream into. And then we put them in garden trash bags and he puts them out just before the garbage men arrive, so the neighborhood dogs don't get at them. For the meat."

He noticed that he was gripping the armrests so tightly that his hands were cramping. He pried them loose and tucked them under his thighs.

"He dragged me into the bathroom. One second, we were rolling around in bed, giggling like kids in love, and then he had me so hard by the wrist, dragging me naked to the bathroom, his knife in his other fist. I had to keep quiet, so that I wouldn't wake Link and Natalie, but he was hurting me, and I was scared. I tried to say something to him, but I could only squeak. He hurled me into the tub and I cracked my head against the tile. I cried out and he crossed the bathroom and put his hand over my mouth and nose and then I couldn't breathe, and my head was swimming.

"He was naked and hard, and he had the knife in his fist, not like for slicing, but for stabbing, and his eyes were red from the smoke at the club, and the bathroom filled with the booze-breath smell, and I sank down in the tub, shrinking away from him as he grabbed for me.

"He—*growled*. Saw that I was staring at the knife. Smiled. Horribly. There's a piece of granite we use for a soap dish, balanced in the corner of the tub. Without thinking, I grabbed it and threw it as hard as I could at him. It broke his nose and he closed his eyes and reached for his face and I wrapped him up in the shower curtain and grabbed his arm and bit at the base of his thumb so hard I heard a bone break and he dropped the knife. I grabbed it and ran back to our room and threw it out the window and started to get dressed."

She'd fallen into a monotone now, but her wingtips twitched and her knees bounced like her motor was idling on high. She jiggled.

"You don't have to tell me this," he said.

She took off the ice pack. "Yes, I do," she said. Her eyes seemed to have sunk into her skull, vanishing into dark pits. He'd thought her eyes were blue, or green, but they looked black now.

"All right," he said.

"All right," she said. "He came through the door and I didn't scream. I didn't want to wake up Link and Natalie. Isn't that stupid? But I couldn't get my sweatshirt on, and they would have seen my wings. He looked like he was going to kill me. Really. Hands in claws. Teeth out. Crouched down low like a chimp, ready to grab, ready to swing. And I was back in a corner again, just wearing track pants. He didn't have the knife this time, though.

"When he came for me, I went limp, like I was too scared to move, and squeezed my eyes shut. Listened to his footsteps approach. Felt the creak of the bed as he stepped up on it. Felt his breath as he reached for me.

"I exploded. I've read books on women's self-defense, and they talk about doing that, about exploding. You gather in all your energy and squeeze it tight, and then blamo boom, you explode. I was aiming for his soft parts: Balls. Eyes. Nose. Sternum. Ears. I'd misjudged where he was, though, so I missed most of my targets.

"And then he was on me, kneeling on my tits, hands at my throat. I bucked him but I couldn't get him off. My chest and throat were crushed, my wings splayed out behind me. I flapped them and saw his hair move in the breeze. He was sweating hard, off his forehead and off his nose and lips. It was all so detailed. And silent. Neither of us made a sound louder than a grunt. Quieter than our sex noises. *Now* I wanted to scream, *wanted* to wake up Link and Natalie, but I couldn't get a breath.

"I worked one hand free and I reached for the erection that I could feel just below my tits, reached as fast as a striking snake, grabbed it, grabbed his balls, and I yanked and I squeezed like I was trying to tear them off.

"I was.

"Now *he* was trying to get away and I had him cornered. I kept squeezing. That's when he kicked me in the face. I was dazed. He kicked me twice more, and I ran downstairs and got a parka from the closet and ran out into the front yard and out to the park and hid in the bushes until morning.

"He was asleep when I came back in, after Natalie and Link had gone out. I found the knife beside the house and I went up to our room and I stood there, by the window, listening to you talk to them, holding the knife."

She plumped herself on the cushions and flapped her wings once, softly, another puff of that warm air wafting over him. She picked up the tin robot he'd given her from the coffee table and turned it over in her hands, staring up its skirts at the tuna-fish illustration and the Japanese ideograms.

"I had the knife, and I felt like I had to use it. You know Chekhov? 'If a gun is on the mantle in the first act, it must go off in the third.' I write one-act plays. Wrote. But it seemed to me that the knife had been in act one, when Krishna dragged me into the bathroom.

"Or maybe act one was when he brought it home, after I showed him my wings.

"And act two had been my night in the park. And act three was then, standing over him with the knife, cold and sore and tired, looking at the blood crusted on his face."

Her face and her voice got very, very small, her expression distant. "I almost used it on myself. I almost opened my wrists onto his face. He liked it when I . . . rode . . . his face. Liked the hot juices. Seemed mean-spirited to spill all that hot juice and deny him that pleasure. I thought about using it on him, too, but only for a second.

"Only for a second.

"And then he rolled over and his hands clenched into fists in his sleep and his expression changed, like he was dreaming about something that made him angry. So I left.

"Do you want to know about when I first showed him these?" she said, and flapped her wings lazily.

She took the ice pack from her face and he could see that the swelling had gone down, the discoloration faded to a dim shadow tinged with yellows and umbers.

He did, but he didn't. The breeze of her great wings was strangely intimate, that smell more intimate than his touches or the moment in which he'd glimpsed her fine, weighty breasts with their texture of stretch marks and underwire grooves. He was awkward, foolish-feeling.

"I don't think I do," he said at last. "I think that we should save some things to tell each other for later."

She blinked, slow and lazy, and one tear rolled down and dripped off her nose, splashing on the red T-shirt and darkening it to wineish purple.

"Will you sit with me?" she said.

He crossed the room and sat on the other end of the sofa, his hand on the seam that joined the two halves together, crossing the border into her territory, an invitation that could be refused without awkwardness.

She covered his hand with hers, and hers was cold and smooth but not distant: immediate, scritching and twitching against his skin. Slowly, slowly, she leaned toward him, curling her wing 'round his far shoulder like a blanket or a lover's arm, head coming to rest on his chest, breath hot on his nipple through the thin fabric of his T-shirt.

"Alan?" she murmured into his chest.

"Yes?"

"What are we?" she said.

"Huh?"

"Are we human? Where do we come from? How did we get here? Why do I have wings?"

He closed his eyes and found that they'd welled up with tears. Once the first tear slid down his cheek, the rest came, and he was crying, weeping silently at first and then braying like a donkey in sobs that started in his balls and emerged from his throat like vomit, gushing out with hot tears and hot snot.

Mimi enveloped him in her wings and kissed his tears away, working down his cheeks to his neck, his Adam's apple.

He snuffled back a mouthful of mucus and salt and wailed, "I don't know!"

She snugged her mouth up against his collarbone. "Krishna does," she whispered into his skin. She tugged at the skin with her teeth. "What about your family?"

He swallowed a couple of times, painfully aware of her lips and breath on his skin, the enveloping coolth of her wings, and the smell in every breath he took. He wanted to blow his nose, but he couldn't move without breaking the spell, so he hoarked his sinuses back into his throat and drank the oozing oyster of self-pity that slid down his throat.

"My family?"

"I don't have a family, but you do," she said. "Your family must know."

"They don't," he said.

"Maybe you haven't asked them properly. When are you leaving?"

"Today."

"Driving?"

"Got a rental car," he said.

"Room for one more?"

"Yes," he said.

"Then take me," she said.

"All right," he said. She raised her head and kissed him on the lips, and he could taste the smell now, and the blood roared in his ears as she straddled his lap, grinding her mons—hot through the thin cotton of her skirt—against him. They slid down on the sofa and they groaned into each others' mouths, his voice box resonating with hers.

He parked the rental car in the driveway, finishing his cell phone conversation with Lyman and then popping the trunk before getting out. He glanced reflexively up at Mimi and Krishna's windows, saw the blinds were still drawn.

When he got to the living room, Mimi was bent over a suitcase, forcing it closed. Two more were lined up beside the door, along with three shopping bags filled with tupperwares and ziplocs of food from his fridge.

"I've borrowed some of your clothes," she said. "Didn't want to have to go back for mine. Packed us a picnic, too."

He planted his hands on his hips. "You thought of everything, huh?" he said.

She cast her eyes down. "I'm sorry," she said in a small voice. "I couldn't go home." Her wings unfolded and folded down again nervously.

He went and stood next to her. He could still smell the sex on her, and on him. A livid hickey stood out on her soft skin on her throat. He twined her fingers in his and dropped his face down to her ear.

"It's okay," he said huskily. "I'm glad you did it."

She turned her head and brushed her lips over his, brushed her hand over his groin. He groaned softly.

"We have to get driving," he said.

"Yes," she said. "Load the car, then bring it around the side. I'll lie down on the back seat until we're out of the neighborhood."

"You've thought about this a lot, huh?"

"It's all I've thought of," she said.

She climbed over the back seat once they cleared Queen Street, giggling as her wings, trapped under her jacket, brushed the roof of the big Crown Victoria he'd rented. She prodded at the radio and found a college station, staticky and amateurish, and nodded her head along with the mash-up mixes and concert bootlegs the DJ was spinning.

Alan watched her in the rearview and felt impossibly old and strange. She'd been an incredible and attentive lover, using her hands and mouth, her breasts and wings, her whole body to keep him quivering on the brink of orgasm for what felt like hours, before finally giving him release, and then had guided him around her body with explicit instructions and firm hands on his shoulders. When she came, she squeezed him between her thighs and screamed into his neck, twitching and shuddering for a long time afterward, holding him tight, murmuring nonsense and hot breath.

In the dark, she'd seemed older. His age, or some indeterminate age. Now, sitting next to him, privately spazzing out to the beat, she seemed, oh, twelve or so. A little girl. He felt dirty.

"Where are we going?" she said, rolling down the window and shouting over the wind as they bombed up the Don Valley Parkway. The traffic had let up at Sheppard, and now they were making good time, heading for the faceless surburbs of Richmond Hill and Thornhill, and beyond.

"North," he said. "Past Kapuskasing."

She whistled. "How long a drive is it?"

"Fifteen hours. Twenty, maybe. Depends on the roads—you can hit cottage traffic or a bad accident and get hung up for hours. There are good motels between Huntsville and North Bay if we get tired out. Nice neon signs, magic fingers beds. A place I like has 'Swiss Cabins' and makes a nice rosti for dinner."

"God, that's a long trip," she said.

"Yeah," he said, wondering if she wanted out. "I can pull off here and give you cab fare to the subway station if you wanna stay."

"No!" she said quickly. "No. Want to go."

She fed him as he drove, slicing cheese and putting it on crackers with bits of olive or pepper or salami. It appeared that she'd packed his entire fridge in the picnic bags.

After suppertime, she went to work on an apple, and he took a closer look at the knife she was using. It was a big, black hunting knife, with a compass built into the handle. The blade was black except right at the edge, where it gleamed sharp in the click-clack of the passing highway lights.

He was transfixed by it, and the car drifted a little, sprayed gravel from the shoulder, and he overcorrected and fishtailed a little. She looked up in alarm.

"You brought the knife," he said, in response to her unasked question.

"Couldn't leave it with him," she said. "Besides, a sharp knife is handy."

"Careful you don't slice anything off, okay?"

"I never cut anything *unintentionally*," she said in a silly-dramatic voice, and socked him in the shoulder.

He snorted and went back to the driving, putting the hammer down, eating up the kilometers toward Huntsville and beyond.

She fed him slices of apple and ate some herself, then rolls of ham with little pieces of pear in them, then sips of cherry juice from a glass bottle.

"Enough," he said at last. "I'm stuffed, woman!"

She laughed. "Skinny little fucker—gotta put some meat on your bones." She tidied the dinner detritus into an empty shopping bag and tossed it over her shoulder into the back seat.

"So," she said. "How long since you've been home?"

He stared at the road for a while. "Twenty years," he said. "Never been back since I left."

She stared straight forward and worked her hand under his thigh, so he was sitting on it, then wriggled her knuckles.

"I've never been home," she said.

He wrinkled his brow. "What's that mean?" he said.

"It's a long story," she said.

"Well, let's get off the highway and get a room and you can tell me, okay?"

"Sure," she said.

They ended up at the Timberline Wilderness Lodge and Pancake House, and Mimi clapped her hands at the silk-flowers-and-waterbeds ambience of the room, fondled the grisly jackalope head on the wall, and started running a tub while Alan carried in the suitcases.

She dramatically tossed her clothes, one item at a time, out the bathroom door, through the clouds of steam, and he caught a glimpse of her round, full ass, bracketed by her restless wings, as she poured into the tub the bottle of cheap bubble bath she'd bought in the lobby.

He dug a T-shirt and a fresh pair of boxers to sleep in out of his suitcase, feeling ridiculously modest as he donned them. His feet crunched over cigarette burns and tangles in the brown shag carpet and he wished he'd brought along some slippers. He flipped through both snowy TV channels and decided that he couldn't stomach a televangelist or a thirty-year-old sitcom right then and flicked it off, sitting on the edge of the bed, listening to the splashing from the bathroom.

Mimi was in awfully good spirits, considering what she'd been through with Krishna. He tried to think about it, trying to make sense of the day and the girl, but the splashing from the tub kept intruding on his thoughts.

She began to sing, and after a second he recognized the tune. "White Rabbit," by the Jefferson Airplane. Not the kind of thing he'd expect her to be giving voice to; nor she, apparently, for she kept breaking off to giggle. Finally, he poked his head through the door.

She was folded into the tub, knees and tits above the foam-line, wings slick with water and dripping in the tile. Her hands were out of sight beneath the suds. She caught his eye and grinned crazily, then her hands shot out of the pool, clutching the hunting knife.

"*Put on the White Rabbit!*" she howled, cackling fiendishly.

He leapt back and she continued to cackle. "Come back, come back," she choked. "I'm doing the tub scene from *Fear and Loathing in Las Vegas.* I thought you were into reading?"

He cautiously peeked around the doorjamb, playing it up for comic effect. "Give me the knife," he said.

"Awww," she said, handing it over, butt first. He set it down on the dresser, then hurried back to the bathroom.

"Haven't you read all those books?"

Alan grinned. "What's the point of a bunch of books you've already read?" He dropped his boxers and stripped off his T-shirt and climbed into the tub, sloshing gallons of water over the scummy tile floor.

When I was two years old,

(she said, later, as she reclined against the headboard and he reclined against her, their asses deforming the rusted springs of the mattress so that it sloped toward them and the tins of soda they'd opened to replenish their bodily fluids lost in sweat and otherwise threatened to tip over on the slope; she encased him in her wings, shutting out the light and filling their air with the smell of cinnamon and pepper from the downy hair)

When I was two years old,

(she said, speaking into the shaggy hair at the back of his neck, as his sore muscles trembled and as the sweat dried to a white salt residue on his skin, as he lay there in the dark of the room and the wings, watching the constellation of reflected clock-radio lights in the black TV screen)

When I was two years old,

(she began, her body tensing from toes to tip in a movement that he felt along the length of his body, portending the time when lovers close their eyes and open their mouths and utter the secrets that they hide from everyone, even themselves)

When I was two years old, my wings were the size of a cherub's, and they had featherlets that were white as snow. I lived with my "aunt," an old Russian lady near Downsview Air Force Base, a blasted suburb where the shops all closed on Saturday for Sabbath and the black-hatted Hasids marked the days by walking from one end to the other on their way to temple.

The old Russian lady took me out for walks in a big black baby buggy the size of a bathtub. She tucked me in tight so that my wings were pinned beneath me. But when we were at home, in her little apartment with the wind-up Sputnik that played "The Internationale," she would let my wings out and light the candles and watch me wobble around the room, my wings flapping, her chin in her hands, her eyes bright. She made me mashed-up cabbage and seed and beef, and bottles of dilute juice. For dessert, we had hard candies, and I'd toddle around with my toys, drooling sugar syrup while the old Russian lady watched.

By the time I was four, the feathers had all fallen out, and I was supposed to go to school, I knew that. "Auntie" had explained to me that the kids that I saw passing by were on their way to school, and that I'd go someday and learn, too.

She didn't speak much English, so I grew up speaking a Creole of Russian, Ukranian, Polish, and English, and I used my words to ask her, with more and more insistence, when I'd get to go to class.

I couldn't read or write, and neither could she. But I could take apart gadgets like nobody's business. Someone—maybe Auntie's long-dead husband—had left her a junky tool kit with cracked handles and chipped tips, and I attacked anything that I could get unplugged from the wall: the big cabinet TV and radio, the suitcase record player, the Sputnik music box. I unwired the lamps and peered at the workings of the electric kitchen clock.

That was four. Five was the year I put it all back together again. I started with the lamps, then the motor in the blender, then the toaster elements. I made the old TV work. I don't think I knew how any of it *really* worked—couldn't tell you a thing about, you know, electrical engineering, but I just got a sense of how it was *supposed* to go together.

Auntie didn't let me out of the apartment after five. I could watch the kids go by from the window—skinny Hasids with sidecurls and Filipinos with pretty ribbons and teenagers who smoked, but I couldn't go to them. I watched *Sesame Street* and

Mr. Dressup and I began to soak up English. I began to soak up the idea of playing with other kids.

I began to soak up the fact that none of the kids on the TV had wings.

Auntie left me alone in the afternoons while she went out shopping and banking and whatever else it was she did, and it was during those times that I could get myself into her bedroom and go rooting around her things.

She had a lot of mysterious beige foundation garments that were utterly inexplicable, and a little box of jewelry that I liked to taste, because the real gold tasted really rich when I sucked on it, and a stack of old cigarette tins full of frayed photos.

The pictures were stiff and mysterious. Faces loomed out of featureless black backgrounds: pop-eyed, jug-eared Russian farm boys, awkward farm girls with process waves in their hair, everyone looking like they'd been stuffed and mounted. I guess they were her relatives, because if you squinted at them and cocked your head, you could kind of see her features in theirs, but not saggy and wrinkled and three-chinned, but young and tight and almost glowing. They all had big shoulders and clothing that looked like the kind of thing the Hasids wore, black and sober.

The faces were interesting, especially after I figured out that one of them might belong to Auntie, but it was the blackness around them that fascinated me. The boys had black suits and the girls wore black dresses, and behind them was creased blackness, complete darkness, as though they'd put their heads through a black curtain.

But the more I stared at the blackness, the more detail I picked out. I noticed the edge of a curtain, a fold, in one photo, and when I looked for it, I could just pick it out in the other photos. Eventually, I hit on the idea of using a water glass as a magnifying lens, and as I experimented with different levels of water, more detail leapt out of the old pictures.

The curtains hanging behind them were dusty and wrinkled. They looked like they were made of crushed velvet, like the Niagara Falls souvenir pillow on Auntie's armchair in the living room, which had whorls of paisley trimmed into them. I traced these whorls with my eye, and tried to reproduce them with a ballpoint on paper bags I found under the sink.

And then, in one of the photos, I noticed that the patterns disappeared behind and above the shoulders. I experimented with different water levels in my glass to bring up the magnification, and I diligently sketched. I'd seen a *Polka Dot Door* episode where the hosts showed how you could draw a grid over an original image and a matching grid on a sheet of blank paper and then copy over every square, reproducing the image in manageable, bite-sized chunks.

That's what I did, using the edge of a nail file for a ruler, drawing my grid carefully on the paper bag, and a matching one on the picture, using the blunt tip of a dead pen to make a grid of indentations in the surface of the photo.

And I sketched it out, one square at a time. Where the pattern was, where it wasn't. What shapes the negative absence-of-pattern took in the photos. As I drew, day after day, I realized that I was drawing the shape of something black that was blocking the curtain behind.

Then I got excited. I drew in my steadiest hand, tracing each curve, using my magnifier, until I had the shape drawn and defined, and long before I finished, I knew what I was drawing and I drew it anyway. I drew it and then I looked at my paper sack and I saw that what I had drawn was a pair of wings, black and powerful, spread out and stretching out of the shot.

She curled the prehensile tips of her wings up the soles of his feet, making him go, Yeek! and jump in the bed.

"Are you awake?" she said, twisting her head around to brush her lips over his.

"Rapt," he said.

She giggled and her tits bounced.

"Good," she said. " 'Cause this is the important part."

Auntie came home early that day and found me sitting at her vanity, with the photos and the water glass and the drawings on the paper sacks spread out before me.

Our eyes met for a moment. Her pupils shrank down to tiny dots, I remember it, remember seeing them vanish, leaving behind rings of yellowed hazel. One of her hands lashed out in a claw and sank into my hair. She lifted me out of the chair by my hair before I'd even had a chance to cry out, almost before I'd registered the fact that she was hurting me—she'd never so much as spanked me until then.

She was strong, in that slow old Russian lady way, strong enough to grunt ten sacks of groceries in a bundle-buggy up the stairs to the apartment. When she picked me up and tossed me, it was like being fired out of a cannon. I rebounded off the framed motel-room art over the bed, shattering the glass, and bounced twice on the mattress before coming to rest on the floor. My arm was hanging at a funny angle, and when I tried to move it, it hurt so much that I heard a high sound in my ears like a dog whistle.

I lay still as the old lady yanked the drawers out of her vanity and upended them on the floor until she found an old book of matches. She swept the photos and my sketches into the tin wastebasket and then lit a match with trembling hands and dropped it in. It went out. She repeated it, and on the fourth try she got the idea of using the match to light all the remaining matches in the folder and drop that into the bin. A moment later, it was burning cheerfully, spitting curling red embers into the air on clouds of dark smoke. I buried my face in the matted carpet and tried not to hear that high note, tried to will away the sick grating feeling in my upper arm.

She was wreathed in smoke, choking, when she finally turned to me. For a moment, I refused to meet her eye, sure that she would kill me if I did, would see the guilt and the knowledge in my face and keep her secret with murder. I'd watched enough daytime television to know about dark secrets.

But when she bent down to me, with the creak of stretching elastic, and she lifted me to my feet and bent to look me in the eye, she had tears in her eyes.

She went to the pile of oddments and junk jewelry that she had dumped out on the floor and sorted through it until she found a pair of sewing shears, then she cut away my T-shirt, supporting my broken arm with her hand. My wings were flapping nervously beneath the fabric, and it got tangled, and she took firm hold of the wingtips and folded them down to my back and freed the shirt and tossed it in the pile of junk on her normally spotless floor.

She had spoken to me less and less since I had fixed the television and begun to pick up English, and now she was wordless as she gently rotated my fingerbones and my wristbones, my elbow and my shoulder, minute movements, listening for my teakettle hiss when she hit the sore spots.

"Is broken," she said. *"Cholera,"* she said. "I am so sorry, *lovenu,"* she said.

I've never been to the doctor's," she said. "Never had a pap smear or been felt for lumps. Never, ever had an X-ray. Feel this," she said, and put her upper arm before his face. He took it and ran his fingertips over it, finding a hard bump halfway along, opposite her fleshy bicep.

"What's this?" he said.

"It's how a bone sets if you have a bad break and don't get a cast. Crooked."

"Jesus," he said, giving it another squeeze. Now that he knew what it was, he thought—or perhaps fancied—that he could feel how the unevenly splintered pieces of bone mated together, met at a slight angle, and fused together by the knitting process.

"She made me a sling, and she fed me every meal and brushed my teeth. I had to stop her from following me into the toilet to wipe me up. And I didn't care: She could have broken both of my arms if she'd only explained the photos to me, or left them with me so that I could go on investigating them, but she did neither. She hardly spoke a word to me."

She resettled herself against the pillows, then pulled him back against her again and plumped his head against her breasts.

"Are you falling in love with me?" she said.

He startled. The way she said it, she didn't sound like a young adult, she sounded like a small child.

"Mimi—" he began, then stopped himself. "I don't think so. I mean, I like you—"

"Good," she said. "No falling in love, all right?"

Auntie died six months later. She keeled over on the staircase on her way up to the apartment, and I heard her moaning and thrashing out there. I hauled her up the stairs with my good arm, and she crawled along on her knees, making gargling noises.

I got her laid out on the rug in the living room. I tried to get her up on the sofa, but I couldn't budge her. So I gave her pillows from the sofa and water and then I tried tea, but she couldn't take it. She threw up once, and I soaked it up with a tea towel that had fussy roses on it.

She took my hand and her grip was weak, her strong hands suddenly thin and shaky.

It took an hour for her to die.

When she died, she made a rasping, rattling sound and then she shat herself. I could smell it.

It was all I could smell, as I sat there in the little apartment, six years old, hot as hell outside and stuffy inside. I opened the windows and watched the Hasids walk past. I felt like I should *do something* for the old lady, but I didn't know what.

I formulated a plan. I would go outside and bring in some grown-up to take care of the old lady. I would do the grocery shopping and eat sandwiches until I was twelve, at which point I would be grown up and I would get a job fixing televisions.

I marched into my room and changed into my best clothes, the little Alice-blue dress I wore to dinner on Sundays, and I brushed my hair and put on my socks with the blue pom-poms at the ankles, and found my shoes in the hall closet. But it had been three years since I'd last worn the shoes, and I could barely fit three toes in them. The old lady's shoes were so big I could fit both feet in either one.

I took off my socks—sometimes I'd seen kids going by barefoot outside, but never in just socks—and reached for the doorknob. I touched it.

I stopped.

I turned around again.

There was a stain forming under Auntie, piss and shit and death-juice, and as I looked at her, I had a firm sense that it wouldn't be *right* to bring people up to her apartment with her like this. I'd seen dead people on TV. They were propped up on pillows, in clean hospital nighties, with rouged cheeks. I didn't know how far I could get, but I thought I owed it to her to try.

I figured that it was better than going outside.

She was lighter in death, as though something had fled her. I could drag her into the bathroom and prop her on the edge of the tub. I needed to wash her before anyone else came up.

I cut away her dress with the sewing shears. She was wearing an elastic girdle beneath, and an enormous brassiere, and they were too tough—too tight—to cut through, so I struggled with their hooks, each one going *spung* as I unhooked it, revealing red skin beneath it, pinched and sore-looking.

When I got to her bra, I had a moment's pause. She was a modest person—I'd never even seen her legs without tan compression hose, but the smell was overwhelming, and I just held to that vision of her in a nightie and clean sheets and, you know, *went for it.*

Popped the hooks. Felt it give way as her breasts forced it off her back. Found myself staring at . . .

Two little wings.

The size of my thumbs. Bent and cramped. Broken. Folded.

There, over her shoulder blades. I touched them, and they were cold and hard as a turkey neck I'd once found in the trash after she'd made soup with it.

How did you get out?"

"With my wings?"

"Yeah. With your wings, and with no shoes, and with the old lady dead over the tub?"

She nuzzled his neck, then bit it, then kissed it, then bit it again. Brushed her fingers over his nipples.

"I don't know," she breathed, hot in his ear.

He arched his back. "You don't know?"

"I don't know. That's all I remember, for five years."

He arched his back again, and raked his fingertips over her thighs, making her shudder and jerk her wings back.

That's when he saw the corpse at the foot of the bed. It was George.

He went back to school the day after they buried Davey. He bathed all the brothers in the hot spring and got their teeth brushed, and he fed them a hot breakfast of boiled mushroom-and-jerky stew, and he gathered up their school-books from the forgotten corners of the winter cave and put them into school bags. Then he led them down the hillside on a spring day that smelled wonderful: loam and cold water coursing down the mountainside in rivulets, and new grass and new growth drying out in a hard white sun that seemed to spring directly overhead five minutes after it rose.

They held hands as they walked down the hill, and then Elliot-Franky-George broke away and ran down the hill to the roadside, skipping over the stones and holding their belly as they flew down the hillside. Alan laughed at the impatient jig they danced as they waited for he and Brad to catch up with them, and Brad put an arm around his shoulder and kissed him on the cheek in a moment of uncharacteristic demonstrativeness.

He marched right into Mr. Davenport's office with his brothers in tow.

"We're back," he said.

Mr. Davenport peered at them over the tops of his glasses. "You are, are you?"

"Mom took sick," he said. "Very sick. We had to go live with our aunt, and she was too far away for us to get to school."

"I see," Mr. Davenport said.

"I taught the littler ones as best as I could," Alan said. He liked Mr. Davenport, understood him. He had a job to do, and needed everything to be accounted for and filed away. It was okay for Alan and his brothers to miss months of school, provided that they had a good excuse when they came back. Alan could respect that. "And I read ahead in my textbooks. I think we'll be okay."

"I'm sure you will be," Mr. Davenport said. "How is your mother now?"

"She's better," he said. "But she was very sick. In the hospital."

"What was she sick with?"

Alan hadn't thought this far ahead. He knew how to lie to adults, but he was out of practice. "Cancer," he said, thinking of Marci's mother.

"Cancer?" Mr. Davenport said, staring hard at him.

"But she's better now," Alan said.

"I see. You boys, why don't you get to class? Alan, please wait here a moment."

His brothers filed out of the room. and Alan shuffled nervously, looking at the class ring on Mr. Davenport's hairy finger, remembering the time that Davey had kicked him. He'd never asked Alan where Davey was after that, and Alan had never offered, and it had been as though they shared a secret.

"Are you all right, Alan?" he asked, settling down behind his desk, taking off his glasses.

"Yes, sir," Alan said.

"You're getting enough to eat at home? There's a quiet place where you can work?"

"Yes," Alan said, squirming. "It's fine, now that Mom is home."

"I see," Mr. Davenport said. "Listen to me, son," he said, putting his hands flat on the desk. "The school district has some resources available: clothes, lunch vouchers, Big Brother programs. They're not anything you have to be ashamed of. It's not charity, it's just a little booster. A bit of help. The other children, their parents are well and they live in town and have lots of advantages that you and your brothers lack. This is just how we level the playing field. You're a very bright lad, and your brothers are growing up well, but it's no sin to accept a little help."

Alan suddenly felt like laughing. "We're not underprivileged," he said, thinking of the mountain, of the feeling of being encompassed by love of his father, of the flakes of soft, lustrous gold the golems produced by the handful. "We're very well off," he said, thinking of home, now free of Davey and his hateful, spiteful anger. "Thank you, though," he said, thinking of his life unfolding before him, free from the terror of Davey's bites and spying and rocks thrown from afar.

Mr. Davenport scowled and stared hard at him. Alan met his stare and smiled. "It's time for classes," he said. "Can I go?"

"Go," Mr. Davenport said. He shook his head. "But remember, you can always come here if you have anything you want to talk to me about."

"I'll remember," Alan said.

Six years later, Bradley was big and strong and he was the star goalie of all the hockey teams in town, in front of the puck before it arrived, making desperate, almost nonchalant saves that had them howling in the stands, stomping their feet, and sloshing their Tim Horton's coffee over the bleachers, to freeze into brown ice. In the summer, he was the star pitcher on every softball team, and the girls trailed after him like a long comet tail after the games when the other players led him away to a park to drink illicit beers.

Alan watched his games from afar, with his schoolbooks on

his lap, and Eric-Franz-Greg nearby playing trucks or reading or gnawing on a sucker.

By the ninth inning or the final period, the young ones would be too tired to play, and they'd come and lean heavily against Alan, like a bag of lead pressing on him, eyes half-open, and Alan would put an arm around them and feel at one with the universe.

It snowed on the afternoon of the season opener for the town softball league that year, fat white wet flakes that kissed your cheeks and melted away in an instant, so soft that you weren't sure they'd be there at all. Bradley caught up with Alan on their lunch break, at the cafeteria in the high school two blocks from the elementary school. He had his mitt with him and a huge grin.

"You planning on playing through the snow?" Alan said, as he set down his cheeseburger and stared out the window at the diffuse white radiance of the April noontime bouncing off the flakes.

"It'll be gone by tonight. Gonna be *warm*," Bradley said, and nodded at his jock buddies sitting at their long table, sucking down Cokes and staring at the girls. "Gonna be a good game. I know it."

Bradley knew. He knew when they were getting shorted at the assayers' when they brought in the golems' gold, just as he knew that showing up for lunch with a brown bag full of dried squirrel jerky and mushrooms and lemongrass was a surefire way to end up social roadkill in the high school hierarchy, as was dressing like someone who'd been caught in an explosion at the Salvation Army, and so he had money and he had burgers and he had a pair of narrow-leg jeans from the Gap and a Roots sweatshirt and a Stussy baseball hat and Reebok sneakers and he looked, basically, like a real person.

Alan couldn't say the same for himself, but he'd been making an effort since Bradley got to high school, if only to save his brother the embarrassment of being related to the biggest reject in the building—but Alan still managed to exude his don't-fuck-with-me aura enough that no one tried to cozy up to him and make friends with him and scrutinize his persona close in, which was just as he wanted it.

Bradley watched a girl walk past, a cute thing with red hair and freckles and a skinny rawboned look, and Alan remembered that she'd been sitting next to him in class for going on two years now and he'd never bothered to learn her name.

And he'd never bothered to notice that she was a dead ringer for Marci.

"I've always had a thing for redheads," Bradley said. "Because of you," he said. "You and your girlfriend. I mean, if she was good enough for *you*, well, she had to be the epitome of sophistication and sexiness. Back then, you were like a god to me, so she was like a goddess. I imprinted on her, like the baby ducks in Bio. It's amazing how much of who I am today I can trace back to those days. Who knew that it was all so important?"

He was a smart kid, introspective without being moody. Integrated. Always popping off these fine little observations in between his easy jokes. The girls adored him, the boys admired him, the teachers were grateful for him and the way he bridged the gap between scholarship and athleticism.

"I must have been a weird kid." he said. "All that quiet."

"You were a great kid," Alan said. "It was a lot of fun back then, mostly."

"Mostly," he said.

They both stared at the girl, who noticed them now, and blushed and looked confused. Bradley looked away, but Alvin held his gaze on her, and she whispered to a friend, who looked at him, and they both laughed, and then Alan looked away, too, sorry that he'd inadvertently interacted with his fellow students. He was supposed to watch, not participate.

"He was real," Bradley said, and Alan knew he meant Davey.

"Yeah," Alan said.

"I don't think the little ones really remember him—he's more like a bad dream to them. But he was real, wasn't he?"

"Yeah," Alan said. "But he's gone now."

"Was it right?"

"What do you mean?" Alan said. He felt a sear of anger arc along his spine.

"It's nothing," Billy said, mumbling into his tray.

"What do you mean, Brad?" Alan said. "What else should we have done? How can you have any doubts?"

"I don't," Brad said. "It's okay."

Alan looked down at his hands, which appeared to belong to someone else: white lumps of dough clenched into hard fists, knuckles white. He made himself unclench them. "No, it's *not* okay. Tell me about this. You remember what he was like. What he . . . did."

"I remember it," Bryan said. "Of course I remember it." He was staring through the table now, the look he got when he was contemplating a future the rest of them couldn't see. "But."

Alan waited. He was trembling inside. He'd done the right thing. He'd saved his family. He knew that. But for six years, he'd found himself turning in his memory to the little boy on the ground, holding the loops of intestine in through slippery red fingers. For six years, whenever he'd been somewhere quiet long enough that his own inner voices fell still, he'd remember the hair in his fist, the knife's thirsty draught as it drew forth the hot splash of blood from Davey's throat. He'd remembered the ragged fissure that opened down Clarence's length and the way that Davey fell down it, so light and desiccated he was almost weightless.

"If you remember it, then you know I did the right thing. I did the only thing."

"*We* did the only thing," Brian said, and covered Alan's hand with his.

Alan nodded and stared at his cheeseburger. "You'd better go catch up with your friends," he said.

"I love you, Adam," he said.

"I love you, too."

Billy crossed the room, nodding to the people who greeted him from every table, geeks and jocks and band and all the meaningless tribes of the high school universe. The cute red-head sprinkled a wiggle-finger wave at him, and he nodded at her, the tips of his ears going pink.

The snow stopped by three P.M., and the sun came out and melted it away, so that by the time the game started at five-thirty, its only remnant was the soggy ground around the bleachers with the new grass growing out of the ragged brown memory of last summer's lawn.

Alan took the little ones for dinner at the diner after school, letting them order double chocolate-chip pancakes. At thirteen, they'd settled into a fatness that made him think of a foam-rubber toy, the rolls and dimples at their wrists and elbows and knees like the seams on a doll.

"You're starting high school next year?" Alan said, as they were pouring syrup on their second helping. He was startled by this—how had they gotten so old so quickly?

"Uh-huh," Eli said. "I guess."

"So you're graduating from elementary school this spring?"

"Yeah." Eli grinned a chocolate smile at him. "It's no big deal. There's a party, though."

"Where?"

"At some kid's house."

"It's okay," Alan said. "We can celebrate at home. Don't let them get to you."

"We can't go?" Ed suddenly looked a little panicked.

"You're invited?" He blurted it out and then wished he hadn't.

"Of course we're invited," Fred said from inside Ed's throat. "There's going to be dancing."

"You can dance?" Alan asked.

"We can!" Ed said.

"We learned in gym," Greg said, with the softest, proudest voice, deep within them.

"Well," Alan said. He didn't know what to say. High school. Dancing. Invited to parties. No one had invited him to parties when he'd graduated from elementary school, and he'd been too busy with the little ones to go in any event. He felt a little jealous, but mostly proud. "Want a milkshake?" he asked, mentally totting up the cash in his pocket and thinking that he should probably send Brad to dicker with the assayer again soon.

"No, thank you," Ed said. "We're watching our weight."

Alan laughed, then saw they weren't joking and tried to turn it into a cough, but it was too late. Their shy, chocolate smile turned into a rubber-lipped pout.

The game started bang on time at six P.M., just as the sun was setting. The diamond lights flicked on with an audible click and made a spot of glare that cast out the twilight.

Benny was already on the mound, he'd been warming up with the catcher, tossing them in fast and exuberant and confident and controlled. He looked good on the mound. The ump called the start, and the batter stepped up to the plate, and Benny struck him out in three pitches, and the little ones went nuts, cheering their brother on along with the other fans in the bleachers, a crowd as big as any you'd ever see outside of school, thirty or forty people.

The second batter stepped up and Benny pitched a strike, another strike, and then a wild foul that nearly beaned the batter in the head. The catcher cocked his mask quizzically, and Benny kicked the dirt and windmilled his arm a little and shook his head.

He tossed another wild one, this one coming in so low that it practically rolled across the plate. His teammates were standing up in their box now, watching him carefully.

"Stop kidding around," Alan heard one of them say. "Just strike him out."

Benny smiled, spat, caught the ball, and shrugged his shoulders. He wound up, made ready to pitch, and then dropped the ball and fell to his knees, crying out as though he'd been struck.

Alan grabbed the little ones' hand and pushed onto the diamond before Benny's knees hit the ground. He caught up with

Benny as he keeled over sideways, bringing his knees up to his chest, eyes open and staring and empty.

Alan caught his head and cradled it on his lap and was dimly aware that a crowd had formed round them. He felt Barry's heart thundering in his chest, and his arms were stuck straight out to his sides, one hand in his pitcher's glove, the other clenched tightly around the ball.

"It's a seizure," someone said from the crowd. "Is he an epileptic? It's a seizure."

Someone tried to prize Alan's fingers from around Barry's head and he grunted and hissed at them, and they withdrew.

"Barry?" Alan said, looking into Barry's face. That faraway look in his eyes, a million miles away. Alan knew he'd seen it before, but not in years.

The eyes came back into focus, closed, opened. "Davey's back," Barry said.

Alan's skin went cold and he realized that he was squeezing Barry's head like a melon. He relaxed his grip and helped him to his feet, got Barry's arm around his shoulders, and helped him off the diamond.

"You okay?" one of the players asked as they walked past him, but Barry didn't answer. The little ones were walking beside them now, clutching Barry's hand, and they turned their back on the town as a family and walked toward the mountain.

George had come to visit him once before, not long after Alan'd moved to Toronto. He couldn't come without bringing down Elliot and Ferdinand, of course, but it was George's idea to visit, that was clear from the moment they rang the bell of the slightly grotty apartment he'd moved into in the Annex, near the students who were barely older than him but seemed to belong to a different species.

They were about sixteen by then, and fat as housecats, with the same sense of grace and inertia in their swinging bellies and wobbling chins.

Alan welcomed them in. Edward was wearing a pair of wool

trousers pulled nearly up to his nipples and short suspenders that were taut over his sweat-stained white shirt. He was grinning fleshily, his hair damp with sweat and curled with the humidity.

He opened his mouth, and George's voice emerged. "This place is . . ." He stood with his mouth open, while inside him, George thought. "*Incredible.* I'd never . . ." He closed his mouth, then opened it again. "*Dreamed.* What a . . ."

Now Ed spoke. "Jesus, figure out what you're going to say before you say it, willya? This is just plain—"

"Rude," came Fede's voice from his mouth.

"I'm sorry," came George's voice.

Ed was working on his suspenders, then unbuttoning his shirt and dropping his pants, so that he stood in grimy jockeys with his slick, tight, hairy belly before Alan. He tipped himself over, and then Alan was face-to-face with Freddy, who was wearing a T-shirt and a pair of boxer shorts with blue and white stripes. Freddy was scowling comically, and Alan hid a grin behind his hand.

Freddy tipped to one side and there was George, short and delicately formed and pale as a frozen french fry. He grabbed Freddy's hips like handles and scrambled out of him, springing into the air and coming down on the balls of his feet, holding his soccer-ball-sized gut over his Hulk Underoos.

"It's incredible," he hooted, dancing from one foot to the other. "It's brilliant! God! I'm never, ever going home!"

"Oh, yes?" Alan said, not bothering to hide his smile as Frederick and George separated and righted themselves. "And where will you sleep, then?"

"Here!" he said, running around the tiny apartment, opening the fridge and the stove and the toaster oven, flushing the toilet, turning on the shower faucets.

"Sorry," Alan called as he ran by. "No vacancies at the Hotel Anders!"

"Then I won't sleep!" he cried on his next pass. "I'll play all night and all day in the streets. I'll knock on every door on every street and introduce myself to every person and learn their stories and read their books and meet their kids and pet their dogs!"

"You're bonkers," Alan said, using the word that the lunch lady back at school had used when chastising them for tearing around the cafeteria.

"Easy for you to say," Greg said, skidding to a stop in front of him. "Easy for you—you're *here*, you got *away*, you don't have to deal with *Davey*—" He closed his mouth and his hand went to his lips.

Alan was still young and had a penchant for the dramatic, so he went around to the kitchen and pulled a bottle of vodka out of the freezer and banged it down on the counter, pouring out four shots. He tossed back his shot and returned the bottle to the freezer.

George followed suit and choked and turned purple, but managed to keep his expression neutral. Fred and Ed each took a sip, then set the drinks down with a sour face.

"How's home?" Alan said quietly, sliding back to sit on the minuscule counter surface in his kitchenette.

"It's okay," Ed mumbled, perching on the arm of the Goodwill sofa that came with the apartment. Without his brothers within him, he moved sprightly and lightly.

"It's fine," Fred said, looking out the window at the street below, craning his neck to see Bloor Street and the kids smoking out front of the Brunswick House.

"It's awful," Greg said, and pulled himself back up on the counter with them. "And I'm not going back."

The two older brothers looked balefully at him, then mutely appealed to Alan. This was new—since infancy, Earl-Frank-Geoff had acted with complete unity of will. When they were in the first grade, Alan had wondered if they were really just one person in three parts—that was how close their agreements were.

"Brian left last week," Greg said, and drummed his heels on the grease-streaked cabinet doors. "Didn't say a word to any of us, just left. He comes and goes like that all the time. Sometimes for weeks."

Craig was halfway around the world, he was in Toronto, and Brian was God-knew-where. That left just Ed-Fred-George and Davey, alone in the cave. No wonder they were here on his doorstep.

"What's he doing?"

"He just sits there and watches us, but that's enough. We're almost finished with school." He dropped his chin to his chest. "I thought we could finish here. Find a job. A place to live." He blushed furiously. "A girl."

Ed and Fred were staring at their laps. Alan tried to picture the logistics, but he couldn't, not really. There was no scenario in which he could see his brothers carrying on with—

"Don't be an idiot," Ed said. He sounded surprisingly bitter. He was usually a cheerful person—or at least a fat and smiling person. Alan realized for the first time that the two weren't equivalent.

George jutted his chin toward the sofa and his brothers. "They don't know what they want to do. They think that, 'cause it'll be hard to live here, we should hide out in the cave forever."

"Alan, talk to him," Fred said. "He's nuts."

"Look," George said. "You're gone. You're *all* gone. The king under the mountain now is Davey. If we stay there, we'll end up his slaves or his victims. Let him keep it. There's a whole world out here we can live in.

"I don't see any reason to let my handicap keep me down."

"It's not a handicap," Edward said patiently. "It's just how we are. We're different. We're not like the rest of them."

"Neither is Alan," George said. "And here he is, in the big city, living with them. Working. Meeting people. Out of the mountain."

"Alan's more like them than he is like us," Frederick said. "We're not like them. We can't pass for them."

Alan's jaw hung slack. Handicapped? Passing? Like them? Not like them? He'd never thought of his brothers this way. They were just his brothers. Just his family. They could communicate with the outside world. They were people. Different, but the same.

"You're just as good as they are," he said.

And that shut them up. They all regarded him, as if waiting for him to go on. He didn't know what to say. Were they, really? Was he? Was he better?

"What are we, Alan?" Edward said it, but Frederick and George mouthed the words after he'd said them.

"You're my brothers," he said. "You're . . ."

"I want to see the city," George said. "You two can come with me, or you can meet me when I come back."

"You *can't* go without us," Frederick said. "What if we get hungry?"

"You mean, what if I don't come back, right?"

"No," Frederick said, his face turning red.

"Well, how hungry are you going to get in a couple hours? You're just worried that I'm going to wander off and not come back. Fall into a hole. Meet a girl. Get drunk. And you won't ever be able to eat again." He was pacing again.

Ed and Fred looked imploringly at him.

"Why don't we all go together?" Alan said. "We'll go out and do something fun—how about ice-skating?"

"Skating?" George said. "Jesus, I didn't ride a bus for thirty hours just to go *skating*."

Edward said, "I want to sleep."

Frederick said, "I want dinner."

Perfect, Alan thought. "Perfect. We'll all be equally displeased with this, then. The skating's out in front of City Hall. There are lots of people there, and we can take the subway down. We'll have dinner afterward on Queen Street, then turn in early and get a good night's sleep. Tomorrow, we'll negotiate something else. Maybe Chinatown and the zoo."

They are stared at him.

"This is a limited-time offer," Alan said. "I had other-plans tonight, you know. Going once, going twice—"

"Let's go," George said. He went and took his brothers' hands. "Let's go, okay?"

They had a really good time.

George's body was propped up at the foot of the bed. He was white and wrinkled as a big toe in a bathtub, skin pulled tight in his face so that his hairline and eyebrows and cheeks seemed raised in surprise.

Alan smelled him now, a stink like a mouse dead between the gyprock in the walls, the worst smell imaginable. He felt Mimi breathing behind him, her chest heaving against his back. He reached out and pushed aside the wings, moving them by their translucent membranes, fingers brushing the tiny fingerlets at the wingtips, recognizing in their touch some evolutionary connection with his own hands.

George toppled over as Alan stepped off the bed, moving in the twilight of the light from under the bathroom door. Mimi came off the bed on the other side and hit the overhead light switch, turning the room as bright as an icebox, making Alan squint painfully. She closed the blinds quickly, then went to the door and shot the chain and the deadbolt closed.

Mimi looked down at him. "Ugly sumbitch, whoever he was."

"My brother," Alan said.

"Oh," she said. She went back around the bed and sat on the edge, facing the wall. "Sorry." She crossed her leg and jiggled her foot, making the springs squeak.

Alan wasn't listening. He knelt down and touched George's cheek. The skin was soft and spongy, porous and saturated. Cold. His fingertips came away with shed white flakes of translucent skin clinging to them.

"Davey?" Alan said. "Are you in here?"

Mimi's foot stilled. They both listened intently. There were nighttime sounds in the motel, distant muffled TVs and car engines and fucking, but no sound of papery skin thudding on ground-down carpet.

"He must have come up through the drain," Alan said. "In the bathroom." The broad pale moon of George's belly was abraded in long gray stripes.

He stood and, wiping his hand on his bare thigh, reached for the bathroom doorknob. The door swung open, revealing the sanitized-for-your-protection brightness of the bathroom, the water sloshed on the floor by Mimi earlier, the heaps of damp towels.

"How'd he find us here?"

Mimi, in her outsized blazer and track pants, touched him on his bare shoulder. He suddenly felt terribly naked. He backed out of the bathroom, shoving Mimi aside, and numbly pulled on his jeans and a shapeless sweatshirt that smelled of Mimi and had long curly hairs lurking in the fabric that stuck to his face like cobwebs. He jammed his feet into his sneakers.

He realized that he'd had to step over his brother's body six times to do this.

He looked at his brother again. He couldn't make sense of what he was seeing. The abraded belly. The rictus. His balls, shrunk to an albino walnut, his cock shriveled up to unrecognizability. The hair, curly, matted all over his body, patchily rubbed away.

He paced in the little run beside the bed, the only pacing room he had that didn't require stepping over George's body, back and forth, two paces, turn, two paces, turn.

"I'm going to cover him up," Mimi said.

"Good, fine," Alan said.

"Are you going to be okay?"

"Yes, fine," Alan said.

"Are you freaking out?"

Alan didn't say anything.

George looked an awful lot like Davey had, the day they killed him.

Mimi found a spare blanket in the closet, reeking of mothballs and scarred with a few curdled cigarette burns, and she spread it out on the floor and helped him lift Grant's body onto it and wind it tightly around him.

"What now?" she said.

He looked down at the wound sheet, the lump within it. He

sat down heavily on the bed. His chest was tight, and his breath came in short *hup*s.

She sat beside him and put an arm around his shoulder, tried to pull his head down to her bosom, but he stiffened his neck.

"I knew this was coming," he said. "When we killed Darren, I knew."

She stood and lit a cigarette. "This is your family business," she said, "why we're driving up north?"

He nodded, not trusting his voice, seeing the outlines of Grad's face, outlined in moth-eaten blanket.

"So," she said. "Let's get up north, then. Take an end."

The night was cold, and they staggered under the weight of the body wound in the blanket and laid him out in the trunk of the car, shifting luggage and picnic supplies to the back seat. At two A.M., the motel lights were out and the road was dark and silent but for the soughing of wind and the distant sounds of night animals.

"Are you okay to drive?" she said as she piled their clothes indiscriminately into the suitcases.

"What?" he said. The cool air on his face was waking him up a little, but he was still in a dream-universe. The air was spicy and outdoors and it reminded him powerfully of home and simpler times.

He looked at Mimi without really seeing her.

"Are you okay to drive?"

The keys were in his hands, the car smelling of the detailing-in-a-can mist that the rental agency sprayed on the upholstery to get rid of the discount traveler farts between rentals.

"I can drive," he said. Home, and the mountain, and the washing machine, and the nook where he'd slept for eighteen years, and the golems, and the cradle they'd hewn for him. Another ten or twelve hours' driving and they'd be at the foot of the trail where the grass grew to waist-high.

"Well, then, *drive*." She got in the car and slammed her door.

He climbed in, started the engine, and put the hertzmobile into reverse.

Two hours later, he realized that he was going to nod off. The thumps of the body sliding in the trunk and the suitcases rattling around in the back seat had lost their power to keep him awake.

The body's thumping had hardly had the power to begin with. Once the initial shock had passed, the body became an object only, a thing, a payload he had to deliver. Alan wondered if he was capable of feeling the loss.

"You were eleven then," he said. It was suddenly as though no time had passed since they'd sat on the bed and she'd told him about Auntie.

"Yes," she said. "It was as though no time had passed."

A shiver went up his back.

He was wide awake.

"No time had passed."

"Yes. I was living with a nice family in Oakville who were sending me to a nice girls' school where we wore blazers over our tunics, and I had a permanent note excusing me from gym classes. In a building full of four hundred girls going through puberty, one more fat shy girl who wouldn't take her top off was hardly noteworthy.

"The family, they were nice. WASPy. They called me Cheryl. With a Why. When I asked them where I'd been before, about Auntie, they looked sad and hurt and worried for me, and I learned to stop. They hugged me and touched my wings and never said anything—and never wiped their hands on their pants after touching them. They gave me a room with a computer and a CD player and a little TV of my own, and asked me to bring home my friends.

"I had none.

"But they found other girls who would come to my 'birthday' parties, on May 1, which was exactly two months after their son's birthday and two months before their daughter's birthday.

"I can't remember any of their names.

"But they made me birthday cards and they made me breakfast and dinner and they made me welcome. I could watch them grilling burgers in the back yard by the aboveground pool in the summer from my bedroom window. I could watch them building forts or freezing skating rinks in the winter. I could listen to them eating dinner together while I did my homework in my bedroom. There was a place for me at the dinner table, but I couldn't sit there, though I can't remember why."

"Wait a second," Alan said. "You don't remember?"

She made a sad noise in her throat. "I was told I was welcome, but I knew I wasn't. I know that sounds paranoid—crazy. Maybe I was just a teenager. There was a reason, though, I just don't know what it was. I knew then. They knew it, too—no one blamed me. They loved me, I guess."

"You stayed with them until you went to school?"

"Almost. Their daughter went to Waterloo, then the next year, their son went to McGill in Montreal, and then it was just me and them. I had two more years of high school, but it just got unbearable. With their children gone, they tried to take an interest in me. Tried to make me eat with them. Take me out to meet their friends. Every day felt worse, more wrong. One night, I went to a late movie by myself downtown and then got to walking around near the clubs and looking at the club kids and feeling this terrible feeling of loneliness, and when I was finally ready to go home, the last train had already gone. I just spent the night out, wandering around, sitting in a back booth at Sneaky Dee's and drinking Cokes, watching the sun come up from the top of Christie Pitts overlooking the baseball diamond. I was a seventeen-year-old girl from the suburbs wearing a big coat and staring at her shoelaces, but no one bugged me.

"When I came home the next morning, no one seemed particularly bothered that I'd been away all night. If anything, the parental people might have been a little distraught that I came home. 'I think I'll get my own place,' I said. They agreed, and agreed to put the lease in their name to make things easier. I got a crummy little basement in what the landlord called Cabbagetown but what was really Regent Park, and I switched out to a huge, anonymous high school to finish school. Worked in a restaurant at nights and on weekends to pay the bills."

The night highway rushed past them, quiet. She lit a cigarette and rolled down her window, letting in the white-noise crash of the wind and the smell of the smoke mixed with the pine-and-summer reek of the roadside.

"Give me one of those," Alan said.

She lit another and put it between his lips, damp with her saliva. His skin came up in goosepimples.

"Who knows about your wings?" he said.

"Krishna knows," she said. "And you." She looked out into the night. "The family in Oakville. If I could remember where they lived, I'd look them up and ask them about it. Can't. Can't remember their names or their faces. I remember the pool, though, and the barbecue."

"No one else knows?"

"There was no one else before Krishna. No one that I remember, anyway."

"I have a brother," he said, then swallowed hard. "I have a brother named Brad. He can see the future."

"Yeah?"

"Yeah." He pawed around for an ashtray and discovered that it had been removed, along with the lighter, from the rental car's dashboard. Cursing, he pinched off the coal of the cigarette and flicked it to the roadside, hoping that it would burn out quickly, then he tossed the butt over his shoulder at the back seat. As he did, the body in the trunk rolled while he navigated a curve in the road and he braked hard, getting the car stopped in time for him to open the door and pitch a rush of vomit onto the roadway.

"You okay to drive?"

"Yeah. I am." He sat up and put the car into gear and inched to the shoulder, then put it in park and set his blinkers. The car smelled of sour food and sharp cigarettes and God, it smelled of the body in the trunk.

"It's not easy to be precognizant," Alan said, and pulled back onto the road, signaling even though there were no tail-lights or headlights for as far as the eye could see.

"I believe it," she said.

"He stopped telling us things after a while. It just got him into trouble. I'd be studying for an exam and he'd look at me and shake his head, slowly, sadly. Then I'd flunk out, and I'd be convinced that it was him psyching me out. Or he'd get picked for kickball and he'd say, 'What's the point, this team's gonna lose,' and wander off, and they'd lose, and everyone would hate him. He couldn't tell the difference between what he knew and what everyone else knew. Didn't know the difference between the past and the future, sometimes. So he stopped telling us, and when we figured out how to read it in his eyes, he stopped looking at us.

"Then something really— Something terrible . . . Someone I cared about died. And he didn't say anything about it. I could have—stopped—it. Prevented it. I could have saved her life, but he wouldn't talk."

He drove.

"For real, he could see the future?" she said softly. Her voice had more emotion than he'd ever heard in it and she rolled down the window and lit another cigarette, pluming smoke into the roar of the wind.

"Yeah," Alan said. "*A* future or *the* future, I never figured it out. A little of both, I suppose."

"He stopped talking, huh?"

"Yeah," Alan said.

"I know what that's like," Mimi said. "I hadn't spoken more than three words in the six months before I met Krishna. I worked at a direct-mail house, proofreading the mailing labels. No one wanted to say anything to me, and I just wanted to disappear. It was soothing, in a way, reading all those names. I'd dropped out of school after Christmas break, just didn't bother going back again, never paid my tuition. I threw away my houseplants and flushed my fish down the toilet so that there wouldn't be any living thing that depended on me."

She worked her hand between his thigh and the seat.

"Krishna sat next to me on the subway. I was leaning forward because my wings were long—the longest they've ever been—and wearing a big parka over them. He leaned forward to match me and tapped me on the shoulder.

"I turned to look at him and he said, 'I get off at the next stop. Will you get off with me and have a cup of coffee? I've been riding next to you on the subway for a month, and I want to find out what you're like.'

"I wouldn't have done it, except before I knew what I was doing, I'd already said, 'I beg your pardon?' because I wasn't sure I'd heard him right. And once I'd said that, once I'd spoken, I couldn't bear the thought of not speaking again."

They blew through Kapuskasing at ten A.M., on a gray morning that dawned with drizzle and bad-tempered clouds low overhead. The little main drag—which Alan remembered as a bustling center of commerce where he'd waited out half a day to change buses—was deserted, the only evidence of habitation the occasional car pulling through a donut store drive-through lane.

"Jesus, who divorced me this time?" Mimi said, ungumming her eyes and stuffing a fresh cigarette into her mouth.

"*Fear and Loathing* again, right?"

"It's *the* road-trip novel," she said.

"What about *On the Road?*"

"Oh, *that,*" she said. "Pfft. Kerouac was a Martian on crank. Dope fiend prose isn't fit for human consumption."

"Thompson isn't a dope fiend?"

"No. That was just a put-on. He wrote *about* drugs, not *on* drugs."

"Have you *read* Kerouac?"

"I couldn't get into it," she said.

He pulled sharply off the road and into a parking lot.

"What's this?" she said.

"The library," he said. "Come on."

It smelled just as it had when he was seventeen, standing among the aisles of the biggest collection of books he'd ever seen. Sweet, dusty.

"Here," he said, crossing to the fiction section. The fiction section at the library in town had fit into three spinner racks. Here, it occupied its own corner of overstuffed bookcases. "Here," he said, running his finger down the plastic Brodart wraps on the spines of the books, the faded Dewey labels.

H, I, J, K . . . There it was, the edition he'd remembered from all those years ago. *On the Road.*

"Come on," he said. "We've got it."

"You can't check that out," she said.

He pulled out his wallet as they drew up closer to the check-out counter. He slid out the plastic ID holder, flipping past the health card and the driver's license—not a very good likeness of his face or his name on either—and then produced a library card so tattered that it looked like a pirate's map on parchment. He slid it delicately out of the plastic sleeve, unbending the frayed corner, smoothing the feltlike surface of the card, the furry type.

He slid the card and the book across the counter. Mimi and the librarian—a boy of possibly Mimi's age, who wore a mesh-back cap just like his patrons, but at a certain angle that suggested urbane irony—goggled at it, as though Alan had slapped down a museum piece.

The boy picked it up with such roughness that Alan flinched on behalf of his card.

"This isn't—" the boy began.

"It's a library card," Alan said. "They used to let me use it here."

The boy set it down on the counter again.

Mimi peered at it. "There's no name on that card," she said.

"Never needed one," he said.

He'd gotten the card from the sour-faced librarian back home, tricked her out of it by dragging along Bradley and encouraging him to waddle off into the shelves and start pulling down books. She'd rolled it into her typewriter and then they'd both gone chasing after Brad, then she'd asked him again for his name and they'd gone chasing after Brad, then for his address, and then Brad again. Eventually, he was able to simply snitch it out of the platen of the humming Selectric and walk out. No one ever looked closely at it again—not even the thoroughly professional staffers at the Kapuskasing branch who'd let him take out a stack of books to read in the bus station overnight while he waited for the morning bus to Toronto.

He picked up the card again, then set it down. It was the first piece of identification he'd ever owned, and in some ways, the most important.

"I have to give you a new card," the mesh-back kid said. "With a bar code. We don't take that card anymore." He picked it up and made to tear it in half.

"NO!" Alan roared, and lunged over the counter to seize the kid's wrists.

The kid startled back and reflexively tore at the card, but Alan's iron grip on his wrists kept him from completing the motion. The kid dropped the card and it fluttered to the carpet behind the counter.

"Give it to me," Alan said. The boy's eyes, wide with shock, began to screw shut with pain. Alan let go his wrists, and the kid chafed them, backing away another step.

His shout had drawn older librarians from receiving areas and offices behind the counter, women with the look of persons accustomed to terminating children's mischief and ejecting rowdy drunks with equal aplomb. One of them was talking into a phone, and two more were moving cautiously toward them, sizing them up.

"We should go," Mimi said.

"I need my library card," he said, and was as surprised as anyone at the pout in his voice, a sound that was about six years old, stubborn, and wounded.

Mimi looked hard at him, then at the librarians converging on them, then at the mesh-back kid, who had backed all the way up to a work surface several paces back of him. She planted her palms on the counter and swung one foot up onto it, vaulting herself over. Alan saw the back of her man's jacket bulge out behind her as her wings tried to spread when she took to the air.

She snatched up the card, then planted her hands again and leapt into the air. The toe of her trailing foot caught the edge of the counter and she began to tumble, headed for a face-plant into the grayed-out industrial carpet. Alan had the presence of mind to catch her, her tit crashing into his head, and gentle her to the floor.

"We're going," Mimi said. "Now."

Alan hardly knew where he was anymore. The card was in Mimi's hand, though, and he reached for it, making a keening noise deep in his throat.

"Here," she said, handing it to him. When he touched the felted card stock, he snapped back to himself. "Sorry," he said lamely to the mesh-back kid.

Mimi yanked his arm and they jumped into the car and he fumbled the key into the ignition, fumbled the car to life. His head felt like a balloon on the end of a taut string, floating some yards above his body.

He gunned the engine and the body rolled in the trunk. He'd forgotten about it for a while in the library, and now he remembered it again. Maybe he felt something then, a twitchy twinge of grief, but he swallowed hard and it went away. The clunk-clunk of the wheels going over the curb as he missed the curb-cut back out onto the road, Mimi sucking breath in a hiss as he narrowly avoided getting T-boned by a rusted-out pickup truck, and then the hum of the road under his wheels.

"Alan?" Mimi said.

"It was my first piece of identification," he said. "It made me a person who could get a book out of the library."

They drove on, heading for the city limits at a few klicks over the speed limit. Fast, lots of green lights.

"What did I just say?" Alan said.

"You said it was your first piece of ID," Mimi said. She was twitching worriedly in the passenger seat. Alan realized that she was air-driving, steering and braking an invisible set of controls as he veered around the traffic. "You said it made you a person—"

"That's right," Alan said. "It did."

He never understood how he came to be enrolled in kindergarten. Even in those late days, there were still any number of nearby farm folk whose literacy was so fragile that they could be intimidated out of it by a sheaf of school enrollment forms. Maybe that was it—the five-year-old Alan turning up at the school with his oddly accented English and his Martian wardrobe of pieces rescued from roadside ditches and snitched off of clotheslines, and who was going to send him home on the first day of school? Surely the paperwork would get sorted out by the time the first permission-slip field trip rolled around, or possibly by the time vaccination forms were due. And then it just fell by the wayside.

Alan got the rest of his brothers enrolled, taking their forms home and forging indecipherable scrawls that satisfied the office ladies. His own enrollment never came up in any serious way. Permission slips were easy, inoculations could be had at the walk-in clinic once a year at the firehouse.

Until he was eight, being undocumented was no big deal. None of his classmates carried ID. But his classmates *did* have Big Wheels, catcher's mitts, Batmobiles, action figures, Fonzie lunchboxes, and Kodiak boots. They had parents who came to parents' night and sent trays of cupcakes to class on birthdays— Alan's birthday came during the summer, by necessity, so that this wouldn't be an issue. So did his brothers', when their time came to enroll.

At eight, he ducked show-and-tell religiously and skillfully, but one day he got caught out, empty-handed and with all the eyes in the room boring into him as he fumfuhed at the front of the classroom, and the teacher thought he was being kind by pointing out that his hand-stitched spring moccasins—a tithe of the golems—were fit subject for a brief exposition.

"Did your mom buy you any real shoes?" It was asked without

malice or calculation, but Alan's flustered, red-faced, hot stammer chummed the waters and the class sharks were on him fast and hard. Previously invisible, he was now the subject of relentless scrutiny. Previously an observer of the playground, he was now a nexus of it, a place where attention focused, hunting out the out-of-place accent, the strange lunch, the odd looks and gaps in knowledge of the world. He thought he'd figured out how to fit in, that he'd observed people to the point that he could be one, but he was so wrong.

They watched him until Easter break, when school let out and they disappeared back into the unknowable depths of their neat houses, and when they saw him on the street headed for a shop or moping on a bench, they cocked their heads quizzically at him, as if to say, *Do I know you from somewhere?* or, if he was feeling generous, *I wonder where you live?* The latter was scarier than the former.

For his part, he was heartsick that he turned out not to be half so clever as he'd fancied himself. There wasn't much money around the mountain that season—the flakes he'd brought down to the assayer had been converted into cash for new shoes for the younger kids and chocolate bars that he'd brought to fill Bradley's little round belly.

He missed the school library achingly during that week, and it was that lack that drove him to the town library. He'd walked past the squat brown brick building hundreds of times, but had never crossed its threshold. He had a sense that he wasn't welcome there, that it was not intended for his consumption. He slunk in like a stray dog, hid himself in the back shelves, and read books at random while he observed the other patrons coming and going.

It took three days of this for him to arrive at his strategy for getting his own library card, and the plan worked flawlessly. Bradley pulled the books off the back shelves for the final time, the librarian turned in exasperation for the final time, and he was off and out with the card in his hand before the librarian had turned back again.

Credentialed.

He'd read the word in a book of war stories.

He liked the sound of it.

W hat did Krishna do?"

"What do you mean?" She was looking at him guardedly now, but his madness seemed to have passed.

"I mean," he said, reaching over and taking her hand, "what did Krishna do when you went out for coffee with him?"

"Oh," she said. She was quiet while they drove a narrow road over a steep hill. "He made me laugh."

"He doesn't seem that funny," Alan said.

"We went out to this coffee shop in Little Italy, and he sat me down at a tiny green metal table, even though it was still cold as hell, and he brought out tiny cups of espresso and a little wax-paper bag of biscotti. Then he watched the people and made little remarks about them. 'She's a little old to be breeding,' or 'Oh, is that how they're wearing their eyebrow in the old country?' or 'Looks like he beats his wife with his slipper for not fixing his Kraft Dinner right.' And when he said it, I *knew* it wasn't just a mean little remark, I *knew* it was true. Somehow, he could look at these people and know what they were self-conscious about, what their fears were, what their little secrets were. And he made me laugh, even though it didn't take long before I guessed that that meant that he might know my secret.

"So we drank our coffee," she said, and then stopped when the body thudded in the trunk again when they caught some air at the top of a hill. "We drank it and he reached across the table and tickled my open palm with his fingertips and he said, 'Why did you come out with me?'

"And I mumbled and blushed and said something like, 'You look like a nice guy, it's just coffee, shit, don't make a big deal out of it,' and he looked like I'd just canceled Christmas and said, 'Oh, well, too bad. I was hoping it was a big deal, that it was because you thought I'd be a good guy to really hang out with a *lot*, if you know what I mean.' He tickled my palm again. I was a blushing virgin, literally. Though I'd had a couple boys maybe possibly flirt with me in school, I'd never returned the signals, never could.

"I told him I didn't think I could be romantically involved with him, and he flattened out his palm so that my hand was pinned to the table under it and he said, 'If it's your deformity, don't let that bother you. I thought I could fix that for you.' I almost pretended I didn't know what he meant, but I couldn't really, I knew he knew I knew. I said, 'How?' as in, *How did you know?* and *How can you fix it?* but it just came out in a little squeak, and he grinned like Christmas was back on and said, 'Does it really matter?'

"I told him it didn't, and then we went back to his place in Kensington Market and he kissed me in the living room, then he took me upstairs to the bathroom and took off my shirt and he—"

"He cut you," Alan said.

"He fixed me," she said.

Alan reached out and petted her wings through her jacket. "Were you broken?"

"Of *course* I was," she snapped, pulling back. "I couldn't *talk* to people. I couldn't *do* anything. I wasn't a person," she said.

"Right," Alan said. "I'm following you."

She looked glumly at the road unraveling before them, gray and hissing with rain. "Is it much farther?" she said.

"An hour or so, if I remember right," he said.

"I know how stupid that sounds," she said. "I couldn't figure out if he was some kind of pervert who liked to cut or if he was some kind of pervert who liked girls like me or if I was lucky or in trouble. But he cut them, and he gave me a towel to bite on the first time, but I never needed it after that. He'd do it quick, and he kept the knife sharp, and I was able to be a person again—to wear cute clothes and go where I wanted. It was like my life had started over again."

The hills loomed over the horizon now, low and rolling up toward the mountains. One of them was his. He sucked in a breath and the car wavered on the slick road. He pumped the brakes and coasted them to a stop on the shoulder.

"Is that it?" she said.

"That's it," he said. He pointed. His father was green and craggy and smaller than he remembered. The body rolled in the trunk. "I feel . . ." he said. "We're taking him home, at least. And my father will know what to do."

"No boy has ever taken me home to meet his folks," she said.

Alan remembered the little fist in the dirt. "You can wait in the car if you want," he said.

Krishna came home,

(she said, as they sat in the parked car at a wide spot in the highway, looking at the mountains on the horizon)

Krishna came home,

(she said, after he'd pulled off the road abruptly, put the car into park, and stared emptily at the mountains ahead of them)

Krishna came home,

(she said, lighting a cigarette and rolling down the window and letting the shush of the passing cars come fill the car, and she didn't look at him, because the expression on his face was too terrible to behold)

and he came through the door with two bags of groceries and a bottle of wine under one arm and two bags from a rave-wear shop on Queen Street that I'd walked past a hundred times but never gone into.

He'd left me in his apartment that morning, with his television and his books and his guitar, told me to make myself at home, told me to call in sick to work, told me to take a day for myself. I felt . . . *glorious*. Gloried *in*. He'd been so attentive.

He'd touched me. No one had touched me in so long. No one had *ever* touched me that way. He'd touched me with . . . *reverence*. He'd gotten this expression on his face like, like he was in *church* or something. He'd kept breathing something too low for me to hear and when he put his lips right to my ear, I heard what he'd been saying all along, "Oh God, oh God, my God, oh

God," and I'd felt a warmness like slow honey start in my toes and rise through me like sap to the roots of my hair, so that I felt like I was saturated with something hot and sweet and delicious.

He came home that night with the makings of a huge dinner with boiled soft-shell crabs, and a bottle of completely decent Chilean red, and three dresses for me that I could never, ever wear. I tried to keep the disappointment off my face as he pulled them out of the bag, because I *knew* they'd never go on over my wings, and they were *so* beautiful.

"This one will look really good on you," he said, holding up a Heidi dress with a scoop neck that was cut low across the back, and I felt a hot tear in the corner of my eye. I'd never wear that dress in front of anyone but him. I couldn't, my wings would stick out a mile.

I knew what it meant to be different: It meant living in the second floor with the old Russian Auntie, away from the crowds and their eyes. I knew then what I was getting in for—the rest of my life spent hidden away from the world, with only this man to see and speak to.

I'd been out in the world for only a few years, and I had barely touched it, moving in silence and stealth, watching and not being seen, but oh, I had *loved it,* I realized. I'd thought I'd hated it, but I'd loved it. Loved the people and their dialogue and their clothes and their mysterious errands and the shops full of goods and every shopper hunting for something for someone, every one of them part of a story that I would never be part of, but I could be *next to* the stories and that was enough.

I was going to live in an attic again.

I started to cry.

He came to me. He put his arms around me. He nuzzled my throat and licked up the tears as they slid past my chin. "Shhh," he said. "Shhh."

He took off my jacket and my sweater, peeled down my jeans and my panties, and ran his fingertips over me, stroking me until I quieted.

He touched me reverently still, his breath hot on my skin. No one had ever touched me like that. He said, "I can fix you."

I said, "No one can fix me."

He said, "I can, but you'll have to be brave."

I nodded slowly. I could do brave. He led me by the hand into the bathroom and he took a towel down off of the hook on the back of the door and folded it into a long strip. He handed it to me. "Bite down on this," he said, and helped me stand in the tub and face into the corner, to count the grid of tiles and the greenish mildew in the grout.

"Hold still and bite down," he said, and I heard the door close behind me. Reverent fingertips on my wing, unfolding it, holding it away from my body.

"Be brave," he said. And then he cut off my wing.

It hurt so much, I pitched forward involuntarily and cracked my head against the tile. It hurt so much I bit through two thicknesses of towel. It hurt so much my legs went to mush and I began to sit down quickly, like I was fainting.

He caught me, under my armpits, and held me up, and I felt something icy pressed to where my wing had been—I closed my eyes, but I heard the leathery thump as my wing hit the tile floor, a wet sound—and gauzy fabric was wrapped around my chest, holding the icy towel in place over the wound, once twice thrice, between my tits.

"Hold still," he said. And he cut off the other one.

I screamed this time, because he brushed the wound he'd left the first time, but I managed to stay upright and to not crack my head on anything. I felt myself crying but couldn't hear it, I couldn't hear anything, nothing except a high sound in my ears like a dog whistle.

He kissed my cheek after he'd wound a second bandage, holding a second cold compress over my second wound. "You're a very brave girl," he said. "Come on."

He led me into the living room, where he pulled the cushions off his sofa and opened it up to reveal a hide-a-bed. He helped me lie down on my belly, and arranged pillows around me and under my head, so that I was facing the TV.

"I got you movies," he said, and held up a stack of DVD

rental boxes from Martian Signal. "We got *Pretty in Pink, The Blues Brothers, The Princess Bride,* a Robin Williams stand-up tape, and a really funny-looking porno called *Edward Penishands.*"

I had to smile in spite of myself, in spite of the pain. He stepped into his kitchenette and came back with a box of chocolates. "Truffles," he said. "So you can laze on the sofa, eating bonbons."

I smiled more widely then.

"Such a beautiful smile," he said. "Want a cup of coffee?"

"No," I said, choking it out past my raw-from-screaming throat.

"All right," he said. "Which video do you want to watch?"

"Princess Bride," I said. I hadn't heard of any of them, but I didn't want to admit it.

"You don't want to start with *Edward Penishands?"*

Alan stood out front of the video shop for a while, watching Natalie wait on her customers. She was friendly without being perky, and it was clear that the mostly male clientele had a bit of a crush on her, as did her mooning, cow-eyed coworker who was too distracted to efficiently shelve the videos he pulled from the box before him. Alan smiled. Hiring cute girls for your shop was tricky business. If they had brains, they'd sell the hell out of your stock and be entertaining as hell; but a lot of pretty girls (and boys!) had gotten a free ride in life and got affronted when you asked them to do any real work.

Natalie was clearly efficient, and Alan knew that she wasn't afraid of hard work, but it was good to see her doing her thing, quickly and efficiently taking people's money, answering their questions, handing them receipts, counting out change. . . . He would have loved to have had someone like her working for him in one of his shops.

Once the little rush at the counter was cleared, he eased himself into the shop. Natalie *was* working for him, of course, in the impromptu assembly line in Kurt's storefront. She'd proven herself to be as efficient at assembling and testing the access points as she was at running the till.

"Alan!" she said, smiling broadly. Her co-worker turned and scowled jealously at him. "I'm going on break, okay?" she said to him, ignoring his sour puss.

"What, now?" he said petulantly.

"No, I thought I'd wait until we got busy again," she said, not unkindly, and smiled at him. "I'll be back in ten," she said.

She came around the counter with her cigs in one hand and her lighter in the other. "Coffee?" she said.

"Absolutely," he said, and led her up the street.

"You liking the job?" he said.

"It's better now," she said. "I've been bringing home two or three movies every night and watching them, just to get to know the stock, and I put on different things in the store, the kind of thing I'd never have watched before. Old horror movies, tentacle porn, crappy kung-fu epics. So now they all bow to me."

"That's great," Alan said. "And Kurt tells me you've been doing amazing work with him, too."

"Oh, that's just fun," she said. "I went along on a couple of dumpster runs with the gang. I found the most amazing cosmetics baskets at the Shiseido dumpster. Never would have thought that I'd go in for that girly stuff, but when you get it for free out of the trash, it feels pretty macha. Smell," she said, tilting her head and stretching her neck.

He sniffed cautiously. "Very macha," he said. He realized that the other patrons in the shop were eyeballing him, a middle-aged man, with his face buried in this alterna-girl's throat.

He remembered suddenly that he still hadn't put in a call to get her a job somewhere else, and was smitten with guilt. "Hey," he said. "Damn. I was supposed to call Tropicál and see about getting you a job. I'll do it right away." He pulled a little steno pad out of his pocket and started jotting down a note to himself.

She put her hand out. "Oh, that's okay," she said. "I really like this job. I've been looking up all my old high school friends: You were right, everyone I ever knew has an account with Martian Signal. God, you should *see* the movies they rent."

"You keep that on file, huh?"

"Sure, everything. It's creepy."

"Do you need that much info?"

"Well, we need to know who took a tape out last if someone returns it and says that it's broken or recorded over or
whatever—"

"So you need, what, the last couple months' worth of rentals?"

"Something like that. Maybe longer for the weirder tapes,
they only get checked out once a year or so—"

"So maybe you keep the last two names associated with each
tape?"

"That'd work."

"You should do that."

She snorted and drank her coffee. "I don't have any say in it."

"Tell your boss," he said. "It's how good ideas happen in
business—people working at the cash register figure stuff out,
and they tell their bosses."

"So I should just tell my boss that I think we should change
our whole rental system because it's creepy?"

"Damned right. Tell him it's creepy. You're keeping information you don't need to keep, and paying to store it. You're
keeping information that cops or snoops or other people could
take advantage of. And you're keeping information that your
customers almost certainly assume you're not keeping. All of
those are good reasons *not* to keep that information. Trust me
on this one. Bosses love to hear suggestions from people who
work for them. It shows that you're engaged, paying attention to
their business."

"God, now I feel guilty for snooping."

"Well, maybe you don't mention to your boss that you've
been spending a lot of time looking through rental histories."

She laughed. God, he liked working with young people. "So,
why I'm here," he said.

"Yes?"

"I want to put an access point in the second-floor window and
around back of the shop. Your boss owns the building, right?"

"Yeah, but I really don't think I can explain all this stuff to him—"

"I don't need you to—I just need you to introduce me to him. I'll do all the explaining."

She blushed a little. "I don't know, Abe. . . ." She trailed off.

"Is that a problem?"

"No. Yes. I don't know." She looked distressed.

Suddenly he was at sea. He'd felt like he was in charge of this interaction, like he understood what was going on. He'd carefully rehearsed what he was going to say and what Natalie was likely to say, and now she was, what, afraid to introduce him to her boss? Because why? Because the boss was an ogre? Then she would have pushed back harder when he told her to talk to him about the rental records. Because she was shy? Natalie wasn't shy. Because—

"I'll do it," she said. "Sorry. I was being stupid. It's just—you come on a little strong sometimes. My boss, I get the feeling that he doesn't like it when people come on strong with him."

Ah, he thought. She was nervous because he was so god-damned weird. Well, there you had it. He couldn't even get sad about it. Story of his life, really.

"Thanks for the tip," he said. "What if I assure you that I'll come on easy?"

She blushed. It had really been awkward for her, then. He felt bad. "Okay," she said. "Sure. Sorry, man—"

He held up a hand. "It's nothing."

He followed her back to the store and he bought a tin robot made out of a Pepsi can by some artisan in Vietnam who'd endowed it with huge tin testicles. It made him laugh. When he got home, he scanned and filed the receipt, took a picture, and entered it into The Inventory, and by the time he was done, he was feeling much better.

They got into Kurt's car at five P.M., just as the sun was beginning to set. The sun hung on the horizon, *right* at eye level, for an eternity, slicing up their eyeballs and into their brains.

"Summer's coming on," Alan said.

"And we've barely got the Market covered," Kurt said. "At this rate, it'll take ten years to cover the whole city."

Alan shrugged. "It's the journey, dude, not the destination— the act of organizing all these people, of putting up the APs, of advancing the art. It's all worthwhile in and of itself."

Kurt shook his head. "You want to eat Vietnamese?"

"Sure," Alan said.

"I know a place," he said, and nudged the car through traffic and on to the Don Valley Parkway.

"Where the hell are we *going*?" Alan said, once they'd left the city limits and entered the curved, identical cookie-cutter streets of the industrial suburbs in the north end.

"Place I know," Kurt said. "It really cheap and really good. All the Peel Region cops eat there." He snapped his fingers. "Oh, yeah, I was going to tell you about the cop," he said.

"You were," Alan said.

"So, one night I'd been diving there." Kurt pointed to an anonymous low-slung, sprawling brown building. "They print hockey cards, baseball cards, monster cards—you name it."

He sipped at his donut-store coffee and then rolled down the window and spat it out. "Shit, that was last night's coffee," he said. "So, one night I was diving there, and I found, I dunno, fifty, a hundred boxes of hockey cards. Slightly dented at the corners, in the trash. I mean, hockey cards are just *paper*, right? The only thing that makes them valuable is the companies infusing them with marketing juju and glossy pictures of mullethead, no-tooth jocks."

"Tell me how you really feel," Alan said.

"Sorry," Kurt said. "The hockey players in junior high were real jerks. I'm mentally scarred.

"So I'm driving away and the law pulls me over. The local cops, they know me, mostly, 'cause I phone in B&Es when I spot them, but these guys had never met me before. So they get me out of the car and I explain what I was doing, and I quote the part of the Trespass to Property Act that says that I'm allowed to do what I'm doing, and then I open the trunk and I show him, and he busts a *nut*: 'You mean you found these in the *garbage?* My kid spends a fortune on these things! 'In the *garbage?*' He keeps saying, 'In the garbage?' and his partner leads him away and I put it behind me.

"But then a couple nights later, I go back and there's someone in the dumpster, up to his nipples in hockey cards."

"The cop," Alan said.

"The cop," Kurt said. "Right."

"That's the story about the cop in the dumpster, huh?" Alan said.

"That's the story. The moral is: We're all only a c-hair away from jumping in the dumpster and getting down in it."

"C-hair? I thought you were trying not to be sexist?"

"*C* stands for *cock,* okay?"

Alan grinned. He and Kurt hadn't had an evening chatting together in some time. When Kurt suggested that they go for a ride, Alan had been reluctant: too much on his mind those days, too much *Danny* on his mind. But this was just what he needed. What they both needed.

"Okay," Alan said. "We going to eat?"

"We're going to eat," Kurt said. "The Vietnamese place is just up ahead. I once heard a guy there trying to speak Thai to the waiters. It was amazing—it was like he was a tourist even at home, an ugly fucked-up tourist. People suck."

"Do they?" Alan said. "I quite like them. You know, there's pretty good Vietnamese in Chinatown."

"This is good Vietnamese."

"Better than Chinatown?"

"Better situated," Kurt said. "If you're going dumpster diving afterward. I'm gonna take your cherry, buddy." He clapped a hand on Alan's shoulder. Real people didn't touch Alan much. He didn't know if he liked it.

"God," Alan said. "This is so sudden." But he was happy about it. He'd tried to picture what Kurt actually *did* any number of times, but he was never very successful. Now he was going to actually go out and jump in and out of the garbage. He wondered if he was dressed for it, picturing bags of stinky kitchen waste, and decided that he was willing to sacrifice his jeans and the old Gap shirt he'd bought one day after the shirt he'd worn to the store—the wind-up toy store?—got soaked in a cloudburst.

The Vietnamese food was really good, and the family who ran the restaurant greeted Kurt like an old friend. The place was crawling with cops, a new two or three every couple minutes, stopping by to grab a salad roll or a sandwich or a go-cup of pho. "Cops always know where to eat fast and cheap and good," Kurt mumbled around a mouthful of pork chop and fried rice. "That's how I found this place, all the cop cars in the parking lot."

Alan slurped up the last of his pho and chased down the remaining hunks of rare beef with his chopsticks and dipped them in chili sauce before popping them in his mouth. "Where are we going?" he asked.

Kurt jerked his head in the direction of the great outdoors. "Wherever the fates take us. I just drive until I get an itch and then I pull into a parking lot and hit the dumpsters. There's enough dumpsters out this way, I could spend fifty or sixty hours going through them all, so I've got to be selective. I know how each company's trash has been running—lots of good stuff or mostly crap—lately, and I trust my intuition to take me to the right places. I'd love to go to the Sega or Nintendo dumpsters, but they're like Stalag Thirteen—razor wire and motion sensors and armed guards. They're the only companies that take secrecy seriously." Suddenly he changed lanes and pulled up the driveway of an industrial complex.

"Spidey-sense is tingling," he said, as he killed his lights and crept forward to the dumpster. "Ready to lose your virginity?" he said, lighting a cigarette.

"I wish you'd stop using that metaphor," Alan said. "Ick."

But Kurt was already out of the Buick, around the other side of the car, pulling open Alan's door.

"That dumpster is full of cardboard," he said, gesturing. "It's recycling. That one is full of plastic bottles. More recycling.

This one," he said, *oof*ing as he levered himself over it, talking around the maglight he'd clenched between his teeth, "is where they put the good stuff. Looky here."

Alan tried to climb the dumpster's sticky walls, but couldn't get a purchase. Kurt, standing on something in the dumpster that crackled, reached down and grabbed him by the wrist and hoisted him up. He scrambled over the dumpster's transom and fell into it, expecting a wash of sour kitchen waste to break over him, and finding himself, instead, amid hundreds of five-inch cardboard boxes.

"What's this?" he asked.

Kurt was picking up the boxes and shaking them, listening for the rattle. "This place is an import/export wholesaler. They throw out a lot of defective product, since it's cheaper than shipping it all back to Taiwan for service. But my kids will fix it and sell it on eBay. Here," he said, opening a box and shaking something out, handing it to him. He passed his light over to Alan, who took it, unmindful of the drool on the handle.

It was a rubber duckie. Alan turned it over and saw it had a hard chunk of metal growing out of its ass.

"More of these, huh?" Kurt said. "I found about a thousand of these last month. They're USB keychain drives, low-capacity, like 32MB. Plug them in and they show up on your desktop like a little hard drive. They light up in all kinds of different colors. The problem is, they've all got a manufacturing defect that makes them glow in just one color—whatever shade the little gel carousel gets stuck on.

"I've got a couple thousand of these back home, but they're selling briskly. Go get me a couple cardboard boxes from that dumpster there and we'll snag a couple hundred more."

Alan gawped. The dumpster was seven feet cubed, the duckies a few inches on a side. There were thousands and thousands of duckies in the dumpster: more than they could ever fit into the Buick. In a daze, he went off and pulled some likely flattened boxes out of the trash and assembled them, packing them with the duckies that Kurt passed down to him from atop his crunching, cracking mound of doomed duckies that he was grinding underfoot.

Once they'd finished, Kurt fussed with moving the boxes around so that everything with a bootprint was shuffled to the bottom. "We don't want them to know that we've been here or they'll start hitting the duckies with a hammer before they pitch 'em out."

He climbed into the car and pulled out a bottle of window cleaner and some paper towels and wiped off the steering wheel and the dash and the handle of his flashlight, then worked a blob of hand sanitizer into his palms, passing it to Alan when he was done.

Alan didn't bother to point out that as Kurt had worked, he'd transferred the flashlight from his mouth to his hands and back again a dozen times—he thought he understood that this ritual was about Kurt assuring himself that he was not sinking down to the level of rummies and other garbage pickers.

As if reading his mind, Kurt said, "You see those old rum-dums pushing a shopping cart filled with empty cans down Spadina? Fucking *morons*—they could be out here pulling LCDs that they could turn around for ten bucks a pop, but instead they're rooting around like raccoons in the trash, chasing after nickel deposits."

"But then what would you pick?"

Kurt stared at him. "You kidding me? Didn't you *see*? There's a hundred times more stuff than I could ever pull. Christ, if even one of them had a squint of ambition, we could *double* the amount we save from the trash."

"You're an extraordinary person," Alan said. He wasn't sure he meant it as a compliment. After all, wasn't *he* an extraordinary person, too?

Alan was stunned when they found a dozen hard drives that spun up and revealed themselves to be of generous capacity and moreover stuffed with confidential-looking information when he plugged them into the laptop that Kurt kept under the passenger seat.

He was floored when they turned up three slightly elderly Toshiba laptops, each of which booted into a crufty old flavor of Windows, and only one of which had any obvious material defects: a starred corner in its LCD.

He was delighted by the dumpsters full of plush toys, by the lightly used office furniture, by the technical books and the CDs of last year's software. The smells were largely inoffensive— Kurt mentioned that the picking was better in winter when the outdoors was one big fridge, but Alan could hardly smell anything except the sour smell of an old dumpster and occasionally a whiff of coffee grounds.

They took a break at the Vietnamese place for coconut ice and glasses of sweet iced coffee, and Kurt nodded at the cops in the restaurant. Alan wondered why Kurt was so pleasant with these cops out in the boonies but so hostile to the law in Kensington Market.

"How are we going to get connectivity out of the Market?" Kurt said. "I mean, all this work, and we've hardly gotten four or five square blocks covered."

"Buck up," Alan said. "We could spend another two years just helping people in the Market use what we've installed, and it would still be productive." Kurt's mouth opened, and Alan held his hand up. "Not that I'm proposing that we do that. I just mean there's plenty of good that's been done so far. What we need is some publicity for it, some critical mass, and some way that we can get ordinary people involved. We can't fit a critical mass into your front room and put them to work."

"So what do we get them to do?"

"It's a good question. There's something I saw online the other day I wanted to show you. Why don't we go home and get connected?"

"There's still plenty of good diving out there. No need to go home anyway—I know a place."

They drove off into a maze of cul-de-sacs and cheaply built, gaudy monster homes with triple garages and sagging rain gut-ters. The streets had no sidewalks and the inevitable basketball nets over every garage showed no signs of use.

Kurt pulled them up in front of a house that was indistin-guishable from the others and took the laptop from under the Buick's seat, plugging it into the cigarette lighter and flipping its lid.

"There's an open network here," Kurt said as he plugged in the wireless card. He pointed at the dormer windows in the top room.

"How the hell did you find that?" Alan said, looking at the darkened window. There was a chain-link gate at the side of the house, and in the back an aboveground pool.

Kurt laughed. "These 'security consultants' "—he made lit-tle quotes with his fingers—"wardrove Toronto. They went from one end of the city to the other with a GPS and a wireless card and logged all the open access points they found, then released a report claiming that all of those access points represented ig-norant consumers who were leaving themselves vulnerable to attacks and making Internet connections available to baby-eating terrorists.

"One of the access points they identified was *mine*, for chris-sakes, and mine was open because I'm a crazy fucking anar-chist, not because I'm an ignorant 'consumer' who doesn't know any better, and that got me to thinking that there were probably lots of people like me around, running open APs. So one night I was out here diving and I *really* was trying to remem-ber who'd played the Sundance Kid in Butch Cassidy, and I knew that if I only had a net connection I could google it. I had a stumbler, an app that logged all the open WiFi access points that I came into range of, and a GPS attachment that I'd dived that could interface with the software that mapped the APs on a map of Toronto, so I could just belt the machine in there on the passenger seat and go driving around until I had a list of all the wireless Internet that I could see from the street.

"So I got kind of bored and went back to diving, and then I did what I usually do at the end of the night, I went driving around some residential streets, just to see evidence of humanity after a night in the garbage, and also because the people out here sometimes put out nice sofas and things.

"When I got home, I looked at my map and there were tons of access points out by the industrial buildings, and some on the commercial strips, and a few out here in the residential areas, but the one with the best signal was right here, and when I clicked on it, I saw that the name of the network was 'ParasiteNet.'"

Alan said, "Huh?" because ParasiteNet was Kurt's name for his wireless project, though they hadn't used it much since Alan got involved and they'd gotten halfway legit. But still.

"Yeah," Kurt said. "That's what I said—huh? So I googled ParasiteNet to see what I could find, and I found an old message I'd posted to toronto.talk.wireless when I was getting started out, a kind of manifesto about what I planned to do, and Google had snarfed it up and this guy, whoever he is, must have read it and decided to name his network after it."

"So I figger: This guy *wants* to share packets with me, for sure, and so I always hunt down this AP when I want to get online."

"You've never met him, huh?"

"Never. I'm always out here at two A.M. or so, and there's never a light on. Keep meaning to come back around five some afternoon and ring the bell and say hello. Never got to it."

Alan pursed his lips and watched Kurt prod at the keyboard.

"He's got a shitkicking net connection, though—tell you what. Feels like a T1, and the IP address comes off of an ISP in Waterloo. You need a browser, right?"

Alan shook his head. "You know, I can't even remember what it was I wanted to show you. There's some kind of idea kicking at me now, though. . . ."

Kurt shifted his laptop to the back seat, mindful of the cords and the antenna. "What's up?"

"Let's do some more driving around, let it perk, okay? You got more dumpsters you want to show me?"

"Brother, I got dumpsters for weeks. Months. Years."

It was the wardriving, of course. Alan called out the names of the networks that they passed as they passed them, watching the flags pop up on the map of Toronto. They drove the streets all night, watched the sun go up, and the flags multiplied on the network.

Alan didn't even have to explain it to Kurt, who got it immediately. They were close now, thinking together in the feverish drive time on the night-dark streets.

"Here's the thing," Kurt said as they drank their coffees at the Vesta Lunch, a grimy twenty-four-hour diner that Alan only seemed to visit during the smallest hours of the morning. "I started off thinking, well, the cell companies are screwed up because they think that they need to hose the whole city from their high towers with their powerful transmitters, and my little boxes will be lower-power and smarter and more realistic and grassroots and democratic."

"Right," Alan said. "I was just thinking of that. What could be more democratic than just encouraging people to use their own access points and their own Internet connections to bootstrap the city?"

"Yeah," Kurt said.

"Sure, you won't get to realize your dream of getting a free Internet by bridging down at the big cage at 151 Front Street, but we can still play around with hardware. And convincing the people who *already* know why WiFi is cool to join up has got to be easier than convincing shopkeepers who've never heard of wireless to let us put antennae and boxes on their walls."

"Right," Kurt said, getting more excited. "Right! I mean, it's just ego, right? Why do we need to *control* the network?" He spun around on his cracked stool and the waitress gave him a dirty look. "Gimme some apple pie, please," he said. "This is the best part: It's going to violate the hell out of everyone's contracts with their ISPs—they sell you an all-you-can-eat Internet connection and then tell you that they'll cut off your service if you're too hungry. Well, fuck that! It's not just community networking, it'll be civil disobedience against shitty service-provider terms of service!"

There were a couple early morning hard-hats in the diner who looked up from their yolky eggs to glare at him. Kurt spotted them and waved. "Sorry, boys. Ever get one of those ideas that's so good, you can't help but do a little dance?"

One of the hard-hats smiled. "Yeah, but his wife always turns me down." He socked the other hard-hat in the shoulder.

The other hard-hat grunted into his coffee. "Nice. Very nice. You're gonna be a *lot* of fun today, I can tell."

They left the diner in a sleepdep haze and squinted into the sunrise and grinned at each other and burped up eggs and sausages and bacon and coffee and headed toward Kurt's Buick.

"Hang on," Alan said. "Let's have a walk, okay?" The city smelled like morning, dew and grass and car-exhaust and baking bread and a whiff of the distant Cadbury's factory oozing chocolate miasma over the hills and the streetcar tracks. Around them, millions were stirring in their beds, clattering in their kitchens, passing water, and taking on vitamins. It invigorated him, made him feel part of something huge and all-encompassing, like being in his father the mountain.

"Up there," Kurt said, pointing to a little playground atop the hill that rose sharply up Dupont toward Christie, where a herd of plastic rocking horses swayed creakily in the breeze.

"Up there," Alan agreed, and they set off, kicking droplets of dew off the grass beside the sidewalk.

The sunrise was a thousand times more striking from atop the climber, filtered through the new shoots on the tree branches. Kurt lit a cigarette and blew plumes into the shafting light and they admired the effect of the wind whipping it away.

"I think this will work," Alan said. "We'll do something splashy for the press, get a lot of people to change the names of their networks—more people will use the networks, more will create them. . . . It's a good plan."

Kurt nodded. "Yeah. We're smart guys."

Something smashed into Alan's head and bounced to the dirt below the climber. A small, sharp rock. Alan reeled and tumbled from the climber, stunned, barely managing to twist to his side before landing. The air whooshed out of his lungs and tears sprang into his eyes.

Gingerly, he touched his head. His fingers came away wet. Kurt was shouting something, but he couldn't hear it. Something moved in the bushes, moved into his line of sight. Moved deliberately into his line of sight.

Danny. He had another rock in his hand and he wound up and pitched it. It hit Alan in the forehead and his head snapped back and he grunted.

Kurt's feet landed in the dirt a few inches from his eyes, big boots a-jangle with chains. Davey flitted out of the bushes and onto the plastic rocking horses, jumping from the horse to the duck to the chicken, leaving the big springs beneath them to rock and creak. Kurt took two steps toward him, but Davey was away, under the chain-link fence and over the edge of the hill leading down to Dupont Street.

"You okay?" Kurt said, crouching down beside him, putting a hand on his shoulder. "Need a doctor?"

"No doctors," Alan said. "No doctors. I'll be okay."

They inched their way back to the car, the world spinning around them. The hard-hats met them on the way out of the Vesta Lunch and their eyes went to Alan's bloodied face. They looked away. Alan felt his kinship with the woken world around him slip away and knew he'd never be truly a part of it.

He wouldn't let Kurt walk him up the steps and put him to bed, so instead Kurt watched from the curb until Alan went inside, then gunned the engine and pulled away. It was still morning rush hour, and the Market-dwellers were clacking toward work on hard leather shoes or piling their offspring into minivans.

Alan washed the blood off his scalp and face and took a gingerly shower. When he turned off the water, he heard muffled sounds coming through the open windows. A wailing electric guitar. He went to the window and stuck his head out and saw

Krishna sitting on an unmade bed in the unsoundproofed bed-room, in a grimy housecoat, guitar on his lap, eyes closed, con-centrating on the screams he was wringing from the instrument's long neck.

Alan wanted to sleep, but the noise and the throb of his head—going in counterpoint—and the sight of Davey, flicking from climber to bush to hillside, scuttling so quickly Alan was scarce sure he'd seen him, all conspired to keep him awake.

He bought coffees at the Donut Time on College—the Greek's wouldn't be open for hours—and brought it over to Kurt's storefront, but the lights were out, so he wandered slowly home, sucking back the coffee.

Benny had another seizure halfway up the mountain, stiffening up and falling down before they could catch him.

As Billy lay supine in the dirt, Alan heard a distant howl, not like a wolf, but like a thing that a wolf had caught and was sav-aging with its jaws. The sound made his neck prickle and when he looked at the little ones, he saw that their eyes were rolling crazily.

"Got to get him home," Alan said, lifting Benny up with a grunt. The little ones tried to help, but they just got tangled up in Benny's long loose limbs and so Alan shooed them off, telling them to keep a lookout behind him, look for Davey lurk-ing on an outcropping or in a branch, rock held at the ready.

When they came to the cave mouth again, he heard another one of the screams. Brendan stirred over his shoulders and Alan set him down, heart thundering, looking every way for Davey, who had come back.

"He's gone away for the night," Burt said conversationally. He sat up and then gingerly got to his feet. "He'll be back in the morning, though."

The cave was destroyed. Alan's books, Ern-Felix-Grad's toys were smashed. Their clothes were bubbling in the hot spring in rags and tatters. Brian's carvings were broken and smashed. Schoolbooks were ruined.

"You all right?" Alan said.

Brian dusted himself off and stretched his arms and legs out. "I'll be fine," he said. "It's not me he's after."

Alan stared blankly as the brothers tidied up the cave and made piles of their belongings. The little ones looked scared, without any of the hardness he remembered from that day when they'd fought it out on the hillside.

Benny retreated to his perch, but before the sun set and the cave darkened, he brought a couple blankets down and dropped them beside the nook where Alan slept. He had his baseball bat with him, and it made a good, solid aluminum sound when he leaned it against the wall.

Silently, the small ones crossed the cave with a pile of their own blankets, George bringing up the rear with a torn T-shirt stuffed with sharp stones.

Alan looked at them and listened to the mountain breathe around them. It had been years since his father had had anything to say to them. It had been years since their mother had done anything except wash the clothes. Was there a voice in the cave now? A wind? A smell?

He couldn't smell anything. He couldn't hear anything. Benny propped himself up against the cave wall with a blanket around his shoulders and the baseball bat held loose and ready between his knees.

A smell then, on the wind. Sewage and sulfur. A stink of fear.

Alan looked to his brothers, then he got up and left the cave without a look back. He wasn't going to wait for Davey to come to him.

The night had come up warm, and the highway sounds down at the bottom of the hill mingled with the spring breeze in the new buds on the trees and the new needles on the pines, the small sounds of birds and bugs foraging in the new year. Alan slipped out the cave mouth and looked around into the twilight, hoping for a glimpse of something out of the ordinary, but apart from an early owl and a handful of fireflies sparking off like distant stars, he saw nothing amiss.

He padded around the mountainside, stooped down low,

stopping every few steps to listen for footfalls. At the high, small entrance to the golems' cave, he paused, lay on his belly, and slowly peered around the fissure.

It had been years since Alvin had come up to the golems' cave, years since one had appeared in their father's cave. They had long ago ceased bringing their kills to the threshold of the boys' cave, ceased leaving pelts in neat piles on the eve of the waning moon.

The view from the outcropping was stunning. The village had grown to a town, fast on its way to being a city. A million lights twinkled. The highway cut a glistening ribbon of street-lamps through the night, a straight line slicing the hills and curves. There were thousands of people down there, all connected by a humming net-work—a work of nets, cunning knots tied in a cunning grid—of wire and radio and civilization.

Slowly, he looked back into the golems' cave. He remembered it as being lined with ranks of bones, a barbarian cathedral whose arches were decorated with ranked skulls and interlocked, tiny animal tibia. Now those bones were scattered and broken, the ossified wainscoting rendered gap-toothed by missing and tumbled bones.

Alan wondered how the golems had reacted when Darl had ruined their centuries of careful work. Then, looking more closely, he realized that the bones were dusty and grimed, cob-webbed and moldering. They'd been lying around for a lot longer than a couple hours.

Alan crept into the cave now, eyes open, ears straining. Puffs of dust rose with his footfalls, illuminated in the moon-light and city light streaming in from the cave mouth. Another set of feet had crossed this floor: small, boyish feet that took slow, arthritic steps. They'd come in, circled the cave, and gone out again.

Alan listened for the golems and heard nothing. He did his own slow circle of the cave, peering into the shadows. Where had they gone?

There. A streak of red clay, leading to a mound. Alan drew

up alongside of it and made out the runny outlines of the legs and arms, the torso and the head. The golem had dragged itself into this corner and had fallen to mud. The dust on the floor was red. Dried mud. Golem-dust.

How long since he'd been in this cave? How long since he'd come around this side of the mountain? Two months? Three? Four? Longer. How long had the golems lain dead and dust in this cave?

They'd carved his cradle. Fed him. Taught him to talk and to walk. In some sense, they were his fathers, as much as the mountain was.

He fished around inside himself for emotion and found none. Relief, maybe. Relief.

The golems were an embodiment of his strangeness, as weird as his smooth, navelless belly, an element of his secret waiting to surface and—what? What had he been afraid of? Contempt? Vivisection? He didn't know anymore, but knew that he wanted to fit in and that the golems' absence made that more possible.

There was a smell on the wind in here, the death-and-corruption smell he'd noticed in the sleeping cave. Father was worried.

No. Davey was inside. That was his smell, the smell of Davey long dead and back from the grave.

Alan walked deeper into the tunnels, following his nose.

Davey dropped down onto his shoulders from a ledge in an opening where the ceiling stretched far over their heads. He was so light, at first Alan thought someone had thrown a blanket over his shoulders.

Then the fingers dug into his eyes. Then the fingers fishhooked the corner of his mouth.

Then the screech, thick as a desiccated tongue, dry as the dust of a golem, like no sound and like all the sounds at once.

The smell of corruption was everywhere, filling his nostrils like his face has been ground into a pile of rotten meat. He tugged at the dry, thin hands tangled in his face, and found them strong as iron bands, and then he screamed.

Then they were both screeching and rolling on the ground, and he had Danny's thumb in his hand, bending it back painfully, until *snap*, it came off clean with a sound like dry wood cracking.

Doug was off him then, crawling off toward the shadows. Alan got to his knees, still holding the thumb, and made ready to charge him, holding his sore face with one hand, when he heard the slap of running footfalls behind him and then Bill was streaking past him, baseball bat at ready, and he swung it like a polo mallet and connected with a hollow crunch of aluminum on chitinous leathery skin.

The sound shocked Alan to his feet, wet sick rising in his gorge. Benny was winding up for a second blow, aiming for Darren's head this time, an out-of-the park *smack* that would have knocked that shrunken head off the skinny, blackened neck, and Alan shouted, "NO!" and roared at Benny and leapt for him. As he sailed through the air, he thought he was saving *Benny* from the feeling he'd carried with him for a decade, but as he connected with Benny, he felt a biting-down feeling, clean and hard, and he knew he was defending *Drew*, saving him for once instead of hurting him.

He was still holding on to the thumb, and Davey was inches from his face, and he was atop Benny, and they breathed together, chests heaving. Alan wobbled slowly to his feet and dropped the thumb onto Drew's chest, then he helped Billy to his feet and they limped off to their beds. Behind them, they heard the dry sounds of Davey getting to his feet, coughing and hacking with a crunch of thin, cracked ribs.

He was sitting on their mother the next morning. He was naked and unsexed by desiccation—all the brothers, even little George, had ceased going about in the nude when they'd passed through puberty—sullen and silent atop the white, chipped finish of her enamel top, so worn and ground down that it resembled a collection of beach china. It had been a long time since any of them had sought solace in their mother's gentle rocking, since, indeed, they had spared her a thought beyond filling her belly with clothes and emptying her out an hour later.

The little ones woke first and saw him, taking cover behind a stalagmite, peering around, each holding a sharp, flat rock, each with his pockets full of more. Danny looked at each in turn with eyes gone yellow and congealed, and bared his mouthful of broken and blackened teeth in a rictus that was equal parts humor and threat.

Bradley was the next to wake, his bat in his hand and his eyelids fluttering open as he sprang to his feet, and then Alan was up as well, a hand on his shoulder.

He crouched down and walked slowly to Davey. He had the knife, handle wound with cord, once-keen edge gone back to rust and still reddened with ten-year-old blood, but its sharpness mattered less than its history.

"Welcome me home," Davey rasped as Alan drew closer. "Welcome me home, mother*fucker*. Welcome me home, *brother*."

"You're welcome in this home," Alan said, but Davey wasn't welcome. Just last week, Alan had seen a nice-looking bedroom set that he suspected he could afford—the golems had left him a goodly supply of gold flake, though with the golems gone he supposed that the sacks were the end of the family's no-longer-bottomless fortune. But with the bedroom set would come a kitchen table, and then a bookcase, and a cooker and a fridge, and when they were ready, he could send each brother on his way with the skills and socialization necessary to survive in the wide world, to find women and love and raise families of their own. Then he could go and find himself a skinny redheaded girl with a Scots accent, and in due time her belly would swell up and there would be a child.

It was all planned out, practically preordained, but now here they were, with the embodied shame sitting on their mother, his torn thumb gleaming with the wire he'd used to attach it back to his hand.

"That's very generous, *brother*," Danny said. "You're a prince among *men*."

"Let's go," Alan said. "Breakfast in town. I'm buying."

They filed out and Alan spared Davey a look over his shoulder as they slipped away, head down on his knees, rocking in time with their mother.

Krishna grinned at him from the front porch as he staggered home from Kurt's storefront. He was dressed in a hoodie and huge, outsized raver pants that dangled with straps and reflectors meant to add kinetic reflections on the dance floor.

"Hello, neighbor," he said as Alan came up the walkway. "Good evening?"

Alan stopped and put his hands on his hips, straightened his head out on his neck so that he was standing tall. "I understand what he gets out of *you*," Alan said. "I understand that perfectly well. Who couldn't use a little servant and errand boy?"

"But what I don't understand, what I can't understand, what I'd like to understand is: What can you get out of the arrangement?"

Krishna shrugged elaborately. "I have no idea what you're talking about."

"We had gold, in the old days. Is that what's bought you? Maybe you should ask me for a counteroffer. I'm not poor."

"I'd never take a penny that *you* offered—voluntarily." Krishna lit a nonchalant cig and flicked the match toward his dry, xeroscaped lawn. There were little burnt patches among the wild grasses there, from other thrown matches, and that was one mystery-lot solved, then, wasn't it?

"You think I'm a monster," Alan said.

Krishna nodded. "Yup. Not a scary monster, but a monster still."

Alan nodded. "Probably," he said. "Probably I am. Not a human, maybe not a person. Not a real person. But if I'm bad, he's a thousand times worse, you know. He's a scary monster."

Krishna dragged at his cigarette.

"You know a lot of monsters, don't you?" Alan said. He jerked his head toward the house. "You share a bed with one."

Krishna narrowed his eyes. "She's not scary, either."

"You cut off her wings, but it doesn't make her any less monstrous.

"One thing I can tell you, you're pretty special: Most real people never see us. You saw me right off. It's like *Dracula*, where most of the humans couldn't tell that there was a vampire in their midst."

"Van Helsing could tell," Krishna said. "He hunted Dracula. You can't hunt what you can't see," he said. "So your kind has been getting a safe free ride for God knows how long. Centuries. Living off of us. Passing among us. Passing for us."

"Van Helsing got killed," Alan said. "Didn't he? And besides that, there was someone else who could see the vampires: Renfield. The pathetic pet and errand boy. Remember Renfield in his cage in the asylum, eating flies? Trying to be a monster? Van Helsing recognized the monster, but so did Renfield."

"I'm no one's Renfield," Krishna said, and spat onto Alan's lawn. First fire, then water. He was leaving his mark on Alan's land, that was certain.

"You're no Van Helsing, either," Alan said. "What's the difference between you and a racist, Krishna? You call me a monster, why shouldn't I call you a paki?"

He stiffened at the slur, and so did Alan. He'd never used the word before, but it had sprung readily from his lips, as though it had lurked there all along, waiting to be uttered.

"Racists say that there's such a thing as 'races' within the human race, that blacks and whites and Chinese and Indians are all members of different 'races,'" Krishna said. "Which is bullshit. On the other hand, you—"

He broke off, left the thought to hang. He didn't need to finish it. Alan's hand went to his smooth belly, the spot where real people had navels, old scarred remnants of their connections to real, human mothers.

"So you hate monsters, Krishna, all except for the ones you sleep with and the ones you work for?"

"I don't work for anyone," he said. "Except me."

Alan said, "I'm going to pour myself a glass of wine. Would you like one?"

Krishna grinned hard and mirthless. "Sure, neighbor, that sounds lovely."

Alan went inside and took out two glasses, got a bottle of something cheap and serviceable from Niagara wine country out of the fridge, worked the corkscrew, all on automatic. His hands shook a little, so he held them under the cold tap. Stuck to the wall over his work surface was a magnetic bar, and stuck to it was a set of very sharp chef's knives that were each forged from a single piece of steel. He reached for one and felt its comfort in his hand, seductive and glinting.

It was approximately the same size as the one he'd used on Davey, a knife that he'd held again and again, reached for in the night and carried to breakfast for months. He was once robbed at knifepoint, taking the deposit to the bank after Christmas rush, thousands of dollars in cash in a brown paper sack in his bag, and the mugger—a soft-spoken, middle-aged man in a good suit—knew exactly what he was carrying and where, must have been casing him for days.

The soft-spoken man had had a knife about this size, and when Alan had seen it pointed at him, it had been like an old friend, one whose orbit had escaped his gravity years before, so long ago that he'd forgotten about their tender camaraderie. It was all he could do not to reach out and take the knife from the man, say hello again and renew the friendship.

He moved the knife back to the magnet bar and let the field tug it out of his fingers and *snap* it back to the wall, picked up the wine glasses, and stepped back out onto the porch. Krishna appeared not to have stirred except to light a fresh cigarette.

"You spit in mine?" Krishna said.

Though their porches adjoined, Alan walked down his steps and crossed over the lawn next door, held the glass out to Krishna. He took it and their hands brushed each other, the way his hand had brushed the soft-spoken man's hand when he'd handed over the sack of money. The touch connected him to something human in a way that made him ashamed of his desperation.

"I don't normally drink before noon," Adam said.

"I don't much care when I drink," Krishna said, and took a slug.

"Sounds like a dangerous philosophy for a bartender," Adam said.

"Why? Plenty of drunk bartenders. It's not a hard job." Krishna spat. "Big club, all you're doing is uncapping beers and mixing shooters all night. I could do it in my sleep."

"You should quit," Alan said. "You should get a better job. No one should do a job he can do in his sleep."

Krishna put a hand out on Alan's chest, the warmth of his fingertips radiating through Alan's windbreaker. "Don't try to arrange me on your chessboard, monster. Maybe you can move Natalie around, and maybe you can move around a bunch of Kensington no-hopers, and maybe you can budge my idiot girlfriend a couple of squares, but I'm not on the board. I got my job, and if I leave it, it'll be for me."

Alan retreated to his porch and sipped his own wine. His mouth tasted like it was full of blood still, a taste that was woken up by the wine. He set the glass down.

"I'm not playing chess with you," he said. "I don't play games. I try to help—I *do* help."

Krishna swigged the glass empty. "You wanna know what makes you a monster, Alvin? That attitude right there. You don't understand a single fucking thing about real people, but you spend all your time rearranging them on your board, and you tell them and you tell yourself that you're helping.

"You know how you could help, man? You could crawl back under your rock and leave the people's world for people."

Something snapped in Alan. "Canada for Canadians, right? Send 'em back where they came from, right?" He stalked to the railing that divided their porches. The taste of blood stung his mouth.

Krishna met him, moving swiftly to the railing as well, hood thrown back, eyes hard and glittering and stoned.

"You think you can make me feel like a racist, make me *guilty*?" His voice squeaked on the last syllable. "Man, the only day I wouldn't piss on you is if you were on fire, you fucking freak."

Some part of Alan knew that this person was laughable, a Renfield eating bugs. But that voice of reason was too quiet to be heard over the animal screech that was trying to work its way free of his throat.

He could smell Krishna, cigarettes and booze and club and sweat, see the gold flecks in his dark irises, the red limning of his eyelids. Krishna raised a hand as if to slap him, smirked when he flinched back.

Then he grabbed Krishna's wrist and pulled hard, yanking the boy off his feet, slamming his chest into the railing hard enough to shower dried spider's nests and flakes of paint to the porch floor.

"I'm every bit the monster my brother is," he hissed in Krishna's ear. "I *made* him the monster he is. *Don't squirm,*" he said, punching Krishna hard in the ear with his free hand. "Listen. You can stay away from me and you can stay away from my family, or you can enter a world of terrible hurt. It's up to you. Nod if you understand."

Krishna was still, except for a tremble. The moment stretched, and Alan broke it by cracking him across the ear again.

"Nod if you understand, goddammit," he said, his vision going fuzzily black at the edges. Krishna was silent, still, coiled. Any minute now, he would struggle free and they'd be in a clinch.

He remembered kneeling on Davey's chest, holding the rock over him and realizing that he didn't know what to do next, taking Davey to their father.

Only Davey had struck him first. He'd only been restraining him, defending himself. Alan had hit Krishna first. "Nod if you understand, Krishna," he said, and heard a note of pleading in his voice.

Krishna held still. Alan felt like an idiot, standing there, his neighbor laid out across the railing that divided their porches, the first cars of the day driving past and the first smells of bread and fish and hospital and pizza blending together there in the heart of the Market.

He let go and Krishna straightened up, his eyes downcast. For a second, Alan harbored a germ of hope that he'd bested Krishna and so scared him into leaving him alone.

Then Krishna looked up and met his eye. His face was blank, his eyes like brown marbles, heavy-lidded, considering, not stoned at all anymore. Sizing Alan up, calculating the debt he'd just amassed, what it would take to pay it off.

He picked up Alan's wine glass, and Alan saw that it wasn't one of the cheapies he'd bought a couple dozen of for an art show once, but rather Irish crystal that he'd found at a flea market in Hamilton, a complete fluke and one of his all-time miracle thrift scores.

Krishna turned the glass one way and another in his hand, letting it catch the sunrise, bend the light around the smudgy fingerprints. He set it down then, on the railing, balancing it carefully.

He took one step back, then a second, so that he was almost at the door. They stared at each other and then he took one, two running steps, like a soccer player winding up for a penalty kick, and then he unwound, leg flying straight up, tip of his toe catching the wine glass so that it hurtled straight for Alan's forehead, moving like a bullet.

Alan flinched and the glass hit the brick wall behind him, disintegrating into a mist of glass fragments that rained down on his hair, down his collar, across the side of his face, in his ear. Krishna ticked a one-fingered salute off his forehead, wheeled, and went back into his house.

The taste of blood was in Alan's mouth. More blood coursed down his neck from a nick in his ear, and all around him on the porch, the glitter of crystal.

He went inside to get a broom, but before he could clean up, he sat down for a moment on the sofa to catch his breath. He fell instantly asleep on the creaking horsehide, and when he woke again it was dark and raining and someone else had cleaned up his porch.

The mountain path had grown over with weeds and thistles and condoms and cans and inexplicable maxi-pads and doll parts.

She clung to his hand as he pushed through it, stepping in brackish puddles and tripping in sinkholes. He navigated the trail like a mountain goat, while Mimi lagged behind, tugging his arm every time she misstepped, jerking it painfully in its socket.

He turned to her, ready to snap, *Keep the fuck up, would you?* and then swallowed the words. Her eyes were red-rimmed and scared, her full lips drawn down into a clown's frown, bracketed by deep lines won by other moments of sorrow.

He helped her beside him and turned his back on the mountain, faced the road and the town and the car with its trunk with its corpse with his brother, and he put an arm around her shoulders, a brotherly arm, and hugged her to him.

"How're you doing there?" he said, trying to make his voice light, though it came out so leaden the words nearly thudded in the wet dirt as they fell from his mouth.

She looked into the dirt at their feet and he took her chin and turned her face up so that she was looking into his eyes, and he kissed her forehead in a brotherly way, like an older brother coming home with a long-lost sister.

"I used to want to know all the secrets," she said in the smallest voice. "I used to want to understand how the world worked. Little things, like heavy stuff goes at the bottom of the laundry bag, or big things, like the best way to get a boy to chase you is to ignore him, or medium things, like if you cut an onion under running water your eyes won't sting, and if you wash your fingers afterwards with lemon-juice they won't stink.

"I used to want to know all the secrets, and every time I learned one, I felt like I'd taken—a step. On a journey. To a place. A destination: to be the kind of person who knew all this stuff, the way everyone around me seemed to know all this stuff. I thought that once I knew enough secrets, I'd be like them.

"I don't want to learn secrets anymore, Andrew." She

shrugged off his arm and took a faltering step down the slope, back toward the road.

"I'll wait in the car, okay?"

"Mimi," he said. He felt angry at her. How could she be so selfish as to have a crisis *now, here,* at this place that meant so much to him?

"Mimi," he said, and swallowed his anger.

His three brothers stayed on his sofa for a week, though they only left one wet towel on the floor, only left one sticky plate in the sink, one fingerprint-smudged glass on the counter.

He'd just opened his first business, the junk shop—not yet upscale enough to be called an antiques shop—and he was pulling the kinds of long hours known only to ER interns and entrepreneurs, showing up at seven to do the books, opening at ten, working until three, then turning things over to a minimum-wage kid for two hours while he drove to the city's thrift shops and picked for inventory, then working until eight to catch the evening trade, then answering creditors and fighting with the landlord until ten, staggering into bed at eleven to sleep a few hours before doing it all over again.

So he gave them a set of keys and bought them a MetroPass and stuffed an old wallet with $200 in twenties and wrote his phone number on the brim of a little porkpie hat that looked good on their head and turned them loose on the city.

The shop had all the difficulties of any shop—snarky customers, shoplifting teenagers, breakage, idiots with jumpy dogs, never enough money and never enough time. He loved it. Every stinking minute of it. He'd never gone to bed happier and never woken up more full of energy in his life. He was in the world, finally, at last.

Until his brothers arrived.

He took them to the store the first morning, showed them what he'd wrought with his own two hands. Thought that he'd inspire them to see what they could do when they entered the world as well, after they'd gone home and grown up a little. Which they would have to do very soon, as he reminded them at every chance, unmoved by George's hangdog expression at the thought.

They'd walked around the shop slowly, picking things up, turning them over, having hilarious, embarrassing conversations about the likely purpose of an old Soloflex machine, a grubby pink Epilady leg razor, a Bakelite coffee carafe.

The arguments went like this:

George: Look, it's a milk container!

Ed: I don't think that that's for milk.

Fred: You should put it down before you drop it, it looks valuable.

George: Why don't you think it's for milk? Look at the silver inside, that's to reflect off the white milk and make it look, you know, cold and fresh.

Fred: Put it down, you're going to break it.

George: Fine, I'll put it down, but tell me, why don't you think it's for milk?

Ed: Because it's a thermos container, and that's to keep hot stuff hot, and it's got a screwtop and whatever it's made of looks like it'd take a hard knock without breaking.

And so on, nattering at each other like cavemen puzzling over a walkman, until Alan was called upon to settle the matter with the authoritative answer.

It got so that he set his alarm for four A.M. so that he could sneak past their snoring form on the sofa and so avoid the awkward, desperate pleas to let them come with him into the shop and cadge a free breakfast of poutine and eggs from the Harvey's next door while they were at it. George had taken up coffee on his second day in the city, bugging the other two until they got him a cup, six or seven cups a day, so that they flitted from place to place like a hummingbird, thrashed in their sleep, babbled when they spoke.

It came to a head on the third night, when they dropped by the shop while he was on the phone and ducked into the back room in order to separate into threes again, with George wearing the porkpie hat even though it was a size too big for his head and hung down around his ears.

Adam was talking to a woman who'd come into the shop that afternoon and greatly admired an institutional sofa from the mid-seventies whose lines betrayed a pathetic slavish devotion to Danish Moderne aesthetics. The woman had sat on the sofa, admired the sofa, walked around the sofa, hand trailing on its back, had been fascinated to see the provenance he'd turned up, an inventory sticker from the University of Toronto maintenance department indicating that this sofa had originally been installed at the Robarts Library, itself of great and glorious aesthetic obsolescence.

Here was Adam on the phone with this woman, closing a deal to turn a $3,000 profit on an item he'd acquired at the Goodwill As-Is Center for five bucks, and here were his brothers, in the store, angry about something, shouting at each other about something. They ran around like three fat lunatics, reeking of the BO that they exuded like the ass end of a cow: loud, boorish, and indescribably weird. Weird beyond the quaint weirdness of his little curiosity show. Weird beyond the interesting weirdness of the punks and the goths and the mods who were wearing their subcultures like political affiliations as they strolled by the shops. Those were redeemable weirds, weirds within the bounds of normal human endeavor. His brothers, on the other hand, were utterly, utterly irredeemable.

He sank down behind the counter as George said something to Fred in their own little shorthand language, a combination of grunts and nonsense syllables that the three had spoken together for so long that he'd not even noticed it until they were taken out of their context and put in his. He put his back against the wall and brought his chest to his knees and tried to sound like he had a belly button as he said to the woman, "Yes, absolutely, I can have this delivered tomorrow if you'd like to courier over a check."

This check, it was enough money to keep his business afloat for another thirty days, to pay his rent and pay the minimum-wage kid and buy his groceries. And there were his brothers, and now Ed was barking like a dog—a rare moment of mirth from him, who had been the sober outer bark since he was a child and rarely acted like the seventeen-year-old he was behaving like today.

"Is everything all right?" she said down the phone, this woman who'd been smartly turned out in a cashmere sweater and a checked scarf and a pair of boot-cut jeans that looked new and good over her designer shoes with little heels. They'd flirted a little, even though she was at least ten years older than him, because flirting was a new thing for Alan, and he'd discovered that he wasn't bad at it.

"Everything is fine," he said. "Just some goofballs out in the street out front. How about if I drop off the sofa for six o'clock?"

"KILLED HER, CUT HER UP, SLICED HER OPEN," George screeched suddenly, skidding around the counter, rolling past him, yanking the phone out of the wall.

And in that moment, he realized what the sounds they had been making in their private speech had been: They had been a reenactment, a grunting, squeaking playback of the day, the fateful day, the day he'd taken his knife and done his mischief with it.

He reached for the phone cable and plugged it back into the wall, but it was as though his hand were moving of its own accord, because his attention was focused elsewhere, on the three of them arrayed in a triangle, as they had been on the hillside, as they had been when they had chanted at him when the knife grip was sure in the palm of his hands.

The ritual—that's what it was, it was a *ritual*—the ritual had the feel of something worn smooth with countless repetitions. He found himself rigid with shock, offended to his bones. This was what they did now, in the cave, with Davey sitting atop their mother, black and shriveled, this was how they behaved, running through this reenactment of his great shame, of the day Danny died?

No wonder Darrel had terrorized them out of their home.

They were beyond odd and eccentric, they were—unfit. Unfit for polite company. For human society.

The phone in his hand rang. It was the woman.

"You know, I'm thinking that maybe I should come back in with a tape measure and measure up the sofa before I commit to it. It's a lot of money, and to be honest, I just don't know if I have room—"

"What if I measure it for you? I could measure it for you and call you back with the numbers." The three brothers stared at him with identical glassy, alien stares.

"That's okay. I can come in," and he knew that she meant, *I won't ever come in again.*

"What if I bring it by anyway? I could bring it by tomorrow night and you could see it and make up your mind. No obligation."

"That's very kind of you, but I'm afraid that I'll be out tomorrow evening—"

"Friday? I could come by Friday—" He was trying to remember how to flirt now, but he couldn't. "I could come by and we could have a glass of wine or something," and he knew he'd said the exact wrong thing.

"It's all right," she said coldly. "I'll come by later in the week to have another look.

"I have to go now, my husband is home," and he was pretty sure she wasn't married, but he said good-bye and hung up the phone.

He looked at his solemn brothers now and they looked at him.

"When are you going home?" he said, and Edward looked satisfied and Fred looked a little disappointed and George looked like he wanted to throw himself in front of a subway, and his bottom lip began to tremble.

"It was Ed's game," he said. "The Davey game, it was his." He pointed a finger. "You know, I'm not like them. I can be on my own. I'm what *they* need, they're not what *I* need."

The other two stared at their fat bellies in the direction of their fat feet. Andrew had never heard George say this, had never even suspected that this thought lurked in his heart, but now that it was out on the table, it seemed like a pretty obvious fact to have taken note of. All things being equal, things weren't equal. He was cold and numb.

"That's a really terrible thing to say, George," is what he said.

"That's easy for you to say," is what George said. "You are here, you are in the *world*. It's easy for you to say that we should be happy with things the way they are."

George turned on his heel and put his head down and bulled out the door, slamming it behind him so that the mail slot rattled and the glass shook and a stack of nice melamine cafeteria trays fell off a shelf and clattered to the ground.

He didn't come back that night. He didn't come back the next day. Ed and Fred held their grumbling tummies and chewed at the insides of their plump cheeks and sat on the unsold Danish Modern sofa in the shop and freaked out the few customers that drifted in and then drifted out.

"This is worse than last time," Ed said, licking his lips and staring at the donut that Albert refused to feel guilty about eating in front of them.

"Last time?" he said, not missing Felix's quick warning glare at Ed, even though Ed appeared to.

"He went away for a whole day, just disappeared into town. When he came back, he said that he'd needed some away time. That he'd had an amazing day on his own. That he wanted to come and see you and that he'd do it whether we wanted to come or not."

"Ah," Alvin said, understanding then how the three had come to be staying with him. He wondered how long they'd last without the middle, without the ability to eat. He remembered holding the infant Eddie in his arms, the boy light and hollowed out. He remembered holding the three boys at once, heavy as a bowling ball. "Ah," he said. "I'll have to have a word with him."

When Greg came home, Alan was waiting for him, sitting on the sofa, holding his head up with one hand. Eli and Fred snored uneasily in his bed, breathing heavily through their noses.

"Hey," he said as he came through the door, scuffing at the lock with his key for a minute or two first. He was rumpled and dirty, streaked with grime on his jawline and hair hanging limp and greasy over his forehead.

"Greg," Alan said, nodding, straightening out his spine, and listening to it pop.

"I'm back," George said, looking down at his sneakers, which squished with gray water that oozed over his carpet. Art didn't say anything, just sat pat and waited, the way he did sometimes when con artists came into the shop with some kind of scam that they wanted him to play along with.

It worked the same with George. After a hard stare at his shoes, he shook his head and began to defend himself, revealing the things that he knew were indefensible. "I had to do it, I just had to. I couldn't live in that cave, with that thing, anymore. I couldn't live inside those two anymore. I'm going crazy. There's a whole world out here and every day I get further away from it. I get weirder. I just wanted to be normal.

"I just wanted to be like you.

"They stopped letting me into the clubs after I ran out of money, and they kicked me out of the cafés. I tried to ride the subway all night, but they threw me off at the end of the line, so I ended up digging a transfer out of a trash can and taking an all-night bus back downtown.

"No one looked at me twice that whole time, except to make sure that I was gone. I walked back here from Eglinton."

That was five miles away, a good forty-minute walk in the night and the cold and the dark. Greg pried off his sneakers with his toes and then pulled off his gray, squelching socks. "I couldn't find anyone who'd let me use the toilet," he said, and Alan saw the stain on his pants.

He stood up and took Greg by the cold hand, as he had when they were both boys, and said, "It's all right, Gord. We'll get you cleaned up and changed and put you to bed, okay? Just put your stuff in the hamper in the bathroom and I'll find you a change of clothes and make a couple sandwiches, all right?"

And just as easy as that, George's spirit was tamed. He came out of the shower pink and steaming and scrubbed, put on the sweats that Adam found for him in an old gym bag, ate his sandwiches, and climbed into Adam's bed with his brothers. When he saw them again next, they were reassembled and downcast, though they ate the instant oatmeal with raisins and cream that he set out for them with gusto.

"I think a bus ticket home is about forty bucks, right?" Alan said as he poured himself a coffee.

They looked up at him. Ed's eyes were grateful, his lips clamped shut.

"And you'll need some food on the road, another fifty or sixty bucks, okay?"

Ed nodded and Adam set down a brown hundred-dollar bill, then put a purple ten on top of it. "For the taxi to the Greyhound station," he added.

They finished their oatmeal in silence, while Adam puttered around the apartment, stripping the cheese-smelling sheets and oily pillowcases off his bed, rinsing the hairs off the soap, cleaning the toilet. Erasing the signs of their stay.

"Well," he said at length. "I should get going to the shop."

"Yeah," Ed said, in George's voice, and it cracked before he could close his lips again.

"Right," Adam said. "Well."

They patted their mouth and ran stubby fingers through their lank hair, already thinning though they were still in their teens. They stood and cracked their knuckles against the table. They patted their pockets absently, then pocketed the hundred and the ten.

"Well," Adam said.

They left, turning to give him the keys he'd had cut for them, a gesture that left him feeling obscurely embarrassed and mean-spirited, even though—he told himself—he'd put them up and put up with them very patiently indeed.

And then he left, and locked the door with his spare keys. Useless spare keys. No one would ever come to stay with him again.

W hat I found in the cave,

(he said, lying in the grass on the hillside, breathing hard, the taste of vomit sour in his mouth, his arms and legs sore from the pumping run down the hillside)

What I found in the cave,

(he said, and she held his hand nervously, her fingers not sure of how hard to squeeze, whether to caress)

What I found in the cave,

(he said, and was glad that she hadn't come with him, hadn't been there for what he'd seen and heard)

What I found in the cave, was the body of my first girlfriend. Her skeleton, polished to a gleam and laid out carefully on the floor. Her red hair in a long plait, brushed out and brittle, circled over her small skull like a halo.

He'd laid her out before my mother, and placed her finger-nails at the exact tips of her fingerbones. The floor was dirty and littered with rags and trash. It was dark and it stank of shit, there were piles of shit here and there.

The places where my brothers had slept had been torn apart. My brother Bradley, his nook was caved in. I moved some of the rocks, but I didn't find him under there.

Benny was gone. Craig was gone. Ed, Frankie, and George were gone. Even Davey was gone. All the parts of the cave that made it home were gone, except for my mother, who was rusted and sat askew on the uneven floor. One of her feet had rusted through, and her generator had run dry, and she was silent and dry, with a humus-paste of leaves and guano and gunk sliming her basket.

I went down to the cave where my father spoke to us, and I found that I—I—

I found that I couldn't see in the dark anymore. I'd never had a moment's pause in the halls of my father, but now I walked falteringly, the sounds of my footsteps not like the steps of a son of the mountain at all. I heard them echo back and they sounded like an outsider, and I fell twice and hurt my head, here—

(he touched the goose egg he'd raised on his forehead)

and I got dizzy, and then I was in the pool, but it didn't sound right and I couldn't hear it right, and I got my clothes off and then I stood there with them in my arms—

(his hand came back bloody and he wiped it absently on the grass and Mimi took hold of it) .

Because. If I put them down. It was dark. And I'd never find them again. So I bundled them all up and carried them over my head and I waded in and the water had never been so cold and had never felt so oily and there was a smell to it, a stagnant smell.

I waded out and I stood and I shivered and I whispered, "Father?" and I listened.

I heard the sound of the water I'd disturbed, lapping around my ears and up on the shore. I smelled the sewage and oil smell, but none of the habitual smells of my father: clean water, coalface, sulfur, grass, and lime.

I picked my way out of the water again and I walked to the shore, and it was too dark to put on my clothes, so I carried them under one arm and felt my way back to the summer cave and leaned against my mother and waited to drip-dry. I'd stepped in something soft that squished and smelled between my mother and my father, and I didn't want to put on my socks until I'd wiped it off, but I couldn't bring myself to wipe it on the cave floor.

Marci's eye sockets looked up at the ceiling. She'd been laid out with so much care, I couldn't believe that Davey had had anything to do with it. I thought that Benny must be around somewhere, looking in, taking care.

I closed my eyes so that I wasn't looking into the terrible, recriminating stare, and I leaned my head up against my mother, and I breathed until the stink got to me and then I pried myself upright and walked out of the cave. I stopped and stood in the mouth of the cave and listened as hard as I could, but my father wasn't speaking. And the smell was getting to me.

She got him dressed and she fed him sips of water and she got him standing and walked him in circles around the little paddock he'd collapsed in.

"I need to get Georgie out of the car," he said. "I'm going to leave him in the cave. It's right."

She bit her lip and nodded slowly. "I can help you with that," she said.

"I don't need help," he said lamely.

"I didn't say you did, but I can help anyway."

They walked down slowly, him leaning on her arm like an old man, steps faltering in the scree on the slope. They came to the road and stood before the trunk as the cars whizzed past them. He opened the trunk and looked down.

The journey hadn't been good to Gregg. He'd come undone from his winding sheet and lay face down, neck stiff, his nose mashed against the floor of the trunk. His skin had started to flake off, leaving a kind of scale or dandruff on the flat industrial upholstery inside the trunk.

Alan gingerly tugged loose the sheet and began, awkwardly, to wrap it around his brother, ignoring the grit of shed skin and hair that clung to his fingers.

Mimi shook him by the shoulder hard, and he realized she'd been shaking him for some time. "You can't do that here," she said. "Would you listen to me? You can't do that here. Someone will see." She held something up. His keys.

"I'll back it up to the trailhead," she said. "Close the trunk and wait for me there."

She got behind the wheel and he sloped off to the trailhead and stood, numbly, holding the lump on his forehead and staring at a rusted Coke can in a muddy puddle.

She backed the car up almost to his shins, put it in park, and came around to the trunk. She popped the lid and looked in and wrinkled her nose.

"Okay," she said. "I'll get him covered and we'll carry him up the hill."

"Mimi—" he began. "Mimi, it's okay. You don't need to go in there for me. I know it's hard for you—"

She squeezed his hand. "I'm over it, Andy. Now that I know what's up there, it's not scary any longer."

He watched her shoulders work, watched her wings work, as she wrapped up his brother. When she was done, he took one end of the bundle and hoisted it, trying to ignore the rain of skin and hair that shook off over the bumper and his trousers.

"Up we go," she said, and moved to take the front. "Tell me when to turn."

They had to set him down twice before they made it all the way up the hill. The first time, they just stood in silence, wiping their cramped hands on their thighs. The second time, she came to him and put her arm around his shoulders and gave him a soft kiss on the cheek that felt like a feather.

"Almost there?" she said.

He nodded and bent to pick up his end.

Mimi plunged through the cave mouth without a moment's hesitation and they set him down just inside the entrance, near a pair of stained cotton Y-fronts.

Alan waited for his heart to stop thudding and the sweat to cool on his brow and then he kicked the underwear away as an afterthought.

"God," he said. She moved to him, put her arm around his shoulder.

"You're being brave," she said.

"God," he said again.

"Let it out, you know, if you want to."

But he didn't. He wanted to sit down. He moved to his mother's side and leaned against her.

Mimi sat on her hunkers before him and took his hand and tried to tilt his chin up with one finger, but he resisted her pull and she rose and began to explore the cave. He heard her stop near Marci's skeleton for a long while, then move some more. She circled him and his mother, then opened her lid and stared into her hamper. He wanted to tell her not to touch his mother, but the words sounded ridiculous in his head and he didn't dare find out how stupid they sounded moving through freespace.

And then the washing machine bucked and made a snapping sound and hummed to life.

The generator's dead, he thought. *And she's all rusted through.* And still the washing machine moved. He heard the gush of water filling her, a wet and muddy sound.

"What did you do?" he asked. He climbed slowly to his feet, facing away from his mother, not wanting to see her terrible bucking as she wobbled on her broken foot.

"Nothing," Mimi said. "I just looked inside and it started up."

He stared at his mother, enraptured, mesmerized. Mimi stole alongside of him and he noticed that she'd taken off her jacket and the sweatshirt, splaying out her wings around her.

Her hand found his and squeezed. The machine rocked. His mother rocked and gurgled and rushed, and then she found some focal point of stability and settled into a soft rocking rhythm.

The rush of water echoed off the cave walls, a white-noise shushing that sounded like skis cutting through powder. It was a beautiful sound, one that transported him to a million mornings spent waiting for the boys' laundry to finish and be hung on the line.

All gone

He jerked his head up so fast that something in his neck cracked, needling pain up into his temples and forehead. He looked at Mimi, but she gave no sign of having heard the voice, the words, *All gone*.

All gone.

Mimi looked at him and cocked her head. "What?" she said.

He touched her lips with a finger, forgetting to be mindful of the swelling there, and she flinched away. There was a rustle of wings and clothing.

My sons, all my sons, gone.

The voice emerged from that white-noise roar of water humming and sloshing back and forth in her basket. Mimi squeezed his hand so hard he felt the bones grate.

"Mom?" he said softly, his voice cracking. He took half a step toward the washer.

So tired. I'm worn out. I've been worn out.

He touched the enamel on the lid of the washer, and felt the vibrations through his fingertips. "I can—I can take you home," he said. "I'll take care of you, in the city."

Too late.

There was a snapping sound and then a front corner of the machine settled heavily. One rusted-out foot, broken clean off, rolled across the cave floor.

The water sounds stilled.

Mimi breathed some words, something like *Oh my God,* but maybe in another language, or maybe he'd just forgotten his own tongue.

"I need to go," he said.

T hey stayed in a different motel on their way home from the mountain, and Mimi tried to cuddle him as he lay in the bed, but her wings got in the way, and he edged over to his side until he was almost falling off before she took the hint and curled up on her side. He lay still until he heard her snore softly, then rose and went and sat on the toilet, head in his hands, staring at the moldy grout on the tiled floor in the white light, trying not to think of the bones, the hank of brittle red hair, tied tightly in a shopping bag in the trunk of the rental car.

Sunrise found him pacing the bathroom, waiting for Mimi to stir, and when she padded in and sat on the toilet, she wouldn't meet his eye. He found himself thinking of her standing in the tub, rolled towel between her teeth, as Krishna approached her wings with his knife, and he went back into the room to dress.

"We going to eat breakfast?" she asked in the smallest voice. He said nothing, couldn't will himself to talk.

"There's still food in the car," she said after some silence had slipped by. "We can eat that."

And without any more words, they climbed into the car and he put the pedal down, all the way to Toronto, stopping only once for gas and cigarettes after he smoked all the ones left in her pack.

When they cleared the city limits and drove under the viaduct at Danforth Avenue, getting into the proper downtown, he eased off the Parkway and into the city traffic, taking the main roads with their high buildings and stoplights and people, people, people.

"We're going home?" she said. The last thing she'd said was, "Are you hungry?" fourteen hours before and he'd only shook his head.

"Yes," he said.

"Oh," she said.

Was Krishna home? She was rooting in her purse now, and he knew that she was looking for her knife.

"You staying with me?" he said.

"Can I?" she said. They were at a red light, so he looked into her eyes. They were shiny and empty as marbles.

"Yes," he said. "Of course. And I will have a word with Krishna."

She looked out the window. "I expect he'll want to have a word with you, too."

Link rang his doorbell one morning while he was hunched over his computer, thinking about the story he was going to write. When he'd moved into the house, he'd felt the shape of that story. All the while that he'd sanded and screwed in bookcases, it had floated just below the surface, its silhouette discernible through the ripples.

But when Adam left Mimi watching television and sat at his desk in the evening with the humming, unscuffed, and gleaming laptop before him, fingers poised over the keys, nothing came. He tapped out an opening sentence,

I suspect that my father is dead

and deleted it. Then undid the delete.

He called up The Inventory and stroked the spacebar with his thumb, paging through screensful of pictures and keywords and price tags and scanned-in receipts. He flipped back to the story and deleted his sentence.

My dead brother had been hiding out on the synagogue's roof for God knows how long.

The last thing he wanted was to write an autobiography. He wanted to write a story about the real world, about the real people who inhabited it. He hit the delete key.

The video-store girl never got bored behind her counter, because she could always while away the hours looking up the rental histories of the popular girls who'd shunned her in high school.

That's when Link rang his doorbell and he startled guiltily and quit the text editor, saving the opening sentence. Which had a lot of promise, he thought.

"Link!" he said. "Come in!"

The kid had put on ten or fifteen pounds since they'd first met, and no longer made Alan want to shout, *Someone administer a sandwich, stat!* Most of it was muscle from hard riding as a bike messenger, a gig that Link had kept up right through the cold winter, dressing up like a Gore-Tex Martian in tights and ski goggles and a fleece that showed hints of purple beneath its skin of crusted road salt and pollution.

Andrew had noticed the girls in the Market and at Kurt's shop noticing Link, whose spring wardrobe showed off all that new muscle to new effect, and gathered from the various hurt looks and sulks from the various girls that Link was getting more ass than a toilet seat.

Her brother spent the winter turning into the kind of stud that she'd figured out how to avoid before she finished high school, and it pained her to see the hordes of dumb-bunnies making goo-goo eyes at him.

That would be a good second sentence for his story.

"You okay, Abby?" Link said, looking concerned. Albert realized that he'd been on another planet for a moment there.

"Sorry, just fell down a rabbit hole," he said, flapping his arms comically. "I was writing"—felt *good* to say that—"and I'm in a bit of a, how you say, creative fog."

Link took a step back. "I don't want to disturb you," he said.

But for all that, she still approved his outfits before he left the house, refusing to let him succumb to the ephemeral awful trendiness of mesh-back caps and too-tight Boy Scout Jamboree shirts. Instead, she put him into slightly fitted cotton shirts that emphasized his long lean belly and his broad shoulders.

"Don't sweat it. I could use a break. Come in and have a drink or something." He checked the yellowing face of the tick-tock clock he kept on the mantelpiece and saw that it was just past noon. "Past lunchtime, that means that it's okay to crack a beer. You want a beer?"

And for all that, her brother still managed to come home looking like some kind of frat-rat pussy-hound, the kind of boy she'd always hoped he wouldn't be.

"Beer would be great," Link said. He stepped into the cool of the living room and blinked as his eyes adjusted. "This really is a hell of a place," he said, looking around at the glass cases, the teetering stacks of books that Andrew had pulled down and not reshelved, making ziggurats of them instead next to all the chairs.

"What can I do for you?" Adam said, handing him a glass of

Upper Canada Lager with a little wedge of lime. He'd bought a few cases of beer that week and had been going through them steadily in the living room, paging through the most favored of his books, trying to find something, though he wasn't sure what.

Link sipped. "Summer's here," he said.

"Yeah," Alan said.

"Well, the thing is, summer. I'm going to be working longer hours and, you know, evenings. Well. I mean. I'm nineteen years old, Andy."

Alan raised an eyebrow and sat back in his chair. "What's the message you're trying to convey to me, Link?"

"I'm not going to be going around your friend's shop any-more. I really had fun doing it all year, but I want to try something different with my spare time this summer, you understand?"

"Sure," Alan said. He'd had kids quit on him before. That's what kids did. Attention spans.

"Right. And, well, you know: I never really understood what we were *doing*. . . ."

"Which part?"

"The WiFi stuff—"

"Well, you see—"

"Stop, okay? I've heard you explain it ten times now and I still don't get it. Maybe after a semester or two of electrical engineering it'll make more sense."

"Okay," Adam said, smiling broadly to show no hard feelings. "Hey," he said carefully. "If you didn't understand what we were doing, then why did you do it?"

Link cocked his head, as if examining him for traces of sarcasm, then looked away. "I don't know. It was exciting, even if I didn't quite get it. Everyone else seemed to get it, sort of, and it was fun to work alongside of them, and sometimes the money was okay."

Which is why she decided to—

Damn, what did she decide to do? That was shaping up to be a really good opener.

Which is why she wasn't surprised when he didn't come home for three nights in a row.

Aha.

"No hard feelings, Link," Adam said. "I'm really grateful for the help you gave us and I hope you'll think about helping again in the fall. . . ."

But on the fourth night, she got worried, and she started calling his friends. They were all poor students, so none of them had land-line numbers you could look up in the phone book, but that was okay, since they all had accounts with the video store where she worked, with their deadbeat prepaid mobile numbers listed.

"Yeah, that sounds great, you know, September, it gets dark early. Just got word that I got into Ryerson for the fall, so I'll be taking engineering classes. Maybe I can help out that way?"

"Perfect," Alan said. Link took a step backward, drained his beer, held out the glass.

"Well, thanks," Link said, and turned. Alan reached past him and opened the door. There were a couple of girls there, little suburban girls of the type that you could find by the hatful in the Market on Saturday mornings, shopping for crazy clothes at the vintage shops. They looked fourteen, but might have been as old as sixteen or seventeen and just heartbreakingly naive. Link looked over his shoulder and had the decency to look slightly embarrassed as they smiled at him.

"Okay, thanks, then," he said, and one of the girls looked past him to get a glimpse inside the house. Andy instinctively stepped aside to give her a better view of his showroom and he was about to offer her a soda before he caught himself.

"You've got a nice place," she said. "Look at all those books!"

Her friend said, "Have you read all those books?" She was wearing thick concealer over her acne, but she had a round face and heart-shaped lips that he wouldn't have been surprised to see on the cover of a magazine. She said it with a kind of sneer.

Link said, "Are you kidding? What's the point of a houseful of books you've already read?"

They both laughed adoringly—if Adam was feeling uncharitable, he'd say it was simpering, not laughing—and took off for the exciting throngs in the Market.

Alan watched them go, with Link's empty glass in one hand and his full glass in the other. It was hot out in the Market, sunny, and it felt like the spring had rushed up on him and taken him by surprise when he wasn't looking. He had owned the house for more than a year now, and the story only had three or four paragraphs to it (and none of them were written down yet!).

"You can't wash shit," is what her mother said when she called home and asked what she should do about her brother. "That kid's been a screw-up since he was five years old."

He should write the story down. He went back upstairs and sat down at the keyboard and pecked out the sentences that had come to him, but they seemed very sterile there aglow on the screen, in just the same way that they'd felt restless and alive a moment before. The sunny day beamed through the study window and put a glare up on his screen that made it hard to type, and when he moved to the other side of the desk, he found himself looking out the window at the city and the spring.

He checked his calendar and his watch and saw that he only had a couple hours before the reporter from *NOW* magazine came by. The reporter—a summer intern—was the only person to respond to his all-fluff press release on the open network. He and Kurt had argued about the wording all night, and when he was done he almost pitched it out, as the editorial thrash had gutted it to the point of meaninglessness.

Oh, well. The breeze made the new leaves in the trees across the street sway, and now the sun was in his eyes, and the sentences were inert on the screen.

He closed the lid of the laptop and grabbed his coat and left the house as fast as he could, obscurely worried that if he didn't leave then, he wouldn't get out all day.

As he got closer to Kurt's storefront, he slowed down. The crowds were thick, laughing suburban kids and old men in buttoned-up cardigans and fisherman's caps and subcultural tropical fish of all kinds: goths and punks and six kinds of ravers and hippies and so forth.

He spied Link sitting on the steps leading up to one of the above-shop apartments, passing a cigarette to a little girl who sat between his knees. Link didn't see him; he was laughing at something the boy behind him said. Alan looked closer. It was Krishna, except he'd shaved his head and was wearing a hoodie with glittering piping run along the double seams, a kind of future-sarcastic raver jumper that looked like it had been abandoned on the set of *Space: 1999.*

Krishna had his own little girl between *his* knees, with heart-shaped lips and thick matte concealer over her zits. His hand lay casually on her shoulder, and she brushed her cheek against it.

Alan felt the air whuff out of him as though he'd been punched in the stomach, and he leaned up against the side of a fruit market, flattening himself there. He turned his head from side to side, expecting to see Mimi and wanting to rush out and shield her from the sight, but she was nowhere to be seen, and anyway, what business was it of his?

And then he spied Natalie, standing at the other end of the street, holding on to the handles of one of the show bicycles out front of Bikes on Wheels. She was watching her brother closely, with narrowed eyes.

It was her fault, in some way. Or at least she thought it was. She'd caught him looking at Internet porn and laughed at him, humiliating him, telling him he should get out and find a girl whose last name wasn't "Jpeg."

He saw that her hands were clenched into fists and realized that his were, too.

It was her fault in some way, because she'd seen the kind of person he was hanging out with and she hadn't done a thing about it.

He moved into the crowd and waded through it, up the street on the opposite side from his neighbors. He closed in on Natalie and ended up right in front of her before she noticed he was there.

"Oh!" she said, and blushed hard. She'd been growing out her hair for a couple months and it was long enough to clip a couple of barrettes to. With the hair, she looked less skinny, a little older, a little less vulnerable. She tugged at a hank of it absently. "Hi."

"We going to do anything about that?" he said, jerking his head toward the steps. Krishna had his hand down the little girl's top now, cupping her breast, then laughing when she slapped it away.

She shrugged, bit her lip. She shook her head angrily. "None of my business. None of *your* business."

She looked at her feet. "Look, there's a thing I've been meaning to tell you. I don't think I can keep on volunteering at the shop, okay? I've got stuff to do, assignments, and I'm taking some extra shifts at the store—"

He held up a hand. "I'm grateful for all the work you've done, Natalie. You don't need to apologize."

"Okay," she said. She looked indecisively around, then seemed to make up her mind and she hugged him hard. "Take care of yourself, okay?"

It struck him as funny. "I can take care of myself just fine, don't worry about me for a second. You still looking for fashion work? I think Tropicál will be hiring for the summer. I could put in that phone call."

"No," she said. "No, that's okay." She looked over his shoulder and her eyes widened. He turned around and saw that Krishna and Link had spotted them, and that Krishna was whispering something in Link's ear that was making Link grin nastily.

"I should go," she said. Krishna's hand was still down the little girl's top, and he jiggled her breast at Alan.

The reporter had two lip piercings, and a matt of close-cropped micro-dreads, and an attitude.

"So here's what I don't get. You've got the Market wired—"

"Unwired," Kurt said, breaking in for the tenth time in as many minutes. Alan shot him a dirty look.

"Unwired, right." The kid made little inverted commas with his fingertips, miming, *Yes, that is a very cute jargon you've invented, dork.* "You've got the Market unwired and you're going to connect up your network with the big interchange down on Front Street."

"Well, *eventually*," Alan said. The story was too complicated. Front Street, the Market, open networks . . . it had no focus, it wasn't a complete narrative with a beginning, middle, and end. He'd tried to explain it to Mimi that morning, over omelets in his kitchen, and she'd been totally lost.

"Eventually?" The kid took on a look of intense, teenaged skepticism. He claimed to be twenty, but he looked about seventeen and had been the puck in an intense game of eyeball hockey among the cute little punk girls who'd been volunteering in the shopfront when he'd appeared.

"That's the end goal, a citywide network with all-we-can-eat free connectivity, fully anonymized and hardened against malicious attackers and incidental environmental interference." Alan steepled his fingers and tried to look serious and committed.

"Okay, that's the goal."

"But it's not going to be all or nothing. We want to make the community a part of the network. Getting people energized about participating in the network is as important as providing the network itself—hell, the network *is* people. So we've got this intermediate step, this way that everyone can pitch in."

"And that is, what, renaming your network to ParasiteNet?" Kurt nodded vigorously. "Zactly."

"And how will I find these ParasiteNet nodes? Will there be a map or something with all this information on it?"

Alan nodded slowly. "We've been thinking about a mapping application—"

"But we decided that it was stupid," Kurt said. "No one needed to draw a map of the Web—it just grew and people found its weird corners on their own. Networks don't *need* centralized authority, that's just the chains on your mind talking—"

"The chains on my mind?" The kid snorted.

Alan held his hands up placatingly. "Wait a second," he said. "Let's take a step back here and talk about *values*. The project here is about free expression and cooperation. Sure, it'd be nice to have a city-wide network, but in my opinion, it's a lot more important to have a city full of people working on that network because they value expression and understand how cooperation gets us more of that."

"And we'll get this free expression how?"

"By giving everyone free Internet access."

The kid laughed and shook his head. "That's a weird kind of 'free,' if you don't mind my saying so. I mean, it's like, 'Free speech if you can afford a two-thousand-dollar laptop and want to sit down and type on it.'"

"I can build you a desktop out of garbage for twenty bucks," Kurt said. "We're drowning in PC parts."

"Sure, whatever. But what kind of free expression is that? Free expression so long as you're sitting at home with your PC plugged into the wall?"

"Well, it's not like we're talking about displacing all the other kinds of expression," Alan said. "This is in addition to all the ways you've had to talk—"

"Right, like this thing," the kid said. He reached into his pocket and took out a small phone. "This was free—not twenty dollars, not even two thousand—just free, from the phone company, in exchange for a one-year contract. Everyone's got one of these. I went trekking in India, you see people using these out in the bush. And you know what they use them for? Speech! Not speech-in-quotes meaning some kind of abstract expression, but actual *talking.*"

The kid leaned forward and planted his hands on his knees and suddenly he was a lot harder to dismiss as some subculture-addled intern. He had that fiery intensity that Alan recognized from himself, from Kurt, from the people who believe.

Alan thought he was getting an inkling into why this particular intern had responded to his press release: not because he was too ignorant to see through the bullshit, but just the opposite.

"But that's communication through the *phone company,*" Kurt said, wonderment in his voice that his fellow bohemian couldn't see how sucktastic that proposition was. "How is that free speech?"

The kid rolled his eyes. "Come off it. You old people, you turn up your noses whenever someone ten years younger than you points out that cell phones are actually a pretty good way for people to communicate with each other—even subversively. I wrote a term paper last year on this stuff: In Kenya, electoral scrutineers follow the ballot boxes from the polling place to the counting house and use their cell phones to sound the alarm when someone tries to screw with them. In the Philippines, twenty thousand people were mobilized in fifteen minutes in front of the presidential palace when they tried to shut down the broadcast of the corruption hearings.

"And yet every time someone from my generation talks about how important phones are to democracy, there's always some old pecksniff primly telling us that our phones don't give us *real* democracy. It's so much bullshit."

He fell silent and they all stared at each other for a moment. Kurt's mouth hung open.

"I'm not old," he said finally.

"You're older than me," the kid said. His tone softened. "Look, I'm not trying to be cruel here, but you're generation-blind. The Internet is great, but it's not the last great thing we'll ever invent. My pops was a mainframe guy, he thought PCs were toys. You're a PC guy, so you think my phone is a toy."

Alan looked off into the corner of the back room of Kurt's shop for a while, trying to marshal his thoughts. Back there, among the shelves of milk crates stuffed with T-shirts and cruft, he had a thought.

"Okay" he said. "Fair enough. It may be that today, in the field, there's a lot of free expression being enabled with phones. But at the end of the day"—he thought of Lyman—"this is the *phone company* we're talking about. Big lumbering dinosaur that is thrashing in the tar pit. The spazz dinosaur that's so embarrassed all the other dinosaurs that none of them want to rescue it.

"Back in the sixties, these guys sued to keep it illegal to plug anything other than their rental phones into their network. But more to the point, you get a different kind of freedom with an Internet network than a phone-company network—even if the Internet network lives on top of the phone-company network.

"If you invent a new way of using the phone network—say, a cheaper way of making long-distance calls using voice-over-IP, you can't roll that out on the phone network without the permission of the carrier. You have to go to him and say, 'Hey, I've invented a way to kill your most profitable line of business, can you install it at your switching stations so that we can all talk long distance for free?'

"But on the net, anyone can invent any application that he can get his buddies to use. No central authority had to give permission for the Web to exist: A physicist just hacked it together one day, distributed the software to his colleagues, and in just a very short while, people all over the world had the Web.

"So the net can live on top of the phone network and it can run voice-calling as an application, but it's not tied to the phone network. It doesn't care whose wires or wireless it lives on top of. It's got all these virtues that are key to free expression. That's why we care about this."

The kid nodded as he talked, impatiently, signaling in body language that even Alan could read that he'd heard this already.

"Yes, in this abstract sense, there are a bunch of things to like about your Internet over there. But I'm talking about practical, nonabstract, nontheoretical stuff over here. The real world. I can get a phone for *free*. I can talk to *everyone* with it. I can say *anything* I want. I can use it *anywhere*. Sure, the phone company is a giant conspiracy by The Man to keep us down. But can you really tell me with a straight face that because I can't invent the Web for my phone or make free long-distance calls I'm being censored?"

"Of course not," Kurt said. Alan put a steadying hand on his shoulder. "Fine, it's not an either-or thing. You can have your phones, I can have my Internet, and we'll both do our thing. It's not like the absence of the Web for phones or high long-distance charges are *good* for free expression, Christ. We're trying to unbreak the net so that no one can own it or control it. We're trying to put it on every corner of the city, for free, anonymously, for anyone to use. We're doing it with recycled garbage, and we're paying homeless teenagers enough money to get off the street as part of the program. What's not to fucking like?"

The kid scribbled hard on his pad. "*Now* you're giving me some quotes I can use. You guys need to work on your pitch. 'What's not to fucking like?' That's good."

He and Link saw each other later that day, and Link still had his two little girls with him, sitting on the patio at the Greek's, drinking beers, and laughing at his jokes.

"Hey, you're the guy with the books," one of them said when he passed by.

He stopped and nodded. "That's me, all right," he said.

Link picked at the label of his beer bottle and added to the dandruff of shredded paper in the ashtray before him. "Hey, Abe," he said.

"Hey, Link," he said. He looked down at the little girls' bags. "You've made some finds," he said. "Congratulations."

They were wearing different clothes now—double-knit neon pop-art dresses and horn-rim shades and white legs flashing beneath the tabletop. They kicked their toes and smiled and drank their beers, which seemed comically large in their hands.

Casually, he looked to see who was minding the counter at the Greek's and saw that it was the idiot son, who wasn't smart enough to know that serving liquor to minors was asking for bad trouble.

"Where's Krishna?" he asked.

One girl compressed her heart-shaped lips into a thin line.

And so she resolved to help her brother, because when it's your fault that something has turned to shit, you have to wash shit. And so she resolved to help her brother, which meant that, step one, she had to get him to stop screwing up.

"He took off," the girl said. Her pancake makeup had sweated away during the day and her acne wasn't so bad that she'd needed it. "He took off running, like he'd forgotten something important. Looked scared."

"Why don't you go get more beers," Link said angrily, cutting her off, and Alan had an intuition that Link had become Krishna's Renfield, a recursion of Renfields, each nesting inside the last like Russian dolls in reverse: big Link inside medium Krishna inside the stump that remained of Darrel.

And that meant that she had to take him out of the company of his bad companions, which she would accomplish through the simple expedient of scaring the everlasting fuck out of them.

She sulked off and the remaining girl looked down at her swinging toes.

"Where'd he go, Link?" Alan said. If Krishna was in a hurry to go somewhere or see something, he had an idea of what it was about.

Link's expression closed up like a door slamming shut. "I don't know," he said. "How should I know?"

The other girl scuffed her toes and took a sip of her beer.

Their gazes all flicked down to the bottle.

"The Greek would bar you for life if he knew you were bringing underaged drinkers into here," Alan said.

"Plenty of other bars in the Market," Link said, shrugging his newly broad shoulders elaborately.

Trey was the kid who'd known her brother since third grade and whose puberty-induced brain damage had turned him into an utter turd. She once caught him going through the bathroom hamper, fetishizing her panties, and she'd shouted at him and he'd just ducked and grinned a little-boy grin that she had been incapable of wiping off his face, no matter how she raged. She would enjoy this.

"And they all know the Greek," Alan said. "Three, two, one." He turned on his heel and began to walk away.

"Wait!" Link called. The girl swallowed a giggle. He sounded desperate and not cool at all anymore.

Alan stopped and turned his body halfway, looking impatiently over his shoulder.

Link mumbled something.

"What?"

"Behind Kurt's place," Link said. "He said he was going to go look around behind Kurt's place."

"Thank you, Link," he said. He turned all the way around and got down to eye level with the other girl. "Nice to meet you," he said. He wanted to tell her, *Be careful* or *Stay alert* or *Get out while the getting's good,* but none of that seemed likely to make much of an impression on her.

She smiled and her friend came back with three beers. "You've got a great house," she said.

Her friend said, "Yeah, it's amazing."

"Well, thank you," he said.

"Bye," they said.

Link's gaze bored into the spot between his shoulder blades the whole way to the end of the block.

The back alleys of Kensington were a maze of coach houses, fences, dead ends, and narrow doorways. Kids who knew their secrets played ball-hockey nearly undisturbed by cars, junkies turned them into reeking pissoirs, homeless people dossed down in the lees of their low, crazy-angled buildings, teenagers came and necked around corners.

But Alan knew their secrets. He'd seen the aerial maps, and he'd clambered their length and breadth and height with Kurt, checking sight lines for his network, sticking virtual pushpins into the map on his screen where he thought he could get some real benefit out of an access point.

So once he reached Kensington Avenue, he slipped behind a Guyanese patty stand and stepped through a wooden gate and began to make his way to the back of Kurt's place. Cautiously.

From behind, the riot of colors and the ramshackle signs and subculture of Kensington was revealed as a superfice, a skin stretched over slightly daggy brick two-stories with tiny yards and tumbledown garages. From behind, he could be walking the back ways of any anonymous housing development, a no-personality grayzone of nothing and no one.

The sun went behind a cloud and the whole scene turned into something monochromatic, a black-and-white clip from an old home movie.

Carefully, he proceeded. Carefully, slipping from doorway to doorway, slipping up the alleyway to the next, to the corner that led to the alley that led to Kurt's. Carefully, listening, watching.

And he managed to sneak up on Krishna and Davey, and he knew that for once, he'd be in the position to throw the rocks.

Krishna sat with his back against the cinderblock wall near Kurt's back door, knees and hands splayed, head down in a posture of supplication. He had an unlit cigarette in his mouth, which he nervously shifted from corner to corner, like a soggy toothpick. Behind him, standing atop the dented and scabrous garbage cans, Dumont.

He rested his head on his folded arms, which he rested on the sill, and he stood on tiptoe to see in the window.

"I'm hungry," Krishna said. "I want to go get some food. Can I go and get food and come back?"

"Quiet," Dewayne said. "Not another fucking word, you sack

of shit." He said it quietly in a neutral tone that was belied by his words. He settled his head back on his folded forearms like a babe settling its head in a bosom and looked back through the window. "Ah," he said, like he had taken a drink.

Krishna climbed slowly to his feet and stood off a pace or two, staring at Drew. He reached into the pocket of his old bomber jacket and found a lighter and flicked it nervously a couple times.

"Don't you light that cigarette," Davey said. "Don't you dare."

"How long are we going to be here?" Krishna's whine was utterly devoid of his customary swagger.

"What kind of person is he?" Davey said. "What kind of person is he? He is in love with my brother, looks at him with cow-eyes when he sees him, hangs on his words like a love-struck girl." He laughed nastily. "Like *your* love-struck girl, like she looks at him.

"I wonder if he's had her yet. Do you think he has?"

"I don't care," Krishna said petulantly, and levered himself to his feet. He began to pace and Alan hastily backed himself into the doorway he'd been hiding in. "She's mine, no matter who she's fucking. I *own* her."

"Look at that," Darrel said. "Look at him talking to them, his little army, like a general giving them a pep talk. He got that from my brother, I'm sure. Everywhere he goes, he leaves a trail of manipulators who run other people's lives."

Alan's stomach clenched in on itself, and his butt and thighs ached suddenly, like he'd been running hard. He thought about his protégés with their shops and their young employees, learning the trade from them as they'd learned it from him. How long had Don been watching him?

"When are we going to do it?" Krishna spat out his cigarette and shook another out of his pack and stuck it in his mouth.

"Don't light it," Drew said. "We're going to do it when I say it's time to do it. You have to watch first—watching is the most important part. It's how you find out what needs doing and to whom. It's how you find out where you can do the most damage."

"I know what needs doing," Krishna said. "We can just go in

there and trash the place and fuck him up. That'd suit me just fine. Send the right message, too."

Danny hopped down off the trash can abruptly and Krishna froze in his paces at the dry rasp of hard blackened skin on the pavement. Davey walked toward him in a bowlegged, splay-hipped gait that was more a scuttle than a walk, the motion of some inhuman creature not accustomed to two legs.

"Have you ever watched your kind, ever? Do you under-stand them, even a little? Just because you managed to get a lit-tle power over one of my people, you think you understand it all. You don't. That one in there is bone-loyal to my brother. If you vandalized his little shop, he'd just go to my brother for pro-tection and end up more loyal and more. Please stop thinking you know anything, it'll make it much easier for us to get along."

Krishna stiffened. "I know things," he said.

"Your pathetic little birdie girl is *nothing*," Davey said. He stumped over to Krishna, stood almost on his toes, looking up at him. Krishna took an involuntary step backward. "A little one-off, a changeling without clan or magic of any kind."

Krishna stuck his balled fists into the pockets of his space-age future-sarcastic jacket. "I know something about *you*," he said. "About *your* kind."

"Oh, yes?" Davey's tone was low, dangerous.

"I know how to recognize you, even when you're passing for normal. I know how to spot you in a crowd, in a second." He smiled. "You've been watching my kind all your life, but I've been watching your kind for all of *mine*. I've seen you on the subway and running corner stores, teaching in classrooms and driving to work."

Davey smiled then, showing blackened stumps. "Yes, you can, you certainly can." He reached out one small, delicate hand and stroked the inside of Krishna's wrist. "You're very clever that way, you are." Krishna closed his eyes and breathed heavily through his nose, as though in pain or ecstasy. "That's a good skill to have."

They stood there for a moment while Davey slowly trailed his fingertips over Krishna's wrist. Then, abruptly, he grabbed Krishna's thumb and wrenched it far back. Krishna dropped abruptly to his knees, squeaking in pain.

"You can spot my kind, but you know nothing about us. You *are* nothing, do you understand me?" Krishna nodded slowly. Alan felt a sympathetic ache in his thumb and a sympathetic grin on his face at the sight of Krishna knelt down and made to acquiesce. "You understand me?" Krishna nodded again.

Davey released him and he climbed slowly to his feet. Davey took his wrist again, gently. "Let's get you something to eat," he said.

Before Alan knew it, they were nearly upon him, walking back down the alley straight toward his hiding place. Blood roared in his ears and he pressed his back up against the doorway. They were only a step or two away, and after a couple of indiscreetly loud panting gasps, he clamped his lips shut and held his breath.

There was no way they could miss him. He pressed his back harder against the door, and it abruptly swung open and a cold hand wrapped itself around his bicep and pulled him through into a darkened, oil- and must-smelling garage.

He tripped over his own heel and started to go over, but a pair of hands caught him and settled him gently to the floor.

"Quiet," came a hoarse whisper in a voice he could not place.

And then he knew who his rescuer was. He stood up silently and gave Billy a long hug. He was as skinny as death.

Trey's phone number was still current in the video store's database, so she called him.

"Hey, Trey," she said. "It's Lara."

"Lara, heeeeeeyyyy," he said, in a tone that left no doubt that he was picturing her panties. "Sorry, your bro ain't here."

"Want to take me out to dinner tonight?"

The silence on the other end of the line made her want to laugh, but she bit her lip and rolled her eyes and amused the girl browsing the chop-socky epics and visibly eavesdropping.

"Trey?"

"Lara, uh, yes, I'd love to, sure. Is this like a group thing
or . . ."

"No, Trey, I thought I'd keep this between the two of us.
I'll be at the store until six—meet me here?"

"Yeah, okay. Okay! Sure. I'll see you tonight."

Brad was so thin he looked like a corpse. He was still tall,
though, and his hair and beard were grown out into long, bad-
smelling straggles of knot and grime. In the half-light of the
garage, he had the instantly identifiable silhouette of a street
person.

He gathered Adam up in a hug that reeked of piss and
booze, a hug like a bundle of twigs in his arms.

"I love you," he whispered.

Andrew backed away and held him at arm's length. His skin
had gone to deep creases lined with soot, his eyes filmed with
something that looked like pond scum.

"Brady. What are you doing here?"

He held a finger up to his lips, then opened the door
again onto the now-empty alley. Alan peered the way that
Davey and Krishna had gone, just in time to see them turn a
distant corner.

"Give it another minute," Blake said, drawing the door
nearly closed again. A moment later, they heard another door
open and then Kurt's chain-draped boots jangled past, headed
the other way. They listened to them recede, and then Brian
swung the door wide again.

"It's okay now," he said.

They stepped out into the sunlight and Bert started to walk
slowly away. Alan caught up with him and Bert took his arm with
long bony fingers, leaning on him. He had a slight limp.

"Where have you been?" Alan asked when they had gone
halfway home through deft, confident turnings led by Blake.

"Watching you," he said. "Of course. When I came to the
city, I worked out at the racetrack for a week and made enough
money to live off of for a couple months, and avoided the tough

guys who watched me winning and waited to catch me alone at the streetcar stop. I made enough and then I went to watch you.

"I knew where you were, of course. Always knew where you were. I could see you whenever I closed my eyes. I knew when you opened your shops and I went by at night and in the busy parts of the day so that I could get a better sense of them. I kept an eye on you, Alan, watched over you. I had to get close enough to smell you and hear you and see you, though, it wasn't enough to see you in my mind.

"Because I had to know the *why*. I could see the *what*, but I had to know the *why*—why were you opening your stores? Why were you saying the things you said? I had to get close enough because from the outside, it's impossible to tell if you're wink-ing because you've got a secret, or if you've got dust in your eye, or if you're making fun of someone who's winking, or if you're trying out a wink to see how it might feel later.

"It's been four years I've been watching you when I could, going back to the track for more when I ran out of money, and you know what? I know what you're doing."

Alan nodded. "Yeah," he said.

"You're watching. You're doing what I'm doing. You're watching them to figure out what they're doing."

Alvin nodded. "Yeah," he said.

"You don't know any more about the world than I do."

Albert nodded. "Yeah," he said.

Billy shook his head and leaned more heavily on Alan's arm. "I want a drink," he said.

"I've got some vodka in the freezer," Alan said.

"I'll take some of the Irish whiskey on the sideboard in the living room."

Adam looked at him sharply and he shrugged and smiled an apologetic smile. "I've been watching," he said.

They crossed the park together and Buddy stopped to look hard at the fountain. "That's where he took Edward, right? I saw that."

"Yeah," Alvin said. "Do you know where he is now?"

"Yeah," Billy said. "Gone."

"Yeah," Adam said. "Yeah."

They started walking now, Billy's limp more pronounced.

"What's with your leg?"

"My foot. I lost a couple toes last year to frostbite and never got them looked at properly." He reeked of piss and booze.

"They didn't . . . grow back?"

Bradley shook his head. "They didn't," he said. "Not mine. Hello, Krishna," he said.

Alan looked to his neighbors' porch. Krishna stood there, stocks-still, against the wall.

"Friend of yours, huh?" Krishna said. "Boyfriend?"

"He offered me a bottle of wine if I let him take me home," Bradley said. "Best offer I had all week. Wanna make it a three-some? An 'ow you say mange ma twat?"

Krishna contorted his face into an elaborate sneer. "Puke," he said.

"Bye, Krishna," Buddy said. Alan put his key into the lock and let them in.

Blaine made a hobbling beeline for the sideboard and picked up the Jim Beam Apollo 8 commemorative decanter that Adam kept full of Bushmills 1608 and poured himself a tall glass of it. He drank it back in two swallows, then rolled his tongue around in his mouth with his eyes closed while he breathed out the fumes.

"I have been thinking about that bottle ever since you bought it," he said. "This stuff is legendary. God, that's good. I mean, that's fucking magical."

"It's good," Andrew said. "You can have more if you want."

"Yeah," Burke said, and poured out another drink. He carried it and the decanter to the sofa and settled into it. "Nice sofa," he said. "Nice living room. Nice house. Not very normal, though."

"No," Andrew said. "I'm not fitting in very well."

"I fit in great." He drank back another glug of whiskey and poured out another twenty dollars' worth. "Just great, it's the truth. I'm totally invisible and indistinguishable. I've been sleeping at the Scott Mission for six months now and no one has given me a second glance. They can't even steal my stuff, because when they try, when they come for my shoes or my food in the night, I'm always awake and watching them and just shaking my head."

The whole living room stank of whiskey fumes with an ammoniac tinge. "What if I find you some clothes and a towel?"

"Would I clean myself up? Would I get rid of this protective coloration and become visible again?" He drank more, breathed out the fumes. "Sure, why not. Why not. Time to be visible. You've seen me, Krishna's seen me. Davey's gonna see me. Least I got to see them first."

And so he let his older brother lead him by the hand upstairs to the bathroom with its damp-swollen paperbacks and framed kitsch-art potty-training cartoons. And so he let his brother put him under the stinging hot shower and shampoo his hair and scrub him vigorously with a back brush, sluicing off the ground-in grime of the streets—though the callus pads on his hands remained as dark with soot as the feet of an alleycat. And so he let his older brother wash the stumps of his toes where the skin was just a waxy pucker of scar, like belly buttons, which neither of them had.

And so he let his brother trim away his beard, first with scissors and then with an electric razor, and so he let his brother brush out his long hair and tie it back with an elastic taken from around a bunch of broccoli in the vegetable crisper.

And so, by the time the work was done and he was dressed in too-big clothes that hung over his sunken chest and spindly legs like a tent, he was quite sober and quite clean and quite different.

"You look fine," Adam said, as Brent fingered his chin and watched the reflection in the full-length mirror on the door of Alan's study. "You look great."

"I look conspicuous. Visible. Used to be that eyes just slid off of me. Now they'll come to rest on me, if only for a few seconds."

Andy nodded. "Sure, that's right. You know, being invisible isn't the same as being normal. Normal people are visible."

"Yeah," Brad said, nodding miserably. He pawed again at the smooth hollows of his cheeks.

"You can stay in here," Alan said, gesturing at his study. The desk and his laptop and his little beginning of a story sat in the middle of the room, surrounded by a litter of access points in various stages of repair and printed literature full of optimistic, nontechnical explanations of ParasiteNet. "I'll move all that stuff out."

"Yeah," Billy said. "You should. Just put it in the basement in boxes. I've been watching you screw around with that wireless stuff, and you know, it's not real normal, either. It's pretty desperately weird. Danny's right—that Kurt guy, following you around, like he's in love with you. That's not normal." He flushed, and his hands were in fists. "Christ, Adam, you're living in this goddamned museum and nailing those stupid science-fair projects to the sides of buildings. You've got this comet tail of druggy kids following you around, buying dope with the money they make off of the work they do for you. You're not just visible, you're *strobing*, and you're so weird even *I* get the crawlies around you."

His bare feet slapped the shining cool wood as he paced the room, lame foot making a different sound from the good one.

Andy looked out the window at the green maple keys rattling in the wind. "They're buying drugs?"

Benny snorted. "You're bankrolling weekly heroin parties at two warehouses on Oxford, and three raves a month down on Liberty Street."

He looked up at the ceiling. "Mimi's awake now," he said. "Better introduce me."

Mimi kept her own schedule, mostly nocturnal, padding quietly around his house while he slept, coming silently to bed after he rose, while he was in the bathroom. She hadn't spoken a word to him in more than a week, and he had said nothing to her. But for the snores and the warmth of the bed when he lay down and the morning dishes in the sink, she might not have been living with him at all. But for his constant awareness of her presence in his house and but for the shirts with cut-away backs in the laundry hamper, he might be living all on his own.

But for the knife that he found under the mattress, compass set into the handle, serrated edge glinting, he might have forgotten those wings, which drooped near to the floor now.

Footsteps crossing between the master bedroom and the bathroom. Pausing at the top of the stairs. A soft cough.

"Alan?"

"It's okay, Mimi," he said.

She came down in a pair of his boxer shorts, with the top-sheet complicatedly draped over her chest in a way that left her wings free. Their tips touched the ground.

"This is my brother Bentley," Adam said. "I told you about him."

"You can see the future," she said reproachfully.

"You have wings," he said.

She held out her hand and he shook it.

"I want breakfast," she said.

"Sounds good to me," Brent said.

Alan nodded. "I'll cook."

He made pancakes and cut up pears and peaches and apples and bananas for fruit salad.

"This reminds me of the pancake house in town," Bart said. "Remember?"

Adam nodded. It had been Ed-Fred-George's favorite Sunday dinner place.

"Do you live here now?" Mimi said.

Alan said, "Yes." She slipped her hand into his and squeezed his thumb. It felt good and unexpected.

"Are you going to tell her?" Billy said.

She withdrew her hand. "What is it." Her voice was cold.

Billy said, "There's no good comes of keeping secrets. Krishna and Davey are planning to attack Kurt. Krishna says he owns you. He'll probably come for you."

"Did you see that?" Adam said. "Him coming for her?"

"Not that kind of seeing. I just understand enough about people to know what that means."

Trey met her at six, and he was paunchier than she'd remembered, his high school brawn run to a little fat. He shoved a gift into her hand, a brown paper bag with a quart of cheap vodka in it. She thanked him simperingly and tucked it in her knapsack. "It's a nice night. Let's get takeout and eat it in High Park."

She saw the wheels turn in his head, meal plus booze plus secluded park equals pussy, pussy, pussy, and she let the tip of her tongue touch her lips. This would be even easier than she'd thought.

"How can you tell the difference?" Arthur said. "Between seeing and understanding?"

"You'll never mistake them. Seeing it is like remembering spying on someone, only you haven't spied on him yet. Like you were standing behind him and he just didn't notice. You hear it, you smell it, you see it. Like you were standing *in* him sometimes, like it happened to you.

"Understanding, that's totally different. That's like a little voice in your head explaining it to you, telling you what it all means."

"Oh," Andy said.

"You thought you'd seen, right?"

"Yeah. Thought that I was running out of time and going to die, or kill Davey again, or something. It was a feeling, though, not like being there, not like having anything explained."

"Is that going to happen?" Mimi asked Brad.

Brad looked down at the table. " 'Answer unclear, ask again later.' That's what this Magic 8-Ball I bought in a store once used to say."

"Does that mean you don't know?"

"I think it means I don't want to know."

Don't worry," Bert said. "Kurt's safe tonight."

Alan stopped lacing up his shoes and slumped back on the bench in his foyer. Mimi had done the dishes, Bill had dried, and he'd fretted about Kurt. But it wasn't until he couldn't take it anymore and was ready to go and find him, bring him home if necessary, that Billy had come to talk to him.

"Do you know that for sure?"

"Yes. He has dinner with a woman, then he takes her dumpster diving and comes home and goes to bed. I can see that."

"But you don't see everything?"

"No, but I saw that."

"Fine," Adam said. He felt hopeless in the face of these predictions, as though the future were something set and immutable.

"I need to use the bathroom," Billy said, and made his way upstairs while Alan moved to a sofa and paged absently through an old edition of *Alice in Wonderland* whose marbled frontispiece had come detached.

A moment later, Mimi joined him, sitting down next to him, her wings unfolded across the sofa back.

"How big are they going to get, do you think?" she said, arranging them.

"You don't know?"

"They're bigger than they've ever been. That was good food," she said. "I think I should go talk to Krishna."

Adam shook his head. "Whoa."

"You don't need to be in between us. Maybe I can get him to back off on you, on your family."

"Mimi, I don't even want to discuss it."

"It's the right thing to do," she said. "It's not fair to you to stay."

"You want to have your wings cut," Alan said. "That's why you want to go back to him."

She shied back as though he'd slapped her. "No—"

"You do. But what Billy didn't tell you is that Krishna's out there with other women, I saw him today. With a girl. Young.

Pretty. Normal. If he takes you back, it will be as a toy, not as a lover. He can't love."

"Christ," she said. "Why are you saying this?"

"Because I don't want to watch you self-destruct, Mimi. Stay here. We'll sort out Krishna together. And my brother. Billy's here now, that means they can't sneak up on us."

"And these?" she said, flapping her wings, one great heave that sent currents of air across the room, that blew the loose frontispiece from *Alice in Wonderland* toward the fireplace grate. "You'll sort these out, too?"

"What do you want from me, Mimi?" He was angry now. She hadn't spoken a word to him in weeks, and now . . .

"Cut them off, Alan. Make me into someone who can go out again, who can be seen. Do it. I have the knife."

Adam squeezed his eyes shut. "No," he said.

"Good-bye," she said, and stood, headed for the stairs. Up-stairs, the toilet flushed and they heard the sink running.

"Wait!" he said, running after her. She had her hand on the doorknob.

"No," she said. She was crying now. "I won't stay. I won't be trapped again. Better to be with him than trapped—"

"I'll do it," he said. "If you still want me to do it in two days, I'll do it."

She looked gravely at him. "Don't you lie to me about this," she said. "Don't you dare be lying."

He took her hands. "I swear," he said.

From the top of the stairs then, "Whups," said Billy. "I think I'll just tuck myself into bed."

Mimi smiled and hugged Alan fiercely.

Trey's ardor came out with his drunkenness. First a clammy arm around her shoulder, then a casual grope at her boob, then a sloppy kiss on the corner of her mouth. That was as far as she was going to let it go. She waited for him to move in for another kiss, then slipped out from under his arm so that he fell into the roots of the big tree they'd been leaning against. She brained him with the vodka bottle before he'd had a chance to recover, then, as he rocked and moaned, she calmly took the hunting knife she'd bought at the Yonge Street survivalist store out of her bag. She prized one of his hands off his clutched head and turned it over, then swiftly drew the blade across his palm, laying it open to the muscle.

She hadn't been sure that she'd be capable of doing that, but it was easier than she'd thought. She had nothing to worry about. She was capable of that and more.

They climbed into bed together at the same time for the first time since they'd come home, like a domesticated couple, and Mimi dug under her pillow and set something down with a tin *tink* on the bedstand, a sound too tinny to be the hunting knife. Alan squinted. It was the robot, the one he'd given her, the pretty thing with the Dutch Master craquelure up its tuna-can skirts.

"He's beautiful," she said. "Like you." She wrapped her wings around him tightly, soft fur softer than any down comforter, and pressed her dimpled knees into the hollows of his legs, snuggling in.

He cried like a baby once the pain in his hand set in. She pointed the knifepoint at his face, close enough to stab him if need be. "I won't kill you if you don't scream," she said. "But I will be taking one joint of one toe and one joint of one finger tonight. Just so you know."

He tried not to fall asleep, tried to stay awake and savor that feeling of her pressed against him, of her breath on the nape of his neck, of the enfolded engulfment of her wings, but he couldn't keep his eyes open. Soon enough, he was asleep.

What roused him, he couldn't say, but he found himself groggily awake in the close heat of those wings, held tight. He listened attentively, heard something else, a tinny sound. The robot.

His bladder was full. He gently extricated himself from Mimi, from her wings, and stood. There was the robot, silhouetted on the end table. He smiled and padded off to the toilet. He came back to find Mimi splayed across the whole bed, occupying its length and breadth, a faintly naughty smile on her face. He began to ease himself into bed again when he heard the sound, tinny, a little rattle. He looked at the robot.

It was moving. Its arms were moving. That was impossible. Its arms were painted on. He sat up quickly, rousing Mimi, who let out a small sound, and something small and bent emerged from behind the robot and made a dash for the edge of the end table. The way the thing ran, it reminded him of an animal that had been crippled by a trap. He shrank back from it instinctively, even as he reached out for the table light and switched it on.

Mimi scrunched her eyelids and flung an arm over her face, but he hardly noticed, even when she gave an outraged groan. He was looking at the little, crippled thing, struggling to get down off the end table on Mimi's side of the bed.

It was the Allen. Though he hadn't seen it in nearly twenty years, he recognized it. Tiny, malformed, and bandy-legged, it was still the spitting image of him. Had Davey been holding on to it all these years? Tending it in a cage? Torturing it with pins?

Mimi groaned again. "Switch off the light, baby," she said, a moment's domesticity.

"In a sec," he said, and edged closer to the Allen, which was huddled in on itself, staring and crazy.

"Shhh," Adam breathed. "It's okay." He very slowly moved one hand toward the end table, leaning over Mimi, kneeing her wing out of the way.

The Allen shied back farther.

"What're you doing?" Mimi said, squinting up at him.

"Be very still," he said to her. "I don't want to frighten it. Don't scream or make any sudden movements. I'm counting on you."

Her eyes grew round and she slowly looked over toward the end table. She sucked in sudden air, but didn't scream.

"What is—"

"It's me," he said. "It grew out of a piece of me. My thumb. After Davey bit it off."

"Jesus," she said.

The Allen was quaking now, and Alan cooed to it.

"It's hurt," Mimi said.

"A long time ago," Andreas said.

"No, now. It's bleeding."

She was right. A small bead of blood had formed beneath it. He extended his hand farther. Its bandy scurry was pathetic.

Holding his breath, Alan lifted the Allen gently, cradling it in his palms. It squirmed and thrashed weakly. "Shh," he said again. His hands were instantly made slippery and sticky with its blood. "Shh." Something sharp pricked at his hand.

Now that he had it up close, he could see where the blood was coming from: a broken-off sewing needle, shoved rudely through its distended abdomen.

"Cover up," Bradley said, "I'm coming up." They heard his lopsided tread on the steps.

Mimi pulled the blanket up around her chin. "Okay," she said.

Bert opened the door quickly. He wore nothing but the oversized jeans that Alan had given him, his scrawny chest and mutilated feet bare.

"It's going to die," Brad said, hunkering down beside the bed. "Davey pinned it and then sent Link over with it. It can't last through the night."

Adam felt like he was choking. "We can help it," he said. "It can heal. It healed before."

"It won't this time. See how much pain it's in? It's out of its mind."

"So what do you want me to do?"

"We need to put it out of its misery," Brad said. "It's the right thing."

In his hands, the thing squirmed and made a small, hurt sound. "Shhh," Alan said. The sound it made was like sobbing, but small, so small. And weak.

Mimi said, "I think I'm going to be sick."

"Yeah," Brian said. "Yeah, I can see that."

She lifted herself out of bed, unmindful of her nudity, and pushed her way past him to the door, to the bathroom.

"Stop being such a baby," she told Trey as he clutched at his foot. "It's almost stopped bleeding already."

He looked up at her with murder in his eyes. "Shall I take another one?" she said. He looked away.

"If I get word that you've come within a mile of my brother, I will come back and take your eyes. The toe and the finger joint were just a down payment on that."

He made a sullen sound, so she took his vain and girlish blond hair in her fist and tugged his head back and kissed his throat with the knife.

"Nod if you understand. Slowly."

T he knife is under Mimi's pillow."

"I can't do it," Alan said.

"I know," Brian said. "I will."

And he did. Took the knife. Took the Allen. It cried. Mimi threw up in another room, the sound more felt than heard. The toilet flushed and Brian's hands were sure and swift, but not sure enough. The Allen made a sound like a dog whistle. Bruce's hand moved again, and then it was over. He dug a sock out of the hamper and rolled up the Allen's remains in it. "I'll bury it," he said. "In the back."

Numbly, Alan stood and began dressing. "No," he said. "I will."

Mimi joined them, wrapped in a blanket. Alan dug and Brent held the sock and Mimi watched solemnly.

A trapezoid of light knifed across the back garden. They looked up and saw Krishna staring down at them from a third-floor window. He was smiling very slightly. A moment later, Link appeared in the window, reeling like he was drunk, giggling.

They all looked at one another for a frozen moment, then Alan turned back to his shoveling. He dug down three feet, and

Brent laid the little Allen down in the earth gently as putting it to bed, and Alan filled the hole back up. Mimi looked back up at the window, eyes locked on Krishna's.

"I'm going inside," Adam announced. "Are you coming?"

"Yeah," Mimi said, but she didn't. She stayed out there for ten minutes, then twenty, and when Alan looked out his window at her, he saw she was still staring up at Krishna, mesmerized.

He loudly opened his window and leaned out. Mimi's eyes flicked to him, and then she slowly made her way back into the house.

> **She took his pants and his shoes and left him in the park, crying and drunk. All things considered, it had gone well. When Trey told her that he had no idea where her brother was, she believed him. It was okay, she'd find her brother. He had lots of friends.**

Alan thought that that was the end of the story, maybe. Short and sweet. A kind of lady or the tiger thing. Let the reader's imagination do the rest.

There on the screen, it seemed awfully thin. Here in the house he'd built for it, it seemed awfully unimportant. Such a big and elaborate envelope for such a small thing. He saved the file and went back up to bed. Mimi was asleep, which was good, because he didn't think he'd be able to fall asleep with her twice that night.

He curled up on his side of the bed and closed his eyes and tried to forget the sound the Allen had made.

> **"What is wrong with you?"**
>
> **"Not a thing," she said. Her brother's phone-call hadn't been unexpected.**
>
> **"You're fucking insane."**
>
> **"Maybe," she said.**
>
> **"What do you *want from me*?"**
>
> **"I want you to behave yourself."**
>
> **"You're completely fucking insane."**

He woke to find Billy gone, and had a momentary panic, a flashback to the day that Fred had gone missing in the night. But then he found a note on the kitchen table, terse: "Gone out. B." The handwriting sent him back through the years to the days before Davey came home, the days when they'd been a family, when he'd signed Brad's report cards and hugged him when he came home with a high-scoring paper.

Mimi came down while he was holding the note, staring at the few spare words there. She was draped in her wings.

"Where did he go?"

"I don't know," Alan said. "Out."

"Is this what your family is like?"

"Yeah," Alan said. "This is what they're like."

"Are you going to go out, too?"

"Yeah."

"Fine," she said. She was angry. She stomped out of the kitchen, and stepped on her own wing, tripping, going over on her face. "Tomorrow, you cut these tomorrow!" she said, and her wings flared open, knocking the light fixtures a-swing and tumbling piles of books. "Tomorrow!" she said.

Good morning, Natalie," he said. She was red-eyed and her face was puffy, and her hand shook so that the smoke from her cigarette rose in a nervous spiral.

"Andy," she said, nodding.

He looked at her across the railing that divided their porches. "Would you like to join me for a coffee?"

"I'm hardly dressed for it," she said. She was wearing a pair of cutoffs and house slippers and a shapeless green T-shirt that hung down past her butt.

"The Greek doesn't stand on ceremony," he said. He was hardly dressed better. He hadn't wanted to go up to the master bedroom and face Mimi, so he'd dressed himself out of the laundry hamper in the basement.

"I don't have *shoes,* Alan."

"You could go in and get some," he said.

She shook her head.

Her shoulders were tensed, her whole skinny body a cringe.

"We'll go barefoot and sit on the patio," he said after a moment, kicking his shoes off.

She looked at him and gave a sad laugh. "Okay."

The sidewalk was still cool enough for bare feet. The Greek didn't give their bare feet a second look, but brought iced coffees and yogurt with walnuts and honey.

"Do you want to tell me about them?"

"It's been bad ever since—ever since Mimi left. All of a sudden, Krishna's Link's best friend. He follows him around."

Alan nodded. "Krishna beat Mimi up," he said.

"I know it," she said. "I heard it. I didn't do anything, goddamn me, but I heard it happen."

"Eat," he said. "Here." He reached for a clean napkin from the next table and handed it to her. She dried her eyes and wiped her nose and ate a spoonful of yogurt. "Drink," he said, and handed her the coffee. She drank.

"They brought those girls home last night. *Little* girls. Teeny-boppers. Disappeared into their bedrooms. The noises they made."

"Drink," Alan said, and then handed her the napkin again.

"Drunk. They got them drunk and brought them home."

"You should get out of there," Andrew said, surprising himself. "Get out. Today, even. Go stay with your mom and find a new apartment next month."

She set her cup down carefully. "No," she said.

"I'm serious. It's a bad situation that you can't improve and the more you stay there, the worse it's going to get."

"That's not a practical suggestion."

"Staying there, in potential danger, is not practical. You need to get out. Staying there will only make things worse for you."

She clenched her jaw. "You know, there comes a point where you're not giving advice anymore. There comes a point where you're just moralizing, demonstrating your hypothetical superiority when it comes to doing the right thing. That's not very fucking helpful, you know. I'm holding my shit together right now, and rather than telling me that it's not enough, you could try to help me with the stuff I'm capable of."

Alan digested this. She'd said it loudly, and a few of the other morning patrons at the Greek's were staring at them. He looked away, across the street, and spied Billy standing in a doorway, watching. Billy met his eyes, then looked away.

"I'm sorry, Natalie," he said. "You're right."

She blew air out her nostrils.

"What about this. You can knock on my door anytime. I'll make up the sofa for you." He thought of Mimi and cringed inwardly. She'd have to stay upstairs and be quiet if there were strangers in the house. Then he remembered his promise about her wings. He bit his lip.

She let out a harsh chuckle. "Will I be any safer there?"

"What does that mean?"

"You're the weirdest person I've ever met, Alvin. I mean, sorry, no offense, but why the hell would I knock on your door?"

She stood and turned on her barefoot heel and took herself away, walking at a brisk and gingerly pace.

Barry moseyed over and sat in her seat. "She'll be okay," he said. He picked up her spoon and began to finish her breakfast. "You know, I can't watch the way I could yesterday, not anymore. Too visible. What do I do now?"

Aaron shrugged. "Find a job. Be visible. Get a place to live. We can have each other over for dinner."

Brett said, "Maybe I could get a job where I got to watch. Security guard."

August nodded. He closed his eyes.

"She's very pretty," Barry said. "Prettier than Mimi."

"If you say so."

"Kurt's awake."

"Yeah?"

"Yeah. You could introduce me to him."

I did it for your own good, you know. She couldn't bring herself to say the words, for the enormity of what she'd done was overwhelming her. She'd found three of his friends and treated each of them to an evening of terror and hurt, and none of them would tell her where her brother was, none of them knew. Maybe they'd been innocent all along.

"Where are you?"

"Far from you," he said. In the background, she heard a girl crying.

I*t's going to happen,* we're going to cover the whole Market," Kurt said. He had the latest coverage map out and it looked like he was right. "Look at this." The overlapping rings of WiFi false-colored over the map were nearly total.

"Are those our own nodes, or just friendlies?" Alan asked, all his confusion and worry forgotten at the sight of the map.

"Those are our own," Kurt said. "Not so many friendlies." He tapped a key and showed a map of the city with a pitiful sprinkling of fellow travelers who'd opened up their networks and renamed them ParasiteNet.

"You'll have more," Buddy said. Kurt looked a question at Alan.

"My brother Brent," he said. "Meet Kurt."

They shook.

"Your brother?"

Adam nodded.

"Not one of the missing ones?"

He shook his head. "A different one."

"It's nice to meet you." Kurt wiped off his palms. Adam looked around the little private nest at the back of the shop, at the small, meshed-in window on the back wall. Danny watched at that window sometimes.

"I'm gonna send a screengrab of this to Lyman, he'll bust a nut."

It made Anton smile. Lyman and Kurt were the unlikeliest of pals, but pals they were.

"You do that."

"Why aren't you wearing shoes?"

Anton smiled shyly. "No volunteers today?"

Kurt shrugged, a jingle of chains. "Nope. Slow day. Some days just are. Was thinking of seeing a movie or something. Wanna come?"

"I can't," Anton said.

"Sure," Brett said, oblivious to the fact that the invitation hadn't really been directed at him. "I'd like that."

"O-kaaay," Kurt said. "Great. Gimme an hour or so and meet me out front."

"It's a date."

He was half a block from home when he spotted Natalie sitting on her porch, staring at the park. Kurt and Link were gone. The patio at the Greek's was full. He was stood in his bare feet in the middle of Kensington Market on a busy shopping day, and he had absolutely nowhere to go. Nowhere he belonged.

He realized that Natalie had never put him in touch with her boss at Martian Signal.

Barefoot, there wasn't much of anywhere he could go. But he didn't want to be home with Mimi and he didn't want to walk past Natalie. Barefoot, he ended up in the alleyway behind Kurt's again, with nowhere else to go.

Blake and Kurt got back around suppertime, and by then Alan had counted every shingle on the roofs of the garages, had carefully snapped the sharps off of two syringes he found in some weeds, and then sat and waited until he was ready to scream.

Blake walked confidently into the shop, through Kurt's nest, and to the back door. He opened it and smiled at Adam. "Come on in," he said.

"Right," Alan said. "How was the movie?"

"It was fine," Kurt said.

"Incredible," Burt said. "I mean, *incredible*. God, I haven't been to the movies in ten years at least. So *loud*, Jesus, I've never heard anything like that."

"It was just A&E," Kurt said. "Asses and explosions."

Alan felt a wave of affection for his friend, and an indefinite sadness, a feeling that they were soon to be parted.

Kurt stretched and cracked his knuckles. "Getting time for me to go out diving."

"Let's go get some dinner, okay?" Andy said to Brad.

"G'night guys," Kurt said, locking the door behind them.

"I'm sorry," she said. There had been five minutes of near-silence on the line, only the girl crying in the background at his end. She wasn't sure if he'd set the phone down or if he was listening, but the "sorry" drew a small audible breath out of him.

"I'm really, really sorry," she said, and her hands felt sticky with blood. "God, I just wanted to *save you*."

Mimi was back in bed when they got home. Alan took a shower and scrubbed at his feet, then padded silently around the shuttered bedroom, dressing in the dark. Mimi made a sleepful noise.

"I'm making dinner," he said. "Want some?"

"Can you bring it up here?" she said.

"Yeah, sure," he said.

"I just can't face—" She waved a hand at the door, then let it flop back down to the bed.

"It's all right, babe," he said.

He and Brad ate dinner in silence in the kitchen, boiled hot dogs with cheese and sliced baby tomatoes from the garden and lemonade from scratch. Bradley ate seven. Mimi had three bites out of the one that he brought up to her room, and when he went up to collect her plate, she was asleep and had the covers wrapped snugly around her. He took a spare sheet and a blanket out of the linen closet and brought it downstairs and made up the living room sofa. In moments, he was sleeping.

This night, he was keenly aware of what had roused him from sleep. It was a scream, at the back of the house. A scared, drunken scream that was half a roar.

He was at the back door in a moment, still scrubbing at his eyes with his fists, and Bennett was there already.

He opened the door and hit the switch that turned on the garden lights, the back porch lights, the garage lights in the coach house. It was bright enough to dazzle him, but he'd squinted in anticipation.

So it only took him a moment to take in the tableau. There was Link, on the ground, splayed out and face down, wearing boxer shorts and nothing else, his face in a vegetable bed in the next-door yard. There was Krishna, standing in the doorway, face grim, holding a hammer and advancing on Link.

He shouted, something wordless and alarmed, and Link rolled over and climbed up to his feet and lurched a few steps deeper into the postage-stamp-sized yard, limping badly. Krishna advanced two steps into the yard, hammer held casually at his waist.

Alan, barefoot, ran to the dividing fence and threw himself at it, going up it like a cat, landing hard and painfully, feeling something small and important give in his ankle. Krishna nodded cordially at him, then hefted the hammer again.

He took another step toward him and then Natalie, moving so fast that she was a blur, streaked out of the back door, leaping onto Krishna's back. She held there for a minute and he rocked on his heels, but then he swung the hammer back, the claws first.

It took her just above her left eye with a sound like an awl punching through leather and her cry was terrible. She let go and fell over backward, holding her face, screaming.

But it was enough time, enough distraction, and Alan had hold of Krishna's wrist. Remembering a time a long time ago, he pulled Krishna's hand to his face, heedless of the shining hammer, and bit down on the base of his thumb as hard as he could, until Krishna loosed the hammer with a shout. It grazed Alan's temple and then bounced off his collarbone on the way to the ground, and he was momentarily stunned.

And here was Link, gasping with each step, left leg useless, but hauling himself forward anyway, big brawny arms reaching for Krishna, pasting a hard punch on his cheek and then taking hold of his throat and bearing him down to the ground.

Alan looked around. Benny was still on his side of the fence. Mimi's face poked out from around the door. The sound of another hard punch made him look around as Link shook the ache out of his knuckles and made to lay another on Krishna's face. He had a forearm across his throat, and Krishna gasped for breath.

"Don't," Adam said. Link looked at him, lip stuck out in belligerence.

"Stop me," he said. "Try it. Fucker took a hammer to my *knee.*"

Natalie went to him, her hand over her face. "Don't do it," she said. She put a hand on his shoulder. "We'll call the cops."

Krishna made a choking sound. Link eased up on him a little, and he drew a ragged breath. "Go ahead and call them," he rasped.

Alan took a slow step back. "Brian, can you bring me the phone, please?"

Link looked at his sister, blood streaming down her face, at Krishna's misshapen nose and mouth, distorted into a pink, meaty sneer. He clenched each fist in turn.

"No cops," he said.

Natalie spat. "Why the hell not?" She spat again. Blood was running into her eye, down her cheek, into her mouth.

"The girl, she's inside. Drunk. She's only fifteen."

Alan watched the brother and sister stare at one another. Blaine handed him the phone. He hit a speed dial.

"I need a taxi to Toronto Western Hospital at 22 Wales Avenue, at Augusta," he said. He hung up. "Go out front," he told Natalie. "Get a towel for your face on your way."

"Andrew—" she said.

"I'll call the cops," he said. "I'll tell them where to find you."

It was as she turned to go that Krishna made a lunge for the hammer. Billy was already kicking it out of the way, and Link, thrown from his chest, got up on one knee and punched him hard in the kidneys, and he went back down. Natalie was crying again.

"Go," Alan said gently. "We'll be okay."

She went.

Link's chest heaved. "I think you need to go to the hospital, too, Link," Alan said. The injured knee was already so swollen that it was visible, like a volleyball, beneath his baggy trousers.

"No," Link said. "I wait here."

"You don't want to be here when the cops arrive," Alan said.

Krishna, face down in the dirt, spat. "He's not going to call any cops," he said. "It's grown-up stuff, little boy. You should run along."

Absently, Link punched him in the back of the head. "Shut up," he said. He was breathing more normally now. He shifted and made a squeaking sound.

"I just heard the cab pull up," Alan said. "Brian can help you to the front door. You can keep your sister company, get your knee looked at."

"The girl—" he said.

"Yes. She'll be sober in the morning, and gone. I'll see to it," Adam said. "All right?"

Brian helped him to his feet and toward the door, and Andrew stood warily near Krishna.

"Get up," he said.

Mimi, in his doorway, across the fence, made a sound that was half a moan.

Krishna lay still for a moment, then slowly struggled to his knees and then his feet.

"Now what?" Krishna said, one hand pressed to his pulped cheek.

"I'm not calling the cops," he said.

"No," Krishna said.

"Remember what I told you about my brother? I *made him.*

I'm stronger than him, Krishna. You picked the wrong Dracula to Renfield for. You are doomed. When you leave him, he will hunt you down. If you don't leave him, I'll get you. You made this situation."

Billy was back now, in the doorway, holding the hammer. He'd hand it to Adam if he asked for it. He could use it. After all, once you've killed your brother, why not kill his Renfield, too?

Krishna looked scared, a little scared. Andrew teased at how that felt and realized that it didn't feel like he'd thought it would. It didn't feel good.

"Go, Krishna," he said. "Get out of this house and get out of my sight and don't ever come back again. Stay away from my brother. You will never profit by your association with him. He is dead. The best he can do for you is make you dead, too. Go."

And Krishna went. Slowly. Painfully. He stood and hobbled toward the front door.

Mimi watched him go, and she smiled once he was gone.

Benny said, "Kurt's shop is on fire."

They ran, the two of them, up Augusta, leaving Mimi behind, wrapped in her blanket. They could smell the smoke as soon as they crossed Kensington, and they could see the flames licking out of the dark black clouds just a moment later.

The smell was terrible, a roiling chemical reek that burned the skin and the lungs and the eyes. All those electronics, crisping and curling and blackening.

"Is he in there?" Alan said.

"Yes," Barry said. "Trapped."

"Call the fire department," Andrew said, and ran for the door, fishing in his pocket for his keys. "Call 911."

He got the door open and left his keys in the lock, pulling his shirt up over his head. He managed a step into the building, two steps, and the heat beat him back.

He sucked up air and ran for it again.

The heat was incredible, searing. He snorted half a breath and felt the hair inside his nostrils scorch and curl and the burning was nearly intolerable. He dropped down on all fours and tried to peer under the smoke, tried to locate Kurt, but he couldn't find him.

Alan crawled to the back of the store, to Kurt's den, sure that his friend would have been back there, asleep and worn out from a night's dumpster diving. He took a false turn and found himself up against the refrigerator. The little piece of linoleum that denoted Kurt's kitchen was hot and soft under his hands, melting and scorching. He reoriented himself, spinning around slowly, and crawled again.

Tears were streaming freely down his face, and between them and the smoke, he could barely see. He drew closer to the shop's rear, nearly there, and then he was there, looking for Kurt.

He found him, leaned up against the emergency door at the back of the shop, fingers jammed into the sliver of a gap between the door's bottom and the ground. Alan tried the door's pushbar, but there was something blocking the door from the other side.

He tried slapping Kurt a couple times, but he would not be roused. His breath came in tiny puffs. Alan took his hand, then the other hand, and hoisted his head and neck and shoulders up onto his back and began to crawl for the front door, going as fast as he could in the blaze.

He got lost again, and the floor was hot enough to raise blisters. When he emerged with Kurt, he heard the sirens. He breathed hard in the night air.

As he watched, two fire trucks cleared the corner, going the wrong way down one-way Augusta, speeding toward him. He looked at Billy.

"What?"

"Is Kurt all right?"

"Sure, he's fine." He thought a moment. "The ambulance man will want to talk with him, he said. "And the TV people, soon.

"Let's get out of here," Brad said.

"All right," he said. "Now you're talking."

Though it was only three or four blocks back to Adam's place, it took the better part of half an hour, relying on the back alleys and the dark to cover his retreat, hoping that the ambulance drivers and firefighters wouldn't catch him here. Having to lug Kurt made him especially suspect, and he didn't have a single good explanation for being caught toting around an unconscious punk in the dead of night.

"Come on, Brent," Adam said. "Let's get home and put this one to bed and you and me have a nice chat."

"You don't want me to call an ambulance?"

Kurt startled at this and his head lolled back, one eye opened a crack.

"No," Alan said. "No ambulances. No cops. No firemen. Just me and him. I'll make him better," he said.

The smoke smell was terrible and pervaded everything, no matter which direction the wind blew from.

Adam was nearly home when he realized that his place and his lover and everything he cared about in the entire world were *also* on fire, which couldn't possibly be a coincidence.

The flames licked his porch and the hot air had blown out two of the windows on the second story. The flames were lapping at the outside of the building, crawling over the inside walls.

No coincidence.

Kurt coughed hard, his chest spasming against Alan's back. Alan set him down, as in a dream. As in a dream, he picked his way through the flames on his porch and reached for the doorknob. It burned his hand.

It was locked. His keys were in Kurt's door, all the way up Augusta.

"Around the back," Bentley called, headed for the fence gate. Alan vaulted the porch rail, crashing though the wild grasses and ornamental scrub. "Come on," Bentley said.

His hand throbbed with the burn. The back yard was still lit up like Christmas, all the lights ablaze, shining through the smoke, the ash of books swirling in it, buoyed aloft on hot currents, fragments of words chasing each other like clouds of gnats.

"Alan," Kurt croaked. Somehow, he'd followed them back into the yard. "Alan." He held out his hand, which glowed blue-white. Alan looked closer. It was his PDA, stubby wireless card poking out of it. "I'm online. Look."

Alan shook his head. "Not now." Mimi, somewhere up there was Mimi.

"Look," Kurt croaked. He coughed again and went down to his knees.

Arnos took the PDA in hand and peered at it. It was a familiar app, the traffic analysis app, the thing that monitored packet loss between the nodes. Lyman and Kurt had long since superimposed the logical network map over a physical map of the Market, using false-color overlays to show the degree to which the access points were well connected and firing on all cylinders.

The map was painted in green, packets flying unimpeded throughout the empty nighttime Market. And there, approaching him, moving through the alleys toward his garage, a blob of interference, a slow, bobbing something that was scattering radio waves as it made its way toward him. Even on a three-inch screen, he recognized that walk. Davey.

Not a coincidence, the fires.

"Mimi!" he called. The back window was blown out, crystal slivers of glass all around him on the back lawn. *"Mimi!"*

Billy was at his side, holding something. A knife. The knife. Serrated edge. Sharp. Cracked handle wound with knotted twine, but as he reached for it, it wasn't cracked. It was the under-the-pillow knife, the wings knife, Krishna's knife.

"You forgot this," he said, taking the PDA.

Then Davey was in the yard. He cocked his head and eyed the knife warily.

"Where'd you get that?" he said.

Adam shifted his grip for slashing, and took one step forward, stamping his foot down as he did it. Davey retreated a step, then took two steps forward.

"He set the fires," Bentley said. "She's as good as dead. Cooked. Won't be long now, she'll be cooked."

Darren looked at him for the first time. "Oh, yes," he said. "That's about right. I never found you, no matter how I looked. You don't get found if you don't want to."

Brent shook his head. "He set the fire, he used gasoline. Up the stairs, so it would spread up every floor quickly."

Aaron growled and lunged forward, slicing wildly, but Davey's scurry was surprising and fast and nimble.

"You're going to stab me again, cut me again? What do you suppose that will get you?"

"He's weaker than he was, then. We got six years, then. He's weaker. We'll get ten years. Twenty." Billy was hopping from foot to foot. *"Do it."*

Alan sliced and stabbed again, and the knife's point caught Danny's little bandy leg, like cutting through a loaf of stale bread, and Danny gasped and hopped back another step.

"He gave you the knife, didn't he? He gave you the knife last time. Last time, he took me to the schoolyard and showed me you and your girlfriend. He explained all about girlfriends to me and about what it would mean once our secret was out. He taught me the words, taught me to say *pervert*. Remember, Billy? Remember how you taught me?"

Andrew hesitated.

"He taught me the ritual with your thumbtip, how to make the little you, and then he took it away from me for safekeeping. He kept it in one of his rabbit cages, around on the other side of the mountain. It's not there now. Have you seen it? Does he still have it?

"He never liked having a little brother, not me or the others, but he liked having that little thing around to torture."

Billy hissed. "She'll be dead in minutes," he said. "In seconds. Another one dead. His doing!

"Killed her, cut her up, buried her," Benny chanted. "Sliced her open and cut her up," he shrilled.

Alan let the knife fall from his hands. Benny leapt for Danny, hands outstretched. Danny braced for the impact, rolled with him, and came up on top of him, small hands in Benny's eyes, grinding.

There were sirens out front now, lots of sirens.

A distant crash, and a rain of glass fell about his shoulders. He turned and looked up, looked up into the dormer window of his attic, four stories up. Mimi's head poked out from the window, wreathed in smoke, her face smudged and eyes screwed up.

"Mimi!" he cried.

She climbed unsteadily onto the windowsill, perched there for a moment. Then she leaned forward, ducked her head, and slipped into the sky.

Her magnificent wings unfolded in the smoke, in the hot ash, in the smoldering remains of all of Alan's life in human society. Her magnificent wings unfolded and caught the air with a sound he heard and with a downdraft of warm air that blew his hair off his forehead like a lover's hand, smoky smell and spicy smell.

She flew.

The sirens grew louder and she swooped over the yard. She gave two powerful beats of her wings and rose higher than the roof, then she circled the yard in great loops, coming lower and lower with each pass. Davey and Benny watched her. Kurt watched her.

Alan watched her. She was coming straight for him. He held out his arms and she fell into them, enfolding them both in her wings, her great and glorious wings.

"Come on," she said. Kurt was already limping for the alley. Benny and David had already melted away. They were alone in the yard, and the sirens were so loud now, and there were the reflections of emergency lights bouncing off the smoke around them. "Come on," she said, and she put her arms around his waist, locking her wrists.

It took five beats of her wings to get them aloft, and they barely cleared the fence, but they banked low over the alley and she beat her wings again and then they were gaining altitude, catching an updraft from the burning house on Wales Avenue, rising so high into the sky that he felt like they would fly to the moon.

The day that Lyman and Kurt were on the cover of *NOW* magazine, they dropped by Martian Signal to meet with Natalie's boss. Lyman carried the pitch package, color-matched, polyethnic, edgy and cool, with great copy.

Natalie met them. She'd grown out her hair and wore it with bangs hanging over the scar on her forehead, just over her left eye, two punctures with little dents. Three surgeries had cleared all the bone fragments from the orbit of that eye, and she'd kept her sight. Once she was out of the hospital, she quickly became the best employee Martian Signal had ever had. She quickly became manager. She quickly undertook to make several improvements in the daily operations of the store that increased turnover by thirty percent. She slowly and reluctantly hired her brother, but his gimpy knee made it hard for him to bend down to reshelve, and he quickly quit.

Kurt and Natalie hugged, and Lyman formally shook her hand, and then shook her boss's hand.

It took less than an hour to convince her boss to let them put up their access point. On the way back, three different people stopped them and told them how much they liked the article, and swore that the first thing they'd do when they got home would be to open up their networks and rename them ParasiteNet.

Lyman handled the thank-you's for this, and Kurt smiled and fiddled with his PDA and watched the sky, looking for a girl with wings as wide as a house.

I went to the house,
(she said, as he tended the fire, turning the yams in the coals and stirring the pot in which his fish stew bubbled)

I went to the house,

(she said, resting up from the long flight she'd flown from Toronto to Craig's distant, warm shores, far away from Kensington Market and Krishna and Billy and Danny)

I went to the house,

(she said, and Andy worked hard to keep the grin off his face, for he'd been miserable during her long absence and now he could scarcely contain his delight)

I went to the house, and there was no one home. I had the address you'd given me, and it was just like you'd described it to me, down to the basketball hoop in the driveway.

It was empty. But it was as I'd remembered it. They'd lived there. I'd lived there. You were right, that was the house.

That was the house I'd lived in. I rang the doorbell, then I peeked in through a crack in the blinds. The rooms were empty. No furniture. Just blinds. It was night, and no one was looking, so I flew up to the third floor, to the window I'd stared out all those times.

The window was unlatched, and I slid aside the screen and let myself in. The room was empty. No carpet. No frilly bed and stuffed animals. No desk. No clothes in the closet, no hangers.

The only thing in the room was a small box, plugged into the wall, with a network cable snaking away into the phone jack. It had small lights on it, blinking. It was like the one you'd had in your attic. A wireless access point.

I remembered their names, then. Oliver and Patricia. They'd been my mother and father for a few years. Set me up with my first apartment. This had been their house.

I slept there that day, then, come nightfall, I set out again to come home to you.

Something woke Andy from his sound sleep, nestled in her wings, in her arms. A tread on Craig's inviolable soil, someone afoot on his brother.

Slowly, he got himself loose of Mimi and sat up and looked around.

The golem standing before him was small, and its eyes glowed red. It bent over and set something down on the earth, a fur-wrapped bundle of smoked meat.

It nodded at him. He nodded back.

"Thank you," he said.

Mimi put her hand on his calf. "Is it okay?"

"It's right," he said. "Just as it was meant to be."

He returned to her arms and they kissed. "No falling in love," she said.

"Perish the thought," he said.

She bit his lip and he bit hers and they kissed again, and then he was asleep, and at peace.

7.5.06
7.5.07 Sunset Bud